Sabrina So Far

MORMON TO MYSTIC, FUNDAMENTAL TO FAR OUT

AN EXPERIMENT IN PHILOSOPHICAL FICTION

PATRICIA YORK

COVER IMAGE BY KEVIN GOLLAHER

BALBOA.
PRESS
A DIVISION OF HAY HOUSE

Balboa Press books may be ordered through booksellers or by contacting:

Balboa Press
A Division of Hay House
1663 Liberty Drive
Bloomington, IN 47403
1 (877) 407-4847

Print information available on the last page.

ISBN: 978-1-9822-0733-5 (sc)
ISBN: 978-1-9822-0735-9 (hc)
ISBN: 978-1-9822-0734-2 (e)

Library of Congress Control Number: 2018907448

Balboa Press rev. date: 11/15/2019

Contents

Chapter 1   Drama with Chops 1

Chapter 2   The George Concept 3

Chapter 3   Rewind 10

Chapter 4   Theory of Everything 17

Chapter 5   Questions with No Answers 20

Chapter 6   Dark Night 29

Chapter 7   In Which Sabrina Reflects on Special
             Relationships and Other Illusions 35

Chapter 8   A Conversation with God in Which Sabrina
             Gets on His Case 44

Chapter 9   The Risk 55

Chapter 10   One True Thing 61

Chapter 11   In Which Sabrina Encounters the Fool 64

Chapter 12   Out 77

Chapter 13   Voices 85

Chapter 14   Of Keys and Kingdoms 93

Chapter 15   Alternate Universe 105

Chapter 16   Night Terrors 114

Chapter 17   The Golden Braid 119

Chapter 18   Return of the Lazy Man 123

Chapter 19   Kierkegaard in the Cafeteria 138

Chapter 20   Republican Rant 147

Chapter 21   Wherein Sabrina Observes the Sabbath and
             Learns More About the Lazy Man 155

Chapter 22   In Which Sabrina Goes Camping and Meets
             Mr. Wright 167

Chapter 23   Mushroom Soup and the Call of the Wild 175

Chapter 24   Down the Rabbit Hole.................................. 180
Chapter 25   The Devil in the G-spot 192
Chapter 26   The Most Terrifying Thing 205
Chapter 27   Surprise.. 211
Chapter 28   The Kiss 215
Chapter 29   What The?...224
Chapter 30   Just a Little Hitch 227
Chapter 31   Sabrina Makes Her Move 233
Chapter 32   George Wright Considers His Plight...................236
Chapter 33   Sabrina On Pause.......................................245
Chapter 34   Amphibious 251
Chapter 35   Borderline... 253
Chapter 36   Sleeping Beauty 267
Chapter 37   Awake...273
Chapter 38   Icons and Infidels 278
Chapter 39   Paradox..286
Chapter 40   It is Written 295
Chapter 41   Lovers don't finally meet somewhere. They
                   are in each other all along. –Rumi 299
Chapter 42   Land Mines 305
Chapter 43   Back to the Future 314
Chapter 44   Out Beyond Right and Wrong.........................322
Chapter 45   The Gift 327
Chapter 46   331
Chapter 47   The Expression Session 335

Epilogue.. 347
Endnotes... 355

Special Thanks To:

Lucille Wayne

Balboa Design Team

Portia Barney

Charlotte Pannell

Mark Gollaher

Kevin Gollaher

Paige Paulsen

Lori Yearwood

Stacey Thompson

1

Drama with Chops

The last thing she saw before losing consciousness was that crazy man, screaming unintelligible anathemas at her, his swollen lips dripping with blood and every scar on his pock-marked face standing out in grotesque relief.

Her head was throbbing and she knew she must have caught him good right in the teeth with that ingenuous backward head slam, because he was holding a piece of his tongue in his hand. So she guessed he wouldn't be threatening anyone else with—

Then suddenly a deafening crack perforated her eardrums and everything had gone quiet like in an old silent movie. Falling to her knees and then sideways onto the ground, she could feel something lovely and warm running down the front of her shirt, accompanied by a blissful flash of light so absolutely still it hurt.

The man with no tongue was hanging over her like he wanted her to believe he was a real bad guy, a true villain, straight out of a DC comic book. Strange how the word, 'villain' seemed irrelevant though. Because just then—as he was filling the entire screen of her mind—there was nothing like an opposite to compare him to; someone who might be, let's say, a hero. No other.

And she didn't know why, but she felt a kind of irrational, unguarded reverence for him. She loved him, overtly and wholeheartedly, and not with any of that sappy, sentimental, romantic kind of love. In fact it was way outside the ordinary affection she'd ever felt for anyone she could remember. She loved him with a love beyond all reason, in a kind of unqualified intimacy that seemed to make them two sides of one coin.

And also she wanted to clobber him—maybe even kill him—before he could do any more damage.

Odd, how Love can take sides like that, she thought, as she faded in and out of a world where that was possible.

Am I hallucinating or is this really happening? she wondered.

"That, my love, is all in the way you see it . . . see it . . . see it . .," echoed a familiar voice somewhere on a distant star.

Then she exhaled herself right out of conscious awareness.

2

The George Concept

In the twilight between worlds the teacher watched as she wandered aimlessly, meandering back and forth without much interest in finding her way. He walked a while by her side, hands behind his back, until at last she noticed him. She was with her teacher and it was safe here; peaceful, free and wonderfully expansive. No pain, no guns, no blood, and no commotion.

"So how're you doing there, Sabrina-girl?" said the Teacher, just as casually as though they'd been walking together like this for light-years, "I have to admit, you're getting some things down pretty well," he said, as he counted them on his fingers.

- Love as much as you can from wherever you are.[1]
- No resistance[2]
- What did you think it was that needed to be loved?[3]
- And . . . when you learn to love Hell, you'll be in Heaven[4]

"These are no small things. In this moment, you just may be my prize student."

"Really? You mean you have others?" She asked, incredulous as she was confused. "How do you find the time?"

He laughed. "You know you're getting this down well enough that you could move on to a dimension beyond time, more attuned to your present sensibilities than the three-dimensional one in which you've been playing.

"And where would that be?" she asked.

"Not so much where. Consider this. Instead of a different star system, you could live in a different thought system."

She had no response for that. It felt good not focusing on thoughts.

"You like the quiet, do you?" he asked. "Then you'd have a wonderful life here in my fifth-dimensional reality, for instance. A lot of space between thoughts. And you would harmonize with anything, wherever you'd find yourself. You wouldn't be much interested in referencing yourself as a body, however. But you'd love the lack of limitation, I think."

For this, she engaged her thinking mind. "Yes, I've heard people talk about the fifth dimension. What is it exactly?"

"It's hard to describe in three-dimensional terms. One might say that it is a playground for the abstract mind, pure awareness. It doesn't deal so much in specifics. It responds equally to everything it knows as true and does not respond at all to anything else. This is not a spatial dynamic I'm talking about. I'm using the word 'dimension' as the idea of a frequency band, a level of consciousness. What I can tell you is how I experience it. It's what people on earth might call, heaven. Here, one appreciates everything one encounters, yet takes nothing too seriously. Boundaries are understood to be imaginary. We see a wall as a mere suggestion, for instance. It says: 'Go around me, if you please, —or through me if you'd rather.'

"Typically, the human mind works in patterns of resistance and lacks an element of . . . of whimsy. It loves to set up problems that are incapable of solution, like squaring the circle and carrying pi to infinity. But all problems, including these mathematical ones, are diversionary tactics so that the limited earthbound mind will never ask the essential question: 'To what purpose'? The purpose or intention of something, will give you its results.

"To access the fifth dimension, one must possess the heart of a poet. Poetry has the elements of fluidity and harmonics, even when dealing with harsh, dissident dynamics. The <u>Leaves of Grass</u>, by your Walt Whitman is a good example of what I am speaking of here. The poetic mind trumps the conventional mind for sheer maneuverability.

"I see," she said, not really knowing for sure if she did. "I think I get what you are saying. In this movie I saw once, <u>Contact</u>, there was a scene where a woman scientist was harnessed into a kind of capsule and then launched into space. So they thought. Actually what happened was something very different than they expected. The spacecraft didn't go anywhere. But she did. And when she finally got herself loose from this crazy captain's chair they'd strapped her into, she just floated like a feather, staring into another dimension.

"I remember it because, for some reason, I was suddenly sobbing out loud, right there in the theater. I couldn't help myself. I suppose that's how I'd felt sometimes when I'd let go of something really tight or rigid. I couldn't remember what exactly, but something painful and big and—con—con—"

"Constricted?" asked the Teacher.

"Yeah, like that. But then she said something so unexpected. She said, '. . . They should have sent . . . a poet.'"

The teacher looked at his student with full appreciation for her apparent comprehension of the principle he was trying to convey.

At last she said, "So . . . would you and I be partners in this fifth dimensional world? Lovers, I mean?"

"Oh," he frowned, "you might not understand it right away, but beings here don't partner up the way you do on the earth plane. We are whole within ourselves. Partnering is kind of a duality thing. Remember when I told you that I was married to the one in front of me the first time we met? It's really like that in the 5th dimension."

"I do remember," she said smiling, "but I'm quite certain that I thought it was a pick-up line. You mean you really don't have relationships, even after that amazing sex we had?"

He was silent for a moment. "Let me put it this way," he started carefully. "Each of us is in relationship to everything and everyone in the exact moment in which we find ourselves. In fact the universe *is* our relations with each other.

But the confusion of physical urges with love is a major perceptual distortion. These urges refract the light by focusing on only one thing, one person or tribe. This puts Conscious Awareness on a trajectory that is only slightly off at first, but eventually moves out onto the edge of creation in a very wide arc, where opposites seem possible. A point of view (like an angle of light) is almost infinitesimal at the beginning, but as it extends further out onto the space/time continuum, it widens into an experience that shows the mind how far adrift one can travel, how far from its Source.

"Let us call this source, God, for now. All pleasure comes from doing God's will, not the limited personal will. Being motivated primarily by personal desire is a denial of the Self we all share. The Christ Mind, some call it.

"Oh. But I thought the goal was to never be in the mind," "I thought we were supposed to live from the heart."

"The Christ Mind, a singularity in scientific terms, is the same thing that you mean when you say heart. It takes the good of all and everything into account. *'He sendeth the rain on the just and on the unjust*[5] remember? That old scriptural reference is an echo of this understanding.

"Now beyond this One Mind is that which we shall call, The Absolute. When scientists talk about the universe at rest before the big bang and when Buddhists speak of 'no-mind', they are essentially speaking of the same thing. The Absolute is prior to the creation of universes, —or of Gods, as a matter of fact. It is a clear, clean canvas, unblemished by any image or thought or conflict. It's nice to remember it now and then. To do so restores sanity, true identity. And it's always there, this eternal pause, in every moment.

"Now. And now. And now. Reset.

"What we did the other night—sex, as you characterize it—was to shift focus a bit from the physical to the energetic, then back again to that Christ Mind. It was a nice synthesis of the corporeal and the higher imagination. That's why it felt sexual as well as visionary. "Because you trusted me, we were able to transcend all your thoughts about it in the moment; thoughts about good, evil, right and wrong.

"When I offer you the opportunity to live in a more . . . permeable dimension, I'm giving you the choice to live from different impulses and to save yourself a great deal of time in terms of suffering. Time is illusory and illusions come to pass rather than to stay. And other, more accurate illusions (because they are more attuned to oneness) take their place. We call this evolution."

"Explain to me again what you mean by illusions, will you?" she asked.

He touched her hair, holding his hand lightly over the crown of her head for a moment. "Think of an illusion like this. The people in an audience are real, but 'audience' is a name for something that will disappear when the people go home. Do you see? In this sense, the audience is an illusion: a temporary, partial, and limited reality. It has no independent, causative existence. . .[6] And thus, as the audience is formed of people, so illusions are formed out of real beings. Indeed, there is no other way to form an illusion except by using what is real.[7]

"But seeing the illusory nature of existence is a way to lessen the pain of time-bound experience. One doesn't clutch so tightly to ideals and circumstances. Most citizens of the third dimension think it is a noble thing to clutch and cling. Patriotism, loyalty, devotion and fidelity, they call it. However, could they but see that all principles, ethics and situations are simply transitory structures of thought, they would evolve much more smoothly and lovingly towards their existential satisfaction. Delaying progress is meaningless in the most expansive view, of course, but it can be truly wretched in time."

"So. How about it? Do you want to change up?"

She was invigorated by this invitation to transcend the physical plane. But something was still nagging at her, something waiting in the third dimension, she thought. And she knew that a sense of her own "nearness" would guide her to the universal latitude and longitude that would become her new 'now'.

Finally the teacher spoke again.

"I often used to tell myself when I was living in your dimension that if it was that easy to get back to space—or Heaven in your terms—why not go back and play in the more limited realities? Is there some idea in the physical world that you still cherish? Something you've left unappreciated fully?"

Then he played a trump card he'd been holding in the back of his mind. "By George, I think I'm supposed to be—"

George! George? . . . I've heard that name before . . . haven't I, she thought. And she let her wide open mind narrow just a little, and deepen into the concept of GEORGE.

A trail of memories, like breadcrumbs, showed her the way. Not as far back as the big bang. Just to the beginning of a little space/time event called:

Sabrina, So Far.

3

Rewind

The strangest thing: Sabrina Ryder had just been thinking she would like to move into a place of her own and how it might relieve the ennui that seemed to dog her like the phantom trickster from Carlos Castaneda, ever since the breakup. Then what do you know, her friend Abby called to tell her about this wonderful old townhouse located within a large conglomerate of newer ones—two bedrooms/two baths—just five doors away from her own place, and could Sabrina come to see it right away because it would surely be snatched up within the week. With a clubhouse, covered parking, two swimming pools, and restaurants and shops within walking distance, it was kind of a miracle.

She went to see it that evening. Her father, who was on hand for a consultation and inspection, met her there at 6:00 sharp. Peering in with keen interest at the breakers, the copper plumbing, the five year old furnace, and the new air conditioner, he announced with confidence that he thought the place was in good shape for its age, and the price? Well, that wasn't bad either. In fact he seemed openly excited about the whole idea, which made Sabrina a little uneasy, though she didn't know why. . .

For the past three years since she'd finished college, Sabrina had lived at home with the family, largely because of pressure from her mother. "Just until I find a place of my own then," she said to her mother almost every week. She had a good job as a junior editor at a small publishing company and honestly, she had tried to move out several times.

But Mrs. Ryder always balked and sniffled and pled, "Can't you at least wait until after the wedding, Darling?" And for a while that had seemed like the best plan since it was assumed from the beginning of her relationship with Ben that marriage was "impending" as her mother was fond of saying.

Sabrina and Ben had found each other in their last two years of college, graduated together, and were crazy stupid in love. For almost two years. Then things started to unravel, and Sabrina began to think that "impending" was exactly what the idea of marriage felt like.

"Doesn't it have the ring of doom, 'impending'?" she asked Abby. "I mean, don't you always hear the two words together: 'impending doom.' I swear every time Mother uses that word to describe the wedding it sounds like an execution. Unlike 'forthcoming,' or 'in the near future,' which have a more relaxed, sort of, 'Oh, yeah, really? We'll see about that,' kind of sentiment."

Abby didn't see the difference, but then Abby didn't love words the way Sabrina did, their use, derivations, and subtle nuances, and all the wonderful ways they could be interpreted. And here was the rub. Sabrina had begun to interpret things. Or reinterpret them, one might say. Not just words either, but whole systems of belief that had been handed down through generations of time, a pioneering dynasty of sacrifice and consecration. A lineage which had been the unifying fabric of all the major themes in her life; beliefs about romance, love, life, eternity and God. All things spelled with capitals. And in the process, her relationship with Ben had come to a screeching— no actually, a slow, uncomfortable, and tedious halt.

But all that was over now and "so is the financial reprieve of living at home," Sabrina said to her mother one day. "I think it's time to find my own place in the world".

One late September evening, as they stood around the large pine table in the farmhouse kitchen of the Salt Lake City home (that her mother loved more than recipes and genealogy), Sabrina listened once more to the tearful lamentations of dashed hopes for a spring wedding and an eternal alliance between herself and Ben. Rehearsing again the litany of untimely decisions that had led up to the fateful end of the relationship, her mother plead with Sabrina to reconsider. As if Ben had no say in the matter at all. As if he would be satisfied with any weak apology Sabrina might make, and go along amiably with a reconciliation.

Sabrina was just about ready to walk out of the room when Mrs. Ryder turned to her husband. Couldn't *he* get her to see reason? Surprisingly, and to Sabrina's great relief, he confessed that he'd always felt a little indifferent towards Ben. Just never could see the attraction, really. And that seemed to put an end to it.

Now here she stood with her ally father, in the middle of a new possibility: this modest townhouse with a mortgage and a kitchen that needed remodeling.

"Your life is going through a bit of a remodel too," he said, "It's a kind of metaphor, isn't it? Give it some consideration, Sabra," he coaxed, with his pet name for her. "A week or so. You'll know if it's the right thing. You've saved some money, and with the inheritance you received from your grandmother two years ago, you'll have enough for a hefty down payment. You've been looking for a while now. This could be it. Why don't you . . . uh . . . meditate on it? Isn't that what you like to do?" he said, running his fingers over the old tile countertops. "I know it's not as big as you wanted, and your mother will hate the idea of your moving so far from us, but who knows? It might be just what you need for a change, and to get over this thing with Ben."

"Pop," she countered (with a childhood nickname of her own from Dr. Seuss), "Losing Ben isn't really the issue. It's the feeling of having made such a colossal mistake that bothers me. And making another one on the heels of it, I just . . ." And trailing off into the outback of her mind, as she was accustomed to do when faced with a challenge, she fell into a momentary silence.

He waited patiently for what he knew would follow, allowing the quiet to work its magic.

"But you could be right," she sighed. "I didn't really want a fixer-upper and it'll probably take me forever to get it the way I want, but it does have a lot of potential and here's the deal. It's huge if you measure it in cubic feet. I mean most of these rooms have 12 foot ceilings."

John Ryder laughed in that easy way he did when they were commiserating and she interjected one of her peculiar insights. And it made Sabrina feel as though she hadn't lost all of her moxie, however ridiculous she may be feeling about certain past decisions.

Then with a sudden burst of passion, Mr. Ryder exclaimed, "And did you see the closet in the master? Why, that alone is worth the asking price! But of course, we should probably come in with a lower offer. See if they counter."

And he had summed it up accurately too, because for all the charm of the old place the most intriguing feature was in the main bedroom, although you could hardly call it a master. It wasn't much bigger than the other bedroom, except for a stunning walk-in closet, sporting two hand-planed cherry wood doors, which swung out on large hand-hammered brass hinges and were attached to a rounded frame on each side, made from the same wood. A seven inch crown molding ran across the top, and an old iron-forged skeleton key stood at attention in a handcrafted lock for easy entry. Gliding soundlessly as they opened, the doors seemed to stand as sentinels into another century. Another dimension.

From the outside, the cupboard had polish and depth and intrigue. Patina. All the things that Sabrina would have said she lacked. But on the inside there was enough room for what she knew she had in spades. A "wholly sufficient wardrobe" (Ben used to call it) of outrageous and whimsical vintage clothes and shoes, along with some wonderful old hats, which made the whole collection look as if it belonged in a consignment store window.

"You're right," she said to her father. "That closet is really something, isn't it?" And then, "Okay, Pop, I'll do it. I'll meditate on it."

And so with one simple suggestion her father had talked her down from the ledge of her own self doubt. And Sabrina knew that this invitation to meditate from her father (a Mormon bishop, no less), was a generous nod of tolerance, a sort of détente of the heart that signified his desire to stay connected to his eccentric firstborn, even though she no longer subscribed to the traditional ancestral religion.

Or mores. 'Standards,' was the word her mother always used for moral guidelines. "How can you live without standards? Guidelines, I mean?" she'd asked many times in desperation since the wedding had been called off and everything sacred was now in question.

"I have standards, Mother," Sabrina would say. "I make them up in each moment, from the most loving place I can think of at the time. Little revelations of the heart."

But Blanche Ryder was of the fundamental persuasion that rules handed down from generation to generation were much more reliable than anything one could think up spontaneously in the moment. For one thing, how could you possibly know if these new rules had been okayed by Heavenly Father? Had someone passed it by Him? Was he even available for that kind of impromptu decision making? It was her experience that it took weeks, sometimes months, to get an answer from a man. And maybe that went double for God, especially since He was much busier now with the baby boomers. And even then how could you know for sure without some kind of backup, a church authority for instance, who could verify your answer with a doctrinal precedent? No. Consensual agreement is what was needed, and from the top down too. Yes, because agreement was— well, agreeable, and without it Mrs. Ryder was sure there would be total anarchy.

But Bishop Ryder took a different tack. He liked Sabrina's willingness to question everything. A physics professor at the University of Utah, he had taught his three children to accept nothing less than the veracity of their own answers. This was sometimes a sticking point with his wife, but for him it was the only path leading to true strength of character.

That Sabrina's answers didn't always align with his own or that they sometimes didn't even appear to be in Sabrina's own best interests, well curiously that didn't bother him too much. He knew that with practice she would eventually find herself. And who can learn anything without practice? The thing was to trust the process.

Believing that truth resided in a particular system of thought, like Mormonism, was a comfort to him. It meant that everyone had to come to it eventually in his or her own time, but that it had to be based on one's own inner search. On personal integrity. That was how he had found the truth and so he knew the power of self discovery.

The trouble was, he could feel the tension building between Sabrina and her mother, who was determined to bring her back into the fold. But the plan was backfiring. And as much as he wanted to keep his daughter close, still he could see that his wife was forcing a standoff that would result in the opposite of her intent. And so he thought if he could diffuse the situation . . . if he could help Sabrina get a place of her own, well he was almost certain she would see everything aright if given the freedom to find it out for herself. And without personal discernment, what good would her faith be anyway? How reliable in times of trouble?

Meantime, she had said she would meditate. This he felt was as efficient as prayer, maybe even better. Less supplicating, more listening. After all, what did God need with our shopping lists anyway?

4

Theory of Everything

"But the idea is worth some consideration, isn't it?" Sabrina asked, parachuting uninvited into the middle of a brainstorming session in the break room at work. She was used to plopping herself down at any table with a free chair and a good conversation going on. And this was as good as it got.

A visiting editor-in-chief from a major scientific journal had stopped by the day before to promote an idea for a book, based on an article published in a popular anthropological magazine, (one of its many imprints); *Is There a Basic Elemental 'Nature' Underneath All Cultural Differences?* Apparently the response from the top had been indifferent. But when Sabrina realized that the idea was still in play a day later? Well, she simply had to meddle.

One of the senior editors had been discouraging the notion, killing every proposal with the ease of a sharpshooter. But Sabrina had some pet theories she wanted to throw into the fray.

"Wait. Isn't this is one of the more intriguing universal themes? It's a thesis for our time, isn't it? I mean, couldn't this be anthropology's answer to the search for a unified field, in a sort of psychological way? Come on! Everybody's looking for the unified field! The Theory of Everything? It's reality with a capitol 'R'. A little creative juice could fuel this idea into something really—I don't know—but weighty and entertaining as well."

Her ideas exploded like clay pigeons onto the conceptual landscape, and what was once an intimate tête-à-tête was now a bristling debate, which was definitely Sabrina's delight. She loved pushing a conversation to its ideological limits. And within minutes, the discussion had become a philosophical brouhaha of some proportion. Turns out, Reality with a capitol R had several special interest groups willing to speak for and against it.

"But the truth about anything is totally subjective," said a young copy editor. "So how could we find the underpinnings of all subcultures to have anything in common with each other, really?"

"Yeah, and that would be some historical sleuthing job!" said another kid from one of the proofreading departments as he stirred cocoa into his coffee, and spilling powder all over the marble countertop, apparently leaving it for someone else to clean up.

"One of us girls", Sabrina said to herself. But her response belied her irritation. "But it is a compelling idea, isn't it, John? And one worth looking into? A primary mind, let's say, from which all basic conditioning springs?

"Uh, I think you're talking about God," said an older woman who usually sat in the courtyard, smoking.

Then an editor from Food and Travel spoke up, deliberately bypassing the reference to deity. "And from that 'primary mind', every subculture gets its cues?"

"Not only that," said an astute young intern, a girl who Sabrina happened to like, "I think we're saying that they get the same cues, but interpret them differently through time and their own experience. Am I right, Sabrina?"

"Well, why not?" she said. "What if we traced these 'cues', as you call them, all the way back, and we were able to see a common thread through all belief systems? Wouldn't that be something? One of the main contemporary spiritual themes right now is 'oneness'. Anthropology could find the proof."

"The observer affects the observed. Heisenberg." said one of the science editors. "We can prove anything we want, based on what we're looking for."

Then from the back of the room, a handsome young production editor spoke up. He worked in another building, but came over occasionally to catch up on the new stuff. Sabrina remembered that he had teased her one day about her style of dress. He was smart and funny and well-spoken and she always watched for him at break time. Unfortunately, he didn't come over often, but today was obviously an exception.

"Has anyone ever read Edward Carpenter's, <u>Origins of Pagan and Christian Beliefs</u>? He has some brilliant theories on the subject, though he wrote it back in the early 1900's, I think."

There was a dead space for a moment, and no one responded. Then Sabrina detonated one last idea before returning to her desk. "You know, someone could weave these ideas into a metaphysical pop-culture story-line. A novel. Get someone like Dan Brown to write it."

And as she left the room, she was almost certain she could hear little caucuses from every department already writing down the bones for a New York Times best seller.

5

Questions with No Answers

Ever since her 23th birthday two years ago, Sabrina's unwavering inclination to examine the conventions of the traditional mindset had put her friends and family in tilt, like a pinball machine gone bonkers. Her doubts seemed to chafe everyone, probably not for the same reasons. They scared her mother, astonished her father, and sometimes amused, sometimes irritated her friends. Although they were maybe not doubts as much as questions. Lots and lots of questions. And the thing about questions is: uncertainty.

"I get it," she had to admit one night, while watching her brother's avid interest in the TV show, Jeopardy. "Answers are just more satisfying to people. They fill you up and leave no room for qualms. I understand wanting answers, but then why do I prefer questions?" she asked no one in particular. Realizing then that she was talking to herself, she answered herself as well. "I think it's because *not* knowing is kind of wild and unsettling, fierce, and wonderfully liberating! I mean, when you think about it, if there are no ultimate answers, if everything is always changing, evolving, then there are no boundaries anywhere that could or should keep us from expanding to greater frontiers."

She posed a question with no answers to Abby and Noah while waiting for a table at Lugano's on their regular Tuesday night dinner date.

"Can we talk about 'family values'? I mean, what does that even mean anymore? Conventional thinking on this subject is so full of religious and political cobwebs they haven't been swept out since the dark ages."

"The last thing I want to do is sweep out the corridors of time. Major janitorial nightmare!" answered Noah, who did not share her enthusiasm for philosophic inquiry and would much rather focus on critical social dilemmas like which girl to ask to the company Christmas party.

"Whatever for darlin'?" Abby asked. "You aren't getting married any more. And what difference does it make anyway? Do you think we're actually going to mend all the problems imbedded so deep in the collective mind that it would take an extreme makeover to fix them all? Just to use a metaphor. I know how you like them." Abby had a point. Obstinate as ever in her Irish stubbornness, she hated dwelling on issues that couldn't be settled within the next five minutes.

"Look, I just want to discuss the possibilities. Can't we just talk about it?" Sabrina asked. "It's fun."

"No, Sabrina, it's not fun," said Abby in her stunning Irish brogue. "Or maybe you could say, it used to be fun; to dropouts and hippies and Communists. This exchange you're proposing is from another era. It's obsolete. Nobody cares about deliberately trying to change social structures anymore. They're changing just dandy, all on their own. Haven't you noticed? Five times the divorce rate and the national debt is soaring? We're much more interested now in maintaining the status quo. Social Security, Medicare, and the ozone layer. We just long for a little stability! Let's talk about how to keep what we got, eh? Now who wants to share a salad?"

"So you're saying there's no need for creative discourse?" countered Sabrina. "I mean, whatever happened to 'agreeing to disagree', 'tuning in and dropping out', 'times, they are a-changing'?"

Abby answered by rolling her eyes, picking up her purse and leaving the table for a trip to the ladies' room. "It went out with Timothy O'Leary and beatnik poetry," she shouted over her shoulder.

"Excuse me! It's Timothy Leary! You can't co-opt everything for the Irish!" Sabrina shouted back. Relentless, she turned again to Noah, who was still looking at the menu. "You know, families are coming apart at the seams, like Abby just said about the divorce rate. Even in *my* subculture, the Mormon one, where tradition reigns supreme, the conventional family isn't doing so well".

Sabrina's parents and siblings could have been the poster family for the popular Mormon idiom, "families are forever". Challenging the cherished concept of infinite proliferation was akin to heresy, but she couldn't help herself. "We try to hide it and sweep it under the rug, but it's almost impossible to cover up." She said. "Maybe the whole concept of family, though, is undergoing a radical redesign. It could be a good thing. What do you think, Noah, really?"

He mumbled something about the psychological architecture of idiots, took a sip of water, and only looked up when Abby returned to the table. She and Noah were determined to order up a large fried onion and turn the conversation to something more palatable, something that went with steak and fries.

The problem, as Sabrina saw it, was that there was nowhere with an open mic for inquiry. Not at parties, not necessarily even at work where fresh viewpoints should have been welcome, and certainly not at church. Oh, and apparently not the dinner table at home either. Because she had tried it there, unsuccessfully as ever, having diplomatically (she thought) raised questions on all kinds of subjects. For instance, the concept of the 'eternal family' that had been discussed in church earlier one Sunday.

"I love the family as much as anybody," she said to her father over the traditional Sunday pot roast. "But is it only defined by biology and tradition? I mean, we don't always bear children out of love do we? Isn't it possible that sometimes we have them out of a desire for security, for instance; the need to create little kingdoms of our own making?"

And when no one commented, she followed it up with a punch. "Like it says in that scripture they are always quoting at church: 'Train them up in the way they should go. . .' and blah, blah, blah . . . they'll be little parodies of ourselves. Their copy-cat lives will belong to the tribe. The—the state. In fact, it's kind of '1984-ish', isn't it, Pop?" she said to her father, who choked on a bite of his parker house roll. "And by the way, whatever happened to 1984? I think it whizzed right by, without so much as a nod to Georgie Orwell. You see what I mean? We think we know how things are going to be, and then it often turns out so unlike what we imagined. So, based on results, how can we keep being so sure of ourselves? I'm just saying. . ."

Sabrina had the feeling that every time she initiated a conversation like this at home, she was putting her relationship with her mother (who used sniffling as her main communication device), at risk. And more often now, even her father, who used to brag about his daughter's "brilliant redirect", remained quiet. And to her chagrin, he even suggested that she might not want to use the editorial "we" when speaking of children, since she hadn't actually had any herself.

It seemed she was growing too old to be excused by her age, but sadly still too much of a neophyte to initiate a spirited discussion among people who already had all the answers.

To her brother Neil's indictment of pseudo-intellectualism, Sabrina snapped back defensively. "I am not. And I'm not cynical either. But I enjoy not knowing. Honestly? It feels more truth-bound, like truth is written somewhere on the outside wall of consciousness, just beyond the things we think we think we know."

But Neil was not convinced. Having just turned 19, he was making plans to go on a mission for his church, like most Mormon boys his age. A two year stint somewhere in the world to preach the gospel, proselyte the faith.

"And I'm glad you're going on a mission," she conceded. "It's the Mormon version of the young English lord's grande tour. You could do worse than go away from home to experience new countries and cultures." But then she had to add, "It's a little heady, however, that your prime motivation is to educate them about your beliefs and traditions, instead of wanting to learn about theirs. Isn't that a little presumptuous? I mean, how can you be so sure that what you have to tell people who live with different customs on the other side of the world is better than what they have already?"

"If they join the Church, that's how I'll know!" he answered in his testimonial voice.

Well, she couldn't argue with that logic. If someone wanted fascinating doctrines and family traditions, they could hardly do better than to join the Church of Jesus Christ of Latter-day Saints. *And being one of the richest churches per capita in the world doesn't hurt either,* she thought. "And as a self sustaining economic and socio-spiritual support system, it's really first rate, and an ideal catalyst for change in third world countries," she conceded to her church friends. And she couldn't help humming under her breath, "It is the very model of a major modern moral code," Gilbert and Sullivan notwithstanding. If what was wanted were the right answers to almost everything, Sabrina had to admit that the Saints could give you that, hands down.

There was endless trouble though if you wanted to question established answers. There wasn't a church for that apparently. You were kind of on your own there. And now at the age of 25, Sabrina just wanted the luxury of asking any question that came to mind without feeling awkward and out of order. Mostly what she felt living under her mother's careful watch, where it seemed to Sabrina that she was under constant scrutiny.

"Everyone suffers when one cell in the body is sick", Mrs. Ryder reminded Sabrina intermittently. "It's about integrity, Darling," she said for the maximum affect. Sabrina didn't like being referred to as a sick cell, but something even more niggling than that was presenting itself. She was beginning to see that this thing she had called integrity was no longer about what she *should* be feeling. It was about . . . well, *what she actually was feeling*, which was quite different from her mother's definition of the word.

That was the beginning of two roads diverging in a very yellow wood indeed. In fact, it was as though autumn had taken up residence in her psyche. She was dropping beliefs all over the place, like the leaves falling from the bright orange and red maple trees lining the street where she lived.

The decision to break with Ben didn't help matters. He was Mormon also, but until he'd met Sabrina, he hadn't been an active participant for many years. From the beginning, he had said that he wasn't sure how he felt about religion.

"I prefer not to think about it," he said. "It's an intuitive thing, best left to the realm of the heart, rather than trying to reason it out in the mind."

That was a really good answer, Sabrina remembered thinking. But she couldn't shake the feeling that he had simply been quoting something he'd read in a book somewhere. And she sensed that he had a kind of childish fear of retribution from external authority, unwilling to face the conflict that would certainly follow if he exposed his real feelings about the old time religion. This seemed insufferable to her, like a timid, childish response to an adult problem.

He had agreed to the traditional Mormon temple wedding, for instance, which pleased everyone, particularly her own family. This meant that he and Sabrina would be married, not just until "death do you part", but for "time and all eternity" which could seem epic in some ways of thinking. But Sabrina suspected that he agreed just to placate them, since he had never expressed the slightest affinity for the notion. And now she too had begun to have serious reservations about the idea. Indeed, she was starting to think that maybe two years was an eternity.

Bottom line, Sabrina couldn't live in this no-man's land of conceptual romantic hyperbole, especially where her own little momentary, transitory life was at stake. One way or another, she was going to have to find a way through this labyrinth of beliefs, and the last thing she needed was to be dragging someone else along who didn't have the balls to choose his own path in life.

The conflict in Sabrina's mind between old and new belief systems seemed beyond repair and soon, and without a shared vision, neither Ben nor Sabrina could find any common ground, much less sacred ground, on which to stand.

When they finally announced their mutual desire to stop the marriage-go-round, Sabrina wanted to have an un-engagement party, to help her mother see that it wasn't such a serious thing, and to give it a light disposition. But Ben didn't agree.

"It's not funny, Sabrina; too much flying in the face of tradition. We probably shouldn't so be happy about this, you know. One of us needs to at least appear to be undone about it." And this is where they disagreed most. Ben wanted to please everyone at the cost of great personal sacrifice. And though he always found a back door out of any circumstance which unnerved him, still it came with a price. Headaches and back problems; and the flu had its way with him at least twice a year. But Sabrina, revolted by pain and congestion, could hardly tell the truth fast enough.

But Ben was right about one thing at least. To their mothers, breaking with tradition was a very serious thing, this falling away from the time-honored path. In fact, it could hardly be seen as anything less than a fatality, not unlike the Jewish tradition. Although cloaks were not rent and the person in question declared null and void, in some ways it was almost worse. Instead of disowning the prodigal, Mormons were always holding out for his/her return. They could even re-baptize you after you were dead if it came to that. And they didn't shun you like the Amish either. Your place at the table was held in conspicuous and hopeful expectancy, your return always warmly anticipated.

"The problem with that kind of hope is that it's torture for everyone," Sabrina wrote one evening in her journal. "because, at some point, the return becomes a different kind of going back. One cannot go backward, but one must return to oneself. And to imagine that we know what that should look like is to keep life from doing its fundamental work, which is to bring us to new plateaus, inner vistas of awakening," she wrote.

She abhorred the feeling of living on the periphery of her mother's life with no way into her heart except through recantation, repentance or changing the trajectory of her life. Sabrina liked the direction she was going. Even though there was an aspect of fear in leaving the beaten path, to walk out onto that figuratively narrow, but experientially open road headlong into the unknown, she often felt lifted to heights she had never experienced in church. For one thing, she was more aware of a depth of feeling that included all passions, light and dark. And whereas it was not always comfortable, still it was strangely pure and honest, as though she were moving towards her Entirety; wholeness beaconed her from radiant, archetypal circles of light.

In the discussions she remembered having with her father in his study on Sunday evenings, he would often use the phrase, "the fullness of the gospel". And didn't 'fullness' tend toward inclusion, an ever widening circle of acceptance and appreciation of all thoughts and feelings?

In fact, stated in the Mormon <u>Articles of Faith</u>, was an odd phrase, attributed to the Apostle, Paul, something Sabrina had never really comprehended before now: *"We believe all things."*[8] Now she thought she could see what that phrase was pointing to. Fullness included 'all things', didn't it? Certainly it wasn't about excluding anything, any feeling or experience, was it?

No. It was all or nothing.

"Every belief is true when believed. That's why 'we believe all things,' in time. But no belief is true forever; believe it . . . or not," Sabrina wrote with a twist of irony.

6

Dark Night

Mormonism had been a beautiful thing in Sabrina's young life, growing up. Warm and secure, a safe harbor from the world, conceived especially for the special, the one true path. Particularly seductive was the unwavering adulation that adults superimposed on their young, touting them as the most prodigious youth in the world. As a pre-teen, Sabrina felt enamored and uplifted by the constant praise and the subtle inducement to set an example, and to be "valiant for righteousness sake". Even the admonition to "avoid the very appearance of evil" had seemed somehow do-able to her.

But as she had grown older, these same admonitions began to feel like the worst kind of separation, putting oneself above others. It seemed to maintain an illusion of specialness, creating the effect of having to reach down to pull the rest of the world up to one's own higher level of understanding. And even if that were true in some instances (for Mormons were generally kind and good people), this seemed to Sabrina an artificial contrivance, and one that emphasized the differences between people instead of the common bond of their humanity.

"Exactly what do you mean by 'our humanity', Sweetheart?" her mother asked one day, while hemming some bedroom curtains.

"Oh, I mean our common ground, our sameness as human beings," she said, handing her mother the scissors. "You know, people everywhere are much more alike than unlike. These imaginary walls we put up between ourselves, causes a subtle movement away from finding true brotherhood. We overlook it and instead we find countless reasons for disagreement until finally, we're marching headlong into battle over property disputes, religion, politics and other illusory boundaries. But we're not that different from each other, not really."

"Mormons are different," said her mother. "We are a 'peculiar people',"[9] she quoted from somewhere in the Mormon catalogue of thought, with a sort of dreamy satisfaction. As if her private version of God played favorites and was especially fond of oddballs.

In an uncharacteristic challenge, Sabrina shot back, "Mother, It feels like you're saying that God is partial to Mormons. Can you imagine that He really thinks that way?"

"'Heavenly Father', dear. You mustn't take the Lord's name in vain."

"But Mom, what about Go—Heavenly Father—being 'no respecter of persons',[10] like it says in the scriptures? And anyway, doesn't every religion wish for specialness? They all think they're peculiar in some way; they just have different words for it. But don't you see how the idea leaves out so much more than it takes in? There's this sense of sitting safely by the lord's hearth of preferential affection," she said with an exaggerated air, "while the whole rest of the world just pines away in sorrow at the outside window ledge."

"Sabrina, you don't know what you're saying. You shouldn't talk about the Lord in that way."

"What way? Isn't it just how you said you experienced Him? And incidentally, do you really think He could be offended by anything *I* could say? Wouldn't that make Him—I don't know—sort of petty?"

"You're twisting my words Sabrina, and making it sound like He's some kind of . . . oh, I don't know what! You're being blasphemous! How can you speak of Him in that way?" cried her mother, and she left the room unable to engage in a conversation that led to any further examination of her cherished beliefs, as though they were just as common as anyone else's.

"Mother, I didn't mean to hurt you. It's not personal. We're just talking about concepts . . . aren't we? I just wanted to—" And trailing off in a wisp of guilt, she knew that she and her mother were already out of range of each other, physically and spiritually.

"I want the path to truth that includes everyone," she decided that day, as a declaration of faith started to form in her mind. "One that's available right now, without rituals and dogma, and a litany of rules and regulations. One that is here waiting in each moment for the simple initiate, that requires nothing more than an open mind and heart. No tests, no badges of honor, and most of all, no specialness. Oh, and no proselyting either, by the way, because each would come to it in his or her own time. Because if we can't find the truth exactly where we are, where should we go in order to find it?"

The problem, at once, was one of enthusiasm and containment: how to share her newly emerging passion without offending prevailing attitudes and beliefs? "Turns out, you can't get there from here," Sabrina realized one day, after a particularly unsatisfying conversation with a church friend about the relativity of right and wrong.

And that's when Sabrina decided to take a Sunday off in order to see if going to church felt in any way essential to her "salvation" (a word rife with ambiguity, she thought). And she told her parents that she wasn't feeling well that weekend which was at least psychologically true, since she was suffering the pangs of an unrequited, comprehensive mental / spiritual exchange.

The experiment proved to be the final blow against a lifelong convention of church going. Not only did she see that church meetings were not a necessary adjunct to divine contemplation, the quiet time gave her an opportunity to investigate her own spiritual moorings. She found out that, indeed, she had some, and that they were not necessarily bound to "the traditions of the fathers," (as was so often quoted in the <u>Book of Mormon</u>, the key sacred text in the Mormon canon of scriptures). She noticed too, that this particular phrase was always applied to the bad guys in that book. The fact that they followed the traditions of their fathers seemed to be the main reason for their lack of personal integrity.

Sabrina could hardly see how this was not a universal problem among the 'good' as well as the 'evil'. That any thought system adhering to strict, unquestioned tradition for generations was bound to run amok somewhere down the bio-sociological chain of events.

Plato had said, "The unquestioned life is not worth living".

And the unquestioned mind? Is a static purgatory. Spiritual inbreeding, she thought."

All this had led her into her version of the dark night of the soul, which was apparently not going away until she had made a clear decision about her path, one way or the other. And she had to admit that moving to the townhouse might just be a way out of this spiritual cull de sac.

But it would mean letting go of the communion of mind she'd always shared with her father. And now, since she had no other man in her life, it would be doubly hard. This she realized was why she felt so uneasy about the idea of moving and why the solution did not appear clear cut and obvious.

Nevertheless, following his advice, Sabrina forayed every morning and night into the spacious, open country of the Big Mind. "No Mind," the Buddhists sometimes called it, referring to a mind free of preconceptions. Meditation, new as it was to Sabrina, always seemed to accommodate her uncertain and limited intelligence with vast canyons of holistic attention.

And what do you know, just as her father predicted, she began to feel something. A sweet resonant sensation that shifted her inner focus from indecision to a kind of open certainty. Yes, this unique little 2000 sq. ft. townhouse felt like just the thing that she needed for the rebirth of her conflicted soul. And even though apprehension loomed in her consciousness like an old familiar dragon, still Sabrina felt a quiet reassurance from within that the cosmos had her back. Which didn't always mean it was going to be smooth sailing. It may well be that her next growth spurt was coming on, which Sabrina had learned the hard way was a euphemism for upheaval and disaster. And even though she was reluctant about following an inner prompt that might lead to another series of unfortunate events, at the same time she couldn't really fight it or didn't want to. The Force was with her and it was living her life just the way it wanted, without a lot of input from her limited fear-based personality either.

But she had given herself over to this wholeness called Truth, and had promised that she would learn to follow her own guidance. This vow to lean inward, to ask her interior self and trust the answers, was a sweeping, no holds barred commitment. And she had no way of knowing where it would take her next or whether she would live through it unscathed. The only thing she knew so far, was that inner guidance did not necessarily equal ego gratification.

For one thing, this path was definitely not about playing it safe. Like it or not, in five weeks she would be writing out a big fat check to the mortgage company for all the money she had saved in the last 5 years, and it would take all her inner chutzpah to do it. Nevertheless, she went forward with a sense of purpose she hadn't felt in months. But this way was not for sissies.

The owners never countered. And so it was on the first Monday of October, 2012, she took up residence in her funky little Mindhouse which would begin a series of new adventures in:

<u>The Life and Times of Sabrina Ryder</u>

A Comedy in four parts

<u>Part one:</u> Into the Closet

<u>Part two:</u> Betrayal

<u>Part three:</u> What the?

<u>Part four:</u> Yadda Yadda Yadda

Forward by Woody Allen

Or maybe Eddie Izzard. Someone really funny though, because one needed a finely-honed sense of humor to appreciate the irony of everything that happened next.

7

In Which Sabrina Reflects on Special Relationships and Other Illusions

On the very night Sabrina planned the big move, she had to turn down an invitation for dinner with What's-His-Name, that cute editor on the production staff at work. And she liked editors too because they could always pare down a story so that it wasn't so self absorbed, plus they knew what questions to ask in order to get you to reveal yourself. It was a social arena she enjoyed and this particular guy was beginning to warm her cockles. And, what do you know, he was finally asking her out.

She loved working at Edwin Ross as a proofreader for prospective metaphysical material, perfect for her new life and times. And some interesting men had come her way since Ben, but she *wasn't biting on that apple anymore,* she often repeated silently to herself. Like a mantra she used it, afraid of going headlong into another exclusive relationship. No, that would be a long time down the road. *Maybe never,* she sometimes thought.

"The special relationship is the ego's most boasted gift"[11], she had read in the big blue book that she came upon one day at Costco, of all places, shortly after meeting Ben. The title she had found a bit sensational: <u>A Course in Miracles.</u> Yet it did get her attention.

And after reading just a few random passages, she found that she resonated deeply with the innate intelligence that seemed to transport her mind on every page:

- *You must learn that only infinite patience produces immediate effects.*[12]
- *The holiest of all the spots on earth is where an ancient hatred has become a present love.*[13]
- *Be not content with future happiness. It has no meaning, and is not your just reward. For you have cause for freedom now.*[14]

There were stacks of them piled onto a table, as though it were the most common thing in the world for wisdom of this magnitude to be lying about for just anybody on their way to buying a case lot of toilet paper. She bought the book without hesitation, and immersed herself in it every moment that she could find the time. Strangely, no author claimed it. It was published by The Foundation for Inner Peace, and was a work that apparently stood on its own merit. And Sabrina noticed that it was written in a rather lyrical, poetic form, maybe meant to override the intellect? Iambic pentameter?

The Voice was clear and certain, and it seemed almost an unspoken requirement that it be read with the heart, and not the strategic mind. For whenever she tried to understand the concepts in some rational way, she felt confounded. Yet had she fallen into a gradual, but deep rapport with it. With herself.

In fact, she couldn't explain how, but she felt that she had been an integral part of writing it for herself. Could that even be possible? Yet this feeling was certainly part of its miraculous nature.

She was moved beyond words by the feeling of love it evoked in her. On the other hand, she could hardly see how such unorthodox interpretations of traditional Christian concepts could work in a dualistic world. Take the one on relationship, for instance:

". . . the fantasies that center around [the special love relationship] are often quite overt . ."[15]

"Most curious of all is the concept of the self which the ego fosters in the special relationship." This "self" seeks the relationship to make itself complete. Yet when it finds the special relationship in which it thinks it can accomplish this, it gives itself away, and tries to "trade" itself for the self of another.[16]

"See how exactly this ritual is enacted . . . an altar is erected in between two separate people . . . Over and over this ritual is enacted. And it is never completed, nor ever will be completed. The ritual of completion cannot complete. . ."[17]

"Love is freedom. To look for it by placing yourself in bondage is to separate yourself from it. For the Love of God, no longer seek for union in separation, nor freedom in bondage!"[18]

She reflected on how this world was all about two separate people coming together over an altar and promising each other specialness in a "ritual of completion". And she remembered one of her favorite pundits, Fran Lebowitz—and who was gay, by the way—who once said, "Do I think gay marriage is progress? Are you kidding me? . . . I am stunned that the two greatest desires for gay rights are gay marriage and gays in the military! Really!!? To me, those are the two most confining institutions on the planet. Usually a fight for freedom is a fight for freedom! This is like the opposite! This is a fight for slavery!"[19]

Anyway, Sabrina resonated with that sentiment. This unquestioned zeal, this headlong romantic swagger into the outward show of pomp and circumstance—The Wedding—annoyed Sabrina no end, especially now that it hadn't worked out for herself.

Outrageously expensive wedding receptions and equally outrageous coming of age parties, like debutant balls, bar and bat mitzvahs, and baptisms, all seemed unwarranted to Sabrina, who loved pointing out to friends and family that change happened much too often to make any of these rituals ultimately meaningful, and certainly not worth all the money and pageantry.

At any rate, "What's-His-Name", the production editor, was going on her list of interesting friends, and nothing more. They would have to wait for another time to get to know each other, because here was the deal; even if all these long-held rituals and traditions could be sorted out to her satisfaction, Sabrina was not going to be heading in that direction tonight. Tonight she was going to be cleaning the debris out of her new/old fireplace, scouring her claw-foot cast iron bathtub and stocking her 18th century reproduction of a French armoire closet. And she had to admit that she was more intrigued with the prospects of hanging clothes, stacking shoes, and folding undies than going on a date with— what was his name anyway? Nathan something, but she had no interest in moving into the specifics of surnames. That might lead to a discussion about family, where do they live, and then dinner with the parents. And well, that was way too far down the road for this cynical romantic Heretic. Although that isn't what she said.

What she said was, "Sorry, but I have to get my house in order," which made it sound like she was dying, and gave him some pretty good material for a clever stand-up routine, a talent she was only just starting to appreciate about him. In between spasms of laughter, Sabrina explained that she was moving into her first house ever, and she wasn't even that polite about turning down his offer to help. "Another time," she laughed, and left him standing there conjuring jokes about the misuse of the death idiom.

She had even turned down offers from her family. Sabrina wanted this night to herself, to just move things around and get a feeling for where things wanted to be.

Yeah, well, and that was another thing that would have been hard to explain. She had a strong sense that the furniture knew best where it should go. Only a few weeks before, she had an almost mystical experience meditating on a lesson in <u>A Course in Miracles,</u> which stated,

"God is in everything I see. . .You will probably find this idea very difficult to grasp at this point. You may find it silly, irreverent, senseless, funny and even objectionable. Certainly God is not in a table, for example. .." [20]

"[Yet] you are making a commitment to withdraw your preconceived ideas about the table, and open your mind to what it is, and what it is for. You are not defining it in past terms. . ."[21]

"You could, in fact, gain vision from just that table, if you would withdraw all your own ideas from it, and look upon it with a completely open mind. It has something to show you; something beautiful and clean and of infinite value . . . Hidden under all your ideas about it is its real purpose, the purpose it shares with all the universe. . . ."[22]

Ever since this meditation, she was sure that even inanimate objects had a kind of intelligence flowing through them, and that they could certainly tell you where they belonged in a room, feng shui be damned. There was a downside to all this intelligence within the inert, however. And it sure as hell could turn against you in the form of a flat tire, or when something went wrong in the middle of a printing job. Or losing a file on the computer that you forgot to backup.

But tonight her main focus had nothing to do with technology. The only goal was to get things arranged so that by the time she left the house the next morning, the closet would be completely put together because here was the deal. To deliberately organize your closet right off was a kind of spiritual metaphor. It was as though your inner life had somehow patched in a direct line to God because you had actually given the heart of the matter (the inner expression of the outward form), some quality attention first. At least that's the way Sabrina had it wired the night she pulled into her new parking space on the fourth level of the parking garage, behind the little row of townhouses that would be her new home.

Examining the green LED–lit house key her father had given her the day she'd signed the mortgage documents, she engaged an inward smile. Nothing anyone passing by would have noticed. It was a private, sentimental gesture acknowledging that it was nice to have a protector, a champion and friend, even if it was her dad. As a matter of fact, "Pop" was too shabby a word for him she decided, and made a conscious decision right then and there to call him "Father" from now on. She felt suddenly more mature in adopting it although she often worried that her life had become rather trivial, making it unworthy of any real advocacy.

But maybe all that was going to change now.

Grabbing a load of clothes out of the trunk of her car, she walked to the elevator and pushed the down button to the well-lit paved alley below. Stumbling towards the row of townhouses and dropping belts and socks in her wake, she entered in the kitchen door at the back.

Earlier that day her father had let the movers in to deliver the furniture, and he'd left a note on the door: "Enjoy your first adventure into the Wardrobe: 'Onward and Upward, Narnia and the North!'"

Cute. And so like him, she thought. When she was ten years old they had read all seven volumes of C. S. Lewis' Narnian Chronicles, together. And since then, they had never lost an opportunity to use references from the stories in their daily life. *Kind of like actors do when they're in a play and they're constantly using lines from the script or songs to enhance whatever they're doing in real life,* Sabrina thought again.

The series of books began with four children playing hide-and-seek in a wardrobe that turned out to have a whole other dimension in its bowels. Hiding in the quiet depths of the closet was an enchanted country, frozen in ice and snow because of a spell held in place by a diabolical—what else?—white witch. Also there were fawns and all sorts of talking animals, and a lion king. Narnia was its name, and a more consummate adventure into the imagination there never was.

It was handy too, Sabrina recalled, that there were several old fur coats hanging on hooks just at the back of the wardrobe, so that the children didn't have to walk through the freezing cold in their shirtsleeves. Stories like this had a way of making one see that life was always supporting you, even when you are facing the unknown, afraid and uncertain.

Replete with Christian symbolism, the Narnian Chronicles was a perfect entry into the world of metaphor for a 10 year old. The lion, named Aslan, was a representation of Jesus. Sabrina learned to see, with the help of her father, that all stories ever written, including the Greek and Roman mythologies, children's fairy tales, and, of course, the time-honored scriptures from all sacred traditions and cultures, were simply stories about finding some idea of God, Good or some idea of truth. And taking the baton from him with intense fascination, Sabrina had found her stride in holding up her end of an on-going conversation about symbolism and metaphor.

Now, envisioning Narnia and remembering the warmth of her father's voice as they read each escalating chapter to each other, Sabrina had a petite mal moment right there in her kitchen. A little seizure of the heart. And for a few seconds she gazed glassy-eyed into a sphere of childhood delight, hypnotized by an exquisite transcendence of thought.

Presently though, a voice from somewhere in the work-a-day mind said: "Fur coats; we don't have those, not real ones any more, do we?"

Shaking her head, and coming back into reality, she thought, *What? I don't have time for spacing out!* Then grabbing a few more blouses and skirts from a nearby garment box, she hobbled up the stairs to her bedroom, where she threw everything on the unmade bed, and sat down on it cross-legged to get a feeling for her new digs.

The tail end of an autumn sunset ricocheting off the eastern mountain range had dappled her bedroom walls in a yellow-orange lightshow. "This is an even better feature than the closet", she whistled under her breath in appreciation. "Anyway, so far, so very, very good," she said, taking in the room lit up with golden luminosity. The walls were painted a rich yellow ochre in an old world Venetian plaster, and with the reflected light it was the perfect place and time of day to spend a quiet hour alone in meditation.

Glancing toward the closet, she noticed the large paneled doors were standing slightly ajar and that the key had fallen to the floor. *Pop must have wanted to have a closer look,* she thought, getting up to inspect it. *And no wonder. You really don't find a treasure like this every day.* It reminded Sabrina of an old antique cupboard she had once seen on Robertson Blvd in Los Angeles, and how surprised she was by the price; almost ten thousand dollars. She and Ben had gone to LA on a short vacation that year, and after looking in all the shops on Decorator's walk they decided that one day they would fill a house with real antiques and Persian carpets.

Now as she smoothed her hands affectionately over the dark stained wood, she thought there was something almost radiant about the doors; luminous, and a bit supernatural. Was it because of the childhood memories that had just flashed through her mind a moment ago?

Someone had taken great pains to make the whole affair look like a freestanding piece of furniture. It was a clever façade in the antique French armoire tradition, circa 1700, via 1986. But in reality it was an 8' X 10' walk-in closet, unusually large for a place that size. There were even the characteristic wormholes, which were probably put there by an ice pick, her father had said.

Peeking in, it felt as though she were embarking on an inner voyage; that Narnia was only a hair breadth away. And so it was that in an age when everyone was coming out of the closet, Sabrina Ryder was going into hers with curiosity and a sense of wonder. Still, the last thing she expected when she stepped into it that October night was—well, what actually happened.

8

A Conversation with God in Which Sabrina Gets on His Case

Betrayal is ugly; big and ugly and worst of all, unpredictable. Sabrina remembered that one of her psychology teachers once said that anyone who had ever lived would almost certainly feel a sense of betrayal sometime in his or her life, that it was built into the experience of being human, and that in many ways it was a highly underrated transformational device. She had always held this theory at bay with wry skepticism, not being familiar with the territory, confident that the "almost certainly" part was written in for someone like herself; an exclusion clause for the fashionably spiritual.

She was much too smart to be betrayed for one thing. And no one, least of all an adoring admirer—a man for instance—could pull the proverbial wool over her eyes.

Why she'd made straight A's in all her psychology classes, hadn't she? And besides, to Sabrina, being a victim was such an ugly trait that no one should ever seriously consider pretending to be one. For one thing, no victim ever lived or died for anything purposeful. Not to himself anyway. That's the point about being a victim. You were always at the behest of someone else's objectives. Anyway she was saving her sympathy for someone who really deserved it.

She was still looking for someone who really deserved it the day she met Ben. He had asked her to breakfast after an early morning sociology class on lower campus, and right away she made a guess that he might be just the one. Well, it wasn't such a stretch. He had a melancholy about him that drew her in immediately. He seemed sad for no reason in particular. It gave him a soft, gentle, unassuming demeanor.

Apparently she made him laugh too, a talent for which Sabrina never thought she had any aptitude at all. He'd heard of her bold tirades in psychology class, for instance, from one of his friends. In a heated debate on sexual abuse, Sabrina was reported to have said, "Here's the part I don't understand. Even if you were three years old and your creepy grandfather came into your bedroom at night, wouldn't you scream? Especially if you were three? I mean, three-year-olds scream if you look at them the wrong way!"

"But what if they love their grandfather or whatever and are too afraid to say no?" said a girl who said she had been abused. "A small child is helpless in that kind of situation."

But Sabrina persisted. "Are you kidding? Have you ever seen what a three year is capable of when something isn't happening the way they want? Let me tell you, it's not a pretty sight. It would take the wind out of the sails of any old blackguard's ill intentions to the contrary! I'm not sure a lecherous old man could handle something that malevolent!"

This elicited not a few snickers and some loud guffaws from the class.

"Okay, very funny!" said the other student. "But I personally have had regressions in hypnosis where I got in touch with some very dark energies, Satanic cult rituals and—"

"Oh really? Wait. What kind of shame are you hiding in there anyway? Sabrina said as she poked a finger at her challenger's forehead. "It may have even happened just the way you think it did, but here's the chilling part. It happens again in your psyche and your emotional body every time you tell it! Do you really want the grief that badly?"

Her cavalier attitude towards victimization had not gleaned her any points for compassion, but she couldn't help it. She wasn't buying any of it. Certainly it wasn't a stance that invoked admiration in the eyes of students and friends, but Ben seemed intrigued. He even seemed to agree. And what the heck? She liked people who agreed with her, especially men.

Sabrina was a good judge of character too, and why shouldn't she be? Her mother was the model of decorum and her father was a gem, a real gentleman and if not a scholar, certainly a—well, you know what?—he was a scholar, that's all. Good judgment was built right into the Ryder DNA and Sabrina was sure she had inherited it. Little double helixes, strung with wisdom beads, flowed all through her biological and genealogical charts.

And certainly a young man like Ben, who seemed to be able to hold his own in a conversation about almost anything, would be someone worth getting to know, right? Besides, he had to see that she was only looking for what was real. After all, she didn't attract scoundrels. Anyone could see that. So if Ben was one, he should have known better than to follow her around. Law of attraction, right?

They finally tested that one out a few weeks later in the back seat of his convertible under the desert sky. Magic.

But before that, when he had kissed her on the back of the neck while standing in line for breakfast at the IHOP? Well he just should have known who the hell he was going after.

Or at the very least, her intuition should have given her a heads up. Sabrina never shied away from doing the right thing if she understood what the right thing was. That is, she was smart enough to make mature decisions if she comprehended the rules for engagement. So why hadn't the Universe given her some kind of warning? A red flag or a blue notice board with the words, "Caution: Dangerous Curves Ahead", or something. Some indication that romantic love was a trap, that men are simpletons when it comes to romance, and that there are some women who are such fierce competitors, they want to win more than they want sisterhood. Oh, that was another kind of betrayal, and she didn't know if it wasn't the worst kind.

But the one she was really furious at, was God.

In some ways, it was much easier when she used to believe in the old anthropomorphic Mormon God, the "Heavenly Father", the great parent in the sky who watched over her and kept notes on her private thoughts and fantasies.

Or the God of the Old Testament. Now there was a deity who was passionate, very much like herself, and sometimes even waxed unaccountably wrathful, again, like herself. It seemed like He could at least understand where she was coming from. Why He could take out a whole city including the women, children and all the animals without so much as a "Woe unto you!" But at least he was someone who could understand her frustration and anger; someone she could whine at when things went wrong. True, he was always changing his tune. But while he was humming a particular tune, you could pretty much count the beats and keep in step if you paid attention.

But now of course, Sabrina didn't believe in those versions of God. She was almost certain that God was not a guy, for one thing, with a body and all its passions and appendages. Because if God were guided by human emotions, and not the tranquil serenity that was the signature of her experience in meditation, then he wasn't any more mature than she was. And where was the wisdom in communing with that?

Sabrina thought she had felt a distinct inner *yes* concerning her relationship with Ben. But then if God didn't have a body, maybe he didn't have a voice either and that sucked. So here was the real frustration in changing one's beliefs about God; who was He anyway? She could see why the fundamental mind clung to objective realities about Him. It was just easier to relate. And of course it was simply expedient to use the male pronoun in referring to the Source of all things, and useful as a metaphor.

And though her new version of God was not likely to be offended by the petty errors of everyday existence, perhaps "He" was not terribly interested in them either, so what could one expect in the realm of personal guidance?

"I mean this thing with Ben felt so right," the Radical Dissenter snarled at Abby one day in the midst of a temper tantrum. "I thought I was being guided by something . . .Someone that cared about my private—I don't know—my private struggles and intrigues. I mean why wasn't I warned that something was off with Ben?! How could I have been so completely fooled by this man; this . . . this boy? I mean, I was blindsided by folly on a level so cosmic, it's beyond reason or rationality! Someone," she said shaking her finger upward at Deus Nobodeus, "should have warned me!"

Abby pointed out that if she was talking about God, almost everything about him was beyond reason or rationality and that this much at least was clear: God was a Mystery.

Okay that was probably true, but you ought to be able to count on your own intuition then, and here was the deal: Sabrina hadn't even noticed how Ben was falling for those cheap stories that Amy Houston was feeding him. Well okay, she noticed, but who'd have believed he'd be swayed by them? That Amy needed him to repair their relationship from past lifetimes? That she was psychic about these things, and that personal expedience had nothing to do with it? Oh please.

I mean, really. Who falls for that stuff? Hello: someone who wants to. Oh she'd heard the stories Ben recounted, with great aplomb incidentally. One night while they were standing in line for a movie, he went off on Amy like she was a character in Modern Family. With typical sarcasm, Sabrina laughed and commented on the manipulative nature of 'the psychic'. She certainly never thought of her own sorority sister—almost three years younger—as a serious threat.

Here was an odd thing too. Amy had always insisted that she had introduced Ben and Sabrina to each other, but that wasn't true because Sabrina remembered they had met in sociology class.

"What Amy really means," the Madwoman said one day in a heated crossfire with Ben, "is that she knew you first, which apparently gives her some kind of a-priori claim on you!"

"She did know me first," Ben had replied, like it was a well known fact with which he concurred, and that that was the point after all.

This just sent the Crazy Girl into fits of prickly exasperation. "Oh really?! Really? Well, what difference does it make anyway, Ben? She's using it to enroll you, initiate you, enmesh you in a relationship with her, like somehow you owe her something. And you always end up care-taking her in kind of a juvenile—I don't know—but it has Jr. High overtones. Anyway, you actually seem to enjoy it. It's not her being your friend that bothers me. It's the quality of your friendship. It kind of bleeds all over everything, the co-dependency of it all. You suck each other's blood. It's a vampire thing. Really, Ben, can't you see it?"

He couldn't of course. And he wasn't laughing this time either. He looked somewhat horrified as a matter of fact, noticing for the first time The Serious One who wasn't that charming, but listen, who could sanction a thing like that? Amy was a pretty girl in her way and Sabrina knew that she and Ben were close friends, but a romance between them didn't track. Because Amy was a needy little shit, and Ben was always saying so.

As a matter of fact, Sabrina thought until then, being needy was listed under the "cons" side of a relationship and she was certain Ben thought so too. Of course Sabrina didn't need Ben. She had always thought it was in her psychological best interests not to need him. No. She was just very fond of the ground upon which he walked.

But maybe this had been his way of telling Sabrina that he liked being needed. Had she simply missed the cues? See, that's what she meant by being warned. Why wasn't she prompted to hear it that way? If she had been, this whole travesty of being deceived and looking like a tragic (or comic, she didn't know which) figure on the romantic event horizon, could have been averted.

But instead, for Sabrina's first trial run at real relationship, she found that needing and being needed actually trumped every other sentiment in the romantic love card deck. And she had to admit she was terribly naïve where these things were concerned.

What did she really know about romance anyway? Following in the tradition of good judgment, she'd always assumed that living in the present was the primary thing about being in relationship, that it precluded the unsettling distraction of lifetimes past. But now she was seeing that there was actually something quite exhilarating, to Ben and Amy at least, about life-hopping. Why was Sabrina so clueless about something so apparently engaging? Was there something wrong with her? Was she a soul with no experience, no resume' of birth, death and rebirth?

The worst part was that Sabrina had been completely unaware of the turn things were taking because. . .well, because she didn't really know that she was supposed to be competing for Ben's attention. And how could she be in the game if she didn't get a copy of the ground rules?

"First you make love. Then you get screwed," Sabrina whined. "That's where the trouble starts apparently; you just can't imagine the situation as it is," said the Raving Martyr to Abby. "And God—whoever/whatever he is—did not protect me from my own foolishness," she ranted, "and isn't that His job after all?" She realized, in fact, that she had cultivated a relationship with him for no other reason than that He should save her ego at times like this. And now who—whom—could she trust? Not Ben. Not God. Not even her intuition. Perhaps she had no intuition. Her only ally was her old friend, Suspicion.

"The ego is therefore capable of suspiciousness at best and viciousness at worst,"[23] said <u>A Course in Miracles</u>. And toward the end of her relationship with Ben, Sabrina simply vacillated from one to the other on any given day.

"Listen, God," she railed. "You're nothing like they told me you were, you know that? And another thing: where's back-up when I need it?" She liked being able to talk to him like this. For one thing, it was good to know right up front if he could handle it. He *was* God after all, right? She honestly didn't know what she believed about him anymore, but she was pretty sure He wasn't someone who could be offended by human frailty and who had strong personal opinions that reverted to methods of inquisition, excommunication and/or burning up whole cities when people didn't agree with Him.

As a matter of fact, it was in noticing how much God had changed from those Old Testament stories to the one in the New Testament, that Sabrina finally understood something. Man had pretty much made God in his own image instead of the other way around.

And just to underscore the idea, right after she had made this discovery there was a bit of a synchronistic moment when she found a book in Barnes and Noble one day called, <u>A History of God,</u> by Karen Armstrong. It contained the most wonderful non-sequitur right there in the title, and seemed to prove Sabrina's own point to herself.

The whole meaning of God having no beginning and end, being omnipresent, omnipotent and omniscient, was that He *has* no history. So if someone had made up a story-line on God, it had to be man himself; the master storyteller. And to Sabrina's way of thinking, that history would reflect perfectly the psychological evolution of the human mind.

In fact, in the New Testament, one could imagine that God had matured a bit, past the trivial mythologies of anthropological middle school, and was now actually relating more tenderly toward his children. At any rate she wouldn't be yelling at a God who wasn't, now would she?

When she was small she worshiped the Heavenly Father just like she adored her own father. Or Santa Claus. She would never dared have spoken to that God like she was speaking to this one. Besides, He was far away and busy with a lot of other civilizations and planets. He had a lot on his celestial plate, although Jesus was right there when He needed someone to stand in for Him.

Sometimes portrayed as a mediator between corporate management and consumer, Jesus was straightforward, no kidding around; handsome and full of lovely surprises, like healing everyone and casting out devils. He had you covered too, even if you made some terrible mistakes. As long as you repented he was there for you. He was even a prince. The Prince of Peace.

All those fairy tales are starting to make sense, Sabrina thought. *A virgin under glass, or maybe one who sleeps for a hundred years, gets kissed and awakened by the handsome prince who comes to save her and they ride off on his white stallion.*

Jesus is the prince, and humanity is the sleeping princess who awakens to find a new world. The white horse is—what? The gospel, as the Mormons call it. Truth, in metaphysical terms. And they ride off to live happily ever after. That would be like heaven, right? Everyone wants to know what Heaven looks like, of course. But it's self explanatory. Hello! It's 'Living happily ever after'. It's just really great, that's all, no exceptions. Are there malls, bowling alleys, amusement parks and good restaurants? Do they have Netflix? No one really knows. But it must be awfully fine.

"Sacred tales of the puerile mind," she mumbled.

And now, standing in her in the middle of her closet sanctuary, Sabrina realized that God was probably smarter than she was and mature enough to hear her anger without reacting in a torrent of fire and brimstone or burning down a city with all the women and children in it. Or giving her grief about the language she used in communicating with Him.

But conversations with God notwithstanding, she still had a bone to pick. The thing is, she had not just been humbled in this thing with Ben. She'd been humiliated. That was a big distinction and God sure must know the difference and didn't seem to care.

This was Betrayal with a capitol B. She felt not only immature, but amateur. And her sense of mortification would not let God off the hook that easily. She should have been warned. But instead, she had been betrayed: by love, by life, by God himself.

Now, how does a girl get over that?

9

The Risk

No, Sabrina wasn't done with God yet. She was going to find some way to get him to take a meeting with her. That was the appeal of meditation really, because maybe before, the problem had been that she simply wasn't speaking his language. She noticed he was silent a lot. Maybe silence was his language. Silence, or something very ancient like Sanskrit. But since she didn't speak Sanskrit, she thought she'd try silence first.

Well, okay, she didn't speak silence very well either. But gradually, through meditation, she thought she could learn to quiet the busy binary brain, and hear the voice for God underneath all the chatter that usually filled her head. She liked the term, "Voice for God". It was the way A Course in Miracles, characterized it.

In Church, they had called it, "the Voice of God", and that sounded rather too definitive for Sabrina. It smacked of, "God's Voice just spoke to me, so you better listen!"

On the other hand, a Voice *for* God could hardly be misinterpreted. It spoke for love, towards love, but not necessarily for the whole truth about anything. More like, "This is what I heard. It seemed like a loving voice at the time. Do you want to hear?" A very different approach, and one that gave everyone his own access to the internal wisdom generally attributed to a Higher Source.

As Sabrina stood admiring the workmanship of the doors, she wished that God were as real and as sincere to her as this closet. She picked the little key up off the carpet, using it to lock the doors together. Then jiggling the key, she opened it again. At first it wouldn't turn, but after a few tries it gave way. Then leaving the key in the lock, she stepped into the dark, quiet, beautifully carpeted space inside. Polished brass rods hung on three walls, with shelving above the rods and on either side of the doors. The light switch, she remembered, was just inside the first shelf, wasn't it? She remembered because, with all of the planning that must have gone into designing this thing, not having a light switch on the outside of the closet seemed like a huge mistake. But now she couldn't find a switch at all, anywhere. Where had she seen it before? There was no overhead light in the bedroom and no lamps to plug in yet. The dimming twilight was making it difficult to see anything, and no matter how many times she ran her hands over the shelves and walls of the closet, she couldn't find the damn switch. Feeling her way to the back of the closet she was irritated at this singular lack of foresight.

In everything that didn't go along smoothly these days (in her terms) she immediately felt thwarted, as though something more potent or comprehensive than her own understanding was running the show. Well alright, maybe that was a good thing, but did everything have to feel like a great big sucker punch to the solar plexus?

She thought as how maybe she had become a bit jaded. Instead of experience softening her into a kinder, gentler version of herself, it seemed to be doing the opposite. In fact, life seemed to be doing its level best to harden her. "Kicking against the pricks," was what they used to call it in church when it felt like this. *Still a very apt description,* Sabrina thought. She was definitely in her hard-ass phase, and too far down the road to deny it. Life may have closed a door, but she was determined to find a great big fucking picture window to climb back through.

Anyway, everything had a bittersweet flavor to it now, with all the old familiar themes and values causing her to be restless and uncertain instead of safe and comfortable. Playing it safe was the way she'd always rolled as a Mormon. She had taught herself to gauge activities with boys and other hazardous objects by these two guidelines:

- Was it safe?
- Did it feel familiar?

Subsets of these questions were:

- Am I going to get in trouble?
- Will it make my parents look bad?
- Will they be really angry?
- Will I look foolish?

Those were the real tests of truth in those days. And suddenly she realized in mild embarrassment, that whatever she thought was her new spiritual path, it was still only ever about these two things really: safety and familiarity. Comfort. Not too different from the path she had just left actually.

"Really?" she whined, "Have I lived for twenty-five years, playing it safe by following someone else's rules, only to end up playing by the same old rules in this new arena?" she asked herself.

They were good guidelines at one time no doubt, but now, didn't she want to take some risks? Wasn't that part of growing up, growing into herself and maturing?

To follow your heart into the darkest part of the forest all alone, like one of the Knights of the Round Table, just you and 'The Sword of Righteousness', she thought. "And what would I like to risk?" she asked herself in that moment, standing in the middle of her awesome, dark closet. Something valuable, she imagined, or it wouldn't really be a risk now, would it? Then it struck her.

"How about my eternal life? Do I have to risk it in order to find it?"

But this was another one of her outrageous theories. You couldn't really risk your eternal life, because eternal life is. . .well, what you are. In fact, she often liked to point to something as inconsequential as a toothbrush or a stack of dirty dishes and say, "I *am* Eternal Life, doing this!"

But so far, it was still just a theory. So why not take the ultimate risk and prove it to herself? Honestly, hadn't she come to this dimension to have experience? If she had, then for twenty-five years she'd been resisting it in the name of some idea of truth. Except that it wasn't in the name of truth at all. It was in the name of propriety and looking good, and lots of other ideas built on generations of conditioning about maintaining a sterling image for the sake of setting an example to a world which seriously needed help. But what if helping the world simply meant to change your mind about it?

She noticed that if she started her day with meditation and instructed her mind to look for peace in every situation, she would actually have a noticeably calm and unruffled day. It was like her mind was a servant of her own clear intentions. If she focused it on love and peace, then that is the day she would have. But when she forgot to focus or set an intention, her days reflected this lack of focus with endless mishaps, frustrations and chaos.

Why would changing her ideas about eternal life work any differently?

So this was the risk she was willing to take. To trade her old ideas about eternal life; that it was somewhere out there far away and separate from her, for this new idea; that she practice *being* eternal life right now. Then see how changing this one thought about it, might change her world.

Ensconced in her closet, and poised on the brink of something auspicious, she thought she really could learn to trust life again, if she were willing to question her old, habitual, conditioned thinking and consciously open her mind to something new.

"Well, then. Let's get started," she said to the elves of the closet world. I'll get my things and begin arranging a new life with new rules in my new space."

Then very slowly, almost noiselessly, hardly noticeable at all, the heavy paneled doors swung shut behind her.

"What the—?"

She tried to adjust her eyes to the dimming light. No, actually, it was quite black now. Like pitch, to use a blatant cliché. Turning around, she felt her way back to the doors and pushed on them. No movement. No handles on the inside either. Pushing hard, rattling the place where the key must have been, they still wouldn't open.

Then she heard a soft click and a dull little thud. Was she imagining it? No. The doors were locked tight and the key had fallen out of the lock, onto the floor again.

She was locked in the closet with no way of letting anyone know. Because in the excitement of grabbing all her stuff out of the trunk, she realized she had left her cell phone on the front seat of the car. She remembered that now, but here was the deal: it was too late. Surely this unconscious, idiotic lack of awareness was not part of the plan.

The feeling was strangely ironic and much too familiar.

Betrayal.

10

One True Thing

It was chilly too. The utilities had been turned on, but she hadn't flipped on the thermostat yet. And—oh—just for added cosmic humor? There were no fur coats hanging in the closet, and apparently not an escape hatch out the back either. No Narnian nether-world waiting to relieve her from the tedium of the next 12 hours.

The manager had said she would probably stop by in the morning, or maybe her father would come. He had an extra key to let himself in if he thought to bring it. But she wasn't expecting any visitors between now and morning. She had made very sure of that. She did have a light sweater on, thank goodness. And there was a small wad of something soft on one of the shelves, she couldn't tell what it was exactly, in case she wanted to use it as a pillow for sleeping. Meantime, she could . . . meditate. Right.

Sitting up straight against the back wall in the crossed-legged yoga fashion, with palms up, she tried to calm her mind . . .

"Oh! Screw it! This is unbearable! Why do these things always happen to me?!" the Indignant One fumed. Feeling helpless against an outer universe determined to expose her for a fool, she realized that this was a running theme in her life. It was her old friend, Humiliation.

If only she could learn to trust things as they occurred, even things like this, instead of feeling conspired against.

"Your passage through time and space is not at random,"[24] she'd read in A Course in Miracles. And typically, she loved the kind of reassurance that that gave her. But in this moment her life felt entirely random and restless, and not aligned with any kind of purpose at all. Honestly, what purpose could this serve anyway?

"And even when someone eventually comes by, I'll feel so stupid calling out for help," she groaned in anticipated embarrassment.

Gradually, however, she wrenched her attention away from The Predicament, and the quiet voice underneath seeped through. That voice felt authentic, attentive. That voice wasn't really a voice at all. It was more like a guidance system built on feeling. *Turns out, simple feeling is trustworthy,* she thought, *and it can lead you to the Holy Grail of anything.*

And how to describe the feeling? Well, it felt like an ancient pre-verbal language. *Like a loving Presence has your back,* she thought. *That acceptance, allowance and appreciation—the three 'A's, I like to call them, are the default position for navigating this wild ride called life. It is the feeling of facing everything with an open heart. And if something else looms on the horizon of my mind—resistance in any form, for instance, I can feel that too, and know right away I'm going in the wrong direction. If I remember to check.*

Buying this condo was her first deliberate attempt at following this subtle yet simple feeling state since the Ben thing. Certainly there must be a way to get her groove back, her hunch reflex, her sixth sense. *This intuitive instinct.*

Times like this you have to use all the tricks in your psychological tool belt, she thought. After all, she did want experience, right? And it wasn't all going to be *only good*, and on her terms. That's what she'd been doing all her life so far. Now didn't she want some real adventure? And not the cheap kind either. The real kind, with pith and poignancy.

Within the first hour the silence had wooed her in a way she never expected. It actually seemed like an entity, a comfortable blanket or a shadow quilt. In fact, it was just like the old traditional scriptures said: 'a comforter'. "I will send you another comforter,"[25] Jesus had said. And this must be it because she was beginning to feel alright. More than alright, she was feeling like this was exactly where she was supposed to be. And in an odd sort of way, there wasn't any place she'd rather be.

It was a good feeling, and one she always went for when she was stuck in traffic or in a situation where resistance was high. Very seldom did she come to such complete surrender, however. But she achieved it now, perhaps because there really was nothing else to be done? And twelve hours was such a long time. Nevertheless, being wholeheartedly present for life was the thing.

It might be the only thing.

11

In Which Sabrina Encounters the Fool

For the next hour she felt as if she were floating on her back in a salt water pool; the quiet mind supporting her in brilliant stillness. Eventually thoughts began to bubble up from subconscious depths:

But I could have influenced so many people for good if I had just stayed on the traditional path. If I had done it another way, and not been so foolish, the logical everyday mind observed. And yet, she couldn't deny that there was some merit, however small, in the way she was actually doing it. Something so satisfying in being willing to make huge mistakes in front of God and everybody. Not that they were intentional, but just the willingness to make mistakes seemed somehow courageous.

A wise teacher had once said, "Don't be careful, you could hurt yourself."[26] Well, she had been being careful her whole life, preserving her image for posterity, and was no better off for it. Now she would give real experience a try.

For one thing she could see how beautifully the Universe supported her in any direction she happened to go. Playing the fool may not be worldly wise, but it was simple and open and easy. She had only to look upon the world with curiosity and awe. Sure, there'd be times when she'd stumble all over herself, or be "hoisted up on her own petard" (Shakespeare always said it best). Or run smack into a psychological cement wall going 60 miles an hour, like a Looney Tunes cartoon. She simply needed to get comfortable with herself as life's straight man. The straight man in a comedy act was the one everyone laughed *at*. Not the one who made all the clever jokes, but the one who looked stupid afterward. Elmer Fudd.

It's important to have a straight man in a comedy act, but who actually wants to be one? Sabrina asked herself. *But what if she were willing? What if she stopped resisting the inevitable? Wasn't she just going to keep getting a pie in the face anyway? Why fight it? If only she could stop taking everything so seriously.*

But that seemed beyond her ken. She'd been raised to do the opposite, the victim of what she liked to call, "Serious-Child Syndrome"—SCS. And this was heavy stuff.

It went like this. She was taught that everything good was sacred, which was synonymous with serious. And the opposite of this kind of serious was not funny, but evil. There was no place for "silly" in the serious mind. Not that living a sober life was completely somber, mind you. There was a difference. Life was just far too important to be flippant about.

Sarcasm, Sabrina decided, was the serious man's humor, and a weapon so brutal as to not be underestimated. She, her mother and brother were skilled in its use. Her father, not so much because he was a convert to the religion of the sacred/serious mind, and already too open and unpretentious by the time he came to Mormonism for sarcasm to have had much of a trickle-down effect on his vocabulary.

In fact, he often tried to get Sabrina to see things through a lighter, less serious lens. "Vision," he called it; a more spacious perspective, he said, that allowed one to see life as a "large vista of stories strung together with no beginning or end, so you can hardly blame anyone for the way it turns out," he would say. To his way of thinking, it was taking things literally that made one solemn and humorless. Even tyrannical. He often repeated in her ear (when they were sharing something beautiful and heartrending) the Anne of Green Gables' quote, "'Such scope for the imagination', eh Sabra?"

Her mother, quite clever really, had a more practical approach to life, and through her considerable piety, she had at least an equal effect on Sabrina. One day, for instance, she quipped with a dry observation, "Good taste hardly has anything to do with getting into the Celestial Kingdom (the Mormon version of Heaven)." Knowing, of course, that good taste was entirely subjective and had nothing to do with it at all, still they'd all recognized that they had been so thoroughly programmed to think that her idea of refinement was directly related to some notion of right and wrong. It was one of those moments when a family joke was born, and they used it whenever they encountered something that was not to their liking. But the distinction between the truth about it, and its humorous undertones had diminished over the years.

"The strain of constant judgment is virtually intolerable," said A Course in Miracles. "It is curious that an ability so debilitating would be so deeply cherished." [27]

Sabrina wondered if it were possible to live without judgment or preferences. Could you be wise and not judge? Better to be the fool she decided, which was probably just another way of excusing unconscious behavior, but what the heck. You can forgive the fool anything, right? Even judgment?

In Elizabethan times there was such a thing as the Holy Fool. Not the sophisticated prankster of the political and social court, but an "innocent," who was the modern day equivalent of a psychic or an intuitive. A mystic, prophet or visionary. Sabrina kind of liked that idea of a fool, but then that fool was rarely thought of as funny. And somehow she knew that what she needed was to inject some kind of madcap humor into her life to lighten the heaviness of the compression of her own judgments and weighty opinions.

Here, in the solace of the closet world, in dark visions, she imagined herself being slashed with the sharp, two edged sword of seriousness and sarcasm and emerging unscathed, *if* she were willing to play the fool entirely without reservation and—more importantly—without defense.

She had been sitting in the dark for so long now that she was beginning to take her thoughts for things. Dressed in the court jester's garb, yellow on one side and green on the other, with bells jangling on the tips of a triple-pointed hat, The Fool danced her way through countless dreamy vignettes calculated to make Sabrina laugh. But here was the thing. She didn't know how. She'd never really learned what it was to feel a deep-throated guffaw bubbling up from the depths of her belly and spilling out all over the place without restraint.

And maybe that was the problem. Once she started laughing, would she ever be able to stop? Eventually she lay down on the carpeted floor of the closet in the fetal position, and drifted off into a reverie halfway between meditation and sleep. Weary of being wary, and exhausted from defending her need to look like she knew something, it seemed she was lost in a whirlpool of collective and personal idiocies, all of them swirling inexorably toward a black hole opening up in her mind.

****

Then somewhere down deep in the thickets of her imagination, her wildest inner landscapes, the visage of a man came to her.

It seemed that he found her on a dampened forest floor, covered in a copse of tangled boxwood, conspiring to keep her sleeping, and far from the life that seemed to be going on up there on the surface of things. At first she didn't know whether he was there to save her, or push her further into the moist, dank undergrowth below. He stooped down though, and gave her a draft of wine. Or at least she thought it was wine. From a tiny chalice it was. He held it to her lips, and it seemed to revive the aguish blood now barely percolating in her cold frame. The wine had a lovely effect on her and she sat up.

"Well now," he said with a kind, indulgent voice, "How did you come to be here on my path? I suppose you're in need of guidance or else some common sense, seeing you've just decided to lie right down in the middle of the road without a thought as to who might trip over you?"

"Am I? In the middle of someone's road?" she yawned.

"I should say you are. My road as a matter of fact, and it's a good thing too, because there's a lot of mischief afoot tonight. You could have done worse. I hear there's been a Fool causing some disturbance in the cosmos," he said, as he helped her onto her feet. "Here, come and sit with me on this log," he said, indicating the spot with his hand. "You're much too silly to be lying there pretending to be dead. No one with half a mind would ever believe you. I certainly don't, but then, of course, I have no mind."

"You have no mind? How is it you can talk then?"

"Well I suppose I shouldn't say, 'no mind' exactly. I just don't identify with it. It's a tool I get out and sharpen once in a while, because I do use it on occasion. You see, I'm a lazy man, but in spite of that, I'm revving it up right now so I can help you out with a few things there, Sabrina-girl."

She revived a little more and sat next to him, as he bid her do. She wanted to see how this mind-as-a-tool thing worked. "Tell me about the Fool," she said. "Is he dangerous, because I was thinking about maybe playing that part myself for a while. Consciously that is. I've already done it very well without meaning to, thank-you very much. It's quite painful that way. It feels like I am the royal butt of some cosmic joke, if you know what I mean. I was hoping to do it differently this time."

"Ah. . . Then you must *see* it differently this time," he said, looking at her with affection. She couldn't really see him that well. It was very dark after all, but it felt like affection, like genuine loving kindness.

"First of all," he said slowly, as if he wasn't used to talking much, "I think maybe you're on to something. You can play the Fool consciously and you'll come out all right. It's not too different than the way you've been doing it, but—like you said—you'll be more aware. And you'll more easily find the humor in things. And you'll get to be right about as often as you are wrong, so good news, huh? But don't attach yourself to that idea. You may be wrong many times in a row. But the Fool doesn't care.

"And you were accurate when you were thinking about your church experience a while back; growing up with the belief that you had a higher understanding of truth than the rest of the world. You should always ask yourself in any situation like that, 'Out of all the perceptions available to me in the universe—why am I emphasizing the ignorance of my brothers?[28] What am I doing in a role where I am the smart one, the enlightened one? What kind of standards am I conceiving, in which so many people are seen to be suffering, while I am the one with the truth?'

"We like to think of ourselves as only kind, good, and wise. We try to be pendulums that swing only to one side.[29] But the more we hate evil, the more evil there is to hate.[30] That which you resist, persists. Jesus said, 'Resist not evil,' and then he gave those wonderful parables about going the extra mile and turning the other check and so on, remember? People don't like to emphasize that part of his teaching. It makes them uncomfortable because we are afraid of our own ignorance, our evil impulses. We'd rather project those qualities onto someone else.

"But the more we withdraw from loving other beings, no matter how evil or ignorant you think they are, the more mass-obsessed we become.[31] Then your vibrations drop to a level, where you find yourself being identified with the serial adventures of the conditioned human mind. But there's nothing holding you down to the mass level except the ignorance of your own thinking and its affect on you. At this mass level of density, you feel pushed around a bit, not in control. You don't feel free when you think of yourself essentially as a body or personality, separated off from the whole of consciousness. After all, so many things seem to be harmful at this level; toxic air, questionable food, contaminated water; other peoples' words and actions, guns, war, pestilence and disease. But strangely, the more you resist this solid, material world, the more you bind yourself to it."

"But, if we don't resist the world as it is," she replied a little defensively, "How can we keep from suffering? And there's so much pain in the world. Shouldn't we help others?"

"Ah, yes. Helping others. But before dashing impulsively into any scenario you've judged problematic, consider this: how can you know that what you are doing in most cases *is* truly helpful and to whom? And from what point of view?"

"What do you mean? How hard can it be to see what's helpful to someone?" she responded. "I could site many instances where what was assumed to be helpful to one, was pretty much an abomination to the other. The Spanish Inquisition, witch hunts, two World Wars, the Berlin Wall. Then of course, there is chemotherapy, pesticides, fireworks, and fire itself. Bad or good? When to burn and when to douse? Then of course, there is slavery, circumcision, amputation, the welfare state, and *what about* Obamacare?"

Sabrina laughed at the lazy man's take on things. "Okay. . .so there are two sides to every—"

"My love, there are too *many* sides to consider, where helping is concerned. Unless you feel prompted by a feeling of great compassion—not pity mind you, or guilt—it might be better for one to simply stay centered in his/her peace. Perhaps it could be said that the Boy Scout aiding an elderly woman across the street is the least terrifying example of helping others. Although, a runaway bus could negate even that good deed."

"Really! You're—that's appalling!"

"Life on the unconscious mass level is appalling, my Love. And—at least where helping is concerned—rarely predictable."

"But still, we have to *try* help people who are suffering . . . shouldn't we? Even if we get it wrong sometimes?"

"Hmmm. But it is elementary, my dear Watson, to understand that it is *your* idea of suffering and pain you're looking at. After all, you are the one defining it thus. And the truth is, your suffering is the direct result of your resistance and lack of peace. But all you need do to get free from the suffering, is to be willing to be aware of anything, absolutely anything that enters your consciousness.[32] The way out, as hard as it is to believe, is not through further resistance or negation, but by being willing to think about it without judgment, by allowing it, in short, which could be seen as a way of loving it, as we should have done in the first place, [33] when it was just a thought. And I'm talking about what appears outside your mind as well as in it; it's all the same, you know."

"Well no, I don't," said Sabrina.

"Ho! Unfortunately, most people with good intentions are trying to deny or eliminate what is already manifest.[34] But everything in the manifest world begins in the mind: and every evil in the manifest world becomes real on the mass level because you refused to conceive of causing it, or denied someone else the freedom to conceive of it.[35]

"I happen to know you like A Course in Miracles. It's a . . . scripture for your time, don't you think? In the workbook, it says,

'All things I think I see reflect ideas. . . . What I see reflects a process in my mind, which starts with my idea of what I want. From there, the mind makes up an image of the thing the mind desires, judges valuable, and therefore seeks to find. These images are then projected outward, looked upon, esteemed as real and guarded as one's own.'[36]

"And I might add, concerning the perception of evil: hidden, and represented as someone else's.

"In short, a thought that is despicable to you is still one of the many thoughts that you *do* have, whether you like it or not. But not liking it—resisting it—won't make it go away. It will just make it more real to you. Attention is a powerful way to fuel a temporary reality. Even an unpleasant one.

"And what can you do about a perceived evil then? A great deal, if your head is clear. So rid your mind of judgment and anger first. My catch-all phrase is: I wouldn't deny that experience to the One Mind.[37] Then once you have cleared your head on the matter, do whatever feels right to you. Because you wouldn't deny that experience either, right?

"Evil occurs as a secondary reality, after you have withdrawn to the lower vibration level of resistance. The seduction of evil gains potency just because it involves us in trying to eliminate it.[38] When your consciousness is open and free, peaceful, any action you take in reference to evil has no more significance than digging a ditch to channel floodwaters away from a house .. . The true enemy—if there is one—is in yourself, in your failure to love enough.[39] Ah, but there's no moral judgment about that either. We can't love before we do!

"Look, it's like this. You can pretend that you are only good. You could even pretend that evil doesn't really exist at your level of consciousness. But take this example: if you refuse to admit that automobiles exist, you are going to get hit by cars, not because you are sinful or neurotic, but just because you are not looking for automobiles."[40]

Sabrina finally had something to say, because she had just been thinking about this idea in regards to Ben; how she had not been aware of the games he and Amy were playing. "Amazingly, I think I understand what you are saying," she said. "I had some experience of that not long ago. So, how can I be the fool and be aware at the same time?" she asked.

"Playing the Fool doesn't mean you are stupid. Being stupid (unaware) is not being able to be in the same mental/physical space as others. You are always responsible for what you condemn in others. Think about it. You are the one defining the dynamics in any situation. Therefore, it is useless to correct anyone's behavior. If he knew what he was doing, he wouldn't be doing it, true enough, but he's just as capable of knowing that as we are. And if he doesn't see it of his own free will, is he any more likely to do so when we tell him?[41]

"By denying him his freedom to be wrong—to be 'stupid', let's say—we are equally wrong.[42] Playing the Fool is to see this clearly and act accordingly. Never try to be right or special or better than. Just let yourself be in the same space as everyone around you. Allow, appreciate, and accept! The 3 "A's". That was a great aphorism you made there, Sabrina-Girl.

"We can call it 'playing the fool', because this attitude intends no harm. You may look foolish to others out there because you are not trying to control or fix or establish rules, boundaries or images of yourself. You are just looking at life without judgment. It really is more like that Elizabethan fool that you were thinking of a moment ago. Innocent, because no agenda. That's what innocence looks and feels like. Do you see?

Sabrina thought she might.

"Giving others the freedom to be stupid is one of the most important and hardest steps to take . . . Conveniently? The opportunity to take that step is all around us every day.[43] And that's what it means to play the fool. Because it feels, for all the world, vulnerable and 'not knowing'. Go for that feeling, sleepyhead, and you will be the Holy Fool having holy encounters every moment of every day."

She sat in stillness, taking in everything he was saying, hoping she could remember it all. She wanted to be the perfect fool. Uh oh— but then that would just be another agenda for trying to be better than others, wouldn't it?

"To be a real Fool, I can't be trying to be the best one, then, can I?" she finally asked.

After a moment's consideration, he said, "At first you may feel a bit lazy. Certainly not driven. You will question your new outlook based on the old conditioned standards your mind is used to following. But stay loose, relaxed and unhurried. Not lethargic, mind you. Pause as often as possible and loosen your mind from all it thinks it knows. Just a few seconds, here and there every so often. The power of Pause is potent.

"At any rate, you are neither greater nor lesser than any other, no matter what it looks like on the outside. Every personality is like a jewel in the crown of Life. Let every jewel remind you of the diamond light of love. And know that the smallest kindness is a facet in the infinite jewel of enlightenment."[44]

"I'm not really a naturally kind person," Sabrina said. "I've been much too serious about being a good person."

"Very nice awareness, dear one," The Lazy Man said. "Keep looking and loving yourself right where you are. The best one, on which to practice being kind, is yourself."

Sabrina heard these words, but she couldn't take in any more wisdom than she'd already absorbed in this dark and wondrous wood. She was feeling tired again and almost ready to nod off.

"You will get the hang of this very quickly my friend. And we'll talk again in time. For now let that last insight give you . . . pause."

And in an instant, it seemed to her that the Lazy Man disappeared into the forest, and she was lying again on the road where he had found her. Or was it the closet floor? Was this a metaphor? Was she on a particular path now? His path?

"Wait! What's your name?" she called out faintly.

But he didn't answer. Too lazy, no doubt. He was gone, and she was suddenly too sleepy to care.

It was as if she had traveled into the woods, far into an unknown part of herself. Would she ever come out? She only hoped she wasn't in anyone else's way. Because just right then, she couldn't have removed herself for anyone. Not even Aslan, the Lion of Narnia.

Patricia York

12

Out

"Sabrina? Sabrina! Are you here?"

Awakened suddenly and startled by several voices calling her name in fretful apprehension, it took her a minute to remember where she was, and she didn't even have time to be embarrassed. She was back in the world of density, of people and places, time and space.

"Dad? Mom? Neil, is that you? I'm in here! I'm in the closet. I think the key is on the floor. Can you see it?"

In a moment there was a wrangling of the key in the lock, and her mother stood backlit by the light streaming though the open closet door. Feeling like Gollum, wandering the underground Mines of Moria, Sabrina unwound herself and stood up, squinting hard at the morning sun coming through the east windows, unshielded as yet by any curtains. Running her fingers through tangles of dark, untamed hair, she patted her head to see if she had on a Jester's hat or anything else that might give away the conversations running rampant through her mind for the last—what? Time was playing tricks on her.

"What time is it?" she asked, squeezing the sleep out of her eyes.

"9:30. What happened, honey?" her mother asked, relieved to find her daughter *not* dead in the alley behind the townhouse or abducted by aliens, either one of which—in her mind—had been a strong possibility only a few minutes before. It was that SCS thing.

"Honey, did you sleep here in this closet all night?"

"Yeah, Mom," said Sabrina, sleepily. "The closet door locked behind me and I couldn't get out."

"Aren't you cold? It's freezing in here!" bellowed her younger sister, Sadie. "I just turned on the thermostat incidentally. Why didn't you call?"

"Why did you close the door behind you if you didn't have a key?" asked her brother, Neil. "That's just the kind of stupid thing you'd do, Sabra." Ordinarily Neil's annotated version of her life had a grating effect on Sabrina's nerves, but not this morning. She was just too glad to be out from under house arrest.

"Yeah, I'm an idiot. Hey everybody, can we get some breakfast? I didn't eat dinner last night. No room service in the closet."

"Let's!" rejoined her father, "But why you didn't call, Sweetheart? Were you afraid it was too late? Because I would have been happy to come over and unlock the—"

"Pop," Sabrina interrupted, "I left my phone in the car. Can you believe it?" And then to Neil, she said, "And I didn't close the door, you jerk. It closed and locked behind me all by itself. I mean, what are the chances? I think I was supposed to spend the night in there; kind of like an initiation thing. Whoa, Sadie, you're right! Thank goodness it wasn't as cold in the closet as it is out here," she said, wrapping her arms around her thin sweater.

Patricia York

"You make it sound like that closet has a mind of its own," said Mrs. Ryder, looking suspiciously at the lock and key. "Why do you insist on making up stories about inanimate objects with personalities, dear? It isn't smart, you know. People will think—"

"It locked all by itself?" said her father in disbelief. "Sweetheart, that's a little hard to believe. Seriously."

"Yeah, I know. . ." she responded thoughtfully. "But don't you think maybe we are inclined to take things *too* seriously, Pop? Maybe we don't need to. I mean maybe nothing is as serious as we think."

"It's creepy if you ask me," said Neil, "like a poltergeist or something. And that's pretty serious."

"Darling, can't you find a spiritual path that doesn't require all these esoteric hijackings?"

"Whoa, Mom! 'Esoteric hijackings'! That's a good one; I'm going to remember that when I write my book," Sabrina said as she locked the front door. She didn't even bother to put on lipstick or comb her hair. The Fool was definitely out in full force (regalia) this morning.

"What book?" asked her mother, hopping a little to keep up. Mrs. Ryder was usually in her own world, straggling behind the others when they went out together as a family. But now everything about Sabrina interested her. She secretly loved adventure stories and this was one; this story that Sabrina was forcing them to live through. So now what? A book? "It's not a memoir, is it? You're not going to write about family secrets are you, Sabrina?"

"Family secrets?!" Everyone laughed, rolling their eyes and jabbing each other with elbows.

"Mom! Our family doesn't have any secrets," Sadie said loudly, so that everyone on the street turned to look.

"Yeah, and anyway, we are the most boring people in the world," said Sabrina. "Maybe in the whole Church. And certainly on the block! I wouldn't write a book about our family. It wouldn't sell. Not to worry, Mom. It was just a figure of speech."

Blanche Ryder was chagrined. Of course they were boring. That was the definition of a nice, well brought up family. No one doing anything to put in a in a tell-all book. But did Sabrina have to say it that way?

"Would it be such a stretch to think that I could write a book though?" Sabrina asked as the family walked toward the car. "I could write something about Joseph Smith. He was always getting into trouble. Now there's someone who was interesting! Visions and Golden Plates, and he was only an "uneducated boy of 14," as they say. Plus he wasn't even a Mormon at the time! Can you imagine, Mom? No Mormons?" she teased. "Incidentally, in case you didn't notice, Mormons are primed for 'esoteric hijackings'. That's how the whole thing got started, isn't it?" she said, opening the front passenger door to the Prius for her mother.

Bishop Ryder shouted out, "Where to everybody?"

"Let's go to that Mexicali place on 21st South," Sadie said. "They have breakfast burritos and some kind of a vanilla drink that's really good."

"The Mexicali place it is!" cried the Bishop. "Get in everyone. Sabra, let that go now and give us the specifics about last night." And so, with everyone talking over each other all the way, Sabrina gave her father the cliff notes on the closet experience (leaving out the part about the Lazy Man for the time being) and she barely heard him when he asked her about the latest book she was amending at work.

"Oh," she called from the back seat over the conversation her mother and Sadie were having about new school clothes, "It's a smart little manuscript about archetypal symbols. I can't make out if it's going to be comprehensive enough to publish on a grand scale or if they'll just print a few to test the market. It could be something that would interest almost anyone in anthropology, psychology, history or maybe even philosophy, since it's all about connecting belief systems through universal images and icons. It follows the tradition of Carl Jung and Joseph Campbell, only not quite so academic."

They pulled into a parking place behind the eatery, and piled out of the car, still engaged in side talk.

"Do you actually think it's possible to find a connection between all belief systems?" her father asked. "Is there a field out beyond our ideas of right and wrong? I'm afraid that's got to be the idealism in you talking again, Sabra." He was referring to Rumi, the Sufi poet, whom he had introduced to Sabrina when she was 19.

Sabrina adored the fact that he could take up this line of reasoning with her, even though she often, especially lately, didn't agree with him. He could have run her over with a convoy, tankers-full of things she didn't know, if he was of a mind to. But he was never condescending. And he rarely shied away from talking about something just because they couldn't agree, although it happened occasionally now that she was in questioning mode.

"That's weird, we were just playing around with these same ideas at work the other day, only it was a discussion about the underpinnings of human nature, and whether it exists commonly throughout all ages. Human nature. Isn't that just another term for the collective mind? And if we share a mind as a human species, couldn't we step outside convention once in a while and observe our collective thinking from there?

"I don't see why not. 'Scope for the imagination'?" he said.

She thought how uncommon it was to stay in a conversation that likely would never be resolved, especially with someone you cared so much about. No one got to be right. No one got to win. There was no finish line and no absolute conclusion on which they would ever likely agree.

Having taught his children to think for themselves, Bishop Ryder realized he must appreciate the fact that Sabrina had at least learned this one lesson well. But what had he really done? He often asked himself this in the middle of the night, waking up in a cold sweat, worrying about his firstborn, this precious life that had been given into his care. In those moments, he felt blindsided. Why had he, in such a cavalier style, simply trusted that freedom of thought could be handled by one so young? Certain church leaders had even warned him about it, but no, he had to uphold some intellectual standard he thought was more correct. Now his pride had led him into this 3-o'clock-in-the-morning labyrinth of bewilderment and guilt.

The problem was she had turned out to be intelligent in a way that no one could have predicted. Being his first child, how could he have known how extraordinary she was? Would he have been more careful if he had known? And anyway, how could her intelligence be a negative thing? They hadn't really discovered this about Sabrina until she was a sophomore in high school when her class had taken a battery of aptitude tests. One of her teachers suspected that she had some extraordinary gifts, and asked for an I Q test along with the other ones. A friend, Ryder's closest confidant at church, was a teacher at the high school and privy to these things. Taking him aside one Sunday, he told the Bishop the amazing news, that his daughter had as high an IQ score as anyone had ever tested in the school district, maybe even the whole state.

They never told her about it. They didn't need to really. Ryder could tell that his daughter knew it without being told; that was part of the gift. Or the curse. That part was yet to be seen. It hadn't made her an anomaly though, not uncharacteristically odd or even terribly nerdy, at least not so anyone would notice. No, she had just enough intelligence to hang herself. Enough for her to trust her own ideas over someone else's. Over his. What, in his eagerness to bring up this child "in the way she should go,"[45] had he done? Had he just deliberately thrown her over to the adversary with no lifeline back?

He had been much more careful with the others after that, discomfited by his overreaching intellectual pride. Meantime, this one, this Sabrina, this bright star, would have to be nourished with as much love as he could possibly muster without smothering her. That was the only way to undo his mistake, and he asked God's help in it every day.

Characteristically, Ryder didn't have much use for resistance or force anyway. He'd never had a day's luck with either of them, perhaps because his own father had used them both without success. J. Ryder Sr. had died, having put as much distance between himself and his oldest son as it is possible to do in a lifetime.

But John Ryder Jr. was determined to take the lesson handed him on a silver belt buckle: force does not equal power. Kindness and listening were much more persuasive, even if sometimes those dynamics could be used as manipulation also.

Had it backfired on him, this dedication to the opposite polarity of his father's rough approach? All he could see now was that his oldest daughter was determined to flower in her own beautiful but terrifyingly singular way.

While everyone ordered at the bar-like food preparation area, Sadie found two tables next to each other near a window, looking southward onto the boulevard. People with cups of coffee and breakfast rolls walked by, *wending their way,* Sabrina thought in an imagined narrative, *to nowhere in particular.* As a matter of fact it was a perfect day to be "wending". It was going to be a crisp Indian summer weekend, and it seemed to her that no one could possibly care about anything but being right down in it. Then, snuggling herself between Sadie and her dad, she looked at them both with a hint of mischief.

This was it. She was going to try it. Sabrina looked directly into John Ryder's brooding eyes with renewed appreciation, and said with glowing self-satisfaction,

"Father? What's the derivation of the word, 'wend'?"

13

Voices

Sabrina thought that after last night's adventure in the closet, it was coincidental that the word, 'wend' which originated in Old English, before 900 BC, just incidentally, meant to proceed along a journey, a course, or route. A path. Why had she picked that particular word to wonder about this morning? Synchronicities like this she thought, were little signposts that pointed, not to anything in particular, but to the importance of being present with that which was in play in the moment.

She had apparently put herself in someone's path the night before. He, whoever he was, had been very clear about that. It was not that she had been blocking him exactly. He didn't seem to mind that she was there lying in his path, but he did claim ownership of it. Was this man a teacher or guide of some sort? And was "the path," in this case, a symbol for learning a specific line of reasoning? An angel from another realm, come to instruct her in a new way of being or thinking? Or unthinking? A romantic idea, she thought to herself, and one that she wouldn't be sharing with her family just yet. Not even her father, who might previously have taken delight in the notion.

No. Best to wait and see if this teacher ever showed up again.

Bishop Ryder was taken aback at her use of the formal title, "father", but almost as quickly he had laughed and seemed to understand that it was simply her desire to pay him homage. He was quick that way and she loved that she didn't have to explain herself, though her younger sister, Sadie, did give her an incomprehensible look.

After eating breakfast, the family went back to the townhouse to help her sort all the boxes into designated rooms. But then she insisted that they could be of no further help. And she gave them hugs, promising never to go into the closet without leaving the doors wide open behind her or, at the very least, taking the key with her. She assured them she would never make that mistake again and walked them to the car, her mother weeping shamelessly into one of her new dishtowels.

"I'm just so lonely without you there," she said handing it over to Sabrina and then suddenly jerking back again, blowing her nose on it and wailing, "I'll just have to take it home with me. Oh, honey, I'm sorry for being such a boob."

"I'll pick it up next time I'm over, Mom," Sabrina said in a reassuring tone, one that implied an imminent visit.

When they had gone, she sat down on a stool in the kitchen, wondering if she should take a nap or keep on going. After all, shouldn't she be exhausted from the night before? She ought to have been of course. Because it seemed that if she could remember everything the teacher had said, she must have been fairly conscious, and thus awake. And that would mean that she didn't get much sleep at all. But strangely, she felt invigorated, not tired.

Suddenly remembering her cell phone, she ran across the alleyway and took the little elevator three floors up into the parking garage. Approaching the car, she could hear the phone ringing. Fumbling wildly between the seats, she retrieved it.

It was Abby, wanting to come over.

"Yes! And we can talk about what to do or your birthday next Sunday," she responded with alacrity.

Abby arrived within minutes. "Have you got any wine, there, darlin'?" she asked, situating herself on a tall chair by the little oriental bar-height kitchen table. "I'm out."

"I haven't found it yet," Sabrina said, opening the tops of several boxes and finding nothing so much as a water glass. "I don't like to upset Mom by having it around when she's here, so I packed it somewhere deep in a—oh here! Here's something," she said, holding up a bath towel and rolling out an opened bottle of Turning Leaf chardonnay. "Is this okay?" And grabbing two plastic cups from a stack in the cupboard, she poured. They sipped and talked about days to come and what fun it would be to live so close to each other.

Abby had grown up Catholic, but when they compared notes on "living in the conditioned mind," (at work, where they first met), they found their comparative upbringing to be very similar. And they were always amused at how much more alike they were than not.

"Even though there was a time when our church called yours, 'the great and abominable church'. I mean, you'd have thought that for all the hype about our differences, you and I would have turned out to be two very opposite sorts of people. But no, you're as bound up in convention as I am."

"I beg your pardon, miss appropriate," Abby snapped back, "but we're not as serious about our religion as you are, never have been.

Catholics are more. . . uh, temperate than Mormons. You take your religion straight up. We've found a way to mix in a little objectivity. I mean we go to church, or not. But the priests handle the big stuff. You? You have a lay ministry. I mean, you're all so resolute and weird about it. Like every day is church."

"Touché," Sabrina said with a sigh. There was no arguing that. In fact it was one of the things that used to make her feel extra special and right about it. She thought for a moment, reflecting on the events of the night before, then asked with measured intonation, "Listen, Abby, with all the sightings of the Virgin Mary in your church, have you ever had one? I mean, have you ever seen her in a vision or a dream?"

Abby glowered. Chuckling, she said, "You must be kidding! I wouldn't even qualify! You have to be like some kind of saint or something for that to happen. And why, silly, are you asking about visions? Have you had any lately? Come to think of it, you'd be just the kind of person Mary would approach. You know why? Because you're always looking for things like that. 'Oh look, Abby—here's an exact likeness of the face of the Virgin Mary in this piece of sourdough bread. Look, she's all excited because Joseph just bought her a new pair of slippers and a little round halo thingy for the baby,'" she said hesitating just a little in order to conjure the most outrageous anecdotal vignette.

Sabrina had to love the lengths Abby could go to make her point, even to the extent of poking fun at sacred icons. Now see? Maybe that's what it took to get past the serious, conditioned mind: a willingness to laugh about things that had previously been sacrosanct. But she wasn't sure how to proceed down that treacherous road. At least it felt treacherous to the Serious One because, well, how do you reconcile reverence and humor? Was there 'a field out beyond right-doing and wrong-doing'? If there was, then it might be the same place where these two possibilities co-existed in harmony.

Meantime, her life felt a bit like a Möbius strip, turning back on itself with twisted surprises on every front. Where once everything had seemed consecrated and significant, now there was a tinge of humor around the edges of each moment, like nothing was so very important after all. It was as though a great burden had been lifted in one sense, all the heaviness and bulk taken out of the overworked, overwhelmed mind. But was that a gift or a penalty for lack of obedience to the old law?

"Well, what if I had? Seen a vision? Or something. . ." Sabrina trailed off in embarrassment. "Not Mary, of course, but someone less. . . renowned. In fact, no one of any significance at all, really. Just a voice?"

"Oh, look! Here's where you put the good stuff!" Abby had been rustling through some boxes under the table and found two bottles of Merlot.

It appeared she hadn't even heard Sabrina's tentative question.

Just as well, she thought.

"What do you mean, 'a voice'?" said Abby, seemingly preoccupied, as she held up the wine bottle considering whether to open it.

"Oh, nothing," Sabrina said, deflecting Abby's absent-minded question.

But suddenly Abby came back insistently. "Listen, you. Are you telling me that you're hearin' voices? I mean, voices besides mine and, let's say, Neil's, aggravating as it is, and the ones in the background on the elevator? Voices that say things like, 'Put on a suit of armor and ride out in front of an army?' Important stuff, you know. Or at least, you think it's important.

"What did it say, this voice? I'll tell you if it's real or not. Sabrina, look at me! Your heritage may be full of crazy books of gold and crap, but mine is much older and more reliable. And I can tell you from centuries of experience, don't listen to those voices in your head! It didn't go well with what's-her-name. Joan of Arc. She ended up in a heap of ashes and what the modern day equivalent of that is, I don't know. But it isn't a pretty picture, I can tell you. The psychiatric ward. Excommunication or some shit. Do you want to be excommunicated from your family, your childhood religion, your whole culture?"

Sabrina looked at Abby, stunned, and laughed out loud. Apparently, she had listened in catechism and the story of Joan of Arc was not lost on her. Who knew? Abby, the history buff.

"Abby, it's the 21st century. I don't think anyone's going to burn me at the stake today for listening to a voice of wisdom, wherever it comes from. But you're right about one thing; your heritage rocks for crazy ass inquisitions and witch hunts. That's exactly why I wouldn't take your advice on voices. . . .

"One spoke to me last night though, when I was locked in the closet, and I can tell you I liked what I heard. Everything he said was a treasure of wisdom."

"Wha—? Locked in the closet? What did it—he?—say then?" asked Abby, all agog.

"Well, for starters, he said, 'I am a lazy man'."

"That's it? Someone came down from the sky to tell you he was lazy? Was it one of the Three Stooges? Because I have to tell you,

Sabrina, that's got to be one of the most inconsequential pieces of trivia that ever came down the heavenly pipeline."

Sabrina laughed until finally Abby joined her in the merciless hilarity of the moment, both falling into fits and snorts until they finally had to sit down and drink a glass of wine to settle themselves.

"But honestly," Abby said after a quiet interlude, "Did you really hear a voice, darlin'?"

"I did", laughed Sabrina, "but I guess you had to be there. And he didn't come down from Heaven, you know. He was just there in my mind. I mean, it wasn't that supernatural. But he gave me an invitation from the universe, to be less serious and more light-hearted. You'd have agreed with everything he said really."

"Well, okay. I won't report you this time," Abby said jokingly, "because you do need to lighten up. That part I agree with. So I don't care who it is, he's on to something. By the way, are you sure this voice had a gender? What was his name then?"

"I don't know. By the time I thought to ask him, he had gone. But I remember everything he said with crystal clarity. And the funny thing is, that if he hadn't copped to being lazy, I don't know that I would have listened to a thing he said. Something about that just grabbed me. Maybe there's a part of me that really values laziness, in a symbolic way. I mean, I just want to rest from all my thoughts about being productive and doing it right, and making a good impression. Do you think that's possible for me, Abby?"

"It's a tall order, I'll say that. And maybe it took voices from another dimension to get you to hear it. You're a tough nut to crack on that account. I'm just glad he didn't tell you to buy some armor and go out and lead an army against the English or whatever. Still,

'I am a lazy man'? Seems like an awfully weird message. Did he have a Charlie Chaplin mustache by any chance?"

"I didn't get a good look at him. It was dark in there," said Sabrina.

"But you know who was the only other famous person to have a mustache like Charlie Chaplin? Hitler. Go figure. The funniest man in the world, and the most terrible man that ever lived. And Chaplin was Jewish, wasn't he? Now what do you make of that?"

14

Of Keys and Kingdoms

At 10:00 Sunday morning, dressed in a 1950's vintage yellow chintz skirt, a red print tunic apron, and her mother's old high school black and white saddle oxfords with bobby-socks, Sabrina was heading out the door for Abby's birthday brunch at Maxwell's downtown.

Finding the shoes had taken a little extra time, so she was running late. But hurrying out the back, and bolting across the alley to the parking garage, she felt like she could have been the central figure in a painting by Matisse, and that the whole city was about to break out in fauvistic glee. It was a dazzling sunny day and several people gave her a look and a wave as though they should know her. Maybe because they lived in the same complex? Or just because she was so, "Hi! I'm wearing red and yellow today!"

And she realized that she was headed into a world made up mostly (with one small exception) of other people. Ah, the philosophic humor of Sartre' had not been lost on this girl! Maybe she was getting the hang of this lightening up thing after all. A little more practice and enlightenment was surely just around some corner out there, and it was going to make her laugh like there was no tomorrow. "Because: there isn't!" she shouted, and it echoed through the parking garage.

Today she felt especially present in her own life. Free of past and future. Everything was so different. For one thing, she didn't have to tell anyone where she was going and when she thought she'd be home. No one was looking over her shoulder, evaluating every move she made.

Okay, maybe no one was actually doing that before, but it felt like it sometimes.

She had argued with her mother, who disapproved of spending 'hard-earned' money to buy a townhouse when she could be living at home for free in the beautiful Harvard/Yale area of Salt Lake. Had it been hard to earn? Sabrina didn't think so. Yet it went against all sorts of practical and personal considerations, not the least of which was that it excluded her mother from whole portions of her young adult life.

They had been best friends up until— well, until Sabrina had dipped her toe into another universe. And she knew that this was the single hardest part for her both of them, that they should not be best friends in the way they had been before, commiserating over traditional spiritual principles and shopping for clothes. And believe it or not, Sabrina mused, those two seemingly unrelated activities actually went pretty well together in her old life.

But now things had shifted and not a little. And when they went out shopping together, Sabrina sometimes chose clothing that no longer reflected the old standards of what her mother characterized as "modest". She was never that good at being unexceptional and reserved anyway, and now it was just too tempting to live right smack on the edge of couture corruption.

And then the things they used to talk about now seemed small-minded and limited to Sabrina's new way of thinking. When she wanted to take the conversation in a direction that included a more

Patricia York

expanded view of things, it was always a little touch and go. Taking into account belief systems that did not have the same ready-to-serve, hot-right-out-of-the-box, for-your-convenience principles was new for Mrs. Ryder, and a little uncomfortable.

Once, as they were going through a stack of t-shirts at the mall, Sabrina responded to her mother's comment about 'depraved and dissolute souls.'

"But Mom, everyone wants to be happy. They just have odd or unconscious ways of getting to it, don't you think? But we can understand them in that at least, the desire to be happy?" And she was stunned at her mother's response.

"No! No, they don't," she replied with not a little vehemence. And it took Sabrina a moment to figure out why this viewpoint felt so unjust and surprising to her.

"But. . .then you're assuming that the things most people do out of a lack of your idea of virtue or good breeding, simply do them because they *want* to do the wrong thing, like on purpose. That *would* make them evil, not just suffering from lack of education or love. Do you realize what you are saying, Mother?"

But Mrs. Ryder was uneasy, believing that this exchange of concepts was a conflict of interest, rather than a harmless examination of ideas between equals.

These were the small wedges, the "motes and beams" that kept them in different worlds. It was difficult for both of them. How to stay true to one's own heart and mind, and still remain supportive of that other out there. That 'other', who was one's very own self?

It shouldn't be this hard, Sabrina thought.

She was hoping that this move to the townhouse would give her a sense of, what? Autonomy? Not really. Separation was a big word in the metaphysical conversation, and it wasn't exactly a good thing. And she thought as how she ought to feel closer to her mother, not more antagonistic. But in truth, the whole thing felt a bit like a divorce, and it wasn't going to be an easy one either.

Sabrina noticed that children who had been entrained to follow their parents' way of thinking, sometimes found themselves (as adults) living with their parents by default. She noticed, too, that this phenomenon existed in some Mormon families. And she was certain that it had something to do with the co-dependent nature of living on unquestioned, second-hand social and personal values, until at last there was nothing for it but to move in and continue the 'uninvestigated life' in the comfort of the old childhood bedroom and Mom's great home cooking.

"Lots of grown children are just one popover away from moving back into their parents' basement. When things get rough at work or in a marriage, I'm telling you, Abby, it's a wicked world out there, and better to be sleeping on the old family room sofa and eating your mother's bacon-n'-cheese burgers, than getting high on cocaine or meth. And believe it or not, in a black and white world, I'm not sure they think there's a lot in between."

Abby could believe it and was not even interested in coming up with a better theory. Anyway it seemed to Sabrina that her only choice now lay between the comfort of her mother's southern fried wisdom and discovering her own values through her own experience.

Now, as she walked towards the garage elevator, she twined her new house key around a large ring that held all the other important keys in her life: the key to the mini Cooper three floors up (her destination at the moment), a key to her mailbox, and one to the scooter she'd left behind in her parents' garage. And then there were two other keys that she realized she had no reference for whatsoever. Was she already living such a complicated life? And how was she supposed to live without her wonderfully imperfect, incongruent, and disparate family? The fact that she had helped make it that way by detaching herself from the "only true religion" didn't escape her. The key now was to find a way to build a bridge between the two worlds.

The key.

She was reminded of the two she hadn't yet identified. *OK, this is interesting*, she thought. "Could be I just don't want to remember?" And then, *Oh, yes! I know! This one is Ben's*. He had asked her to hold onto the small silver key to his trailer on their last camping trip together. But on the second night, while cooking a late supper on the little two-burner gas stove, Sabrina had burned her hand and they had quarreled (she couldn't even remember why), after which they had split up for good. And truthfully, almost anything would have made for a good end-of-game argument.

Fortunately, by then Mrs. Ryder was almost glad to see Sabrina done with the whole business, seeing how far she and Ben were drifting from the ideas of a traditional Mormon lifestyle.

Something about their openly sexual behavior . . . Or, no, it wasn't the behavior exactly. It was more the easy attitude they took toward it, like it was somehow not even that important.

It wasn't sacred. That was it!

On one hand it seemed much more natural than Blanche Ryder had ever experienced it when she was her daughter's age. But then, being so comfortable with one's sexual nature took the mystery and romance out of it, didn't it? Were they so relaxed about it because they were already familiar with each other in that way? Or were they just not that attracted?

Either way, the prospects, to Blanch Ryder's way of thinking, were daunting. And then Sabrina was so enigmatic, acting almost as if it were none of her mother's business.

For instance, on the subject of sexual abstinence, Sabrina said to her one day, "I think being very aware is better than restraint or discipline where sex is concerned. Simply being deliberate and observant in a relationship is one of the best ways to maintain one's integrity in sex, as with everything."

Blanche had no idea what Sabrina was talking about. Did she mean to be so cryptic?

And later, after the breakup, Sabrina had said, "In fact, that's what gave me the first hint that something was off a little with Ben Chandler and Co. I was watching my stream of thoughts in meditation one day, and for the first time in forever (and a little late, mind you), this very clear inner voice pointed it right out to me. 'Sabrina,' it said, 'he is not really present when he's with you.'"

Mrs. Ryder didn't follow.

"Okay," said Sabrina, "In the modern vernacular it means, 'he's not that into you'. And then the voice said, 'I know this seems like a subtle thing, but he's much too worried about how he appears to you and to others. He may not want a partner, an equal, that is, as much as an admirer'. Whew! That was a revelation!"

"You got all that in a meditation?" asked her mother. "I've prayed for weeks to get an answer that clear. How do you do this meditation thing? Oh. Never mind. Just tell me if you are still a . . . virgin," she said shaking her head as though she had just used a four letter word.

That had been nine months ago and except for the nagging guilt about having wasted such a lot of time on a relationship that had gone so absolutely nowhere, Sabrina had never regretted the decision to end it. The peace that ensued in the weeks following was reward enough. It was the difference between a panic attack and the long, smooth, even breaths she had learned to take in meditation at the Zen Buddhist Center.

Now, mindlessly pushing the elevator down button, she thought as how she ought to call Ben later that day and ask him if he'd like the key back, but then thought better of it. He was already wading with hip boots into a complicated tryst with Amy, and Sabrina knew that calling him would be more problematic than helpful, given the jealousy factor. Anyway he mustn't care so much about the key or he'd have called about it himself before now. Perhaps he would call when the demand for drama was keener. That seemed to be a big part of the equation in his relationship with Amy. *They were always dog-paddling around in the shallow end,* thought Sabrina. *Who, but the most boring people, need that kind of cheap melodrama anyway?*

But this other key, what was it? Deep in thought about the mystery of keys and their obvious value as metaphor, she stepped into the elevator, turning to face the closing doors. Silently, she flipped through the files of her disordered mind. *Wait. Doesn't this second key have something to do with something to do with—*

"Hello there!" An unexpected voice rang out with a kind of boisterous good humor, ricocheting off the four walls of the elevator.

—some old books? she thought, finishing the sentence in her head and then turning to find the source of this unexpected salutation.

But here was the thing. She could have sworn that no one was in the elevator when she stepped into it.

"Old books? Love them! No end to their charm, is there? I mean, they are— well, they're old for one thing and often full of intriguing recipes, arcane and esoteric, of the most delightful and occult mysteries of life. Thaddeus Golas, here."

And a hand shot out, suspended in air, apparently waiting for Sabrina's own to engage it. It was attached quite confidently to a broad masculine shoulder, leading in turn to a body and a face, the likes of which Sabrina had seen only in movies about . . . well, about romance. High adventure. He was an amazingly handsome, "swashbuckling" vision of a man. Theatrical. No really. Positively histrionic, as though a sword should be hanging from his belt, with gloves and lace tucked in somewhere.

Swashbuckling? she thought. *Why would I think of that ridiculous word? It's like out of another era—Victorian, or—that's it!* She came to herself with a start, and suddenly remembered a cabinet full of old Victorian erotica in the rare books department at the library. She'd been working there part time, during the summer.

That's what the key is for! she thought to herself, a bit confused in the timing of two simultaneously interesting discoveries, the key and the man.

Hesitantly, she took the hand that was extended to her.

"Certainly that must be it!" said the curious stranger, "Queen Victoria did it with the key in the library! But why is it, do you suppose, that no one has noticed its disappearance before now? That, my dear Watson, is a question for the inquiring mind!"

"Why— What?" Sabrina stammered, unable to fathom how the stranger, however friendly and good looking, could be so intimately involved in a conversation with her own private thoughts. "What do you mean?" she asked, her eyes narrowing to two little slits. "How do you know about the library?"

"Did I say library? Well, I meant the game, you know." "Clue?" You said, 'that's what the key is for', and I was— I was playing with you."

"Oh. But I don't think I said it exactly. I only thought it. And you mentioned its disappearance. I don't believe I—"

"Yes, the interesting thing is still why you forgot that you had it in the first place. Or maybe why it was forgotten in the third place, having been overlooked in second place."

Sabrina puzzled over this maze of tangled thought. And here she surprised herself with a defensive posture. "Are you kidding? No one around there ever looks in that cabinet. It's practically in its own room. Hardly anyone even knows it's there. And I took this key because—Because Mrs. Gollaher said it was off limits to everyone but researchers and historians. And I knew I'd never get a chance to see the books if I didn't sneak a peek on my own. Victorian erotica, 18th century," she said, lifting her eyebrows up and down, Groucho style. And then speaking sotto voce, as though spies might be listening in, "They're going to dispose of the whole collection within the year. Some buyer from Chicago."

"So I borrowed the key while I had the chance," she said in a more matter-of-fact tone. "They have two other ones; and obviously they haven't missed it, because no one's said a thing about it!"

"Oh, no need defending yourself to me," he said conspiratorially. "I rather like research myself," And leaning toward her with his elbow on the wall, he whispered, "But I believe its 19th century".

"Who *are* you?" Sabrina replied suspiciously, annoyed at his offhand grasp of trivia, and so early in the morning too. "Why are you acting like you know anything about this at all? And why are you in my elevator? Are you married?" she heard herself asking, to her profound chagrin.

What other dimension had she stepped into? A place where people shared each other's private thoughts, and felt comfortable asking the most improbable personal questions?

"I don't," said Mr. Blah–blah-blah. "That is, I hope I'm not acting like a know-it-all. I am, however, somewhat intuitive. A mystic of sorts. And I'm in this elevator because you— now how shall I put it? Because you called me fourth out of the great (and here he stopped to consider just the right words to make his point) . . . possibility plasma, let us say."

Silence for an internal second. *Come on. That wasn't the primary question on her list. How about that last thing? Possibility plasma? Oh please.*

Then sucking in a great gulp of air, he said, "And yes, I *am* married!"

"Why does he treat that like a given?" she thought. She didn't know why, but she could've sworn he wasn't.

"That is, I'm married to the one in front of me! And that my pickled plum, would be you, in this moment."

"Pickled—? " *Oh, he was good.* "Well that's convenient, isn't it, Mr.—" she stammered. "What is it? Bolbus, did you say?"

"Golas. Thaddeus Golas. And yes, it's indeed very convenient because, you see, then I can be fully engaged to anyone I please, which is a lovely thing when it happens, don't you think?"

Sabrina looked at him from clear across a universe of preconceived notions about men. "Well, you're certainly adaptable, if not downright noncommittal," she countered. "But then why should you bother to commit if you're married to . . . to whoever—whomever—you happen to be with . . . in this moment? Did you actually say that?"

"Well, that would certainly be a less direct way of putting it. I forget that in this dimension, I must be more circumspect."

"Oh, never mind! . . . Anyhow, it's a handy philosophy. How has it worked for you so far?"

"So far, so fine. I'm batting a thousand. Well, a lot. As a matter of fact, I'm not really counting. You see, I just rarely refer to past or future. As far as I'm concerned this is the only moment there is. And so you, my sweet, are the only one I have ever loved. Simple that way, yes?"

"Really?" Sabrina replied, doubting that very much. "Well, I have to agree, it does keep things simple. You men certainly have a wonderful way of compartmentalizing everything." She would ordinarily be turned off by this whole bogus line of reasoning, but then why was he otherwise so absolutely, perfectly her notion of the ideal man? One hardly ever met someone as attuned to one's own actual preferences. Yet there he was. And stating that he was already married to her, sort of.

OK, so in another way of seeing it, he was weird, precocious, and a know-it-all. But then she rather liked know-what-all's. They were fun to spar with for one thing, and (she imagined) good in bed for another. Not exactly the boring type anyway. Then waving her hand dismissively, she quipped, "well, I don't even know why I asked you if you were married anyway. Probably you can tell me, since you're— since you're a mystic (emphasis on the doubtful sarcasm) or whatever." That last word there was chock full of wondrous variations on a theme. Whatever. And she thought, *He might be a number of things more interesting than 'mystic'.*

Her usual flirting style was to go with the free flow of repartee' and then see what came of the situation. But it was far too early in the morning to flow or flirt, and she wasn't inclined to just let the moment happen on its own. *In other words,* she thought, *I had better take the situation in hand. He might overpower me. Or even worse . . . he might get away.*

Meantime, he was definitely bringing that "whatever" dynamic into view. What was it exactly? She leafed through the thesaurus in her head, because you know, she loved words like most people love their pets. *Was he too agreeable, too content with himself? No. It was commensurate with uh. . . pleasant, homey, relaxing, —lazy even. At ease? No. He was . . . close. Too close for comfort.*

But just as she thought she was getting the upper hand, Mr. Wonderful, with arms folded, leaned against the elevator emergency stop button, halting it on route to ordinary life.

15

Alternate Universe

It occurred to Sabrina that there was something she had to do, somewhere to go, probably a whole universe of things that needed her attention. But right now, just in this moment? Well, maybe not.

"What are you doing?" Sabrina said in a husky, kind of dawdling voice. "Why are we stopping? What about the others? Other people have to use this—".

Mr. Whatever-His-Name-Was leaned over and —no. Of course he didn't kiss her. That was too cliché. Even Sabrina knew that. He just leaned in, and the possibility of forever seemed to stretch into something really meaningful.

". . . have to use this elevator. . . you know. . ." Sabrina finished. Now where did that come from? A thought she had started to in a previous lifetime? Was she just going to keep on blurting out incomplete sentences? It was like being on pot; she couldn't remember how she had begun and where she was going with this. But oh well. She felt a little stupid. And shy. Which was interesting, because stupid and shy were not even in her repertoire where men were concerned. Without looking down at her purse she dropped her keys into it, unwilling to interrupt his steady gaze.

"May I call you Sabrina?" He said with his mouth so close to hers she could feel his breath with every word.

"Hmmmm?" she said, absently.

"May I call you by your name?"

"Well that depends," she said, "I'm not absolutely certain you should know my name," trying very hard to remember what it was herself.

"But I do know your name; that's rather apparent, isn't it? Sabrina?"

Still dreamy, she replied, "Okay, but why do you have to ask? I mean we're married, aren't we?" she said, as a silly grin spread sideways across her face.

Now he smiled and pulled Sabrina toward him, and with great ease he placed her head beneath his chin, right against his heart. And far from resisting this uncommonly personal gesture, she leaned into it and thought she could hear the heartbeat of eternity ticking away its precious moments, each one replacing the last with its own preeminence. No beat more important than the next. And the next. And the next. Each one, in its turn, made the ticking of the universal clock a reality.

Gradually, she felt herself drawn into a current of such magnitude it overcame her in oceanic wave-like proportions, just as the experience in the closet had done. Only this was a whirlpool of unfathomable depths, with no latitude or longitude, and it was pulling her inward faster and faster. "Resist nothing," she heard him say. And in spite of gripping fear, she gave herself up to just free fall into it without concern about where she should land. And she felt as though she were falling toward the best of all possible worlds: ultimate security and complete freedom.

It was a trip into the very heart of God.

And then, something even more peculiar happened. Silence. Bodiless, weightless Silence.

Not like before in the closet. Not quiet. Quiet needed an opposite to be itself. This Silence had no opposite. It was beyond time: Eternal. It was beyond space: Infinite. One guessed from the pure non-experience of it, that science and religion had got these two ideas all wrong. With a canopy as high as Forever, and a floor as deep and wide as Forgotten, It had been there all along, waiting underneath everything . . .

So this is what all the fuss was about. THIS.

Presently against the cavernous depth, a tiny thought floated by. Why it must have been floating on its own like that for thousands of years, like a tiny hummingbird feather caught in the current of a mighty soundless wind. *I wonder if meditation could ever feel like this.* And the words showered into the magnificent, boundary-less space like a comet. Yet the Silence was endlessly accommodating, infinitely patient.

After an eon, another thought floated by.

Yes, my darling girl, meditation could feel exactly like this, it said.

And just in that moment, the rich, unending, radiant Silence that could never be contaminated or overlooked —was. It seemed to go underground. It was there, underpinning all of life. Yet for all intents and purposes, it had vanished. For a moment, an age? The hundred years of Sleeping Beauty fame?

And she knew with absolute conviction that subtlety was a quality she would need to cultivate if she ever wanted to call forth this Vastness again. And yet the Silence had respectfully withdrawn to dwell beneath the level of her focused conscious awareness. *How long would it be until I encounter it again,* she wondered.

Meantime she would try to remember its effect on her, how it felt like her own 'nearness', how wonderful to get lost in it. If one could call anything God, it would be that . . . that universal love she had just opened into, opened *as*. And when she had all her attention on it, it was the only thing there was. And it was before all things and through all things and after all things. And it wasn't separate from life, anywhere. Not even separate from Sabrina Ryder, that odd little cartoon character down in that peculiar Mormon vignette, with which she was so familiar.

"Remember me?" a voice seemed to call out from somewhere.

Of course, I remember you, she answered. *I used to think I was you, as a matter of fact. Now I'm not sure who I am. But we're going to find out. And, if that love is in everything, then it's in you too, Sabrina Ryder. Just for a minute there, it felt like I—we—were joining with the whole universe! Like everything coming together in one place, until it eclipsed my very self. And what is the point of all that ecstatic joining if it's not going to bless you, Sabrina Ryder, and everyone with whom you come in contact? In fact, can't we take it with us where ever we go? Into the little townhouse? The closet? Can we take it into the marketplace?*

The marketplace. The brunch!

At once, her mind took down the "do not disturb" sign and revved itself up. "Oh, my gosh!" she cried, pushing away the Silence, the comfort, the peace. The Embrace. "I'm late for Abby's birthday brunch! What time is it?" she yelled at Mr. Wonderful. "How long have you been holding this elevator? What are you—crazy? What am I doing here? It's like I've been asleep!"

"No," he said gently but emphatically, "You are actually going to sleep right now. If you forget this space, Sabrina Ryder, you *will* *be* the sleeping beauty, my love. Do not doubt it."

But Sabrina turned away from him, banging on the elevator doors, pushing persistently the button. Door open, door open! Nothing. Door open, Door open!

Then suddenly, the lights went out.

In shock, she stopped all the shouting and banging. Here was darkness so compelling that it demanded silence from her. And she wasn't just silent. She was Silence Itself.

Feeling/being it again, just for a moment, this Silence with no opposite, she lapsed back into its magnificent peace. And this time, great tides of feeling slapped up onto the shores of the heart, washing over long-held, strained emotions. Like a tsunami it was, like an orgasm exploding right through her crown chakra and out beyond the stars. Tears of release and joy! A rainbow of passion flashed across her mind.

Where did these tears, this deep well of feeling, come from? What ocean? And what was there to cry about anyway? Calling out between halting sobs, she wailed, "What is happening? Hello? Mr.—Mr. Globus?"

Abandonment. As though one were alone on some distant moonscape, the dark side.

Then momentarily, from somewhere seemingly far away, she heard breathing, deep and cleansing. And from behind, she heard the familiar voice, " Good, darling girl, you have it this time. Remember me. Watch for me in your dreams. You'll find me there." And she fancied that he placed his hands on her shoulders.

Before she could respond however, the lights came on and the doors suddenly clattered open. And for a minute, all her mind could do in its bumbling state was to think of things like, "Where's my phone? What the—? Where did I put my keys? Is it still Sunday?"

Compared to the other, this was a shabby reality. A world of conflict, clanging doors, unending crises, a universe of separated things, dense and stifled, clogged with feelings that can't get out, bound with emotion that won't flow through.

Sabrina was just Sabrina again, a trifling flesh and bone configuration, a little bit of vacillating willow-the-wisp consciousness that sometimes took the shape of a loud hurricane of thought.

And something else: overwhelming shame. It seemed to piggyback on every thought that identified itself with this little limited ego-mind named—what was the name again? Never mind. Suspicious at best, and vicious at worst. This was its earthly inheritance. Not the ocean-like emotions from before, nor the wild untamable Love that had swallowed her into Itself.

Just the small, petty little recycled thoughts with no real source.

Thank God there was no one standing there outside the elevator waiting to get in. She took a moment to compose herself, to check for damages. Except for the inability to stuff all of her feelings back into the tiny psychological frame of reference in which they have been so tightly packed before, she was alright.

But she also knew that she would never be the same.

And as for this man she had just spent the last—what—eternity with? Well, he had pissed her off on so many levels. He had made her late for Abby's birthday breakfast, for one thing. Shit, he had probably made her late for several lifetimes. Searching for a tissue to dab her blotchy red face and blow her nose, she thought as how he had lulled her away from our own sense of identity, of certainty and control, into this uncanny alternate universe, which just about had her convinced that It was real, instead of her.

What was so great about Silence anyway? Booooring. No place to show off your rhetoric, your talents, and hello: this was not okay, being late for her best friend's birthday brunch! She was never late! She wheeled around to let him know that none of this was very funny and what did he think he was doing anyway— But clearly, there was no one there.

She stepped outside the elevator, looking to find perhaps a shadowy figure dashing across the covered parking lot. Nothing. Then rifling her cell phone out of her purse, she checked the time. 10:48. It was exactly 3 minutes from the moment she remembered glancing at the clock on the kitchen wall as she locked the back door behind her, the exact amount of time it must have taken her to walk to the elevator.

What had she just experienced then? This was only her first week in the trenches of living on her own, and she'd already had an out-of-body experience and an in-the-closet one as well. Was this the way of it? Were these abductions going to be habitual? *I'll take the other elevator tonight just to be sure,* she thought, *even though it's clear on the other side of the parking garage.*

Then, with the back of her hand, she wiped the perplexity from her face, and hurried to her car.

****

For the rest of the day she rejoiced that she was back in a user-friendly world, but in her heart she grieved that none of the ethereal nonsense from the early morning elevator ride could have been real. At the birthday brunch, she mused over the peculiar event, occasionally mumbling out loud to herself.

"My name . . . how did he know my name?"

"What?" asked Abby, "Who? Who knew your name, Darlin'? Was he cute?"

"No. I mean, no one. It was. . .just someone I met in the garage elevator.

Well, genius, you made him up, she said, only in her mind this time. She didn't dare tell Abbey about this. Anyway, after a few hours it began to have the same effect as a dream. Some of it she already couldn't remember and in retrospect, it seemed a bit off-putting. Certainly nothing you could just casually drop into a conversation with someone.

"Oh incidentally, I met a guy. He knew my name and he took me to another dimension. We were with God but God didn't say anything. Turns out He doesn't talk much. Or have a body. Or, well, you know, he doesn't play dice, like Einstein said. But really, you should have been there. Well, no that's not true because no one was there, and it wouldn't have been possible for you to be either. It's a little hard to describe. Listen, do I sound crazy?"

She fell asleep that night trying to find the words to describe what she had experienced, but no luck. It was impossible, ineffable, laughable.

Just before she dropped off around midnight, she thought she saw him, the guy, the Thaddeous Bogus one, sneaking around the edge of the universe. He sported a black cape that covered his face, except for his eyes, which were sparkling and laughing at Sabrina. Trying desperately to catch up with him, she could only move in slow motion since the leggings of her fool's costume kept tripping her up. Also the joker's hat with the bells kept flying off her head, and it seemed like she had absolutely promised to keep it safe and never let it out of her sight. But it kept rolling just a few feet in front of her, so *that* was a thing.

But soon enough, Bogus sloughed her off completely and disappeared over the horizon of her mind. And she fell into a dark and troubled slumber, still running after the cap and bells.

16

Night Terrors

Sabrina had promised a friend that she would cover her shift for the whole day on Saturday, at the Salt Lake City public library downtown. Even though it meant she had to give up half her weekend, she loved working there. It was a bit of an architectural wonder for one thing, with floor-to-ceiling glass and open flights of stairs zigzagging from level to level, looking down into a central mall with cunning little shops and restaurants.

By 11:30 that morning she had completed her first assignment, and was given leave to take her lunch break early. Curious to see whether the Victorian erotica still occupied its own special case in the rare books section, she had decided to use this time to investigate. Finishing off a protein bar bought from a vending machine, she hurried to the third floor desk, where, with special permission, she was allowed to enter the holy of holies.

Stepping through the glass doors of the lush and quiet rooms, she felt as though (she wasn't sure) the same as in the elevator, or that night in the closet? Anyway, it was as though this room had been allotted an extra ration of silence, that the rules for library etiquette went double for this space. In fact, it reminded Sabrina of the reverence that was emphasized in her church-going days. And it occurred to her that reverence was simply a way of giving homage to the silent consciousness underlying all of life. Although It didn't seem to want respect or deference as much as—what—recognition? Yes, a 're-cognition' or remembering, a return to what was always waiting there. *A journey without distance,*[46] she thought, *to a place I've never left.*

The Mormons had a concept: the restoration. And Sabrina mused that perhaps, once again, *everything had been interpreted too literally. To restore Christ's original church to the earth, as the Latter Day Saints had it wired, may have even larger implications. What if 'the restoration' was just a metaphor? The Mormon expression of finding mystical wholeness? To 'restore' the separated ego mind to its original state of completion/peace/rest and creativity? And what if this 'original state' of being was calling each of us in our own language to awaken into all its light and intelligence?*

Right here in the rare books department of the Salt Lake City public library, all this seemed apparent and inevitable to Sabrina. *Funny that a mystical experience with God should feel just the same as being in a room full of books with explicit sexual content though,* she thought as she headed toward the little case with the Victorian erotica, and opened it with the purloined key.

In fact it didn't really matter, did it, what the content of life was? *This Conscious Awareness was in all and through all things, forever holding all of life in its loving embrace. That is it. That's what unconditional love is,* she thought. *It's the Context in which all content is revealed or experienced.*

Well now, who'd-a-thunk?

She took the rest of her breaks there too, and at the end of the day she went back one more time and read until the library closed. Her fascination with the stuff was short lived. Most of it wasn't completely rough and raw, like today's western porn. Some of it even had a kind of sensitivity to it, like being cherished was part of the sexual exploit. It was highly dualistic in nature, pitting exaggerated innocence against its dark counterpart, all kinds of sexual vagaries. And just incidentally, she noticed it *was* mostly a 19th century phenomenon.

She tired quickly of the content itself, but was astonished by the range of passion it brought up whenever she thought about the stranger in the elevator. Still, by the time she locked the bookcase just before closing time and returned the keys to the head librarian, she had to admit that she was quite sated with the stuff.

The day had been a beautiful Indian summer one and the evening was unusually warm for October, and so riding home in her little mini Cooper with the top down, it was no surprise that a bit of Walt Whitman came to her on a breeze, whispering his sensual words in her ear. In the original Adamic language, it seemed:

The welcome nearness, the site of the perfect body, lying and floating,

The female form approaching, I pensive, love-flesh tremulous aching,

The divine list for myself or you or for any one making,

The face, the limbs, the index from head to foot, and what it arouses,

The mystic deliria, the madness amorous, the utter abandonment,

(hark close and still what I now whisper to you),

I love you, O you entirely possess me,

O that you and I escape from the rest and go utterly off, free and lawless,

Free and Lawless,

Two hawks in the air, two fishes swimming in the sea, and not more lawless then we![47]

Arriving at the garage, Sabrina decided to go ahead and take the same elevator that she had that eventful Sunday morning a few days ago. To her great disappointment however, nothing out of the ordinary happened. For one thing, the elevators were very busy late in the evening. Turned out, they were a great place to meet new friends who owned or rented townhouses in the same complex. A law student hailing from New England (a nice looking young man) had even tried—rather unskillfully and without success—to get her number. But he seemed dull in comparison to Bolas which begged the question: would she ever find any one as interesting as the fantasy man she'd conjured up three mornings ago for her own amusement? Indeed, she was beginning to think that her imagination was not so much a gift as it was an obstacle to real space/time relationships.

Her body was pure electricity by the time she opened the kitchen door, threw down her purse and keys, and slipped off her shoes, kicking them across the floor with abandon. Unbuttoning her blouse, she flung it away from her where it landed softly like a parachute on the fireplace screen. Bra and panties she hung capriciously on a lamp in the living room.

Living by yourself had a few advantages and here was one. You could masturbate without shame, all night if you wanted to.

And she did. To Walt Whitman, to the Victorian erotica, and to—oh, yeah—that intrusive stranger, Tobias Globus, whoever or if ever he was. With incendiary urgency she shouted, "How dare you come to me in that way and then leave without so much as a—" and she rode him into the late night hours, exhausted and unsatisfied. Something about the thought of him just enraged and engorged her with passion at the same time, but she could not control his coming and going in her mind, for all her resolve. In fact, she clearly was not in command of her feelings where he was concerned. Her physical response to just the thought of him was a revealing exposition of her most private fantasies, and an indictment of her wild, disobedient and altogether unruly sensual nature.

Once, in the middle of the night, she was awakened abruptly by her own body heat, trying desperately to ride the crest of an undulating wave of pleasure, his maddeningly calm voice whispering in her ear. A few screams into the pillow relieved the mounting force of energy that ripped through her body without permission. Could someone be raped by a thought, a memory, a desire personified?

Screw it, she thought. *I'll kill him if I ever see him again! I swear I'll scratch his eyes out with my library key!*

Sleeping fitfully the rest of the night, she dreamt of wild animals and earthquakes. Nothing subtle to be sure. Once he appeared as a panther, stalking her until she turned to face him in a rage. Shape-shifting then, he took the form of other animals, slinking into the undergrowth nearby or watching her from a cliff high above. What was the meaning of his presence in her psyche anyway? Was he there to protect her? Or kill her, thrusting her lifeless body about with his black nostril, tearing into her flesh with his fierce, white teeth and rough tongue?

Or worse. Was he just going to torment her endlessly, hunting her like prey but purposefully never catching her, like a game of cat and mouse? It seemed that the Great Silence (her only respite from this wild inner chaos) was light years away.

17

The Golden Braid

Sabrina, Abby and Noah got a half-day reprieve from work on Tuesday. Something to do with the electricity being shut off in their part of the building. So they drove together in Abby's car to the Oasis, downtown. It was a little café attached to a bookstore called the Golden Braid on fifth east.

Sabrina first heard about it through some friends at the Zen Center. Accepting an invitation to walk and eat with them after meditation, she'd fallen in love with the place immediately. The café was wonderful enough, but the bookstore was absolutely seductive, and not just because of the books. There was a spicy eastern smell, which was, she found out later, an East Indian incense called Nag Champa. Longing to smell the scent, hear the chimes, and see the little stone Buddha's sitting tranquilly near fanciful indoor fountains, she convinced Abby and Noah that it was a place they would relish as well.

"It is a feast for all the senses," she said, "not just your taste buds."But it was the music that assaulted her senses most and carried her off into other-worldly realms of silk and saffron. Crystal bowls rang shrill in her bones, *disintegrating patterns of old calcified beliefs,* she thought, *like barnacles on a battleship.* Ancient dispositions, customs, rituals and dogma (religious, social and political), all were shattered and scattered like so much pyramid dust collected over the centuries in the habituated, provisional mind.

"The center will not hold!" chanted a voice in apocalyptic clarity, as she held the door for Noah and Abby.

See? Just by walking into the Golden Braid, whole systems of belief are loosened and fall away, she thought. And for some reason, she knew that this was a good thing.

They were led to an outdoor table by a fresh-faced girl in an apron.

Sabrina had been reading about the conditioned mind. The uncharted territory, for her at least, of collective, catalogued thought down through the ages, educated and set in stone like ancient mosaic murals on Byzantine walls. Odysseys, theories, and philosophies all seemed to gain strength as though in the re-telling, they were given the façade of truth. But to Sabrina's way of thinking, these ancient thought forms were much more like the myriad flickering shadows in Plato's cave, always shifting while attempting to appear stable and unchanging.

And she was determined to explore this Maya-mind just like Magellan or Columbus had explored the (explicate) explicit outer world; like Bohm, Planck, Einstein and Capra had explored the (implicate) implicit quantum world. And like all the poets, prophets and philosophers who had ever entered the forbidden halls of Dante, navigating those tricky unsubstantial realms leading from the head to the heart and beyond.

And by the way, weren't all the prophets in the traditional scriptures just the guys who actually went for Truth instead of following established rules? They were the generally the rascals, the rebels, weren't they? she thought. *Isn't that exactly had characterized them as prophets and mystics?*

After a leisurely chat over a salmon and gorgonzola salad, Sabrina trolled the isles of books, looking for her next fix. Anything on nonduality would do: Eckhart Tolle, Krishnamurti, David Hawkins, Byron Katie, or Douglas Harding. And of course, anything by the poet, David Whyte, just about had her in fits of phonic orgasm. In fact, she must remember to think of *him* the next time the M-word reared its beautiful phallic head. So many articulations of Truth: words, phrases, paradoxes, poetry, all pointing homeward.

Reading these books was not so much a discipline as it was an addiction for Sabrina. It was like she couldn't help herself. But she didn't read them to retain information. Far from being a source of worldly wisdom, these books were dazzling gateways into the unknown.

Now, as she moved toward the end of the second row of books, a tiny blue volume, a hardback, almost leapt out at her. It appeared to have been stuck hastily onto the shelf and as she walked by, it literally fell into her hands. The title made Sabrina chuckle: <u>The Lazy Man's Guide to Enlightenment</u>.

Luckily she was a few isles away from Abby and Noah, who were talking to someone at the counter about tarot cards. Because there it was. His name. Thaddeous Golas.

She'd had trouble remembering, but this was it, she was sure. Right there on the cover. There were pictures too. They were vaguely reminiscent of the image of him in her head, but not very flattering. Nothing like her idea of him anyway. His early pictures when he was a young man at her age, were most like her recollection of him. But he would be long past his prime now, if he were even alive that is.

Her heart waited for the cue to start beating again. "Okay. This. . .this is. . .too weird," she said to herself under a breath that took just a little too long to exhale. Feeling faint, she slumped down on a bench behind the stacks, where no one could see the apprehensive look that must have been showing on her face. Or hear what might transpire in this—now she was quite sure— schizophrenic condition coming on. Because it was definitely one of those 'caught-in-the-closet-with-no-way-out' moments. She couldn't speak or call to anyone for help. She was dumbfounded. In fact she was dumb, speechless, which was even more of a conundrum.

Because truthfully, how often does that happen to a real top-notch, pure bred know it all?

18

Return of the Lazy Man

Surely she wouldn't be taken hostage again by some strange out-of-body experience right here in the bookstore. But there it was, that feeling of being in the presence of something otherworldly. And it was quite overt, like a takeover of the mind, not exactly hostile, but certainly unbidden.

She felt herself adrift, in and out of conscious control. Would people think she was having a seizure? One of the quirky characteristics of dimension-hopping was the time factor. She hadn't really worked that part out yet. If she went once more into an alternate reality, would the store be closed by the time she came out? Or would it take no time at all like the last encounter? The mind had many concerns. Sabrina had only one. Would she look like the fool that she feared so much? Momentarily, however, she stopped caring about anything else but the conversation taking place on the inner stage of her psyche. It was that voice "underneath", the same voice as that night she was held prisoner in the closet.

"These are the things I see that seem to give you the most grief: you resist everything you don't like, and you clutch at everything you do. In combination, these qualities give you everything that is expressed in your life as you know it, Sabrina, including me. You know all this of course, but I can't seem to get through to you most of the time. I watch. I wait. I listen to the constant chatter in your mind; but there is no gap between your thoughts for me to slip in. You are a yapper. For instance, I saw the stair you almost tripped on a while ago when you came into the store, but there was nothing I could do to warn you because you were preoccupied with so many other superfluous things.

"You are rarely present for your own experience, living off other people's insights." I can't begin to show you the font of your own wisdom until you consciously invite my presence. There's nothing to be done for it except to stay close and wait for a point of entry. Unfortunately, the opportunity usually only comes when a problem arises that makes it so difficult for you to go on that you are forced to stop. A headache. A car accident. A relationship that doesn't pan out. Ahem. Those are the things that have worked in the past.

"Suffering can be an attention grabber, alright." Often only then is there a place for me to slip in to let you know that I am here. But you are just as likely to forget that we ever connected. You might even remember it as a conversation with a friend or something you saw on television or in a movie.

"Your attention span is petite, to say the least." Yet I can wait forever because I need nothing. Delay goes unnoticeable in eternity, but in time? It is quite tragic. Truthfully, I don't really care how long it takes you. You can make any decision you want and your life will automatically correct itself in this or some other lifetime. I'm just here to observe, to encourage your authentic expression, and remind you that suffering is an option, not a necessity at all.

"In me resides an amazing resting place for the weary mind, especially one that has been caught up in its own story line for a while." I have no needs of my own, like I said. I'm just here for the ride, the journey, the wonderful way of it.

"So here we are together, between Nowhere and Somewhere, having once again a chat, away from the 'madding crowd'".

"Don't you mean, 'maddening'?" she finally asked.

"The word is 'madding'. It means, 'acting in a way that suggests or reveals the presence of a psychiatric disorder'. The whole world is madding, conflicted, just a little crazy stupid, don't you think? But here in the quiet, beyond the busy world of your mind, some peace might be possible. Or maybe we are the madding crowd. What do you think, Sabrina? Can two minds joining, feel like a crowd if one of them is yours?

"Oh, for God's Sake!"

"Yes. I agree. For God's Sake. Let it be for that. What other than God?

"What I mean is, what the—? Why do you keep jerking me around like this? Are you for real? Hey listen, am I going to look foolish here, right in front of all these people? Because last time I—"

"Look around. Do you see anyone here but us chickens?" he asked.

Sabrina did look around. No books or bookshelves, people or clocks or sounds or benches or Abby. And she was sitting on . . . well, nothing to be exact. Sitting on nothing and talking to no one. Startled, she jumped up and stood up on—oops—nothing again. Aside from the disconcerting fact that she was completely alone, without any artifacts of a hitherto bustling civilization, it was quite serene. Then glancing down at her feet, she saw that even they were starting to disappear; everything was flickering out of sight, right up to her—

"Yikes!—is this really happening?" she yelped as though the breath had just been knocked out of her. "What's going on here?!" Just to feel safer, she put her hands over her eyes, which she suspected weren't there anymore either. She couldn't bear watching the disappearance of a whole universe, finishing off with her own head.

It was all so trippy. But she was thinking, that much was clear. Whatever she was or wasn't, she could still think. Descartes came to mind. And in that moment, she thought perhaps Descartes had got it backwards. *I mean, shouldn't it be, 'I am, therefore I think'?*

And instead of everything being in darkness, like the other times, the perception now was of Light. It was all light with a capital L. How could she tell? Because the thought of darkness was there. A memory, an opposite.

Then suddenly the moment was completely clear of all the debris of the little ego mind. Nothing to distract, so she could concentrate. Well not really concentrate, because concentration was only needed in a world of multiplicity. Here there was only one thing happening. But she was really, really there for it. Completely present.

"Ahem. Now that I've got your attention, let's listen to a reel of your thoughts on Tuesday last, shall we? It was the day after you moved into your new place. You were looking into the mirror and wondering about— Well, let's take a peek from the other side of the looking glass, shall we?"

Sabrina saw and heard herself talking as she peered into the bathroom mirror. *Panache. That's what I need. I used to have it and now it's gone. Lost somewhere in the middle of my relationship with Ben. Where did I set it down exactly? Was it when I started defending myself? Or maybe when I began ranting about Amy Houston's many flaws? You can't be pointing the finger at someone else and keep your panache, at least not when you're invested. There has to be a kind of distance between you and your target, like no one would ever want to be on any side but yours because you're panache is so scathingly brilliant. But I don't have that kind of flair for a funny, contemptuous retort. Whenever I get defensive, I lose it; I became awkward and ridiculous. The madder I get, the stupider. So my panache has been crushed under a train wreck of angry emotions. Too bad, because it was kind of a good thing to have, like a taffeta slip. It barely pokes out from the bottom, but it gives the whole ensemble a kick. Ben didn't know it, but that's why he liked me, I'm sure of it. Panache isn't something you get about somebody right away. You just know there's a prize in there somewhere. It's hidden, but working its magic. That is, until it's commandeered by some expression of clumsy jealous graceless inept— You know what? It's just gone that's all. A splash of panache, that's what I lack. Also? It's hard to get over the notion that most (maybe all) men are not that fastidious. Social ADD. But if I had my panache back - I might still be able to find a way to use it on some hapless male-of-the-species chappie. But without it? Well, I'm just not that attractive.*

"You see what I mean?" the voice said. "No gaps. At least nothing long enough for me to slip in and give you pause. "I give good pause, incidentally."

"Very funny," she said out loud. "Okay, duly noted: I have an active mind. But can't that sometimes be a good thing?"

Pause.

"So you're saying that it isn't? You want me to have gaps in my thinking? They have names for that you know. Alzheimer's, dementia. Besides, I think you should know, I meditate a lot and sometimes I can go 5 minutes without thinking. Well anyway, I'm not thinking about those things you just scolded me for. And if you don't want me thinking about whether I have panache, or how to get and hold onto a man, why did you show up so—so— I mean, why did you make yourself into just the kind of one I like? Come to think of it, I actually have a bone to pick with you, Mister. I've had some pretty sleepless nights because of—"

"Hold on there, little darlin'!"—and just then the small blue book she had been holding before was now floating remarkably on the air in front of her. And soon enough a large masculine hand coalesced around it and shimmered right down into an image of Apollo himself.

"Yeah, like that!" barked Sabrina. "How come you show up all ch-charming and charismatic and—I don't know what—like someone I read about once in a cheap romance novel? And just incidentally, you don't look a thing like those terrible pictures in your book! That *is* you, right? How come you didn't tell me before that you wrote a book?

Pause . . .

"This isn't too different from what I was saying, is it?" countered the voice-now-made-flesh. "No gaps? By the way, can you actually see me?"

"What? Well of course, I can. You're right there standing in front of me, aren't you?"

"Well, that depends. Where are you?"

"I'm— oh." She'd already forgotten about the disappearance of the universe. Looking down again, she tried to get her bearings. She did have her body back, but there was still literally no floor or walls or ceiling to reference herself against. "Whoa—!" she yelped, "Good question. Where am I? Is there something here to hold onto?" Steadying herself, she grabbed hold of the only thing around; the strong arm of this wholly redoubtable man. "Listen, am I being abducted again?" she wailed.

"I think it's the other way around. You said yourself that I don't look a thing like my picture. So where did this image come from?" he said, with a self-referent gesture. "I'm just a figment, I'm afraid."

"A figment? You mean a figment of my imagination?"

"Yes, if you want to be redundant. That's what a figment is, something from your imagination. An alter-ego maybe? And I think I'm someone you made up, not the other way around. Think about it. Don't I look exactly like your idea of the perfect man?"

". . . A little bit arrogant there, aren't you Mr. Bogus Figment? You certainly make yourself out to be some kind of Utopian dreamboat guy, don't you now?"

"Or maybe it's you making me out to be the ideal man? You're kind of keen on the idealistic there aren't you, Sabrina-girl?"

She was still holding onto his arm because, well, that was all there was. And she didn't dare look down again. Holding her gaze steadily on his, she frowned and would have liked to stamp her foot if she thought there was something to stamp on. But besides the ridiculous notion of there not being an accompanying sound to accentuate her irritation if she did, it seemed unlikely that her usual "pout and stamp" routine would be as effective as it had been with Ben. Besides, in this place there was no past and so there was no knowing what worked and what didn't based on previous experience.

"Wait. You mean you're just an extension of myself? Do you know what I'm thinking then?"

"Yes, but go ahead and tell me anyway."

"No, I mean do you know what I'm thinking, before I think it?"

"I'm fairly certain I possess a degree of wisdom that you are not exactly lacking, but have forgotten about, or at the very least, covered over with a veil of interpretations." Then thumping her forehead with his finger, he said, "Except in here, you are aware of the power of the mind. Most of the time you are not. But in here with me, you become conscious of so many things you've blocked out.

"What do you mean, 'in here'? Where are we?"

"Inside your mind—the natural, unconditioned mind. Not the one you use on a typical day. It's the spacious, less concrete one. It's more fluid, like in your dreams. Here, you can relax and enjoy your thoughts without judgment. Out there your mind works as a control mechanism to keep yourself from being overwhelmed. It does this by breaking things up into little bits and pieces; segments of time and space. This idea is reflected in the scientific subatomic realm as 'quantum packets'.

"But 'in here' you allow all things to be exactly as they are. You simply don't defend or resist, and so your thoughts don't scare you so much. You are aware of the sheer delight of being aware. Aren't you? And that gives you a feeling of allowing, accepting and appreciating everything that you think, no matter how dark or un-evolved your thoughts may happen to be.

"When we travel together in this dimension, you will have many experiences that you would typically not permit into awareness in a world of solid matter, because your fear makes many things seem untenable. But when you see everything for what it is, simply your thoughts taking form, the fear is less overt.

"Everyone in the external world experiences fear and it's easy to see why. Typically, people do not appreciate the real power of the mind, and no one is fully aware of it all the time. But the mind is so powerful, it never loses its creative force. It doesn't actually sleep, creating every instant. In fact, thought and belief combine together into such a surge of power that they literally can make or move mountains, as the expression goes.

"At first, you're tempted to believe that your mind having such power is arrogant, and so you deny this power in yourself. But the real reason you prefer to believe that your thoughts don't have any actual influence is because you are quite afraid of them. In fact, the whole external world is a picture of the thoughts you've pushed away, or projected out from you, because of this fear. And here's the crazy thing: you are as afraid of your most magnificent thoughts as you are the darkest ones. Projecting thoughts away from you and pretending that they are out there and 'not you', may keep you from feeling guilty about the arrogance of believing in such power of the mind, but at immense personal cost. Now you are impotent.

"Think about it, my love: If you believe that what you think is ineffectual, you might not be afraid of your mind, but you're hardly likely to respect it either. Am I correct? The truth is, Sabrina, none of your thoughts are 'idle'. All thinking generates form at some level. But the thoughts you think of as 'your own' are really just thought forms that have been running through the collective human mind for thousands of years. You, as a separate personality, attach to the ones you like and resist the ones you fear. When you attach to a belief, whether out of fondness or fear, there is an accompanying feeling. These feelings build into emotions (energy-in-motion) over time. Soon it feels like there are lifetimes of emotions to deal with. But that's only an illusion in time. And time is just another construct of the mind. You really only have this moment, and the feeling or thought that you are dealing with right now."

"Wait a minute. There's a difference between feelings and emotions?" Sabrina asked with deliberate emphasis on each word.

"Feelings + Time = Emotion. Time changes everything, I'm sure you've heard."

Sabrina looked down at her hand clinging to his arm and then at her feet, standing on nothing. Instinctively grabbing at his shirt, for a moment she teetered and felt as though she were going to faint or fall or both. This was a lot of information and she was wishing she had some time and space modules to put it in.

"A bit daunting?"

She took a deep breath, and then with no small irritation, she said, "You know what? *You* are a bit daunting, Mister." Then closing her eyes, she asked plaintively, "Listen, can we go somewhere else and talk?"

Apparently a simple request was all that was needed. Because suddenly, the store shimmered back into existence and there they were, standing on the floor behind a shelf of books in the Golden Braid bookstore, emanating its distinctive sounds and smells, all playing on Sabrina's senses as before. Or her senses were making them real, she wasn't sure how it went anymore. But the incense smelled good either way, backwards or forwards.

"Thank-you," She said, expelling her relief in a long outward breath.

"Oh, don't thank *me*", said the figment, standing with his arms extended toward her as if to give her the stage. "You're the one running this show."

"But that can't be right. I'm the one who's the hostage here! Surely you don't think I wanted you to be stalking me in my dreams and playing with my head right in the middle of the store and the elevator and my sleep and the—" Then grabbing the book from his hand and poking his chest with the corner of it, she took the offensive. "Are you dead? Did you write this?"

"Well now, those are questions for the Gods," he said, gesturing upwards. "In your world I am 'dead'. 1997, I think it was. I'm not good with dates. But did *I* write this? Let's just say it came through me at a time when I could least afford to give it the merit it required. No money, you see." And he seemed to be referring to someone, several dimensions up, who was getting an earful no doubt about it.

"Yeah, so how did *you* like being hijacked, Mr. (she stole a glance at the name on the cover, just to make sure) Mr. Golas? It's not so fun as all that, is it?"

"Oh, you have no idea, Miss Ryder. Without personal computers, scanners, printers and digital editing, with nothing but a hotpot to cook in, some Wheatberry bread and Velveeta cheese to live on—not to mention I had to stop taking LSD because I knew I could never finish the book unless I was earthbound—you cannot begin to imagine the hurdles, the bodily discomforts, the anxiety—" Then suddenly, He stopped mid-sentence with a strange look on his face.

"Velveeta cheese! Are you kidding? You lived on Velveeta cheese? No wonder you're dead! That stuff will kill you! So are you a ghost or what? Anyway, for all intents and purposes, you don't even exist as far as I'm concerned, so why are you appearing to me?"

"My pet, I don't expect you to understand it all right now," and putting his hand to the side of his mouth, he whispered, "but let me point out that you *are* having a conversation with a figment."

And he indicated with his eyes that she might want to take a look behind her.

She turned and saw Noah, Abby and two other women, a man and a small boy staring at her. Keeping her eyes on them, she asked out of the corner of her mouth, "They can't they see or hear *you*, I'm guessing?"

Pause.

"Really?" she said to him in a strained voice. Then to Abby and the others, "Okay. This is sticky, You know what? I just need a moment here. Do you mind? Everyone?"

No one minded, but no one moved either. They seemed to be a little afraid of the Crazy Girl, in fact.

"Abby!" she whispered loudly as if to wrench her attention from the collective eye-poppers. "Would you—could you—go . . . somewhere else and just give me, you know, some privacy for a minute?"

Still no one moved.

"Okay. Well, I guess *I'll* just go out the back door then. Don't follow me!" Handing the book to Abby, she motioned for Mr. Wonderful to follow her outside. "Abby will you buy this book for me? I'll pay you when we get home. Buy the book, get in your car and wait for me. I'll be there in— You know what, it won't be long. Just go."

When she and the figment were standing outside the door in a little alley, Sabrina hammered him pretty good. "Is this going to keep happening, because I don't like it one bit. How can you say that *I'm* doing this? Because this is certainly not anything I would choose," she seethed, staring at him, her eyes growing large and menacing.

"Little one—"

"Don't 'little one' me!"

"Well then, darling girl—"

"Oh, don't 'darling girl' me either! Terms of endearment are not going to work here!"

"Will you look at my book? It's an easy read. You'll probably understand most of it. Then we'll talk. How about that?"

"Just stay out of my dreams, okay?" she said, with venom.

"Well, you know I can't promise—"

"Oh!" squinting her eyes hard, she said, "I don't care what you do as long as you stop skulking around in my mind—"

"Skulking?"

"Yes, and—quite honestly?—making me sexually frustrated!"

Pause.

"Did you hear me?"

"Really? I'm making you sexually frust—"

"Yes! Will you stop it?"

"Okay. But I think that you're over—"

"Just don't be so, you know, 'swashbuckling' or whatever! You're making me crazy."

He stood looking at her, undefended and open, without guile.

"And could you not do *that*?!"

"What?"

"That. That thing you do with your eyes and your mouth and your whole body. And your mind. Just quit it. Stop being who you are." She said, realizing she had probably said that before, in her mind at least, to friends and family. Okay, so that was a bit of an outrageous request, but—

Just then Abbey and Noah rounded the corner in the car. The passenger door flew open. "Get in, Sabrina. You've obviously had too much. . . incense, or whatever. You? Honestly? Shouldn't come here that often. You're scaring me, Sabrina, really."

Sabrina turned to sign off with Golas. But he had vanished. So like him, she thought. She stood a moment trying to remember if she'd gotten a response about the sex thing.

"Did you buy the book?" Sabrina asked as she slid into the passenger seat.

"Will you put your seat belt on? Yes, I bought the book. It was $21.00. And it's not a book, it's a glorified pamphlet! Twenty dollars!" she emphasized with disgust. "What the hell, Sabrina? What is all this about?" she yelled as she pulled away from the curb. "Are you completely out of your little mind?

That was probably an apt description of what she was.

In the back seat, Noah flipped through the pages of the book. "This book is weird. It's about space and matter. . . . energy and LSD. You won't even understand it," he said, handing it over to Sabrina with a look. "Pluto the dog. Weird stuff."

"Abby, Noah, you both need to forget about all this," and she wished she had one of those little silver pen things that the Men in Black used to erase people's memory. "I promise not to scare you like this again."

But even as they got onto the freeway, and the late afternoon sun exploded into their eyes, Sabrina knew that she'd never be sure she could keep a promise like that. It reminded her of all those movies where the hero would tell a child in the midst of some holocaust or the world coming to an end: "I will never let anyone hurt you. I promise I'll always keep you safe!"

Oh, really? And then comes the aliens or the bombs or a pestilence of frogs. Which isn't too different from all the promises almost everyone makes at one time or another, about honoring and obeying, in sickness and in health, to do my duty to —etc. etc. etc.

Promises are impulsive, romantic word nosegays, she thought, *with about as much punch and power as the scent of a rosebush. It's quite lovely when you're up close to it, but walk a few feet away and you lose the scent of it pretty quick. I'm not being cynical, I'm just saying, no one can ever know in the moment they make promises that they can be kept. You might drop dead the very next day.*

Or get whisked away in the tumult of a cosmic head storm.

19

Kierkegaard in the Cafeteria

Mired between boxes of bric-a-brac, towels, linens and kitchen equipment, Sabrina worked tirelessly every day after work, dusting, folding and putting away every last item until she dropped from exhaustion at 10 or 11 o'clock each night. Nevertheless, within the first week, and in spite of a life that seemed to take her on unscheduled detours, still her new space was beginning to feel like home.

The mystical closet was at last stocked and organized, and she even had a light switch installed on the outside wall, leaving the one on the inside (a tiny space between two of the shelves she found later) in working order, just in case.

"Just in case" had become her watch-cry because she never knew when she might need an exit strategy. It wasn't exactly an improbability for her to back right into another dimension just any old time a probable version of reality got a hankering. In fact she really thought that her whole life should be backed up on some kind of external hard drive, since there was never any guarantee that she would come back to the same world she'd left.

I mean, what if I end up staying in this other dimension next time? Should I always carry an extra pair of, you know? Or maybe I won't be human anymore and I'll need to buy a whole new wardrobe for someone with three legs or something. She wasn't about to be caught with her proverbial closet doors locked again, anyway, that was for sure. No sir-e-bob.

And it turned out the furniture did know a thing or two about its own placement. She had purchased a spectacular old leather sofa at a garage sale up in the avenues for $150 on Saturday morning and spent the whole afternoon moving it back and forth against two walls of the living room.

She felt like Oscar Wilde, who once said, "I was working on the proof of one of my poems all the morning and took out a comma. In the afternoon—well, I put it back again."

By late Sunday evening, she was thinking she'd made a huge mistake in buying the sofa. Laying down on the uncooperative divan in frustration, she stroked the smooth surface, smelling the leather. Rolling onto her back, she thought momentarily of the several cows whose hides it took to make it, and felt almost like she was stroking one of the four hoofed creatures. It was not unlike the Native American tradition, where gratitude was expressed after killing an animal—not for sport—but for survival of the tribe through a long winter's night. She felt a little prayer glide up through her arms and lovingly crossed her heart with her hands as she lay there, her mind entirely still for a moment.

Had you thought of taking the coffee table out of the configuration?

Voila! Now, where did that thought come from? Never mind, she did exactly that, and the sofa slid easily into a sweet spot, right in front of the antique Danish pine cupboard with the television in it. Practically in the middle of the room it was. The sofa had found its place.

A wonderful bright colored cotton-weave carpet, set on the diagonal, finished it off so perfectly she had to keep glancing back at it from the kitchen while she made a sandwich for lunch. The unusual positioning made it look like she knew a thing or two about decorating. And no one even had to know that all she did was talk to the furniture. Because here was the deal. She wouldn't want anyone to hear her praying to a cow hide or dialoging with a sofa. Her mother would have every right to be concerned about that one.

But it worked. How do you figure that?

Now if she could just communicate like this with her computer, word pad, and the cable TV, life would be sweet indeed. *I mean, how hard can it be?* she thought to herself. *They're communication devices for God's sake.*

Yes. For God's sake, let everything be for that. Especially communication. Every thought a prayer.

"I heard that!" she said with her mouth full of tuna fish on rye. Spinning slowly around in the center of the room, with a glob of tuna on her lip, and talking to no one in particular she "prayed" out loud without embarrassment. "I am grateful for cowhides and sofas and fish and all creatures great and small!" Was the sofa a creature? It was to her, she decided, the closest thing to a pet she would ever have, given her busy schedule.

But this inner voice was like— like having a second opinion about everything. What had she invited into her life anyway? In spite of the chronic anxiety Sabrina always felt over her close encounters of the weird kind, she had now had three wonderful nights' sleep since the episode in the bookstore, with no untoward events to keep her from her simple third dimensional life.

And she was just about to go for a fourth when she got a call from Nathan, the production editor from work. He said he was interested in seeing her new place and could he take her for a late supper? He was sorry he hadn't called sooner, but—one thing and another—he just hadn't got to it till now.

A little put off by the invitation being so late, Sabrina wondered if this was a booty call. Ben had never made that mistake even when they were in relationship. For the most part her sexual encounters with Ben were confined to late afternoon/early evenings because she was still living with her parents then, and his place was shared with another guy who pretty much wanted things wound up by eleven.

And to be honest, Sabrina wasn't sure anymore *what* to expect in the dating world, having been thrown off her game a bit. She could still flirt with the best of them around the espresso machine at work but in real time, how to proceed? A three year relationship with one guy had taken her out of the realm of having to guess, what's next?

So when she hesitated, Nathan sensed the problem. And he said in his strong and sexy New York accent, "Oh, I don't mean *that*—no. We can look at your place another night, if you like. How about we just meet for a drink, can we? I'm not a late night person usually, but I find that I get to know someone best between the hours of 8 PM and midnight."

Pause.

"Okay, that didn't come out right either. Let me start over. I'd really like to get to know you better, Sabrina. Will you meet me at Green Street in say, 20? It's not too far from where you live."

Pause.

"Hey. Do you remember that time we were talking about Kierkegaard, the philosopher, and you said you thought I had a strong moral compass? Try focusing on that right now. Truth is, it's Friday and we'll have to wait a whole week before we can get together if we don't do this now. I have something tomorrow, and Sunday is a work night. I don't do work nights."

"What's tomorrow night?" she blurted out, feeling suddenly invasive. She didn't know why she was asking, but there it was.

He accommodated her question though. "Okay, so the oddest thing. I mistakenly called another girl that I thought was you last week, and asked her out for tomorrow night, So that's why I don't have it free."

Pause.

"Hello? Could you just say anything, please? This *is* Sabrina, isn't it?"

This pausing thing that Golas had taught her was quite effective. She was going to use it more often. By the time she paused five times, it was entirely possible she could hear his whole back story.

Finally she said, "So. It is imperative I go with you tonight at this ungodly hour, because you've already asked a girl—whom you thought was me—for tomorrow night at a reasonable hour? You know what? In my whole life, I've only ever heard one other line better than that one."

"What?"

"What do mean, 'what'?"

"What was the line?"

"Easy cowboy. What is her name?"

"Whose name?"

"The Saturday night girl. The one who gets all the respect."

"Well, that's the thing. I thought it was Sabrina. It said S-something Rhyner on the napkin. I called early in the morning, because you said you were an early riser (just checking) and guess what? You were up. I find that unusual in working girl on a Saturday. Your voice sounded exactly like it always does. You know, kind of sweet, but on guard?"

Wait. On Guard?

"Honestly, I had talked to you for about twenty minutes, when you finally said, 'How come you keep calling me Sabrina? You know it's Sally, don't you?' Well I thought I'd wet my—but you should know, Miss Rhyner, you and I had a great thing going there for a while."

Now it was her turn to laugh. And she was getting really good at it too. Kind of like a thing. She could laugh, who knew? Plus this guy was funny! Stand-ups probably paid a lot to get routines like this. And she countered with, "Well, apparently so. You asked her out. My name is Ryder, by the way: R-Y-D-E-R. Tell me, 'Nation', how could you get so many things wrong before nine o'clock in the morning?"

"Well I couldn't just hang up without asking her for a drink or something, could I? And the only night I had open was this Saturday. It was earmarked for you but sorry, you just lost out to a 'shadow of your former shelf'," he said in some kind of old movie star accent. Sean Connery maybe.

"Also, you need to know," she catapulted back, "I would *never* give a guy my number on a napkin. It's so tawdry."

"I can't say you're wrong about that. I'm actually not that keen on calling numbers off napkins, myself. It's kind of like a bathroom stall thing, isn't it? 'Call S. Rhyner for a good time!' But it was you dammit! Don't you see? I had to overcome all my bashful reservations and call anyway!"

"No. It wasn't me, because I don't—"

"Excuse me. It *was* you, in my mind. In fact, I even remember thinking, how could such a sophisticated girl like Sabrina Rhyner give me her number on a napkin? It's so tawdry. Well, she must really be into me, I thought. What else?"

"Ryder. Kierkegaard? We talked about Kierkegaard? Do I know him?"

Chuckling, he said, "He's one of the more interesting philosophers, you said. Come on, tell me you really don't remember the conversation down in the cafeteria?"

"Must have been that other one. Sally from Yonkers. That cafeteria has a lot of napkins."

"No. It was you. I remember you had on a leather-fringed scarf with an old pin that belonged to your grandmother. You said she was a Grande Dame, and that's where you learned to dress like that. You said she was very eccentric and you hoped you could follow in her footsteps—no. Fill her shoes. Literally; you've still got them in your closet."

Patricia York

"My closet? You know about my closet?" she shot back in extraordinary defensiveness. *Come on, girl. Get it together; no one is going to know what goes on in the privacy of your own—*

"We talked about true character and what it means to be in real integrity. You said that integrity means something different to you now than it did before; what you are actually feeling, not what you ought to be feeling. That's what you said, and I remember it because I liked the flavor of the conversation. It was authentic and somewhat droll. To be honest, it appealed to my inner smartass," he said in his sexy New York accent.

Well okay then, she thought. Finally. A guy who enjoys a conversation enough to actually remember it. She agreed to meet him in an hour, instead of making a formal date sometime far in the future. She even decided to dress: a long sleeved black raw silk vintage jacket with a short flared ruffle attached at the waistline, and some of her good jeans. Shoes by who else? Jimmy Choo.

It took 15 minutes to get ready and another 10 minutes to Drive to Green Street in Sugar House. She let the valet park the car. It was too late to waste any more time walking across the parking lot. Arriving shortly after him, she had the waitress take her to the table he'd secured a few minutes before.

"Wow!" he said. "You look—" stopping short to just stare at her for a minute. She let him gawk, neither of them uncomfortable with the silence. She was glad he didn't feel the need to fill it up with words, even though he probably knew some good ones.

"Sit," he said finally, "But I'm still editing my notes on your outfit: 'smooth, sleek style; a perfect fit for Miss *Ryder* (he said with emphasis) in her Ralph Lauren jeans and elegant black jacket, with a little swirly thing around the waist, for a chilly night out on the town. Chic and fashionable, right down to her Jimmy Choo shoes—"I'm just guessing, riffing. But such panache!"

Sabrina stopped in her tracks there for just a minute.

What the—? He does know some good words. Panache! Hey, maybe it's back.

"Got to get it right," he said. "It's for Vogue, and you know how spiky they can get when the captions don't suit the picture." He was working on a book by one of the writers for Vogue magazine, as the production editor, Sabrina knew.

Again, a few seconds of silence went by. Simple eye contact was a wonderful way to begin Sabrina thought, already glad she had decided to come. He certainly knew how to kick off a relationship. Taking her seat, she peeled back the napkin, and placed the silverware to one side.

Then with a wink, he put his hand lightly on hers and said, "What's for dessert?"

20

Republican Rant

"I beg your pardon", Sabrina said with mock umbrage. "You got everything right but the 'swirly thing'. I assume you mean the peplum on my jacket? You got everything right, but that doesn't mean I'm going to put out, I hope you know."

"Always on guard, Ryder, like I said. Are you a Mormon then?"

Now she was taken aback and not just for laughs. This might go in a serious direction, and she took a moment to consider her answer. "Culturally," she said, shaking the napkin into her lap. "I grew up Mormon and it was very sweet. But for now, I'm keeping my options open. Got any suggestions?"

He didn't apparently, and remained silent.

"I claim it like a Jew claims his ethnicity, but not the religion part. It's like that, only not so historically tragic. Although, come to think of it, we do have our collective persecution persona. I guess we're not about to be outdone in that arena," she said with a gleam in her eye, "Haan's Mill, Winter Quarters, Johnson's army, the whole polygamy thing. In fact I'd say harassment seems to be the burden of proof where Mormonism is concerned. I mean, no one would go through all that pain and suffering if it weren't the only true thing, right? God loves it when His special people get all caught up in suffering and sacrifice. It's a real turn-on, apparently."

"Whoa. You're not just a lapsed Mormon. You're a little cranky there, Ryder."

"A 'lapsed Mormon'?" she laughed. "That's cute. Cranky am I? Well, I'm new at this. I just recently stopped being actively involved. It's only been a few months and let me tell you, it's rough on the family. They're pretty great, and awfully sad about my choices, I can tell you. Why do you ask?"

"Oh, I had a girlfriend in high school who was Mormon, back in Albany, New York. She was pretty committed, always trying to enroll me in going to church."

"Yeah. When you have the True Religion, you've got to make sure the word gets out you know, so everyone has at least a *chance* to join up. Otherwise, you'd feel terribly guilty if you thought—." She stopped for a moment and then went on. "Well, let me just say it starts to feel like a heavy weight. 'The eyes of the world are upon you'; that kind of thing. You've got to wonder though why Life would set it up that way though; why give the Truth to such a small percentage of people and expect them to get the word out to the whole rest of the world? It's a bit like selling vacuums, door to door, an overwhelmingly colossal project. No commission either. Or you could say that the commission is all the people who come to agree with you about what truth means. And I guess that's always a lovely thing when it happens. Like-minds, you know. How did your girlfriend fare?"

"What do you mean?" he replied distractedly, as though not really paying so much attention to her exact words, as to the way she said them.

"Did she finally get you to go to church with her?"

"Oh. Yes. Well, yes and no. Yes, a couple of times, but no, not for the long haul. And you of all people must know, it's kind of an eternal thing, right?"

"You got that right, Mr. But you mean 'forever', don't you?"

"I guess so. What's the difference?"

"Well, eternity isn't really a time-based concept is it? I mean, it's not exactly a description of a long period of time. Isn't it more like a sort of timelessness? Or maybe you could say that it's the intersection of time with the present moment?

He seemed thoughtful, waiting a moment before replying. "Really? You think? Well, I accept your definition of eternity, Miss Ryder, and raise you two correlating concepts: infinity and perpetuity. Are they as equally ambiguous?"

"Okay. No," she said, smiling a little at his quick response. This was just the kind of thing she liked. Someone who could make a conversation feel like a tennis match. "I think those words actually carry the meaning that most people think of as eternity, particularly in the conditioned way of thinking: an indefinite amount of time."

"So what's your take on the conservative right and Mr. Romney?" he asked, changing the subject. "Is he your man? I mean, maybe you are a Jack Mormon as they say, but who would turn against such a formidable candidate just to make a point? I take it that conservatism runs through your veins like the blood of Israel in the tribes of Judah?"

"Yeah. Well, I'm covered either way there. Because first of all, Mormons believe they *are* the blood of Israel, so mazeltov to me,

I guess. Non-Mormons are even called 'gentiles', believe it or not." She waited to see how he might react to that bit of information, but he said nothing. He was generous in his conversational style, open and easy.

"I'm just saying, it's kind of sweet how they adopted themselves into the House of Israel without so much as a 'How d'ya do there?' to their Jewish brothers. I don't know *what* the Jews think of it," Sabrina said sotto voce. "They're probably not used to that sort of flattery, I should think.

"And second? I'm not a Jack Mormon. That's someone who still subscribes to the religious teachings, whether out of apathy, guilt or fear, but just can't live by the rules. Do I strike you as apathetic about anything?"

He smiled and started to answer, but she kept on.

"Sorry—rhetorical question. I lived by the rules very well, thank-you, when I valued them. But for me now, rules are simply suggestions, however loving, that come from an external authority, which I'm not that keen on anymore; and thirdly—"

"Hold on there, pious one," Nathan responded laughingly, "I only asked about your political leanings."

"I was getting to that part. By the way, is it just me or is politics still a matter of secret ballot? And why the wild assumptions? Because I would *never* vote for a rich white man over this cool (and by that I mean, unflappable) black man, who has repeatedly extended the hand of bi-partisan cooperation across the board. So he's not a backslapper or a good ole' boy! You have to consider what the president is as a symbol. Because whoever expects the president— *any president*—to do everything he promises, is just hankering for disappointment on a level so colossal, we might as well be voting for the Second Coming.

What Obama symbolizes is a calm and steady presence, an invitation to a larger conversation than just the average political banter. But the offer to come to the table and discuss things like grown-ups is apparently beyond the aptitude of the average Republican! And you know it's not about policy. It's all about making Obama look impotent. I can hear all the little caucuses in the back rooms right now: 'Don't give this guy an inch! We don't know why, but it will make us look weak, do you hear?! We need to wop his skinny black ass! Because we can't appear to be doin' bi'dness with the Devil!'"

Sabrina was just about out of breath when she remembered to add, "And all this wide-eyed Fox-News-Enquirer-Gossip-Magazine indulgence in fear-mongering? It's enough to put us back two centuries!

"It's like they want you to believe that nothing that is happening now is as sacred or important as what took place two hundred and thirty-six years ago when the constitution was written, as though people back then possessed some kind of wisdom we don't have access to now. Like our ancestors knew something about the future, the one that we're living in, that isn't available to us now that we're living in it. You see? That's the problem with thinking in terms of past and future; you are never really available for the wisdom of the present moment.

"Personally, I think that the best anyone can do in the present is to be tapped into his own internal wisdom as much as possible. And maybe that's what the designers of the Declaration of Independence did do that we don't always do so well today. But there's a field of awareness here in this very moment, surrounding us just like it was them. But are we tapped into it?

"No! Apparently, we're too busy trying to get elected. Or actually it's crazier than that; we're too busy trying to make sure that the other guy *isn't* getting elected. It's not even a positive forward movement! It's about resistance and defensiveness; scrambling over each other to keep the opposition from even appearing to get anything done. Like crabs in a bucket. But who's minding the store, I ask you? Who's doing the work of government?"

Nathan opened his mouth to comment, but Sabrina wasn't stopping for traffic.

"Shame on the Republicans! From the moment Obama was elected, their only goal was to put up roadblocks to his administration to make him look bad. And the heightened emotional energy around this is so obvious you'd think any intelligent Republican could see it. But fear had the average conservative by the balls. So the Republican congress just stopped doing the jobs they were hired to do, and sat right down in the middle of everything and refused to cooperate; like toddlers having a tantrum because they lost the ball on the playground. All that happened was they lost the ball! They didn't lose their jobs. But the last 4 years has been all about getting control of the ball. Nothing to do with working together to heal the economy. Obama is all on his own there. And they want to blame it all on him?

You thought I was cranky about religion? Well, politics has me in full metal rage!

"It's like they believe Obama is this Dark Prince, leading us down a shadowy path toward some arcane collectivism, images of ancient terrors. Socialism, Communism, but what do those words even mean today? We separate ourselves from our own economic healing with concepts that used to carry a political punch, but don't anymore. And listen, if they want to make government smaller, they should start by backing quietly out of our bedrooms!

"And I ask you, which is scarier, that they really understand how manipulative and divisive they are, or that they are completely unconscious about it and just running in fear?

Again, Nathan started to answer, but no entry available.

"I mean, there's no impulse to find common ground and work together, because how can you find common ground with . . . with Evil? Yes, they've actually convinced themselves that the political opposition is not just wrong or different from theirs, or even dimwitted. It's Eeevil," she said, stretching out the word while lowering the pitch of her voice.

"Simply speaking, The Republican party, for the last four years has been a living, breathing fear machine." Then leaning over the table in a whisper, she said, "Is it possible that their desire for an apocalypse or the battle of Armageddon is so fascinating, that they are unconsciously trying to make it happen because of some romantic (and I use that word in the most pedestrian sense) need for the Deus ex Machina? What would they do if they got elected?

"They couldn't actually govern because fear only knows how to resist and control. When people think in terms of absolutes— absolute right and absolute wrong—the only solution is for Absolute Right to win, isn't it? And then the assumption is that if the right/ godly/good candidate wins, God will take it from there. Hence, they don't need a plan.

"Which might even work, if God is Love. But here's the chilling part. They aren't really aligned with God or love, because all this time they've been listening to that other voice, the fearful One. And that voice tells them they have to win at any cost, never mind the means they have to use. And *that's* why Romney can't answer any serious questions, because his only plan is to win. Do you see how that works? The end justifies the means. And that kind of reasoning is extremely shaky, because it's the foundation of every tyrant's belief system.

"When will we get it? The *ends* and the *means* are the same! Listen, are you listening? This isn't just a cautionary tale. I'm saying that this is a metaphor for life. Government is a global symbol of what's going on in our private minds."

Then Sabrina took a long breath, and for the first time in about 10 minutes, looked directly at Nathan who was, quite frankly, rapt. Suddenly, then, feeling sheepish enough to choke on her own words, she did.

"Don't you. . . Don't you think?"

"Honestly?" he said, "I hadn't thought of it like that; about most of what you just said, actually. But it's an interesting perspective. I'm Republican myself and—"

"Wait. You're Republican? How is that even possible?!"

"Well, I think you've given me something to think about there, Ryder. You're all passion, aren't you? And when passion speaks through you, it doesn't fool around."

"Oh, I'm so sorry, I—"

"No, you go girl," he said with a half smile, the kind of smile when you know that something you just said is being taken seriously. Now she liked him even more, which confused her a lot.

Because she would never have deliberately liked a Republican.

21

Wherein Sabrina Observes the Sabbath and Learns More About the Lazy Man

Sunday had become her favorite day and at 9:30 am Sabrina was still in bed, delighting in the new mattress she'd purchased for the antique sleigh bed that had been stored in her parents' garage for the last year and a half.

Symbolism was her new religion. So what did the bed represent? Making the unconscious conscious? Living the Good Dream? Whatever. Today she was languishing, in spite of that great rap from Nathan about being an early riser. She liked that he liked that she liked to get up early. So few people understood the gentle seduction of the early morning hours; The God Hours, she called them.

Turned out that Nathan, the smartass from New York, had an authentic inner core. He was a bit of a philosopher too and it was probably what she enjoyed most about him. In fact, the night before last, over chips and beer, they had agreed that a dynamic conversation was as good as sex. Of course, as far as Sabrina was concerned, that theory wasn't likely to be tested for a while.

"But good conversation *is* the best foreplay," she thought as she lay there naked in existential luxury and wrapped in a goose feather quilt.

She was glad that he had not been offended after she'd gone off on Republicans the way she did. Why had she assumed that he was a Democrat anyway? Could it have been something so simple as a coffee break conversation when he had mentioned Aaron Sorkin's, West Wing TV series? It was one of his favorites he said, and he suggested that they watch it together sometime.

"Okay, great," Sabrina agreed quickly, "How long is it?"

"Seven years," he had said with a wink, "but we don't have to watch it all at once. We can take our time." He was a clever young man and a deep thinker, although his understanding and use of metaphor was not as sharp as she would have liked.

Plus now, he was a Republican, which meant that he must be at least something of a conservative in essential ways of thinking, politically and otherwise. For instance, Sabrina thought he seemed deliberate and graciously aware of her own desire to keep things between them informal and light. Well, except for that wild display of political passion on her part. But in spite of the fact that he had actively pursued her in the last couple of weeks, still he seemed disinclined to hurry things sexually.

She wondered if perhaps he was a Christian with a strong moral code about premarital sex. Or maybe he really was put off by her 'rant'. Whatever it was, it suited her just fine, since she'd made up her mind to hold off on the physically intimate part of any new relationship, no matter what other form it should take. The only real intimacy that Sabrina was interested in right now was the one with her own Deep Wisdom. And quite frankly, so far? Nothing could even compare to it.

Still the discourse with Nathan didn't exclude flirtatious banter with a little sexual innuendo thrown in for spice. And for Sabrina, it was quite enough that he had a talent for rhetoric, because here was the thing: a tongue can be used in many creative ways, and his was an absolute first-class forecast of pleasure.

Reflecting on the nature of the 'romantic endeavor', she watched her thoughts float by like puffy little white clouds in a cerulean blue summer sky. And after staying up late the night before, unpacking and folding up the very last of the moving boxes, she was inclined to just go on lying there, suspended in this rummy contemplation . Usually, anything short of getting straight out of bed and into an early morning sitting meditation, she would have called languorous or lethargic. But today she wasn't going to be bossed around by big words. And also, self-reproach was a concept now on trial in her mind. Words like languid, lazy, indolent and undisciplined (mobilizing technology for the guilty-minded) were words she had always used to flog herself into submission when necessary. Not so much anymore. Not today. Today, she was looking at the whole idea of guilt head-on, realizing that it just didn't have the same motivating clout that it used to have.

"The happy learner cannot feel guilty. . .This is so essential it should never be forgotten. The guiltless learner learns easily because his thoughts are free. Yet this entails the recognition that guilt is interference. . . . and serves no useful function at all."[48] ACIM

I used to suffer when I thought I was being lazy and unproductive, she thought, But now I wonder if maybe no one is ever really lazy. Maybe they're just . . .waiting. . . for some insight. And maybe it's okay to wait, to ponder, to stop running around in circles and to be open to larger perspectives, new possibilities. She remembered that in John Milton's, Sonnet on his Blindness, he said, "They also serve, who only stand and wait." She loved that Sonnet.

Then turning on her side to face the windows, she considered the immensity of life beyond the walls of her little townhouse. A set of small French doors stood slightly open onto a tiny balcony and a slight breeze rustled the leaves on the ficus tree in a corner of the room.

Instead of hanging the heavy opaque draperies she had purchased the week before, she opted for some lightweight translucent curtains instead. Now hanging loosely in puddles on the floor, they seemed to invite the whole outdoors in. Indeed, last night the moonlight had shone through the paned glass and cast strange, elongated patterns along the walls, the floors, and across her body.

Utah had what she liked to call text-book weather, with very little humidity. Seasons appeared like clockwork, and in summer, no matter how hot the day, it almost always cooled off significantly at night. A temperate autumn, like the one they were experiencing now, often lasted well into November, ending in a classic snowfall by Thanksgiving. Winter didn't usually last longer than three months, and one could expect the first crocuses to appear as early as the end of February.

But what Sabrina cherished most was the majestic Wasatch mountain range, which rose right up against the city like a great castle wall. She called them "designer mountains" because instead of the pine trees that filled the canyons, the open faces were covered with low shrubbery which had the effect of a rich woven carpet, green in the spring and summer, red and orange in the fall, and white in the winter. She wondered as she looked out onto these beloved landscapes, now dotted with rich fall colors, if she'd ever find a man who could share her love for bringing the outdoors into the boudoir.

Most people she knew liked to keep their bedrooms dark, allowing them to sleep late into the morning. Ben was of that ilk and toward the end, when they were throwing out all the old rules of sexual decorum hoping to infuse some life into the relationship, she had tried to open the curtains one night in his bedroom, to let in a small slit of moonlight. "Look! It's God's flashlight!" she'd exclaimed, as he threw his hands up to cover his eyes. Assaulted with the unexpected intensity of light, he yelled at her to close them and when Sabrina laughed, he was annoyed. After that she decided she would rather go home to sleep in her own bed.

Her parents liked that arrangement. They shared a fantasy that if she were coming home at night, she must still be holding to the cherished standards of sexual propriety before marriage. But it was the morning and evening light that seduced her like a lover and lured her home to sleep and wake in its grandeur.

And so she knew that if she couldn't find someone to share this feral infatuation, she would be faced with the possibility of living alone the rest of her life. Or at the very least, she and her partner would have to have separate bedrooms, like she'd read about in the Victorian erotica. "Could be sexy," she tried to tell herself.

As her thoughts pulled her focus inward, she shifted her vision from telescopic to microscopic, and something caught her eye. Something immediate and razor-sharp, as though a plucky little bluebird had just fluttered silently onto the table next to her bed. On the linen tablecloth, a farmhouse style lamp and a bouquet of peonies stuffed into a glass jar stood guard over a short stack of Sabrina's favorite books.

And there it was.

Wedged into the middle of the stack, was the little blue book she had just purchased a few days ago, with the help of her madcap friends et al, at the Golden Braid Bookstore:

<u>The Lazy Man's Guide to Enlightenment.</u>

Consumed by unpacking and organizing, she'd thought she'd lost it. But here it was, and what better time to peruse it than now? This wonderfully dreamy Sabbath morning. The idea of the Sabbath was a holdover from church days. And what a wonderful precept it was. After every six days of work; finally, a day of rest.

Except in church, no one had actually rested. There were meetings and more meetings to *prepare* for more meetings, and well, it had never been all that relaxing. The Sabbath was a beautiful idea, but to Sabrina's mind, the obligations of church work kept everyone so distracted that it rarely trickled down to an actual experience.

Except maybe for "fast Sunday". That was the day everyone (8 years old and over) didn't eat or drink for 24 hours. And blessing of blessings, fewer meetings.

That first Sunday of every month stood out in her memory as possibly the Real Thing. Fasting wasn't that difficult for Sabrina, and the rewards of staving off the material world in terms of something as basic as food, had an amazing affect on her; a direct pendulum swing into the realm of spirit. It was her first taste of "the bread of life" (truth) that Jesus had spoken of in the New Testament; and drinking from the "living water" (spirit), of which he promised one would never thirst again. She had seen herself as the woman at the well, and Jesus her first real guru, although in those days she wouldn't have put it that way exactly.

On those special Sundays, she sometimes experienced being carried away in a kind of other-worldly dimension. Not definable in words, it was beyond all ordinary experience. Here were moments of pure revelation, without subject or object, a peaceful feeling given and received from whom and by whom she couldn't say. Just this keen sense of knowing that she was loved. When she tried to put it in objective terms, it lost its savor. So she would just let it *have* her. On other Sundays it seemed like her mother cooked all day, and the kids spent a lot of time cleaning up the dishes after dinner, when personally, Sabrina would rather have been reading. Or maybe just doing nothing?

Now, in the privacy of her own little townhouse, her very own Life, she could truly celebrate this principle called the Sabbath. Reaching for the little blue book—a pamphlet, Abby had called it— she opened it to the preamble - introduction for this 1995 edition, after it had been, apparently, 23 years in continuous publication. And she read:

"Dear Readers, thank you for all the lovely messages you have sent me over the years. What can I say that will not fall short of your imagination about me? I am mortal, your equal, and that's the message I was trying to deliver: we can all do it."[49]

". . .In 1969 . . . the very weekend I was having a pamphlet published with my theories . . . I was offered LSD and went Home . . . I decided I wouldn't advertise my personal illumination, but would try to show it by my behavior and by what I produced. And it seems I succeeded, miraculously, with <u>The Lazy Man's Guide to Enlightenment</u>. I did not at all anticipate the kind of experiences I had on LSD. I had never taken refuge in castles in the air.[50]

"I read enough metaphysics to check out my theories. But I was rooted in the earth and spent more time scanning scientific works to see if anything that was known to be true contradicted my lines of thought. . . I never varied from my determination to evolve hard information. . . I was so ruthless in testing, suspecting every sentiment, that I came to feel I was the destroyer of ideas, and indeed my books are based on what I could not demolish. Anyone who wants to tear these books down will have to work harder and longer than I did. At times on my psychedelic trips I was distinctly aware of myself as an unmoved watcher. . .[51]

"I had a strong intuition that the rules we make for others apply to ourselves, and I would have to be extremely careful about what I told people. I understood that the way up is just as easy as the way down, and it would not be honest to tell people that enlightenment was a long or difficult learning process. Strange and sticky perhaps, in the light of reason, but not laborious."[52]

Then there was a short history of why and how he had written it and the somewhat diverse and *adverse* means of getting it published. He had worked as a production editor for 2 very fine publishing houses: Ballantine Books and Fawcett Publications. Quitting his job in order to concentrate on the final re-write of LMG, he lived a Spartan, half-starved life in a "frenzy of concentrated effort".

Here was a short philosophical treatise on space, energy and matter, just like Noah had said. But it was really about spiritual concepts; love and enlightenment, expansion and contraction of consciousness. Each chapter was only a few pages long and it was just about the most wonderfully abbreviated discussion of universal principle Sabrina had ever read. And Noah was right. You had to be ready for this little gem, as it was a weird and wonderful description of practically everything. Talk about your Unified Theory.

He had been a classic hippy living in the 60's and 70's on California Street in San Francisco, in a one room flat that he paid for with VA checks. Go figure. Had the writing not been impeccable, Sabrina would certainly have questioned the source of such material. But like every book she valued on non-duality, it communicated "the reality of spirit, beyond the literal meaning of its sentences".

And here was an interesting note: In 1972, when a second printing was needed, he received a call from a man that he called a "drop-out Mormon", and whom he claimed "are the most reliable people to do business with", and it was this man and his wife who saved this classic nugget for posterity.

For Sabrina.

As a matter of fact, she read it in one sitting that Sabbath Day and felt certain that it belonged on her bedside table as a reduction version of the five larger volumes she held equal to it:; A Course in Miracles; I Am That (a classic book of dialogues with Sri Nirsagaddatta Maharaj, an East Indian mystic); and A Thousand Names for Joy, by Byron Katie (her interpretation of The Tao Te Ching); and Pathways Through to Space, by Franklin Merrill Wolfe.

And now, this "pearl of great price", for those who didn't appreciate being washed overboard in a river of words and poetry; this small offering for anyone who wanted only the bare bones, unmoved by anything that seemed too overwhelming or rich in scope and appearance. Sabrina could appreciate both. But really, how had this hippy, this Thaddeous Golas guy, been able to condense all that insight into one tiny volume? That alone was a miracle.

"My book was apparently a feature of the New Age movement," said the author, "but I felt embarrassed at being identified with much of the nonsense being promulgated. To those who are offended, I can only say that, The Lazy Man's Guide to Enlightenment, is an authentic expression of space (highest) consciousness, and I am the kind of person it took to write it . . ."[53]

"When I started to write, I found that many of the things I had been saying were stored in my mind as if taped . . ."[54]

At this Sabrina stopped short.

Because it sounded very much like some other references to this style of writing she had heard about. The first was Helen Schucman (a professor of medical psychology at Columbia University who transcribed <u>A Course in Miracles</u>): "That was my introduction to the Voice," Mrs. Shucman said. "It made no sound, but seemed to be giving me a kind of rapid inner dictation . . .It could be interrupted at any time and later picked up again. . . It seemed to be a special assignment I had somehow, somewhere agreed to complete."[55]

And the second was (believe it or not), Joseph Smith, whose wife described his transcription process like this: "acting as his scribe, your father would dictate to me for hour after hour; and when returning after meals, or after interruptions, he would at once begin where he had left off, without either seeing the manuscript or having any portion of it read to him . . . It would have been improbable that a learned man could do this; and, for one so ignorant and unlearned as he was, it was simply impossible."[56]

Sabrina thought. *Is this the way of it? Does the universe speak to us if one just listens, or (in the case of some mystics), they are literally forced to listen? And to what end? Does the Universal Mind just plunk these crazy downloads into the minds of some unsuspecting soul (who then often becomes a prime object of ridicule, by the way)? Has all this data been backed up on some internal hard drive, and when it's time, it just explodes onto the event horizon of the world?*

These thoughts avalanched across the inner terrain of her mind, and Sabrina suddenly had a laser respect for the way information gets transmitted from the Whole to the Part. *The quality of the information conveyed obviously varies from generation to generation,* Sabrina thought. <u>*The Book of Mormon,*</u> *for instance, contains little of the truly remarkable wisdom that practically bleeds through the pages of more modern manuscripts. But then it was written in the 1800's, and in the style of traditional scripture, however dubious the historical value. Still, there are stories in that book that are among the finest of all the mythologies of the world. And aren't all stories, all histories, just 'mythologies' in a way? Isn't the value of a myth like Noah's ark, for instance, simply that it elucidates present moment awareness? Otherwise, what good are they? Because no one voice can tell the whole truth about any circumstance or set of ideas. It would always be just one point of view in any case: that particular historian's, novelist's, poet, journalist, prophet or philosopher.*

Is it possible to transfer data from a broader, wiser mind or self to a lesser one who was open to it or capable of translating higher wisdom into words that bypass the rational mind? Isn't that what poetry is?" All these questions Sabrina asked herself.

She thought as how Handel had 'channeled' the Messiah, using Charles Jennons' compilation of lyrics, largely from Isaiah and Psalms, two forms of biblical poetry. And Handel wrote the music manuscript in a miraculous 24 days. In fact, it was quite well known that when he got to the Hallelujah chorus, his assistant/servant found him in tears saying, "I did think I saw heaven open, and saw the very face of God."[57] How is that different from Joseph Smith or Helen Schucman? Or Thadious Golas, for that matter?

"Can any document or creation contain the whole truth? It can only ever be an approximation. And when music or literature approximates truth at a new level, why can't we say that it is channeled or inspired?"

She thought that <u>A Course in Miracles</u> was perhaps the most explicable, if effusive, synthesis of Christian concepts and the terrifying beauty of Eastern spiritual philosophy. Leading her further and further into depths of the unknown, there were moments she had pierced the dense veil of solid matter into a euphoria of pure unobstructed certainty, although it was not the certainty of anything in particular. That was the strange thing. But it was like passing through clouds into direct sunlight, and you could look right into this light without hurting your eyes. It did not contain stories or histories, but it seemed to reveal the true meaning of all Christian symbolism. Still, <u>A Course in Miracles,</u> was not for everyone.

But it was her path, no kidding around. It was her LSD.

22

In Which Sabrina Goes Camping and Meets Mr. Wright

Nathan Bridger turned out to be a relentless suitor. He cajoled and charmed Sabrina every day until she finally agreed to go camping with him the first weekend in November. The weather was still uncommonly warm and some of his friends from California were coming in for three days, and had planned a trip to Moab, the desert country in south eastern Utah.

As much as Sabrina wanted to keep this thing from turning into a serious relationship, she was still compelled by Nathan's easy manner and clearly attractive openness to life. "Resistance creates the opposite of its intent," she remembered Golas telling her. What if she stopped resisting Nathan's blatantly humorous advances? If she turned around and faced him in the heat of the chase, would he retreat and lose interest? Would he stop asking for her time and attention? And would that be a good or a bad thing? She noticed that she was beginning to wait in an ever-so-slight anticipation for his phone calls every evening. There was a growing pleasure in the push-me/pull-you of their late night talks. So by now she wasn't sure which outcome she wanted.

At the office, he stayed close to his desk, which was quite a distance from her own, so she rarely saw him there. Impressed by his ability to stay focused on his work, she was also amazed at how suddenly he could put the spotlight of his attention (and it was a bright light indeed) directly on *her* in the evenings. He couldn't be spending this much time with other girls as well. So what did that mean?

These were questions she might have asked him because they both were pretty clear that nothing was off limits in their conversations. But would this be a bridge too far? Maybe asking direct questions like that would break some inviolate rule, the one she ought not to breach?

She'd been as surprised as he when they had both blurted out—each in their own way—one evening that keeping their relationship at a 'friends' level was preferable to escalating it to something more intimate. But here was the deal: they obviously moved in opposing political circles. Yet he hadn't said a word about it since that first night, so she didn't know exactly what he believed. On the other hand, she had revealed her own position so completely that there was nothing left for him to conjecture at all. So he was definitely holding the high ground there. His quiet surrender was enough to let her know that he might hold equally strong for the opposition. And so embarrassed was she over the whole matter, that it could hardly be given more focus without putting 'the fool' squarely in his line of vision. Yet it was the most obviously ignored subject in their cornucopia of conversation.

An elephant in the room, she said to herself. *No pun intended.* She was beginning to see that standing boldly for an ideal was possibly the worst way to convince others to see the truth. And that was entirely separate from the outrageous assumption that one was in possession of the truth in the first place.

On Friday morning Nathan came early in an old pickup truck he'd borrowed from a friend. It was loaded with foodstuffs, tents, blankets, pillows, a box of starter firewood, water and a sun shower for those inclined. They were going to wait for his three college buddies and their dates at a local greasy spoon, where they would eat lunch and then drive in three separate vehicles into the heart of the desert.

Nathan looked like a picture straight out of a camp guide magazine with his new hiking boots, khaki shorts, and a brand new baseball cap. Little wisps of dark curly hair stuck out behind his ears. Sabrina looked like a child in grade school, her thin legs rising out of thick red wool socks and yellow leather boots, and a vintage smock over some old baggy shorts.

Nathan, unlike most men she dated, seemed to notice and admire the way she put old and new styles together. Observant in that way, he often made a to-do over her choices. Today was no different. "It's like an art form, your clothes. It's as though you're sculpting with textiles and buttons, belts and ribbons, the way you put it all together. You're like a walking art exhibit, a 'movable feast' for the eyes."

She blushed and stammered out a thank-you.

Reaching the lunch grill before everyone else, they found a large table and ordered coffee and sandwiches.

"So how did three of your best friends end up together in Sacramento?" asked Sabrina as she twisted her long thick hair, banding it into a sloppy knot at the back of her neck.

Nathan, having just taken a bite of his muffin, swallowed hard to answer. "They don't actually live that close to each other. But they love California and always said they wanted to live there. I never knew what the fascination was. The ocean, I suppose. Not that it isn't beautiful, of course. But I fancy the open panoramic views, the bucolic pastureland of Utah. And the wild sunsets blazing off the face of the mountains are something beyond, I don't know, but compared to the rather vacant landscape of the sea, they just blow me away. But I suppose that's all just an excuse really, because I was following my inner muse and I have no idea why it brought me here. It seemed the only option that was clear at the time though."

"Really?! Do you listen to this muse a lot?" Sabrina asked. "Is it a voice? Does it speak in complete sentences or just feelings? I mean how does it—"

"Hey old buddy!" a voice shouted from across the room, "What's for breakfast? And who's this beautiful woman you've brought along?!" And quite out of nowhere it seemed, there were four grown men at the table hugging and slapping each other, all claiming to have never been so glad to be in one place since the beginning of creation.

Sabrina, and three girls who had come with Nathan's friends, stood watching the reunion, smiling and introducing themselves to each other. There was Marty, Helena and Elaine, all with California tans and varying shades of blonde to red hair. Apparently they'd been traveling since early morning from somewhere in northern California, where they had spent the night together in a luxury hotel with the boys. They were friendly enough and seemed to enjoy each other's company, as though they'd known each other for years. Whether or not they did, she couldn't tell.

How wonderful to be so at ease, thought Sabrina, already a little anxious about what the next two nights would reveal. She and Nathan hadn't talked about it, but she realized that her expectations and his may be very different, considering the company and the general atmosphere of gaiety and apparent intimacy.

"Sabrina, these men are my very best friends since high school. We've been through it all together: Sam Reardon, Joshua Levinson, and George Wright. You've met the girls I see," said Nathan in his easy, straightforward fashion. Apparently he was acquainted with at least two of the girls. For some reason Sabrina had not expected that. One of them, Marty, gave him a peculiar look and then shifted her gaze quickly away when she saw Sabrina watching her.

"George is going to be our guide into the desert wild," Nathan said to Sabrina. "He knows where there are some great old Anasazi Indian ruins hidden away out there. He used to be a trail guide back in the day." George wasn't an "aw shucks" kind of guy, and the few profuse complements that Nathan dispatched, he took on calmly without disclaimers.

After everyone ordered and began eating, Nathan stood up and announced that he and Sabrina would be leaving to get a head start on the trip down, having agreed to buy a large portion of the fresh groceries closer to the destination. "So we'll see you all in about three hours at the predetermined spot," he shouted back. "But keep in touch in case there are any problems or delays. We're still going to caravan into the desert together, right? Since there are no marked roads?" They all waved in agreement. Grabbing Sabrina's hand and heading to the exit, Nathan waved back at them one more time and said, "See you soon then, 'you Princes of Albany, Kings of New York!'"

Once on the road, Sabrina petitioned Nathan to tell her about his friends; when and how had they met and become so close; what were their common interests and did they do these kinds of things often? When had the girls come on board? Were some of them old friends as well (as she suspected) and then, finally, against all her better judgment, something prompted her to stare down the elephant in the room: were his friends all Republican too?

"Funny you should ask," he said, seemingly unsurprised by her direct hit to the political jugular. "We—the guys that is—helped in the last Republican campaign. Mostly we wanted to learn the ropes, just to see for ourselves if it was possible to actually accomplish a perceived goal within all of the chaos of the political context. Josh and Dan are real go-getters; probably anyone would sort them out on the extreme right of things. Tea-partiers for a while.

"But George, now, he is a cut above. He's got something, a subtle but unwavering quality that should be patented. He's steady, and he drinks from a very deep well. As a matter of fact, that night when you described Obama as 'unflappable', I thought, 'Eureka! That's what George Wright is. Unflappable.' And that's no small gift, is it? You'll see what I mean. Sometimes I think I love the man," he said with a deflective laugh.

Sabrina was blown away by Nathan's candor, his zeal for friendship, which she had suspected anyway, his insight and now the forbearance it must have taken to hear her go off on Republicans the way she had, and yet stay calm and unmoved.

"Methinks thou art the unflappable one, Mr. Bridger. How did you keep from striking me down that night with this kind of passion burning in you?"

Nathan bellowed with laughter. "Are you kidding? You were actually speaking my language. For a minute there, I thought I was hearing the Voice of God. I had been hoping that no one from the Left would actually notice how steeped in fear the conservative right was, and I had just about convinced myself that it wasn't all that bad. Then I started listening to Bill Maher and, well, he's a bit of a loose cannon, and much too crass for most people, but I began to think that he was right on about some things.

"I even considered for the next few days after listening to you, that I was playing on the wrong team, but then I remembered George Wright. He is the original Republican; what a Republican ought to be. And if there's even one of them left, I'll stand my ground with him."

"Yes, I see that," said Sabrina in measured response. "Of course it would be the only thing to do. But tell me, would George ever consider switching over?" she asked carefully.

"Interesting question. I actually don't think he cares, or I should say he doesn't think it matters. He looks for any entry into the political conversation, you could say, and then steps right into it with a gusto that rivals the likes of Benjamin Disraeli. Are you familiar with him?"

Now it was Sabrina's turn to hear the voice of God. "I have! I've only read a little bit about him, but I like what I read. I saw an old PBS mini-series on him once, and if he was anything like how he was portrayed there, I know exactly what you mean. Is George really that persuasive? Able to let circumstances flow around and through him, and still keep his center?"

"You've hit it right on the nose, Miss Ryder! That's exactly how I'd describe George, and Mr. Disraeli. Cut from the same cloth. In fact I've wondered if maybe George is a reincarnation of him. Do you think that's possible? I've never considered it before, but you're kind of kinky that way. What's your take on it?"

Chuckling at his perception of her, she replied, "Actually, I don't know much about reincarnation. Or should I say, I don't really think it matters whether we lived past lives or not. I mean it's a moot point, isn't it? You couldn't use it on a campaign poster: Vote George Wright, an authentic reincarnation of Benjamin Disraeli! Mr. Wright is standing waste deep in a completely different set of circumstances that he'll have to learn to navigate in his own way. Is admiration necessarily emulation? I'm not so sure."

"You know what? I hope you get to know George a little this weekend, Sabrina. I think you two would hit it off."

She sat quietly for the next 20 minutes. What was he telling her? This man was an enigma of the first rank. He was about to take her into the wilderness and sleep for two nights by her side. She didn't think he meant to give her any trouble on that score; they had been clear about their boundaries so far. But she was about to find out.

"And did he just say he was in love with a man?" she asked herself. "And why was he saying that he hoped I would develop an interest in this George guy? Is Nathan using me as a foil to get close to another girl? Perhaps an old flame?"

She watched her mind wind itself as up as tight as an old watch spring, all the while the truck doing its bump and grind towards their destination in the desert. Eventually she let it all go, content to live in 'the mystery' of Nathan Bridger, which seemed no less compelling than hopping from dimension to dimension with Mr. Thaddeous Golas. In fact, without needing to know all the answers she noticed she was quite satisfied with everything, just as it was actually unfolding.

23

Mushroom Soup and the Call of the Wild

The campfire was blazing in mythological proportions by dinner time, some of the flames leaping as high as eight feet into the air.

Everyone had spent the first hour after arrival searching for driftwood, while George supervised the construction of a fire pit about 6 feet in circumference, marking it with some large stones that Sabrina and the girls found near the camp site. Nathan brought out the box of wood chips from the truck and following George's careful instructions, he set the driftwood in teepee-like fashion over the kindling.

By the time the sun was setting and the desert sky was marbled with wisps of smoke, George finally—after some cajoling—put down the screwdriver he was using to tighten the leg of a camp stove. He stood up, rubbing his neck, and his profile struck a dark silhouette against the raging blaze of bonfire, highlighting his somewhat fierce countenance.

Sabrina thought he looked like a seasoned backwoodsman who probably knew his way around a campsite better than the City Creek Mall. Watching him intently, she saw how careful he was, deliberate, kind, and showing an almost tender patience with the other men, who didn't seem to know the first thing about tying a slip knot or where to place a tent stake. He had everyone put their tents in a circle about eight feet away from the fire pit with the open flap facing towards it. Apparently, it could get very cold at night and he seemed personally invested that everyone be as comfortable as possible.

He was a natural leader out here in the wilderness, but what of this other thing? Would his amiable nature translate into a larger socio-political arena? Here, while he was engrossed in all things practical, Sabrina couldn't really see him giving a stump speech on a fairground somewhere in the mid-west, driving home a point on supply side economics. Not so hard to imagine however, was the possible effect his rugged charm might have on people, as his thick dark hair blew in the breeze against a moody "Atlas Shrugged" landscape. And one had to admit he would be a strong candidate for the women's vote.

Unpacking her sleeping bag, toothbrush and pajamas, Sabrina put them neatly on one side of the tent where she imagined she would be sleeping. She had contributed some comfortable folding chairs and Nathan had set them up nicely in front of the fire. Sitting with him quietly there, she watched the others while they finished their own preparations for the evening. What would everyone want to do these two nights together, Sabrina wondered. Roast marshmallows? Sing camp songs? She rued the thought. Nothing could be more boring as far as she was concerned. And she hadn't even thought to bring a book to read. They were going to hike all day tomorrow, but tonight and the next? Why had she not thought ahead? Perhaps living in the moment was overrated.

But she needn't have worried about being held hostage, singing 99 verses of something-or-other. After a quick dinner of hotdogs, beer and some wonderful homemade sweet potato fries, Elaine fished out of her pocket something small and white. Twirling it between her fingers, she held it to her lips for Dan to light. After taking a long drag and holding in the smoke like her life depended on it, she motioned to Dan to take the second hand smoke from her. He grabbed a toke instead, and she moved to Helena who took a long mouth-to-mouth from her friend with great relish. The entertainment was on, apparently.

Marty had been stirring something in a pot for some time. She poured some of the concoction into a large plastic cup and took a long sip. "Mmmm," she murmured, "This batch is even better; I put onions and celery in it. Try some." Handing it to Joshua, she sat down in the sand in front of the fire to warm herself. Quietly they all partook of one delight or the other until it came around to Nathan and Sabrina.

"Interested?" Nathan asked with a gleam in his eyes.

Sabrina thought as how she ought to keep her head. Decisions had to be made later and she wanted to be there for them. Nathan handed her the cup, and took a long slow drag on the reefer himself.

Gazing deep into the mug, Sabrina watched her mind for a moment; all the calculations, the fears and judgments she had going on. And then without further deliberation, she made a conscious decision to partake. She'd never done mushrooms before. But it felt like the soup was calling to her and it went down smooth.

It wasn't too long before she felt a sensation that was somehow strangely familiar, as though her mind was about to be commandeered by a higher, more spacious consciousness. Taking several more sips, and blessing it with a strong intention for self realization, she heard a voice calling her from within:

"Let go now, Sabrina-girl. Get your blanket and Nathan's baseball cap and come out under the desert stars with me. . ."

After taking one more long draught of the soup, she went into the tent, grabbed her heavy wool fringed blanket and stood for a moment in front of the fire. "May I borrow your hat for a while, Nathan? I want to take a little walk."

"Sure. Do you want me to come with you? You don't want to get lost." He said.

"I can hardly get lost. There's a six foot fire blazing and no hills or shrubbery to speak of for miles. Besides the moon is bright. I'll be fine. Do you mind?"

"Not at all," he said. "This time is for whatever you want to do. I'll be here when you get back," he said, tipping back in his chair and waving.

As usual, she was grateful for his accommodating nature. Looking across at the others, she saw some of them already deeply engrossed in furtive conversation, while one or two were sitting quietly in meditation. Nathan looked over at them lovingly, and then up at Sabrina. "They're great, aren't they?" he asked.

"They are," she said, turning toward the open desert landscape. "I'll be back. Thanks for understanding. And you? Go play," she said, motioning to the others. He smiled, but closed his eyes, and settled into a deep reverie.

Sabrina knew she was about to go into a time warp and wondered what effect the mushrooms would have. But she trusted her Guide completely, and walked out onto the open desert floor. Just before stepping away from the circle of light, however, she looked back once more at the camp. Thin purple clouds, tinged with red and gold around the edges, straggled close to the horizon. George, standing off by himself, had propped his foot up on the bumper of the truck. Like a lion he was, watching over his pride. It appeared he wasn't interested in substances for recreation, and Sabrina felt the slightest twinge of guilt for having given in so easily. He seemed much taller than the rest, or maybe he was just a little closer to her than the others. He was looking at something far away. She couldn't exactly make out what it was. Then suddenly she realized.

He was looking at her.

24

Down the Rabbit Hole

Wandering off into the desert night alone was remarkable enough, but with the enhancement of psilocybin, Sabrina was astonished by the intensity of it all. The moon was of course her guiding light, and when it was full like this and the stars were beyond counting, there was really no need for any enhancement to find ecstasy in the here and now. The world was hallucination enough. And what could a drug do anyway that she couldn't experience on her own without just letting go of her need to control whatever reality wanted to reveal itself next?

"So why did I drink the Kool Aid?" she asked herself.

Shuffling across the still warm sand, she saw a ways off what looked like a little plateau. Strange she hadn't noticed it before, but she thought it was something she could sit atop and have a wider perspective than her line of vision could observe here on the desert floor. Within 20 minutes, she was standing in front of it. It was larger than she imagined and she wondered if scaling it was even possible.

Suddenly however, and without any effort at all, she felt as though she were being swept up—like a prophet of old she'd once read about. Was it the mushrooms or did she just find the climb so easy because, no resistance? She had surrendered fully to the mushroom experience and it was as though nature now supported her in whatever object or idea she gave her attention to. Spreading the blanket out onto a flat rock, she stood on it with her eyes closed and opened her arms wide to the natural world.

A soft breeze lifted the hair off her face, and a rush of memories formed themselves into a string of vignettes. There was her younger sister, Sadie, brushing Sabrina's hair while they watched TV together on a winter evening. Then a scene with her father who was reading to her by the fire, from The Book of Mormon. Then some things not so good. A fight with her mother, and the time she'd forgotten to pick up Neal for an important job interview.

Abruptly then, she felt as if she were falling down a rabbit hole, plummeting deeper with each thought, the conditioned mind pulling her into its vortex of guilt. And it grew stronger with each unholy recall: times she had lied or at the very least, not told the whole truth; friends she had hurt or gossiped about. Now she was cursing herself for more recent things that she had heretofore thought were entirely good and open-minded, by her new standards. Sex, questioning authority, going against the teachings of her parents and the Church. That old world of dos and don'ts, of rights and wrongs, crowded into her conscious mind and left no space for mercy. When Sabrina realized the potency of the temptation to go even deeper into guilt, it took great effort to pry her eyes open and wait for a moment to settle on the reality at hand:

Ah. This beloved ground, this present moment. Now. The endeavor to stay in the present was stabilizing. Not only that, it was incredibly peaceful.

She saw that the universe she beheld was created by thoughts. And she made a decision to have no allegiance to guilty images tonight. This night was for another purpose, and so some vigilance was needed to keep her mind clear. This night was about enjoying the elements of the desert landscape which were, she saw, not separate from her. They were right there, an arm's length away, and not even that. She could trace with her fingertips every star in the sky, some tinged with orange and purple light. Was that a space station out there? Or a planet? It was so big. Even the hazy dark purple clouds close to the horizon did not seem too distant, but within easy access. It was all of a piece; one thing, and not something separate from what *she* was. Reaching out to touch it, it responded like quicksilver, making ripples in a sea of life, a living hologram.

"The universe is made of one kind of whatever-it-is, which cannot be defined,"[58] she heard an inner voice reciting from <u>The Lazy Man's Guide,</u> as she surveyed the nightscape with awe.

Momentarily then, she felt she was leaning back into the arms of Something Familiar and safe. That again. Yet always new. Always now.

"So did you read the book?"

"Well, hello there Mr. Golas. Fancy meeting you here," and she turned to see if he was actually in her same universe or just speaking from—well—somewhere in a distant rarified atmosphere that she couldn't see.

"Yes. Fancy that," he said, solid as a Joshua tree in a bedrock of clay. There he was, as real as Nathan or any of her other friends had been only forty-five minutes ago.

And still her favorite Notion of a Man.

Looking down on the tiny faraway campsite where the firelight was still blazing, she wanted to make sure it stayed there in the periphery of her mind; a sort of touchstone while she was up and away, visiting another ambient reality.

"Yes, I read your book," she said. "I couldn't put it down, as a matter of fact. Turns out I didn't have to. It's so short I read the whole thing in one sitting. I kept thinking, 'how did he manage to condense all this wisdom into one tiny volume?' Not that I understood it all, mind you. I'm going to have to read it a few more times I think.

"And listen, you should know, I think I'm high on mushrooms, so I don't know if anything we say to each other counts. Maybe I won't even remember—"

"You'll remember. The thing about drugs is, you give them too much power. You want to say that it is the drug that gives you the experience, but it's the other way around, don't you see? It's your mind that gives the drug its meaning and purpose. Intention, as always, is everything. But when you see it backwards, it's easy to forget things as they happened. Like in a dream. But your current waking reality is the dream. You—as you are accustomed to think of yourself—are the dream. The expanded state you travel to on the right drugs is actually closer to your primary reality than your everyday consciousness. And after a moment of silence he said, "Why did you take the mushrooms, Sabrina?"

"I don't know," she said.

He took her firmly by the shoulders and holding her gaze, looked directly into her eyes. "Yes you do. You do know. Why did you do it? There was an intention, however unconscious." And stern as he was, she knew that he didn't mean for her to feel shamed by him. "I want you to be accountable, Sabrina, to be very clear about this. Did you make the decision from an expanded or a contracted place in your psyche? Ultimately it doesn't matter which, but you should be aware of your intention. Because it will make a difference in your experience. Consequences are tied to intentions. Be still for a minute and it will come to you."

She became as still as the desert. Still as night. These were the teachers of Silence beaconing her into a kind of inner twilight, rich and luminous. A darkened light.

Finally, she ventured, "I wanted to feel free to do something without the mind getting in the way, I guess. I was thinking how you loved LSD and that mushrooms were a kind of natural version of that drug. I *think* it was basically from a thought about expansion, but it's hard to tell. I'm so used to using my mind to manage and control things. I don't know how to trust an idea to unfold on its own without forcing it. So I might have thought that I could force you to come to me. Meantime, I noticed that following certain trains of thought on this 'medicine' can be a little scary. Guilt, you know. And fear."

"Yes," he said. "The conditioned mind wants to creep in everywhere and reroute the natural experience of being present. It tells you that you will do something wrong without it's help, and the proof it gives, is all the perceived mistakes of your past. It uses the past to make you suffer in the perfectly lovely present. The most amazing thing is that it is completely innocent in this. It can't do it any differently, really, until you're on to it. And even then it seems one can only detach from it after much observation. Eventually you see that it has been running on automatic all these years. So why bother to interfere with its little games? One just stops chasing it down the rabbit hole. Like you did a minute ago."

"Yeah, I could sort of tell. It's as though it thinks it's in charge of keeping me safe somehow. As though I'd commit some horrible error without its input, because it must know that I'm mostly unaware, and stumbling around in the dark: 'The secrecy of my work prevents me from knowing what I am doing'," she murmured in her detective voice. "Like I never did anything wrong following its advice!"

"Do you think it's true," he said, "that most of the time you don't know who you are and what you are doing? Right now—even on mushrooms—is that really true? Are you ever without your Self?" he said as he sat down, cross legged on the blanket, pulling her down to sit in front of him. She leaned back against his shoulders and his voice tickled her ear. "Tell me," he reiterated.

"No. Not really. I guess. . ." she said snuggling backward into his arms. "I mean, I don't kno— Oops," she said, realizing that that wasn't going to be an acceptable answer.

"Yes. You do," he said softly. "Are you unaware of who you are right now for instance? And what you are doing?" He circled his arms around her and strengthened his grip.

"No. In fact, I feel more alive, more aware than usual. I mean, it kind of feels like I could actually be bigger than the circumstances I find myself in. It makes me feel less afraid. Like I passed through a kind of 'fear barrier' when I walked away from the light back there at the camp."

"The perceived light. Can you really walk away from the light? Where is it now?"

"Oh. . . . I guess I'm *in* it now," she said with some amazement. "Or, it's in me? Not like the light of the fire or the moon. They are pale in comparison to this light. It's not something coming from my physical senses either. It's weird, not the way I thought it would be. It's beyond all the *beliefs* I had about light. . . like it's what I Am. Wow. Could that be true?"

"Yes. You are that Light. And you can't walk away from it except in the most dismal nightmares, which can never be real." Then after a moment, he asked candidly, "What did you want to be free to do, by the way?"

It was strange how natural it felt to be talking to him like this. And a strong sexual urge spiraled up from the base of her spine, arching her back, and flowering into the heart chakra. She shivered in response. *Physical impulses are misdirected miracle impulses,*[59] she reminded herself. And she started to quote it. "The Course says—"

"Uh-u. Don't get ahead of your own evolution. This is about total personal accountability. Who is accountable here for your feelings and thoughts? The Light will use everything you give it, so don't be afraid to look deep within, Even at this. So what did you want to be free to do, Sabrina?"

"I wanted. . . . you," she said with some hesitation. "To be with you just like this. I suppose I thought I could force your presence into my consciousness. I wanted to be as open to any kind of encounter with you as possible. Even. . .a physical one. A sexual one. But I thought that I needed the help of this drug. It's like you said, I gave the drug the power to do what I couldn't, so I could pretend that I didn't have anything to do with it. 'The devil [drug] made me do it.' There. How's that for accountability?"

"Dissociation is nothing more than a decision to forget?"[60] He asked, using ACIM for emphasis.

"Something like that," Sabrina said, smiling back at him over her shoulder. "You've really got that Course stuff down."

"I do now, now that I've been hanging out in your mind. I may have said it in a few thousand words less. LSD is laser, but it doesn't come close to the poetry of classic literature."

"That's true," Sabrina said in quiet affirmation.

He continued, "The <u>Course</u> says that worldly perception is upside down and backwards. That's exactly what I meant when I suggested in my book, that you 'turn the whole game upside down'. Stop trying to get enlightened. Instead, ask yourself how an already free and self-determined Being agreed to lock itself into a body and play hide and seek on the physical plane."

"Yeah, it's like playing 'let's pretend," she said. "But then we feel such guilt about it."

"Oh, insidious guilt!" he exclaimed with Shakespearian intonation. "It seeps through all the cracks, and even drugs don't affect it much. Although the right drug can open up the mind—that is if you expand into it and give yourself over to it in love, just like any experience you'd call spiritual. You are always either expanding or contracting, according to your comfort—or consciousness—level.

"But then of course, it's true that many people start to rely on a particular drug as the source of their experience. That's why drugs have a universal cautionary label: 'Take at your own risk!' Although Dante' said it better: 'Abandon all hope, ye who enter here!' Because hoping for eternal bliss can be the worst kind of drug. One must abandon hope—which is usually associated with some future ideal—and live entirely in the present.

"Drugs can take down the prison walls and let the mind soar beyond itself to the space level, for a moment in time anyway. Although, at first, guilt and fear about losing control can cause terrible contractions in the mind. It's a bit like going through a birth canal. 'Darkest before the dawn,' you know. One runs into all kinds of havoc because of the guilt that 'lurks in the minds of men.'"

Sabrina thought of the fear that she had encountered every time she went for something new or even asked for more insight on a particular subject, especially something about herself. Never mind drugs. Fear and guilt *did* lurk around the edges of all of life, particularly where it comes in contact with the unknown.

"I just thought of something," she said. "There's a story about the boy prophet that started the Mormon Church—of which I was a faithful participant, until recently. Joseph Smith? When he went into the woods to pray, he said that he was overcome by a dark presence. 'Satan,' he said it was. I don't believe in Satan, of course, but I do think 'he' might be a personification of fear. So anyway, this fear pinned him to the ground and almost killed him before the Light came and shone around him. That's the way he told it back in the 1800's. Maybe he would tell it differently today, but I think it's a metaphor for what we're talking about. Could it be that the conditioned mind has such a hold on us collectively, that almost everyone who looks to find Truth is bound to face some kind of terror?"

"Terror is always within us to encounter, but even that can be experienced with a fully expanded awareness. And when we are *with* our fears in total awareness, often, they're no longer fearful. They might even be funny. What are your fears, Sabrina? In this moment, what are they?"

"I—," she blew out a little puff of air. She wouldn't fall into the trap of saying that she didn't know again.

In one sense it was true that she didn't know anything. But she had a belief that questions and answers were polarities—the two sides of a coin—in any given moment. And that was a kind of knowing that was not arrogant; just the wisdom of an instant. The Holy Instant, A Course in Miracles called it. Here, in the Holy

Instant (the present moment) *"The problem and the answer have been brought together,"*[61].

So then, looking straight into the now darkened sky, Sabrina charged forward in the demi-truth of her feelings. "The fear I'm feeling right now is subtle. It's more psychological. It's—I told you before, but you seemed to act as though I was making it up, that it was all in my head. That's the part that scares me. If my experiences in life are just an out-picturing of my own thinking, and I don't know how to control my thinking, then how can I keep them from haunting me?"

"Perhaps there's no need to control them so much, as to observe them. Your thoughts haunt you?"

"Sometimes. And it's distracting. I think I want one thing, but then my thoughts trouble me about all kinds of other things. And I feel somehow that I should be able to stop them from doing that," she said.

"And what are these thoughts that trouble you?"

"You know what they are. I've told you."

"Tell me again. I want you to be as clear about this as possible."

"Well. I think you are the most beautiful man I've ever met. Or conjured. Or whatever. I'm so mesmerized, awestruck maybe. Spellbound. You just make me quiver. No I mean really, all the time, whenever I think of you. Now what's that about? I can't seem to access any understanding around it. It baffles me sometimes and angers me at other times. I'm inflamed by this lust or love or—you know? I'm just undone by it, that's all. I have the thought that this is what we humans do. We just make up stuff, and project all of it onto some hapless creature, like yourself. It's unfair, I know, but I'm not sure I can help it. And I was so glad to think that I was over that stage of my life too. Then you came along and—listen you—I was never going to want a special relationship again! Especially not with someone I can't. . can't even—"

"Control?" he asked menacingly.

"I had a plan, okay?! I was going to keep my head! I was certainly not going to make something up out of thin air! So why do you think you've come to me? I didn't want this!"

"Keep your head?" he asked, with a hearty, unapologetic laugh. "Weren't we just talking about the drawbacks of that?" and he leaned back onto the blanket and with one hand, pulled her around, squarely on top of him. Facing him, she was.

"I believe that what you want—or possibly what Life wants through you—is beyond our limited understanding," he said. "Of course, you have certain ideas about how it should look and feel. You are a sexually oriented being after all; a human being with strong physical impulses that can hardly be suppressed, nor should they be. Remember, It's all right to have a good time. And No One at the space [highest consciousness] level ever puts barriers or tests in the way of someone who is earnestly trying to raise his level of understanding, even if he or she is sexually charged in the moment."

"Well I'm fairly impetuous, it turns out," she said. "And I don't believe I should trust myself there, or at least I've taught myself that I shouldn't trust those kinds of feelings. That's why the drug. I just wanted this struggle in me to stop. To do one thing or the other. For God's sake, can't I just be wholehearted about *something*? I think I love you; that's as close as I come. But you don't even live in my same universe. So what's the point anyway?"

He smiled and kissed her. Right on the lips too. "Mmmm," she murmured. This was not what she expected, but then when had he ever done anything she expected? He searched her eyes with an uncharacteristic look of puzzlement. Then quite out of character—because it seemed to surprise even himself—he said,

"Oh. My darling girl, what have you gone and done?"

And the desert floor opened up, and swallowed them both into the bosom of The Great Mother's Love.

25

The Devil in the G-spot

Sabrina thought she could hear the strains of an ancient Song, long forgotten. Yet she knew it as well as she knew her One True Self. Each note was like a chime vibrating on the edge of a crystal bowl. She could hardly breathe for the intensity of each tonal—well there was only one way to say it—ejaculation. She and the Teacher seemed to be moving in rhythm with the Universe. And not only that; they were traveling, whipping through space/ time continuums like the Star Trek Enterprise at warp speed.

"To infinity and beyond!" she felt like yelling out in comic hyperbole, but it wasn't really possible to exaggerate this kind of thing. Here was a sensuous voyage of such magnitude it was hard to say exactly if there were any boundaries to it. And to be absolutely honest, they were not actually traveling through time; not in any ordinary sense of the word. No, it was more like *time* was traveling through them.

Talk about your life review! Only this wasn't her individual life. It was the life stream of the whole planet—the one in her head?— swirling around her like still frames on a movie reel. Or one could say that each of the frames were radiating out from stillness, but full of the movement and vitality of the age they represented. It was like Life Magazine, from the Mind of God Publishing Co.

And she was not in her physical body—she knew that—but still there was an accompanying sensual quality to all of it. The intense visceral feelings she had projected onto her Teacher were now somehow percolating, saturating down into countless historical constructs, as if she were watching a sensual chronological overview of the human race; a terrestrial elucidation originating from One Great Passion of Mind.

Now were continents forming; now turbulent seas; now mountains and valleys, fire and ice; volcanoes, polar caps and blistering sun, and frozen winter forest. It seemed that the mind imagining this wild and divergent terrain was at cross purposes, separating and polarizing, labeling and opposing certain aspects of its Self. This separated part, this smaller self soon became a symbol for the mind playing in separation—and was called Adam in some stories; Atom in others. The Universal Song that each part of the whole had known so well was soon forgotten, replaced by lesser strains, isolating and dispersing the now millions and billions of separated parts.

Of course, from this high place, it could be seen that all this was illusion; 'sounding brass and tinkling cymbal.' Nevertheless, she watched time and space contract into a dimension of solidified thought, where reality was experienced as 'a lone and dreary world,' and mankind, a prodigal who had lost the inheritance of its cherished Eden.

Here a band of nomads foraging, struggling, scrambling for shelter. There, a system of agriculture; pastures, little stone walls and skirmishes. Then time to plant, sit by the fire and weave stories under the night sky. Soon castles on the horizon; great walls, cities, populations and plagues.

One lone man, sitting under a Bodhi tree, vanquishes an army of demons, their weapons turn to flowers simply by seeing the illusory nature of all this thought run rampant. The divided adversarial mind turned to Silence, emptying out all its cankered contents into a psychological black hole; Emptiness.

"With what then, should we fill this spacious Empty Vessel; this Mind, cleansed of all its demons?" asked a Voice from that Void.

In response, an implant of such Inexpressible Love impregnated the world consciousness. The story represented as a babe in a manger: Innocence and simplicity, to challenge man's most unnaturally complex and crude beliefs: sickness, suffering, pain, and finally death itself.

As Sabrina watched from above, she saw that full half the world looked up from their preoccupations at least once a year: to sing the songs of this Babe in a Manger, of Peace, Good Will to Men. And like the Buddha, just for a moment, they emptied their separated minds from conflict and war. And listened to words of wisdom from a Sermon on a Mount.

Then back to business as usual.

And so the crusades, witch hunts and inquisitions! Now the discovery of new continents, ships of commerce heaving with rum and slaves, justice and miscarriage of justice, each in its turn. Cotton, tobacco fields, political and religious upheaval, revivals and revolutions, industrial and political. Renaissances. Each space/time event in living, inexorable color, piercing with the consciousness of each age, shot through with every feeling—horrifying and exhilarating—that accompanied the unfolding panoramic spectacle in 3D Technicolor, wide angle lens, surround sound Theater of the Universe.

Clutching at Golas as each epoch phenomenon passed through them, Sabrina felt giddy: *"celestial speedup"*, one might have called it. And in the midst of this wild panoply came a sensation full and dynamic—inside her—an orgasm moving through the whole Universal Body! Yes! And Oh God—Yes! Looking into the eyes of the Teacher, she felt his hands, his mouth against her ear, coaxing her into an agonizing ecstasy. If she let it go on, she would die, that much was certain. No, this was serious; she *would* explode and evaporate into the ethers! A sudden thrust filled her up like a torpedo from the base chakra to the heart. One more and she would be gone.

"Let go, my darling, relax and let me take you. No resistance, remember? That's my girl. I've got you. Can you relax into it? Just allow me to drive this thing, and—you—you just go with it."

"Go with—? There's no—No, I don't think so! Am I—Am I naked? Where are my clothes—wait; what was that I just saw whizzing by? —was that the signing of the Declaration of Independence?

But wait. Something was penetrating even deeper, as if that were possible. And it *was* possible, apparently, because it kept growing, sealing up every empty chamber. And then—miracle of miracles—it shot up through every tendon and sinew right up to the base of her neck. It wasn't even possible, was it? The G-spot—that wonderful place the whole universe had been looking to find and to mark with some kind of raging neon 'X-marks-the-spot' sign, so that it would never get lost again—was it really there, just at the tip of the medulla oblongata? "Watch out—Oh that's it—That's the spot!" she yelled, climaxing right through the third eye and out into the Cosmos!

"Mark it for posterity! Oh, Oh! Ahhh!" Screaming into the Empty Silence, at the top of her lungs; arching, bucking, wailing, sobbing, all of it without shame, yet unflinchingly present without a mind, without a care; and all and all and all the Universe with her.

"Ahhhh," she wailed, as an inner explosion of such magnitude seized her, she could no longer hold it, and had to let it go on through. She—as she had known herself—was gone, no longer a noun, or even a pronoun. And throughout the entire history of the world it seemed, was each tremor registered:

Elijah peeked out from his cave.

Isaiah wrote another cryptic verse.

Moses dropped his staff and the Red Sea came flooding in on the Pharaoh's soldiers.

Descartes wasn't thinking now!

Isaac Newton missed the falling apple altogether, as it ricocheted off his head.

Thomas Jefferson stopped penning. John Hancock too. "This is big!' he exclaimed.

Benjamin Disraeli halted in the midst of a rousing speech in parliament, for which—it's almost certain—he lost another election.

The great impressionists? Were impressed.

Emerson wrote another essay: "On Cosmic Orgasm".

H. D. Thoreau sighed, and thought perhaps he'd had enough of the little house on Walden Pond.

Walt Whitman, to whom she gave a special shout, wrote a whole new Leaf of Grass: "There sails my muse—that comet of a girl!" he saluted back at her.

Joseph Smith set aside his precious golden plates and wondered for one tiny moment: Did he really want to start another world religion?

Andy Warhol ruined the first silkscreen of Marilyn Monroe.

Okay, this was getting weird—

Oops, No? Not done? Still more?

"Not until you've felt every single withhold; every niggling little embarrassment, each tiny impulse to cover up," said the Voice of her Teacher. "Let's find out everything you've been hiding under that fig leaf!

"Stand undefended at the stake, ready to be burned for your craft. Lie still on the rack, waiting for the ropes to pull at your limbs. Your head in the lion's mouth. Your last coin spent and children left to feed. Don't close your eyes or turn your head from any of it, my love!"

Uh oh. Now she was looking deep into the eyes—not of the Teacher—but of a stranger; a man who was so vacant, so lost, so empty of love that he could only try to steal from her the beauty, the youth, and innocence he saw there. When she realized it wasn't her Guide, her instinct was to scream, to turn away and stop this insane hallucination. But apparently this was not an option.

"Look at me!" he growled, heavy with the sweat and filth of battle. Little rivulets of his sour saliva ran down her neck and onto her bare breast. "Look at me, Goddamit!" he yelled, slapping her with the back of his scarred hand, shouting with hatred born of generations of oppression. "I will have thee, ya little bitch! Whether or no' ye like it! This is for all me brothers that yar' father tartured and killed!"

"See it all. Feel it all. Embrace it all," said the Voice. "Without your resistance, is any of it real?"

And whether because the orgasm was still reverberating through her frame, or because the words of her Teacher had given her a sort of raw courage, she softened and moved with the rhythm of this man she would have called an adversary. The Enemy. She moved with him in his exhausted outrage—not smiling because that might have been interpreted as derisive—but with her whole wide open heart. She gave herself in love to him; weeping for the sins of this man, who was once a blameless child; now a foul-smelling, rancid, malevolent old man. He might have only been 30 years of age, but already ancient with hate.

She looked into his eyes. She did not turn away. She took in his terrifying bequest, with every blow of his heavy weight upon her. She would die right here, right now, under the ugly belly of Life in its foulest disguise, and she would love life *for* this, not in spite of it. Exactly because it was as hideous, revolting, and repulsive as it was beautiful. The submission was so complete there was no thinking about it, no way out. No need. It was simply a moment like any other. And you know what?

The fear was gone.

And something else. There was a tiny recognition, so unexpected she almost missed it. Like a strangled, half-eaten mouse set on the master's doorstep by the old house cat, it was. And it was this: She saw herself in this miscreant. And she knew she was on the receiving end of a very large pendulum that had been swinging for thousands of lifetimes in this world of "eye for eye and tooth for tooth".

Wasn't it the whole point of reincarnation, purgatory, and the Mormon notion of "spirit prison" after all? To get back in the fray and seek revenge—or absolution—in this life or another? Payback for misdeeds? For a lost arm or a missing loaf of bread? It didn't seem to matter the extent of the offence. It had to be atoned for. Six hundred head of cattle taken in payment for a damaged coat of arms or a flag trampled in the mud. A smoking castle, decaying bodies, a small broken toy—wheels still spinning in the ditch—no matter the heinous (or trivial) nature of the grievance, it must be paid for, right? For this was a world of Payment on Demand.

Unless it wasn't.

Unless all those things could finally be overlooked because, at last, we were looking for Something Else: A respite from holocausts. What if we passed by the all the images of rape, incest, murder, and all the offenses conceivable. What if Jesus had really been on to something? "Forgive them, for they know that what they do?"

Yeah, because what if every time anyone had ever done anything to hurt another, they just really didn't know what the hell they were doing? Like everyone gets off on an insanity plea. "Hey, I thought I was doing God's work, I really did. I mean it seemed like a good idea at the time. Sure I felt a little guilty, but the guilt just made me act out more. And I had to project all of that guilt onto someone, didn't I? It was way too hard to bear it all on my own."

And where had *she* raped innocence? Forced her will on someone, or tried to take what was not hers? Where had she projected goodness and beauty outside herself, and then tried desperately to take it back? Yes, she was a part of it all, a contributor simply by being part of the consciousness that had given its attention to it all in some form, some time, in some way. Simply by agreeing to this collective reality. It was called "consensual" for a reason, right?

Yet here was something: the attention she now gave it was not in the form of resistance. It was an accepting of atonement, a reconciliation of all that ever was; an embracing—fair or unfair—of all that was ever thought to be the consequence of a life lived out of fear and contempt. Even as she lay there panting and barely alive it seemed, love was growing within her, consuming her in a firestorm of expiation.

But now with great force, the stranger drew himself up and pulled a large dagger from his belt, holding it over her left eye. *Well perfect,* she thought. *An eye for an eye; so be it.* And steeling herself for the kill, she noticed . . . that she couldn't. (*Steel* herself, that is.) Because it wasn't within her to do anything but watch it all happen with incredible impersonal curiosity. This wasn't *her* life after all. It belonged to Something Larger. It belonged to Experience, to Love. To Life. And they were welcome to it.

"Who did you think it was that needed to be loved?" she heard the voice of the Teacher say.

And with a slight shift in focus, the grim foreboding image above her changed suddenly back into the handsome one she knew. He was beautiful again, the picture of her preferences; the ideal man.

Although. . .

There was something disconcerting here. He was handsome again, but with a strangely macabre countenance, his upper lip curling into a sardonic grin. Now this was actually *not* okay, even by the standards she herself had just invoked. Because this was conscious evil. "Something wicked this way comes," said the Ray Bradbury character on the inner stage of her mind. In fact, this face, this man, seemed to have an archetypal look about him. Just a little too pretty, too perfectly perfect. Something serpentine. . .

"Who did you think it wassss," he snarled, as he repeated the Teacher's words. Could this be —well—Satan? The Devil himself? Had she been wrong to submit to that lesser evil? Had she opened a can of worms so vile that it would now cover the earth with a plague of evil in Biblical proportions?

"Of course, that is the fear, isn't it?" she thought. The overriding, terrifying fear of dealing with any kind of enemy; if you show them mercy, that they will come back en masse to do more harm? Will "Satan" find a way to take over the world because of some silly misunderstood sentiment about Love Unconditional?

Certainly, loving the enemy had very seldom been the way of it in this world, even though Jesus had really said it. She remembered a story of a people in the <u>Book of Mormon</u>. They had decided to go out and greet the adversary, bowing down—not so much in surrender—as in honor and love. A thousand or so were indeed slain by the sword that day, but then something unexpected happened. The army of the enemy stopped in the midst all of the slaughter, and asked themselves what they had really accomplished. And it was said that more people were converted to love that day, than died.

"Intention. Their intention was clear," Sabrina said as she thought of the words of her Teacher. "And the intention wasn't to win, or even to get God to play His hand in their favor," She thought. "It was just pure unadulterated Love."

Now suddenly this new Adversary—"Satan"—was enraged. Handsome and Thaddeous-like in one light, chillingly ghoulish in another, he was certainly going to finish her off, and no doubt, get around to the rest of humanity by noon. Perhaps she should go back and replay that last scene with more resistance. Perhaps her unwitting submission had given entry to an evil even more malevolent. What Pandora's box had she just opened? Because there is not really anything scarier than Conscious Evil; someone who's just bad to the bone. On purpose.

"I suppose running is still not an option?" she asked the Teacher.

Pause.

"Seriously? You're going quiet on me at a time like this?!"

Let all things be exactly as they are,[62] She remembered. This simple lesson from <u>A Course in Miracles</u> had always stumped Sabrina. But now she thought she understood. Perhaps—before acting on something—it was just good sense to accept a situation as it was. Not so much to submit, but to stop resisting. Because resistance was one way to make something even more real—to make it bigger—in one's experience. And she remembered something the Teacher had said:

"Go beyond reason to love. It is safe. It is the only safety."[63]

Maybe without realizing it, this is was what she had just done. And it was what the people in the <u>Book of Mormon</u> story had done too. She gave this insight some room in her conscious mind. It seemed to lighten the situation and give her confidence.

Well, what did this Satan guy want with her anyway? Her blood? Her soul? Her vintage tie collection? For a minute Sabrina couldn't understand what she was feeling. For one thing, "Satan" should have been a lot scarier than this, but here was the deal:

This Icon, this Image of Evil that mankind had used for centuries to 'put fear into the hearts of men' wasn't really that scary when, just for a moment, she stopped resisting it. It was like the story, "There's a monster in my closet", where the kid just had to turn around and look at it to see that it was a fairytale, a psychological bug-a-boo. A part of oneself that needed attention? Some love?

And anyway I'm pretty sure that evil, by definition, is unconscious, Sabrina thought. *Like, if we knew what we were doing—perpetuating pain and suffering—we'd stop.*

"Forgive them for they know not what they do." J. C.

"You can only feel pain when you are stupid." T. G.

Okay, so two terrific Teachers had said the same thing in different ways.

Because this Satan-Devil-Guy was just so obviously an 8 X 10 glossy caricature of man's worst fears. But as soon as anyone becomes conscious of the fear and guilt underneath their violent acts, the rug is pulled out from under them, and all the air let out. The cosmic joke is seen. Everyone goes home for lunch. Cancel the rape. Call off the war. Withdraw the troops. Revoke the call to arms. Send everybody home with— flat feet. Stigmatism. No energy. Can't get it up. Hangnail. Paper cut.

Battle called on account of: **There's no such thing as *Conscious* Evil!** Because evil, by definition—no matter how much the offender thinks he is getting away with something—is really just being unaware of the way the universe works.

So she looked right into the eyes of this Satan Person and called his diabolical bluff. Because what she wanted to do? Was laugh. Long and hard. And that's just what she did, because—no control over that. She laughed until she cried, until she finally got it.

"It's like we've spent thousands of years on this planet, doing to each other the most hideous kinds of things (most of them in God's name by the way) and then we're going to worry about some place called hell?" she said to the Satan caricature. "Like spending eternity with *you* could be any worse? What could be more hellish than this world, the way we've rigged it? You couldn't do anything to me that I haven't already done to myself a million times, you sorry excuse of an archetype! You're nothing but a caricature of all my worst fears!"

In one last volley of fear, Satan tried to become bigger and bigger, except Sabrina didn't care. She had never felt so free in her life, and the laughter just poured out of her. Deep, long, lusty, belly laughs, ones that sucked all the wind out and zipped that Devil backwards in a zigzag phoooot, until he was just a little piece of red stretched out rubber lying in the grass.

A grand hoax come to rest on the lawns of Heaven.

26

The Most Terrifying Thing

There was a feeling that she had just about faced every fear known to man and maybe *now* she could go home for dinner and a nap.

Oh, but one more little thing. How about this: The Most Terrifying Thing of All.

Now she was looking into the eyes of something entirely real. And it felt like the second coming. Only this was no metaphor. It was REALITY of such proportion, that she knew she was in the presence of an Original Awakened One.

"Jesus!" she gasped. "No, I mean really. Is it? Are you Him?" she swooned. "Listen, I'm not sure I'm up for this one—for one thing I'm not dressed for it—". But He was holding her with such tenderness, ever so lovingly inviting her to embrace Him with her whole self, just as she had the villain.

But here was the deal: she found it much harder to embrace this part of herself, than that despicable one. And the crazy thing was that her hesitation was all about the little things: her petty irritations, jealousies, the nagging unworthiness, not wanting to be presumptuous, saying yes when she meant no and vice versa. Forgetting to pay the utility bill. Things so trivial, they were hardly noticeable when you had your makeup on right. Such an odd assortment of existential guilt, but really, really formidable in the Presence of Light and Truth.

This must have been her mother's doing, she started to think; to get her so bound up with politeness and manners that she couldn't actually accept with gracious poise the one Gift she had been longing for her whole life. And from this superman, this symbol of love she had adored as a Savior, a teacher, an elder brother.

Here was the Handsome Prince come to call, and she wasn't up to it? What—she had a headache?

Sabrina watched her guilty mind with simple curiosity, and saw how it would use anything, even the concept of "Mother" to stave off unconditional love. There you go; when all else fails, blame the mother, right? She can take it.

In fact she had born this curse since the beginning of time: "Eve—she gave me of the fruit, and I did eat," said that simpleton, Adam. Okay, maybe they were both a little scared, but did he really think that was going to fly? Yet this cowardly excuse had stood and was still relied upon in times—well, times like this. Well, shit then, she was not going to add one more crime to this woman's laundry list of curses and woes. The buck was going to stop right here, right now in this moment.

In one last horrifyingly embarrassing moment, she looked down at the fig leaf that the serpent had told her she should use to hide her shame and vulnerability. As if. And like a compliant agreeable servant of Mammon, she'd been covering up ever since with aprons, headscarves, prairie skirts, heavy brocade gowns, girdles, bustles, jewelry, chainmail chastity belts, burkes, and other "sacred" garments, some of which the Mormons were especially familiar. But were these really a protection, or were they just talismans; a kind of rabbit's foot for the afflicted, tormented and guilty mind? And what did she need protection from, if it wasn't this? This shameful cover-up? This imprisonment of Living Grandeur in brocade and chains?

"And instead of seeing all this for what it is," she thought, *"we've just become more sophisticated, more modern. Now we cover up with degrees, doctorates, titles of all sorts, licenses and diplomas, resumes, Emmys, Golden Globes and Oscars."*

Seeing all that the fig leaf represented, she reached down and plucked it off. No more significant than a feather it was, yet it had obscured and suppressed the exquisite Beauty of Ages: this unique expression of God; of Life in its flowering female form.

Now without shame, she turned to face her Prince. She was not asleep under glass nor on a bed with tangled vines, or in a tower with no way out. She was free of all restraint and she melted into the beautiful image before her; into all the beliefs and fears she had ever held about this God-Man. Every thought she had ever held—idealistic or fearful—concerning Him was welcomed and undone, washed clean in her mind, as she dissolved into His Brilliant Uncompromising Light. As The Light bore down upon her, she had one final urge to shrink and fall back into the shadows.

But—oops— there weren't any.

"No shrinking," said the Voice. "You are not who you think you are anyway. Aren't you glad? Just in this moment, aren't you glad? Stand firm, my love. Stand in the light, without flinching. Do not blink. You are entirely worthy."

"Yes, I Am" she answered. And it seemed to be an answer for all time. In fact, "YES," was an excellent answer for every question that had ever been asked. In it was full disclosure and total embrace of every consequence sustained by the distracted, unfulfilled, wandering mind. Once again she laughed at the thought of how this unwieldy, limited and rootless mind— could have caused so much pain and suffering.

"It is as though you wandered in without a plan of any kind except to wander off, for only that seems certain,"[64] she heard Jesus say. *"No one who understands what you have learned, how carefully you learned it, and the pains to which you went to practice and repeat the lessons endlessly, in every form you could conceive of, could ever doubt the power of your learning skill. There is no greater power in the world. The world was made by it, and even now depends on nothing else. The lessons you have taught yourself have been so over learned and fixed, that they rise like heavy curtains to obscure the simple and the obvious*[65] *. . . .your power to learn has been strong enough to teach you that your will is not your own, your thoughts do not belong to you, and even [that] you are someone else. . .*[66]

"Temptation has one lesson it would teach, in all its forms, wherever it occurs. It would persuade the Holy Son of God he is a body, born in what must die, unable to escape its frailty, and bound by what it orders him to feel. It sets the limits on what he can do; its power is the only strength he has; his grasp cannot exceed its tiny reach.

"Would you be this, if Christ appeared to you in all His glory, asking you but this: Choose once again if you would take your place among the saviors of the world, or would remain in hell, and hold your brothers there. For He has come, and He is asking this[67] *. . . For we have reached where all of us are one, and we are home."*[68]

"We are home," she heard herself repeat. And she suddenly felt denser than she had a moment ago.

"Sabrina," she heard her name called by a familiar voice, though she wasn't sure who's. For one thing, that old name Sabrina was so remote it didn't track. It wasn't who she was, and she knew it. Still, the voice seemed to be asking her to focus all her attention on it. "Sabrina, you are about to come back into the body. When you wake up, you will be in your tent."

"Tent? What on earth?" she mumbled.

"Exactly. You are re-entering the earth's atmosphere. You will wake up in a world you left behind a while back. You'll be aware of everything you just experienced, but don't try to comprehend it all with your limited mind. Give it a few days to steep. It will all come clear."

Suddenly she was aware that she had on clothes, which felt confining and all wrong somehow, and she opened her eyes—her physical eyes—and tried to focus them on the reality at hand.

"Remember, I am with you always," said the Voice she had learned to love with all her heart.

And shuddering with the last convulsion of an orgasm so long and deep, she grabbed the closest thing to stop the tremor.

It was Nathan.

27

Surprise

"Sabrina! Where have you been? Are you all right?" he demanded. "You had me scared. I couldn't find you. The others are still out looking. Sabrina? Answer me. Focus up."

"I'm . . . I'm okay", she moaned. "No, really, Nathan." She sat up and inhaled a deep breath. He gave her a drink of water. "But how did I get here? Is this our tent?"

"Yes. You came out of the desert and practically stumbled into the fire a few minutes ago. I helped you lay down on your sleeping bag. But I couldn't wake you out of your stupor. For a minute there, I was really worried," he said.

"No need, Nate. I'm just fine. I—I probably just need to sleep a little. Could you call to the others, and tell them I'm okay?"

Just then, a commotion of harried and anxious faces barged in at the opening of the tent: the disquiet of the old world, the fears and apprehensions of a life so foreign to the one still vibrating in her mind and senses. But strangely, Sabrina was indifferent to the intrusion, witnessing it all with open equanimity.

"Where did you go?" Marty yelled.

"Now, Marty, don't be miffed. She's here and safe," said George.

"But is she really alright?" said someone else.

"She's fine, really," said Nathan. "You can all rest now."

She sat up and faced them all with an apologetic smile. There was no doubt that the tale she could recount of moments past would trump every campfire story ever. But here's the deal: it was still just a story. True, it had the flavor of the Hero's Journey, but without bona fide corroboration, who'd believe it? That was the thing about these intra-dimensional excursions. You'd be hard pressed to make a story like that stick. So no showing off.

"You know what does stick though?" she thought to herself as each of the campers sighed with relief, recounting their tales of the early evening, and the last anxious moments when they weren't sure if they'd see Sabrina until daylight. "We were afraid you'd been bitten by a rattler or something," Helena said.

"What stays is the wonder, the awe, the feeling of always being entertained by angels," Sabrina said out loud without realizing it. "That's what you are." She said. "You are my angels. Each one, a bright star of the east. That's how I found my way home. And I think I *was* bitten by a snake, Helena, metaphorically perhaps. So thank-you, Marty, for the soup. It was . . . well, it exceeded my wildest expectations, let's put it that way."

Marty snorted, "Yeah. That stuff can sneak up on you."

And after a moment of uncomfortable silence, everyone turned to exit the tent, resuming their chatter, which was mixed with audible sighs of relief at the evening's outcome. The last one to leave was George, who was quiet and still seemed a little disconcerted. He turned to Sabrina with eyes that bore down on her as though he were privy to something; maybe her prior nakedness and complete lack of shame? Piercing right through to the other side of whatever veil there might have had between them, he said,

"You— Do I know you?"

"From before, you mean?" she asked hesitantly. "Honestly, George, I don't think so. Do I look like someone you've met before?"

"Regarding her question with a slight frown, he said finally, "No. Not at all." And without another word, he walked out of the tent.

Sabrina took off her shorts and put on sweat pants and the warm flannel shirt which used to belong to her dad. She pulled her sleeping bag close to Nathan's and slipped inside it. She noticed that he looked disturbed or concerned about something.

"What is it Nathan? Have I made you too crazy to sleep now?" she asked. "I'm so sorry. I didn't mean to—"

"No, I'm not upset. But I have something I've wanted to tell you about for a while now. Honestly, I should have told you before but I just haven't been absolutely sure about it—you have to believe me on that. I was prepared to talk to you earlier in the evening if you'd come back sooner. But then when you didn't—".

"What do you want to tell me Nate?" she asked with compassion and surprising clarity for someone who had just traveled light years from another universe. "Please, you can say whatever you need to. I'm cool with whatever; you can't imagine how cool," she said in complete sincerity.

"Okay," he began. "But I thought it was just like a—I don't know—a phase or something. Look, you're going to think I'm just the most—"

"Never mind, Nathan. This isn't about what I think. What do you want to say? Say it with no disclaimers," she said, pressing him for full disclosure. Why did it take so much effort to get people to simply be vulnerable and open here? She stopped pressing him for the moment, and let the Pause take over. She noticed how it could be a respite for inner reflection, or the perfect punctuation in an intimate conversation.

"I'm—" he began again. "Sabrina. . .I think I'm. . .gay.

Glorious Pause.

For some reason Sabrina was afraid he was going to say that he was in love with her or wanted to be in a relationship or something. And after the events of the evening, that particular request would have been hard to respond to right then. But this? This was just more than alright. And there was only one response Sabrina could give. She reached for him and took his hand, laughing with all the good will she possessed, which was a lot right then.

"Oh, Nathan, my dear, dear friend. You are just so absolutely perfect. You *think* you are gay? Well, you know, I'm not sure *I* could have guessed. So maybe you're allowed to be a little uncertain," she said, taking his face in her hands.

"Oh, I'm so glad you aren't angry, Sabrina. I've seen you angry and I was really worried,"

"Well I should probably be offended by that," she chuckled, turning over on her back. And then looking up at the stars through the screen at the top of the tent, she said, "But tell me, darling boy, when do you think you'll know for sure?" And she laughed again, doubling up with her arms around her middle, ending in a sigh of exhaustion. Then turning again on her side to look at him, she put one arm around his waist and drifted off with secrets of her own, lingering somewhere near the edge of her conscious mind.

Well. The universe was certainly full of surprises tonight.

28

The Kiss

At breakfast the next morning Sabrina felt surprisingly alert with no negative repercussions from the night before. And Nathan was in high spirits because he had finally outed himself to her, and could now be completely honest with all of his friends, only some of whom had suspected the truth. He was a hard one to read in that respect, and Sabrina wondered why he had tried to keep a hetero-sexual image for so long.

Over scrambled eggs and blueberry pancakes, Nathan answered some of her questions. "I've always felt so comfortable with the women in my life, it's been difficult to admit that I am really more attracted to men. I grew up with sisters, but I wasn't sure how to be with men. I've always known all the right moves with women. I found that I knew what they liked and how they would respond down to the slightest nuance. It was just second nature to me, but men? So coming out for me has required a degree of personal honesty I didn't think I had. I'd have to learn a whole new way of thinking and responding.

"Up until now," he said, "I used a kind of manipulation as a way of navigating intimate relationships with women, telling myself that what I really wanted was aberrant and wrong. And I only resorted to remote gay bars when I was too tired of fighting the urge. I actually could hold off quite easily because I'm sorry to say that I liked being admired as much as anything and women have always given me that at least. That is the real problem as I see it now. I never had to work that hard with women. They seemed to fawn all over me, willing to give me whatever I wanted; even "space", when I asked for it, which I did —a lot.

"But the more I allowed myself to accept what I knew was my bottom line reality," he said, "I realized that I had to take the risk of being open about it before I could initiate a relationship with someone of my own gender. Honestly? It takes more courage than I realized. I kept putting it off because I wasn't sure I could actually go for that kind of intimacy with a man anymore than I'd been able to do with women. Intimacy is the crucial thing, of course; the thing I believe I'm ready for. But that's a whole other thing altogether. Growing up in a strict Catholic home," he confessed, "it was hard to envision myself with a man. But finally I had to admit that that's where I felt more comfortable and less inclined to use my image as collateral."

"In fact, the only time I've ever been completely honest in a relationship was with this kid in high school. We were truthful with each other, and it felt so cleansing, so pure," he said with emotion, "and believe it or not—so strangely and profoundly decent."

"Oh, I believe it," said Sabrina, looking at his flushed, open countenance. "I suspect that the real love affair we want is with Honesty. She is an ardent, relentless lover, that one. How did you get so smart, Mister?" Sabrina said in admiration. "Hardly anyone I know is this savvy about their own personal motivations and instincts."

"I had an uncommonly good friend," he answered with enthusiasm, "who invited me to be very clear; really truthful with myself."

"Really?" Sabrina said, astonished to hear the same words that her Friend and Teacher had used only a few hours ago. "How did he do that? I mean what did he say? Or maybe it was a woman; how did she extend this invitation? Do you mind me asking?"

"Of course not. This is the best feeling, you know, Sabrina, being able to have this conversation with you. In fact you're the reason I could actually give myself this gift of openness. I saw how free you were to express yourself, not holding anything back. Full disclosure is such an amazing drug isn't it? Ah! How I love a cup of candor in the morning!" he crowed, toasting himself with his coffee cup.

"And—what do you know—here is the very friend of whom I speak," Nathan said, referring to someone standing behind her. She turned around and saw Marty, who was smiling like she had just won the lottery. And behind her, almost a foot taller, stood George Wright.

"Are you two ready to go on a hike?" he said, "I'm afraid it's going to take some resolve after last night. Are you up to it?" he asked, not with condescension, but real concern it seemed.

"I think I can handle it, thank-you George. How far is it?" said Sabrina.

"We'll drive out into the desert a few miles, and then walk a mile or so. We'll be climbing a bit too; down a very steep ravine and up the other side of the mountain where the ruins are. It's worth it though. Very few people get to see these. An old buddy of mine showed me where they were a few years ago. Nathan, my friend, are you ready?"

"At the risk of sounding like a cliché, I've never been so ready!" He boasted. Circling his arms around both Marty and George, he looked back at Sabrina in pride. "There never was a finer 'band of brothers'," he said laughing at Marty's sideways glance.

Everyone had packed their own lunches and water, and George brought some first aide items in a larger backpack as well. They drove the truck, three in the cab, and five of them sitting in the truck bed, emptied of all the gear from the day before, out to the site where they would begin hiking.

After a half hour's drive, they parked the truck near a clump of Yucca trees and started the hike in earnest. It was still morning and they were given to understand that they wouldn't be starting back until late afternoon.

George led out and no one seemed to have any problem keeping up. Even Sabrina could hardly believe how good she felt, how easy it was to hike, after the ordeal of the night before. By noon, they had reached the ravine and could see the ruins across the way, and they were every bit as impressive as George had said. In another half hour they were down at the bottom of the ravine and already climbing their way to the small cave dwellings about a quarter of a mile up the other side. George admonished everyone to watch their feet rather than looking up. It was smooth rock and one could slip and slide swiftly down the open faces if they weren't careful.

By one o'clock, they were standing in the cool huts carved out of the side of the mountain by the Anasazi. It would have been a wonderful place to sleep for one night if they had thought about it, Sabrina thought. The huts were dug into the rock in a long row, complete with tiny shelves, windows, chimneys and fire pits in the middle of some.

One of the dugouts had a patio-like effect extending out into the side of the little mountain. They sat on a low rock wall, fatigued and eager for food, water and rest. Nathan was talkative and in his element now, speaking openly and robustly about his new unguarded perspective on the world.

Sabrina decided to go exploring a little on her own, and stole away quietly, climbing from one dwelling to the next. They were cunning and sanctuary-like. After reaching the last of the little shelters, she looked out across the canyon and the view was spectacular. "Whew!" she whistled under her breath, "Frank Lloyd Wright, notwithstanding." And she stood for a moment on a small precipice, gazing down on the open face of the mountain they had just scaled.

"Did someone say Frank Lloyd Wright?" a masculine voice called out behind her. Turning around, she saw it was George. She smiled and motioned for him to come to edge of the cliff.

"Oh. . . .You're not related are you?" she asked.

Shading his eyes with his hand, he looked across at the desert plain where they had parked the truck in the little patch of Yuccas. But it wasn't visible from this vantage point apparently.

She stared at him, waiting for an answer.

"He was a great uncle on my father's side," he said. "I never got to meet him of course. He died in 1959 I think. I saw a documentary on him not long ago though. He was a real maverick. I don't know if I hope some of it rubs off or not. I'm interning at an architectural firm in Oakland. But I can't say yet which part of me will win out: architect or philosopher."

"Really?" Sabrina asked. Why was she not surprised about that? "A philosopher, huh? Would you teach?"

"Well, that's just it. There's not a lot to do with philosophy but teach. Or write. And I don't think I want to do either. But honestly, it's what I spend all my free time reading. It seems to pull my focus in a way that architecture doesn't. I don't know why, but I think I have to *do something* with it, which is a kind of irony, since philosophy is mostly reflective. But to understand the underpinnings of the universe, to know who I am in a comprehensive sense, seems paramount somehow, though I can't tell you why. In some respect, it feels—" and then he stopped abruptly to look at her.

"I heard what you said to Nathan back there at the camp, about honesty being an ardent lover? You have an interesting way of seeing things. Nathan told me some about of the discussions you've had with him over the weeks. Hope you don't mind. We're very close. He really likes you, Sabrina. To hear him talk, you'd think he was in love. To be honest, I'm not sure I believe that he has completely switched to the other side."

"Oh, I think you better believe it, Skippy," she shot back. "People don't like it when you challenge them on things like that. Something to do with the courage it takes to open up, I would guess. Anyway, real change takes a little longer deep down in the psyche than it does on the surface of things, don't you think? So I think we need to give him some time. Besides, gays have always liked me," she laughed. "I'm just lucky that way."

"Are you always this clear about things? I would have thought you'd have been a little put off by the whole business, at least."

She bent over to tie an errant shoelace. "Some people would say I'm the most confused person they know," she said, thinking of her mother and some of her friends at church.

"Is that right?" he laughed. "Seems to me that that would have to be a case of classic projection."

"By the way," she said over her shoulder, "why don't you have a New York accent like the others? I mean, you grew up there, didn't you?"

"Oh. I moved to Albany from Missouri when I was 15. My father and I had some issues, and I always wanted to go to New York anyway. I met Nathan at a high school debate conference and well, we stayed in touch—" And then, with a kind of enigmatic intensity, he asked, "Sabrina, do I know you? I don't mean from somewhere else. This isn't a pickup line.

"Look at me, would you?"

She stood up and gazed intently at him. "I—I don't—" And then she remembered how Golas had not let her off the hook, how he'd challenged her to be clear, to wait before she gave an answer. And in pausing for reflection, something did click. In fact, it seemed that a little lock which had been jammed for a million years just broke open in her mind. No key. It just fell open, as if it was meant to, right at that moment and no other. She might have said that it was something in the past, but that didn't feel right at all. It was more like the present had opened itself to them in all its perfection, sponsoring this intimate liaison as though it were an ad for www. HolyShit.com.

And there was this feeling of Eternity in it. Which was exactly what she'd been trying to say to Nathan before; eternity as a timeless moment without a future or a past? A direct opening into the present. She couldn't remember ever meeting George, yet it felt so right to be standing there with him—

Suddenly, he grabbed her by the shoulders and planted a kiss right on her open, dry mouth; just the most cheap, overrated, romance novel kind of—you know—unwarranted, buckle-your-knees, bodice-ripping, Redbook kind of kiss you could ever imagine.

And she didn't even struggle or whatever you're supposed to do in that kind of situation. In fact, after the first second or so, she responded with equal enthusiasm, and she had a strong impulse to grab his hair and pull on it. But she didn't. It would have made it all way too cheesy, not that it wasn't heading there anyway.

He stopped as suddenly as he had started. And he wasn't panting, thank God, but it didn't seem like he was the least bit sorry either. Not a hint of embarrassment.

After a long pause and a little too late for speculation, she said, "I can't imagine how you'd know me . . . I'm not sure what you mean exactly," her voice shaking a bit. And that was possibly because it was the biggest lie ever, since he obviously knew her well enough. As a matter of fact, she had to admit that she did know exactly what he meant, though she just couldn't find the words. Then with a short burst of laughter, she smiled uncomfortably and looked down, like you do when you've been wrong about something and you're just so damn glad you were.

He stood looking a little baffled himself, over the way the moment had just kind of used him—used them both really—for this idiotic sentimental gesture; this prosaically fevered stunt.

Blowing out a puff of air, she just kept staring at the ground until at last he said to her with some confidence, "I *do* know you, Sabrina. Maybe a more accurate question is: Do you know me?"

And just at that moment Marty and Elaine came bursting into the little dwelling where she and George stood, still a bit awkward from The Kiss. And there was a moment of quiet discomfort. Was it obvious that something was going on between them? Because Sabrina had the feeling that Marty was partnered with George on this trip. She scratched her head, and dug into her pocket for a soft rubber band to bind up her hair, and everyone just stood around watching while she wrapped it, like she was doing something really timely and significant.

Momentarily, Marty backed out of the tiny doorway and hailed Elaine to come with her. "Anyway, we're eating," she called back.

George watched them go and turned back to wait for Sabrina's answer.

She waited till she could hear their footsteps echoing in another chamber and whispered, "Yes, okay. I do know you George. I do. But not from anywhere in the past that I can remember; either here or in some . . .some other lifetime. It feels more like it's from—I know this sounds crazy—but from some place that exists . . . what— parallel? . . . to Now."

"That's it!" he burst out in a kind of innocent wonder, which was a little uncharacteristic for him, she imagined. "That's the answer I knew you'd give! Last night when I was sleeping, you were there in my dreams and you said, 'I know you, not from somewhere else; but from Now'. Jesus. What do you do with something like that?!" he exclaimed, like a child who had just got everything we wanted for Christmas.

She smiled weakly and shook her head. Who knew about anything these days? But here was the deal: He was human, he was in this dimension, he had dreamt about her, and that kiss! That kiss was something, no kidding around. She thought he wanted to take her hand but he hesitated, and so they simply walked shoulder to shoulder, back to meet the others.

29

What The?

When they returned, everyone was eating lunch and enjoying a light conversation about nothing in particular. Sabrina and George remained conspicuously quiet, neither of them interested in engaging in the thin veneer of socially polite chit-chat, when so much seemed to be going on at a deeper level.

After an hour or so, everyone gathered their trash, stuffed it into their backpacks, and set out for the climb and the hike back to the truck.

Sabrina thought that Marty seemed a little antagonistic to George when he had offered to help her on with her knapsack. She was almost sure she hadn't seen The Kiss however, so how bad could it be? She just needed to stay cool, knowing how her mind could run away with these things. Her job was to watch: watch her mind, draw no conclusions about herself or Marty. Or George. And that was a big enough assignment.

She was doing a good job, too, until half way up the other side of the mountain. She and Nathan had stopped to rest in a little clump of Junipers near the top of the gorge. The others were still climbing the open face of the rock, and George was pulling up the rear, making sure no one fell behind.

Then suddenly, they heard a scream echoing off the canyon walls.

"What happened down there?" Nathan called out. "Is someone hurt?" Helena was behind them and she called down to Josh who was below her.

After a few minutes, Josh climbed up beside them and said breathlessly, "It's Marty. She slipped and fell quite a few feet. Got some scrapes and hit her head, I think—there's a lot of blood—and a really bad sprain. Or maybe it's broken. We'll have to see. I have to go back down and help bring her up. Sabrina, would you girls go on and find the truck, and bring it as close to the edge as possible?" he asked with some urgency. "Nathan, we'll need *you* down there, I expect. We'll probably have to *carry* her up."

Nathan looked at Sabrina. "Can you get to the truck on your own, sweetheart?" he asked. "I left the keys under the mat somewhere. But, here's an extra one; you might as well take it."

She nodded and put the key in her pocket.

"Good girl," he said. "We'll be a while I bet. I'm going to keep my water, but I think there's more in the truck if you need some. Take Elaine and Helena with you. The guys will get this."

She waved and waited for the two girls to climb up beside her. They watched for a few minutes to see how things were going, but couldn't see much from where they were. And momentarily, they started back to the truck.

"Did you see what happened?" Helena asked Elaine. "How did she fall?"

Elaine shot an odd look at Sabrina and said, "I think she was kind of upset about something. I'm not really sure, but she wasn't paying attention, like George told us to do. I saw her looking back at him more than once, and then she slipped and her foot caught on a jagged piece of rock or something. Maybe it was a twig from a tree. She fell backward anyway, twisted her ankle, and hit her head pretty hard. At first I thought she was all right, but I guess she's really hurt. She can't walk apparently."

Sabrina didn't have the luxury of feeling guilty. Her job right now was to get back to the truck and bring it as close to the edge of the ravine as possible, like Josh had asked. She decided to concentrate on that. And because they'd spent more time than they planned at the ruins eating lunch and talking, they were already heading into the late afternoon. There wouldn't be much light in another few hours. So the girls walked fast without talking much.

Within an hour, a beautiful golden light began to cast auras around all the edges of things, including the girls' tired faces. The closer they got to the site, however, the more Sabrina felt that something wasn't quite right. Walking wearily into the little bank of Yucca trees where they had parked the truck, they looked at each other in bewilderment. This was surely the spot. They all agreed on that.

But the truck wasn't there.

30

Just a Little Hitch

"What could have happened?" Elaine asked fearfully.

Sabrina closed her eyes and fell silent for a moment. Even though she noticed that her mind wanted to run the show, to think of something quick, to figure it all out, she wouldn't let it get the best of her. Not now. Not when clarity mattered most.

"Sabrina!", Elaine cried, " What the hell are you doing? We need to find the truck. I don't think we can afford to just stand here and use our psychic powers," she said with a hint of reproach.

Sabrina glanced up at her, but remained silent.

"Oh, come on," said Elaine. "We've got to go look for it. We've got to do something!" She motioned fearfully.

"Why?" replied Helena. "The only thing that could have happened is that someone hotwired it and took it."

"Oh my God!" cried Elaine suddenly. "No one had to hot-wire it! Nathan said that he left a key under the mat!"

"Well, there you go. And, honestly, if someone took it, I don't think there's a chance of getting it back now, Helena said. "Sabrina may have the best idea yet," she said. "Let's give it a minute and just think about it. I mean, why not? What else can we do?"

"Oh for God's sake—" Elaine murmured. Panicked and exasperated, she ran out onto the open plain, looking for a glimpse of the truck.

Sabrina did have a strong sense that the truck was nearby, and that they should wait. For what, she didn't know. But this Gap between thoughts had a lot of wisdom in it. That much she was sure of.

In a moment, Elaine came running back, out of breath and spitting fire. "Fuck. Someone out there *has* got it. I can hear them driving around. And I could see a little ball of dust way out there on the horizon. What should we do?" she asked, bending over with her hands on her knees, panting in agitation.

"Let's see if they come any closer," said Sabrina. "It would be crazy to go running after them, I think." The sun was now a big ball of hazy reddish-yellow light and would soon be descending into a tiny mountain range far off in the west. And there would be no daylight. So maybe whoever had taken the truck would have to turn on the headlights, she thought.

Putting an arm around Helena's shoulder, Sabrina thought as how there was a peculiar kind of certainty in moments like this. Not the kind of certainty where you knew what was going to happen exactly; just a sense that you could kind of trust how things were actually happening.

Elaine, on the other hand, was sitting on a rock near a small cactus, crying softly in despair. "I've got so many blisters. I hate this place! Leaving the key under the mat! Smart!" she whined.

Well, that's another way of handling the situation, thought Sabrina. We've all got to wait in our own way. And she remembered something from the little blue book. "Whatever you're doing, love yourself for doing it." And she chuckled at the wisdom of this little gem. Helena half-smiled at her, not knowing what to make of things, but willing to go with it.

And soon enough, the truck came into view and Sabrina decided to go out and hail it down. It came—at high speed—right toward her. She flinched, but decided that it was unlikely they would actually run her over, and if she remained cool it might even give her the upper hand. Whatever. She was just going by her instincts now and as the truck came closer, she could see that there were three men in it. It looked like they were having a good old time driving in circles and spinning out all over the place, laughing and probably high or drunk, she thought to herself.

"Put up your hand and give them the peace sign," the voice of her Teacher said. She did, and they drove right up beside her and stopped in a whirl of dust, making Sabrina sneeze and sputter, to their apparent delight.

"Is this here your truck?" a pock-mark faced man—looked to be about 45—asked her. "We was just takin' it for a ride. Wanna come?" The three of them laughed and that's when Sabrina saw it.

The one on the passenger's side had a gun.

"Oh, she's gonna come with us, Gordie," he said with conviction. And he took aim at her with two fingers. "I think we can coax her." The man in the middle looked a little scared, but pretended to think it was funny.

Elaine, still sitting with her head buried in her hands, cried, "Oh shit, I knew something like this would happen!" But Helena moved away cautiously and started to walk slowly in the direction of where the boys and Marty might be coming up soon from the canyon. Then rather suddenly, Elaine stood up, and followed her. Sabrina watched the man grab his gun, kick the passenger door open with his boot, and point it in the two girl's direction.

Sabrina took a big risk, and it worked. Making a quick bold movement, she got his attention, and swinging around smartly, he focused the gun on her. Then, with a coolness she wouldn't have believed possible, she leaned on the car door and said to the driver, "You men having a good time?" Something jogged in her memory: lying underneath that loathsome man the night before, in whatever kind of world that was, she remembered the feeling of moving in rhythm with what was happening, instead of resisting it. So rather than pull away, Sabrina leaned in with her elbows across the open window.

"Dude, you don't know the half of it," said the man with the gun, as he slipped back into his seat. We killed us a couple a' snakes and three prairie dogs back 'ere." Then to his friend in the driver's seat, he said menacingly, "What do ya say now we take us a nice little filly, huh?" The pock-marked driver stuck out his tongue and tried to lick her face. She leaned back a little and laughed, hoping to keep the repartee going until the boys returned. Although it would be even better if she could humor these crazies into some kind of deal before that, because the more people that were added to the mix, she thought, the more unpredictable the outcome.

"I wonder what you guys would think about giving us back our truck now? We'll drive you to where ever you need to go. Where's your camp anyway?" For some reason, she felt less and less afraid.

"You girls is pretty," said the driver to Sabrina, with a sickening smarminess. "What is you sweet things doin' clear out here in the middle of nowhere anyway? Maybe *we* should take ya'll to *your* camp. " he said, spitting some tobacco out of his mouth, narrowly missing Sabrina's arm.

"Ah, come on Gordie. We're not goin' to any camp," said the guy with the gun. "Let's just take the damn truck and leave 'em here." He said it as though he really meant it. Still Sabrina was unmoved. It was a miracle that she felt no resistance whatsoever, almost like *she* was in charge of this whole charade.

Maybe it was because the Teacher seemed to be holding her tight in another universe, and his voice said, "Tell him you've got some mushrooms back at your camp."

"We have some mushrooms," she said without hesitating. "Why don't you let us give them to you? Then we'll drive you to wherever you want," she negotiated coolly in her sexy 'come-hither' voice.

"Shit! You're kiddin' me! This little lady say she got some 'shrooms back 'ere." The driver yelled to his buddies. "Shit. We just hit the jackpot, Suddy. But I'm not lettin' this'n go," he said and suddenly he grabbed her wrist. "Get in here, little girl. Hell, you don't seriously think we're goin' to hand this truck back over to three helpless little girls, do ya?" he said, laughing and twisting her wrist as he opened the door and got out. "Forget them others," he said to his friends. "We cain't take the trouble to chase *them* down now. Besides there's only one of her and three of us. Much better odds," he said to the guy in the middle. "You get in the back, you mother-fucker. She's ridin' up front with me."

Switching hands, he quickly grabbed her and threw her up against the cab. He was quick, and much stronger than he looked. Even then, Sabrina remained cool. He was lifting her up with his leg between hers and his tough, stringy little arm around her waist, when they heard a voice behind them.

"What do you gentlemen think you are doing with . . . with my . . . girlfriend?" the voice said in a measured but commanding tone.

She saw with relief that it was George.

Or maybe it wasn't relief. Because now she noticed she *was* afraid. Just a little hitch: the shotgun was now leveled right at him.

31

Sabrina Makes Her Move

"Whoa, dude, what girlfriend is 'at you're talking 'bout?" said the little man, holding Sabrina with unmistakable ownership. His grip was hard and unyielding, stronger than she had imagined it could be. He was a skinny little cuss, but his friend's gun gave him a kind of crazy bravado. She didn't make a move to resist though, hopefully encouraging him to feel as if he were in control. Why? Well, because it just felt like the right way to play it.

"I didn't see no ring on your finger, little pussy girl," he said, loud enough for George to hear. Her legs were up on the sideboard, bent to give him a push. "This girl belongs with the truck. She just done tol' me! She got me all kinds a ways, hot and bothered," he said, licking the side of her face again with his tongue. What was with the licking thing? "She's my little filly now, ain'tcha, sweetheart?" he whispered in her ear.

Sabrina could see the tendons hardening in George's neck. She supposed that the other men were staying back out of sight with Marty and the girls, waiting to see what happened. That was prudent, she thought, and probably George's idea. But perhaps her desire to keep things light and friendly with this redneck had backfired. She remembered George had told her, that she had spoken to him in a dream. So could she communicate to him that way now? Did they have some kind of telepathy going between them? "Pause. Pause,

George. Listen into the gap between all the thoughts running wild in your head right now, you beautiful, beautiful man. And don't do anything crazy, okay?"

But her assailant was getting more and more agitated. He clearly wanted to get her into the truck and take off. Should she give in and save the others some grief? Surely she could get free eventually. "Because these guys were about as dumb as a damn toilet seat," she thought in her JD Salinger voice. But no. She might let them take *her*, but then she couldn't let them take the truck. They would need that to get Marty into town. So she had to do something quick. The fowl-smelling guy licked her again and the stench of his chewing tobacco was slathered across her cheek, and he tried to lift her from behind into the cab with his bony knees. Resisting, she reached up to grab the little metal frame inside the cab with her fingers.

Then glancing back at George standing helplessly by, she smiled wickedly. And with all her strength she reared back, slamming her head directly into the face of her abductor. It hurt more than she could have imagined and she felt dizzy and sick with pain for a moment.

Then came a wild careening sound, "Shiee! She cu ma fuchki-hongue off! Goh- damn, Fuchki biiikhhh!"

In spite of dizziness, she turned slightly to see the damage she'd inflicted. Through bloodied lips, he was screaming at her, but his words made no sense, and she realized that her head slam had taken a greater toll than she could have hoped. Between throbbing pulses, she saw that he was holding a large piece of his tongue in his hand. Full half of it, it seemed.

A resonant crack split the air asunder, and a fierce pain vibrated upward from heart to head. The feeling was wild and sensual and it took her breath away, literally. She had this insane desire to laugh, but when she opened her mouth to try, something sticky and wet came trickling out. And anyway there was no sound in this part of the known universe to lend her laughter any real credibility. Either she'd gone deaf or the universal sound button had been turned off.

"Am I hallucinating?" she thought, "Or is this really happening?" She was fading fast and she winced as everything was torn from her conscious mind: the truck, the landscape, the world, and that amazing—*almost believable*—crazy ass villain.

Oh yes, and that lovely illusion called, George.

32

George Wright Considers His Plight

George Wright sat motionless as the Buddha himself next to Sabrina, who was still comatose in the ICU. He hardly knew this girl, yet he felt as though they were somehow connected in a sort of inexplicable way. Maybe she would contact him like she had the other night if he would just make himself available. But he wished it didn't matter so much. It hurt like hell when things mattered, he noticed. And he wished the ache of being alive in this particular body with these particular feelings would just stop.

Why had everything happened just the way it did anyway? Why had he kissed her and made Marty so angry that she got distracted and fell? And why hadn't he taken the bullet instead of Sabrina? It was hard to imagine that he deserved anything less than the dire consequences which were now presenting themselves. He had always thought self-deprecation was a terrible waste of time. Maybe comedians could get away with it, but ordinary people like himself? It was almost arrogant to spend that much energy hating oneself. It was narcissistic and— But it was no use making himself feel guilty over feeling guilty. Now he was just being redundant.

Mr. Ryder and his wife and family were—well—amazing. They had been there—one or all of them—for the last 34 hours, around the clock, and never once had they asked George to leave or explain himself. Yet they hadn't even met him until this catastrophe; this one that *he* had put them in, this crisis starring their lovely Sabrina, in a showdown with death.

After she had smashed that jackass in the face, causing him to lose a couple of teeth and bite off his tongue, the idiot had stood screaming at her with surprising venom, as though she were the one who had forced *him* into the situation.

In the commotion, his gun-happy pal—who had the rifle trained on George up until then— jerked the damn thing around so fast, that it went off without warning, surprising even the gunman himself.

On the recoil, George had jumped in and grabbed the gun with a fury that would have stopped an AGM Hellfire missile. And before that hick could say 'Jack Daniels,' George had thrust his steel-toed boot right on the damn fool's neck. The idiot had fallen to the ground, turning on his back just in time to see the coming of the Apocalypse: the barrel of his own gun cocked and aimed right between his eyes. It was a hell of a rush, George remembered thinking.

"You *better* start running, you mother-fucking son-of-a-bitch!" he yelled as the man attempted to get on his feet with his hands up. And then, "Wait!" stopping him long enough to pull out the wallet from the bulgy back pocket in his piss-stained jeans. "I'm going to need this," he said, and holding it gingerly between two fingers, he flipped it into the cab of the truck.

The three men had started running for their lives when they saw how things were going down, and it felt good to get off a couple shots above their heads as they ran desperately into the desert. Meantime, Nathan was at Sabrina's side in a flash. "She's a bit faint, but I think she'll be okay. Man, she really socked it to him!" he yelled to George from the other side of the truck. "Whoa—she must have really hit that son of a bitch good! There's blood everywhere!"

The fact that they didn't realize that the gunshot had actually hit Sabrina was a matter of immense stupidity George thought. He should have run over to her immediately instead of doing the crazy Indiana Jones thing. But oh no, he had to follow some macho instinct, which was probably just an overreaction to his feeling of helplessness in the whole situation.

Then suddenly Nathan had cried out, "Wait. —George? I think she's been shot! She's—she's been sh—shot! Get over here!" And he started howling like a child.

Stranger still, when George had run around to the other side of the truck and seen Sabrina fading from consciousness; she'd been smiling! In fact she looked like she wanted to laugh but didn't have the strength. He must have looked to her like the clown he was, and he felt like the hapless cowboy comic in one of those old 1940's B-movies.

Now, as often as he'd gone over it in his mind, he couldn't turn back time and make it come out differently. Had Sabrina deliberately coaxed the gun on herself by slamming her head into that bastard? Did she mean to pull the gunman's focus like that? What had she been thinking? He could actually remember feeling like she was trying to tell him something, but he didn't know what.

Without delay, they had lifted both Marty and Sabrina into the truck bed on top of a blanket or two. Sabrina didn't appear to have any spinal damage, and anyway they had no other choice but to expedite things as quickly as possible. Helena and Elaine rode in the cab with Nathan, while George, Josh and Dan rode in the back with the wounded girls.

Nathan drove like the wind, which made for a lot of bouncing, and Marty in particular felt it keenly because she was conscious. George made a pillow for her head and the broken foot with the boys' shirts, and then held Sabrina's head in his lap. Because there was no way to apply a tourniquet on her shoulder, he simply held pressure on the wound, hoping that it would be enough. Nevertheless, blood seeped out all over his hands and shorts and legs. He kept checking to see if she was still breathing. But more than anything he was afraid she might wake up while they were still bouncing around in the truck, and there'd be nothing he could do for the pain.

They didn't stop to get their camp gear and tents, but called 911 as soon as they could get service, and sped directly out onto the highway where they met the paramedics, who drove Sabrina and Marty to the closest full facility hospital, in Moab. From there Sabrina had been given emergency care and then life-flighted to the University hospital in Salt Lake.

When the boys finally got there behind the EMT's, George was covered with so much blood, that the ER team at the Moab hospital kept asking him to lie down and be checked. After refusing several times, he finally got so angry they simply let him go.

"Fuck you," he heard one of the PAs say. George understood. Still in shock, he felt the same way about almost everyone he encountered that evening.

Marty was x-rayed and had her foot set in a cast, which turned out to be broken in a couple of different places. She also had a slight concussion. Within a few hours, however, she was discharged with pain killers and a prescription for bed rest. She wouldn't even talk to George, who asked Nathan if he would drive her to a hotel in Salt Lake, which he would pay for and where she could recoup in comfort.

Meantime, George and the other boys went back to get the camping equipment and the cars. George then drove his car from Moab at breakneck speed to the hospital in Salt Lake. Once he was there, the boys had phoned him every few hours to get an update on Sabrina. They stayed two nights at the Marriot with Marty, until she finally felt good enough to ride back to California with them on the third day.

Nathan had come directly to the hospital after leaving Marty and the boys at the hotel, but George told him that he needn't stay the night. Sabrina wouldn't be waking anytime soon and both of them didn't need to lose sleep. Nathan obliged, seeing now how personally George felt about it, and he did the only thing that made sense: he went back to help with Marty.

Now, as George sat alone with Sabrina, still struggling for life, his mind kept going over the scene in the desert. It could have played out differently if he'd just done—what?—something else. He thought of the anger he felt, pulling that lowlife up by the scruff of his neck. And just remembering the smell of whiskey and sweat that permeated his clothes, he wanted to heave.

He had talked to the Moab police, and given them the wallet and the approximate location where it all had happened. "I don't know where they were camping, but it had to be close, and they'll probably have to come into town to get a doctor to look at that tongue. I would keep a couple of officers here at the hospital, and watch all the clinics around," he said, preoccupied with his thoughts about Sabrina.

When the boys had told Sabrina's family the next morning how quickly George had reacted and with what composure, under what duress, they made it sound like George was some kind of superhero, and Mrs. Ryder was all over him like syrup on a pancake. But what could he do? If he told them how it really went down, that the gun was meant for him and not Sabrina, it would just have made the family suffer more than they were already. Later, if he ever got the chance he would tell them the truth.

Thankfully Sabrina did not regain consciousness before they took her into surgery. But by then, George almost wished she had, just to know that she was alright. And later, when the doctor made his made his report to the family, George stood close enough to hear.

"Luckily, the buckshot missed her heart, but nicked the inside of the left lung." he said. "We were able to place a chest tube in and it looks like the lung is doing well. But because it was a shotgun, it tore her up pretty good inside. As you know, it took several hours, but we were able to repair the clavicle, shoulder and sternum. And we had to give her a lot of blood. She'll need to have a cosmetic surgeon look at it, but she is expected to recover. We'll know in a day or two for sure." he said, as though it was still just a hopeful theory. "Also she'll need extensive physical therapy," the doctor concluded.

Next morning, the doctors said that they weren't sure Sabrina was out of the woods yet. Now it was just a waiting game to see when she'd wake up. It may be another day or two, they had said. Maybe more. They'd all just have to be patient.

Now, on this particular morning (three days after the incident) Mr. Ryder had asked George if he could stay with Sabrina for a few precious hours so they could handle some things at home, and so that he and Mrs. Ryder could go to the Mormon temple with their son, Neil—to pray he guessed—not knowing exactly what else they did there. Something about "a mission"? He had no idea what that was. And Sadie, the younger sister, had an important tryout for something at school. And he'd promised them all, that he would call them personally if she even fluttered her eyelashes.

He phoned his boss in California, who put up no resistance to letting him stay another week. Not only was he one of the firm's most talented young interns, George had worked tirelessly, putting in hours of overtime for several weeks before the trip, in order to finish a huge assignment on an Oakland inner city housing project. And now that it was done, business had slowed down a bit till the next big undertaking in December.

His suggestion that the police keep an eye on the doctors' clinics paid off. They were waiting when the three culprits had shown up in distress at an Insta-care on the edge of town and George had identified them all with photos taken by the Moab police and sent through the internet. "Of course it would take some time for that son-of-a-bitch-without-a-tongue to talk," George thought. "And if he never says another coherent word, it'll be too soon for me," he told the investigator.

Meantime, sitting in the lounge chair next to Sabrina's bed, he tried to sleep. But it was the restless slumber of the unrighteous. Tormented with guilt and remorse, he got up and paced the floor as he tried to think of what he would say to her if she woke up and no one else was there. Would she even know who he was? Often in an accident like this the victim didn't remember the event itself, he thought, which was probably a good thing.

"My only real connection to her was in the last few hours before it all happened, so there's a good chance she won't remember me at all," he thought as he went over it again and again in his head. Still, he was glad if he could be there when she awakened, so that he could—what? Apologize? Throw himself on her mercy? Agitated and disconsolate, he glanced around for something—anything—to take his mind off his angst.

That's when he saw the books on the table next to her bed.

"When she wakes up, and if she's up to it, maybe you could read to her a little?" Mr. Ryder had asked before he left the hospital that morning. "This is one of her current favorites apparently," he said. "Abby says she's poring over it for days. Will you tell her I left it? There's also a <u>Book of Mormon,</u> from her mother."

"Sure. Of course," George had said. He picked up the book of scripture and perused it for a while. Then he looked at the title of the other book: <u>The Lazy Man's Guide to Enlightenment</u>. Well, naturally, she would be into something like this, from all he'd heard. 'Eccentric' was the word Nathan had used to describe Sabrina, and George thought he'd even heard her father use a similar description of her to one of his church friends who'd stopped by.

The book was written by a Thaddeous Golas. Now that was odd. Hadn't he heard Sabrina calling out "Golas" a couple of times in her fevered ramblings, in the truck? Did she know the author? He sat down and began to read. At least he could see what sort of ideas moved and impassioned her. He wasn't too sure about this "enlightenment" stuff, however. He thought that Nathan had said she was over the traditional Mormon dogma, so what was this? Spiritual replacement therapy? Still, if she knew the author, it might be a different matter.

Then he thought of something. He could Google this Thaddeous Golas character, and read all about him, which he did on his iphone. "Interesting," he thought. "He's dead. And if he died in 1997, let's see . . . she'd only have been around 10 years old." Had he been a close friend of the family? But her father had made no reference to him and acted as though he wasn't familiar with the book at all. So then it was a mystery again.

He read the first line: "We are equal beings and the universe is our relations with each other."

"Okay," he thought, "that sounds reasonable". And sitting back in his chair, still with one hand on Sabrina's, he devoted himself entirely to the text in front of him.

33

Sabrina On Pause

Sabrina was moving toward something discrete, she knew, but couldn't tell what it was. It required a sense of concentration that seemed foreign to her, since she'd been free of all concerns in the particular for— for what? An Eternity, it seemed. In fact, she'd been living in the abstract, free of material concerns for long enough that it seemed difficult to even want to try and focus her mind back onto the physical plane.

And she realized that she wasn't so much moving toward it, as it was moving toward her. Momentarily then, she saw a mirage-like figure and waited for it to fully materialize in front of her. Was this someone she should know? Through an obscure mental haze, she stared at this beleaguered, tired-looking young man. He appeared to be preoccupied with something, gazing intently down at it without looking up.

Presently though, she felt his hand on hers. In fact, that's how she first realized that she *had* a hand! He'd taken it, but apparently was not the least bit interested in communicating with her, which suited her just fine by the way because she wasn't much in the mood for talking either. His disheveled hair kept falling into his face. Occasionally he would jerk his head to shake it out of his eyes. She thought it strange that he couldn't see the logic in letting go her hand, which would make it easier for him to tuck the long strands of his hair behind his ear, once and for all.

For some reason, a bed had just appeared out of nowhere too, and she seemed to be lying on it, though she wasn't really sure why she needed a bed. But it was nice anyway because her right shoulder twinged with pain something awful sometimes, and also her head ached like an anvil had been dropped on it from 10 feet up. And through all of it, she lay there drifting in and out of some rather crazy dreams.

The first one came in fragments. There was a closet, an elevator, a bookstore, all very odd locations for scenes of mystical madness. Because that's what it was no doubt about it. The main character in these vignettes was one of those—well there's no other way to put it, she thought, except to say that he was an adventurer, a time-traveler, a primo teacher and who knows what else? Apparently though, his dimension was in a different zip code from hers. And they did things differently there. Anyway, there was no end to the things he had taught her.

The next dream was a finely-honed adventure story that Sabrina wanted to call, "The Desert Affair", and she was the star of it alright. She had two leading men, both fine actors. One was supposed to be gay although, personally, she wouldn't have guessed it. But he played that role for the run of the show. The other one seemed to just follow her around with his eyes, which were dark and piercing and seemed to be asking something intangible from her.

Last was the "The Mountain Men Caper", a wacko ersatz escapade. No one ever would believe it because it was so contrived, she thought. There were guns and shooting and hightailing it out of there, and all kinds of melodrama that doesn't actually happen in real life. But then sometimes it *seemed* quite real. *Which is why I left,* she thought.

And all the while, between these dream segments, people were fading in and out of her awareness, bringing flowers, sitting and talking to each other, and to— . . . the Heavenly Father, was it?— and about *her* it seemed. So now there was this God with a kind of grandfatherly aire; a Persona with a capitol P. Wow. And they supplicated Him to bless Sabrina, as if she weren't already the most blessed creature in all the known universe.

It was like they wanted this Magnificent Being—this God—to care specifically about one outcome over another, and all for her sake. But all she wanted was what Life wanted for her. Why would anyone want more? Or, as a matter of fact, less? Indeed, she could feel that their ideas about this Deity all seemed to coalesce around concepts of duty, obligation, honor and sacrifice. And she could see that 'He' was perceived as an objectified image, separate from ones' self. Not only that, but with a persona of great sentimental value who could then be worshiped, rather than integrated.

Versions of this relationship between man and his Deity resided in the many belief systems that emphasized specialness and ownership of The Truth. In fact, this 'Specialization of Truth' seemed to run rampant in the world. And it was all done in the name of this God, which was pretty crazy considering God was the Name for Everything. Yet here was a whole planet dedicated to making God the symbol of Something-in-Particular. In short, there seemed to be a constant *battle* between the Good God and the Not So Good UnGod.

But how did this UnGod come about? What were they thinking? Well, that was it really. They weren't, it seemed. They were lost in repetitive, compulsory, reflexive patterns of belief initiated centuries ago; beliefs which hadn't really been reexamined since their primitive inception. A whole system of duality had propagated in the wake of these simplistic and unquestioned beliefs. It could even appear that evolution was at a temporary standstill on planet earth.

And apparently *this* was the dimension from which she had just come, and might be going back to. Confusion reigned on the surface of this world and sometimes it looked like Armageddon. Sabrina could see that a serious collective baptism was needed here, a re-birthing, perhaps an ascension in consciousness? But what could *she* do about it?

"Well, it is your world, your dimension of thought," she heard the Teacher say. "Why not give it a shot?"

"Wait—are you saying that I've dreamt up this nightmare?" she asked defensively.

"Who Else?"

"Well— That makes no sense at all. Why should I do that? I mean, what purpose could I find in all that tragic dualism?"

"What indeed?"

"Listen you—quit answering questions with questions—I don't—"

"I thought you liked them; questions."

"I don't like them if they take me further into confusion and—and guilt!"

"The Confusion could be a gift," he said. "It's the feeling you get when your limited ego mind is on override, which from a broader point of view could be a good thing. It could bring your busy mind to a standstill; the Great Silence. Guilt? Well, you're on your own there. That's your misinterpretation."

"So, you're saying this is all in my mind?"

"Well, it's not that simple or that personal. Maybe you could call it a collective trapped fascination. A shared psychic constipation from a steady diet of millions of separated minds stuck on wanting to know everything for certain. No wiggle room. No appreciation for the Unknown. So no, you—as a person; as Sabrina—are not wholly responsible for the problem. How could you be? You—like most of the people in your world—have been asleep. But now that you see it clearly, you *are* responsible for accepting the correction, are you not?"

"Well, I guess. What's the correction anyway?"

"First of all, acknowledging the error; that you are part of a mind that agreed to a dream of separation, violence and suffering. And now, you are responsible for seeing it all with forgiveness. Or better still, seeing that there is nothing to forgive," he said. "Let it all go and leave this nightmare. Just don't leave in a way that hangs you up. Exit with your blessing on it; laughing, if you will."

"Hangs me up? Hangs me —what kind of hippie jargon is that?" she frowned. And she started to feel anxious, like she should do something, something really big and important.

Rapping his knuckles gently on her forehead, he said, "Leave that 'figure-it-out-and-fix-it' mode behind; the lessons are all built into the experience anyway. Try to remember it the way I taught you."

Then like a miracle, in the midst of her confusion, she did remember, this most wonderful thing:

The Eternal Pause.

And she forgot all about the ideas she'd been trying to work out a moment ago, and just sank into this one lovely Idea. Because here was an idea that was *worth* letting it all go. It was so expansive she knew she could use it forever and ever with more and more effectiveness. It was the only idea which, when contemplated, would leave no trace of itself; no anxious footprint of guilt or fear in the mind. Plus it left space for all other ideas. In fact it was the birthplace, the Source of ideas.

"I mean really," she thought, "there's no downside, no attrition, no entropy, and nothing that would make it turn on you. It's not a two-edged sword. It's addictive, but it can't hurt you and you can never wear it out. The more you use it, the better it works and the better life works. And when your life is all finished The Eternal Pause will take you right back into Its Self, no questions asked."

Sabrina felt the peace of that. And even as this new awareness took hold, she contemplated her life in the context of the frail and wounded body that was back in the 3rd dimension. And as she continued her walk with the Teacher, they fell into a kind of meditation together, far away from the world she had sometimes called home.

Patricia York

34

Amphibious

And so it was that for a time Sabrina continued to shuffle back and forth from this Eternal Space she shared with her Teacher, to sit betimes outside the heavy veil of earthly consciousness, contemplating its woes and wonders. On one of those visits, she encountered someone so familiar that she thought to arouse herself into the physical plane, if only for a moment. As though she were swimming toward the surface of life, she made a desperate attempt to pull herself into the body, forcing the breath up through lung and nostril, opening her eyes onto a world of solid matter. Born again. And there he was; the one she had loved since time immemorial.

Pulling herself out of the endless deep, she whispered, "Hello," and moved her hand ever so slightly, although he didn't seem to notice. By the way, where was that other younger man who had been keeping vigil over her these last few days? Well, never mind. *This* one she knew with all her heart. He was . . .

"Father," she strained to speak a little louder this time.

"Oh!" he turned to see her and cried. "Oh, my darling girl! Nurse! She's awake! She's awake! Someone call my wife and let her know!" Then turning all his attention to Sabrina, he wept with his head bent toward his hands holding onto hers. "We didn't know—I mean, after you didn't come round those first few days, we—oh, I'm just so glad you can speak. Can you see me, Sabra?"

"Yesh," she heard her voice squeak past the plastic tubing that slithered up into her throat and mouth from somewhere deep inside a painful body.

"It's alright Sweetheart, don't talk. I just wanted to hear you for a—oh! Oh, I'm so happy you've come back to us! I was worried there for a while that you'd decided to stay – well, wherever you were, you know." As she shut her eyes from the bright lights, he said, "Don't go too far this time, will you Sabra? I have so much to share with you." And he spoke earnestly to her for the next half hour, telling her how he wished he had been a better father, as though he'd somehow failed her. He seemed to be saying something about her coming back to "the church", which made her laugh inwardly.

She couldn't remember exactly what the idea of "Church" meant in this world, but it felt warm and inviting and she knew she had good associations with it; as though it were something she'd always done and would keep doing. Although it wasn't a structure really but more a feeling of joining. So what could he possibly mean that she should come *back* to it? Yet he seemed so determined. In fact, he seemed to be in a lot of pain over the idea. She wanted desperately to tell him about the Eternal Pause, but she didn't have the strength. So she just became semi- present and hoped it would do her father some good. He did seem to calm down a bit, and after a while, simply stared at her in love and wonder.

Presently she felt the weight of sleep coming over her again, and drifted back down below the conscious thoughts of that world, just as though she were some kind of amphibian, breathing underwater.

35

Borderline

In the rarified air of a less encumbered mind, Sabrina examined the concept of 'Church' more closely. From her frame of reference while inside the body, she thought she could remember why it meant so much to her father. But—just as an idea—how had it become so treasured by the whole world, and at the same time so divisive? Everyone seemed to have different notions about which expression of the idea of 'Church' was the best. It was supposed to make people loving, to give one support and unity in the context of others, yet from a broader perspective she could see that it had been the font of almost every contention in the human experience.

Here in the twilight between worlds, free of conditioned thinking, she was liberated from the pain and suffering, the harsh laws of that solid walled reality with all its tubes and needles and monitors. And churches.

In a soft light emanating from a beautiful chapel, she saw her Teacher sitting on the altar near a tall arched leaded window. Only it wasn't lead, it was gold, Sabrina decided. A voice inside wanted to object. "Oh, come on. Gold; really?" it seemed to chide.

"Well, why not?" she laughed, "This is my church after all."

The walls and decor in this cathedral were mere suggestions anyway, not solid facts. Everything was ephemeral here—all of it energy—and, best of all, her feelings were attuned to the open mind and heart, not to the tight, contracted mind and nerve endings of a physical body. She fairly floated down the aisle to the altar. The teacher opened his arms to her and she melted into him.

At last he said, "Did you have a nice visit with your father?"

"Yes. Well . . . sort of. . . " she said hesitantly.

"By now you must know that you and your father have been together as learning companions for a long time. And here we are again, looking at Life from above the battlefield, 'far from the madding crowd,' as we did once before, remember?"

She thought of the last time he'd used that image and said, "Yes, I remember. But how does that relate to this cathedral of light? What are we doing here?" she asked.

"We are standing as Awareness for two dear souls, father and daughter, each struggling with their own mortal lessons. The father has come to an impasse, you see, my dear. He thinks he has failed his daughter in some immense, immeasurable way. And he's about to depart from this world, thinking he will never get the chance to amend this awful mistake. Let's say in this moment, I represent his Higher Self, the 'Holy Spirit', in his terms. I'm here to take him from his body into the bosom of his True Reality. But because of the confusion he's feeling he won't go peacefully, and that will make for rather a rough transition. Would you like to make things a little easier for him? I mean, as long as you are here anyway—in this timeless place?"

"Wait. Are you talking about my father? And I'm the daughter in this scenario? He's— he's dying you say? Right now? He's leaving?

But what if I decide to go back! I—I can't bare it if he's not there! He's got to—"

"My dear, it isn't like that. We are standing apart from the world of time, remember? Seeing events from beyond it? All dimensions exist simultaneously here. You'll have plenty of time to go back, to live with him, and say goodbye if that's what you decide.

"But here—in this moment—on the borderline between the physical and nonphysical, where he will one day be taking his leave from the body, you can speak to him as the angel you are. You see, he is convinced—in the wake of your 'near death' – that he must get you to see reason and return to the old Mormon paradigm. Not understanding fully the nature of Eternal Life, he thinks that *yours* is in jeopardy and that it is his fault."

"Really? He can't see that my path is. . .well, that I am Eternal Life? Doing this? And that he is too? And that we are one? That I am with him always?—He can't see all that? I always thought he knew—doesn't he understand what Jesus meant when he said, "I am the Way, the Truth and the—the—?" And she stopped midsentence, cut off by her own incredulity.

"No. Not in this moment, my dear. He still believes that Jesus was speaking only of himself as a person, and not from the Eternal Timeless Self that we all share; the Christ mind in all of us. And he has had such a scare with your 'near-death' it seems, that an existential anxiety has a fierce hold on him. He thinks that your choice to leave the traditional Mormon path places you outside the Kingdom of God, the kingdom of his very own heart; that you have lost some essential part of yourself, and that this means you might be lost to him forever.

"But—"

"Wait. There's more, my angel. Related to this fear is something else. Something dark, that you won't understand at first. He's never shared with you the chaos of his upbringing, I suspect? His relationship with his own father? The abject terror he lived in as a child?"

Sabrina stood motionless and shook her head slowly; curious, but a little afraid. "Something dark?" she stammered. She couldn't remember her father *ever* saying anything about his childhood, as a matter of fact. She only knew that his parents had died before any of the grandchildren could get to know them. And she thought now that on the one or two occasions when she had asked about them, her father had quickly rerouted the conversation to something else. And she was a bit embarrassed to admit that she'd never pressed him further. No. Her life was all about her, wasn't it?

The Teacher went on. "Somewhere he made a decision to wall himself off from that harrowing experience. And one of the ways he was able to do that was by embracing the Mormon faith, which (in his mind) guaranteed that he would not have to let his father anywhere near him—or his family—by virtue of the doctrine of 'the three kingdoms of glory'.

"As you know, this doctrine wisely says there is no hell, but replaces it instead with three degrees of glory, unto which it is believed every man must qualify after death. Although the idea stands fairly well on its own symbolically, it is never good to take any belief too literally, and your father, of all people, should have understood this. But because of the severity of his childhood fear (never having addressed it, and hiding it deep inside his psyche instead), it seemed in this case vital, that he accept the figurative as absolute fact.

"For you see, while it did not condemn his father to the eternal torment of fire and brimstone, still it was certain that it would keep this drunken misfit, this hardened scoundrel, far from his own precious family." For whichever kingdom your father proved worthy, surely *his* father would attain the lesser. In all these years, though it was not in his natural way of reasoning, a literal interpretation of this precept guaranteed him a measure of safety from the tyranny of his childhood. It was a psychological refuge, you might say, which is perhaps all one can ask of a religion.

"But now this unquestioned belief will not only keep his father out of his reach, but also you. For no one in this closed thought system, who is not aligned with the 'Only True and Living Church' (that is, the Mormon one) may enter the highest kingdom. It's an Idea as old as time and almost every religion in the world has had to face the mortality of such a doctrine. But the Mormon faith, relatively young in its inception, is still infatuated with the idea of having the only access to God. Not too different from the Muslims, actually. These two religions make a strange paradox, two sides of one coin; the ancient and modern (latter-day) versions of Truth in its static form.

"And here lies the rub where your father is concerned: what if you—in your reckless abandonment of Truth (in his mind) were sent to the same kingdom in which his father now resides (again in his mind)?" You see how it stands? He risks not only losing you, but abandoning you to a realm in which his father may be waiting to hound and stalk you, as he did himself as a youth. It's all very 'Orwellian' in literal terms, but there you have it. Just like Love, fear follows no necessary logic.

"And now, he's even worried—because it is also a part of the Mormon ideology—that you might be sent to a kind of 'outer darkness', not realizing, of course, that it is *he* who experiences outer darkness every time he chooses—by very thought—to set anyone outside his heart. Like his own father, for instance. And whether or not he remembers it, he *does* love his father."

"Outer darkness— But this is crazy! What can we do?" she cried, "Besides, outer darkness—what could be so awful about that? It's where I go, in a sense, whenever I meditate. Okay, well then, 'inner darkness', but what's the difference? He loves that I meditate. How could he think it would be anything less than— than complete peace and a rich inner solace? What can I say to him, what can we do?!"

"It is what he must do, I'm afraid. And it isn't so much a 'doing' as an 'undoing'. Nevertheless, you might get him to see how to forgive his father, and that there is no need for walls on this side of things, nor even for separate kingdoms. Then he will be open to the more generous, unconditional response that the idea of the 'three kingdoms of glory' is not about hierarchies in some future Heaven, but rather symbols of various states of consciousness in any given moment.

"It has been an intense drain on his spirit to leave his own father out of his conscious good will. Yet it was needful for his healing until now, because now the integrity of his True Heaven, (which is ultimate joy, however one defines it otherwise) depends upon his forgiveness. For one must always ask oneself, "If, in the company of God, Angels, and these Witnesses, I am the only one—by my lack of forgiveness—to keep another out of Heaven, would I really choose it?"

She saw immediately the dilemma. When we take our thoughts too seriously, literally—even if they seem comforting from one point of view—we eventually suffer. The only way to eternal peace/joy is to see our thoughts, however cherished, as symbols instead of fact.

Truly, her father must have been weary entertaining such inner conflict for so long.

"Well, he must be exhausted from the struggle. How hard can it be then, to get him to forgive, and to let go of this terrible burden?"

"This is no common request for mercy, Sabrina," The Teacher replied. "It means he must *embrace* his father. Not only that, he must see the gift his father has been to him; and to welcome this man, into the highest kingdom of his own heart. Kind of a backwards version of the story of the Prodigal Son? And you are aware now of what I'm talking about. You've had two very clear experiences like unto it, haven't you?" he said, referring to the events of the last week.

"And so you, Sabrina," he said rather too intensely for her liking, "are the key to this forgiveness, for he can see his way to forgive you anything, because he knows his heart would break if he did not. What he doesn't know is that his heart will never settle for anything less than full psychological integration with his father as well.

This is not as personal as you might think, for this is the condition of the whole world as you know it. He will do this work for the whole of consciousness, but it will mean that he has to pass through so rigid a barrier, (for to him, it feels like a literal brick and mortar prison) to overturn a verdict of incontrovertible justice in his mind. The problem is, he—as the symbolic jailor of this prison—is no more free than his father, bound by his need to keep him behind this barricade. 'It's called 'the veil' in the Mormon tradition. But in your father's case it is more like the Berlin wall, and it won't come down any easier.

"Look now to that tiny fortress there," he said, pointing to a structure not far away. "There is your father, surrounded by a citadel (made in his own private mind) of stone and cement, and no apparent way out, though it were finer than gossamer. It represents years of anger and defense built up in protecting his mother and brothers from his father's malevolent rage; and then the final decision to cut him out of his life entirely. It feels to him like a passageway that has been sealed up for eternity, a drawbridge nailed shut and surrounded by a lake of repressed emotion; impenetrable. But in fact, this citadel is so unsubstantial that a feather could pass through it. And so you must get him to see its illusory nature. Focus on that, and you may have a chance to change his mind."

Sabrina thought she would give her own life in trade for her father's, if it were possible, since she was halfway predisposed anyway. But apparently it required more subtly than that. Grand gestures wouldn't do here. She had instead to find the tiniest linchpin that would undo this fortress of judgment. She walked over to it, around it, and saw in this imagined stronghold a man in such misery, so desolate, as to make his visage unlike the father she knew in every way.

Yet it *was* him; of that there was no doubt. And to think he had been lugging this heavy affliction around his whole life, with no one the wiser. How much effort had it taken to hide it from the world while still believing in its reality? For here stood a man besieged and care-warn, heavy with the tremendous weight of his own judgment and fears.

"One cannot carry this kind of burden for so many years without a terrible inner scarring," said the Teacher. "A mighty healing is needed here. An integration."

Suddenly her father didn't seem so much like the parent she had always known. Indeed, he seemed more like a child. But how to convince him to cast this millstone from his neck—this albatross— before drowning in the deluge of his own malice?

"Father," she choked with such emotion she could hardly hold back the tears.

Yet he remained unresponsive. Was he unreachable? For it was sure that nothing could pierce this fortress without his permission, his whole-hearted consent. But where was she to find the wisdom to make that appeal, and he, the will to answer?

Sabrina waited, listened. She stood in the Marvel of the Eternal Pause, and gave her whole heart to its Great Silence. Momentarily, she tried again. "Poppy," she said from the earliest, most tender place in her memory. And he looked up ever so slightly. Had he heard her voice?

His great dark eyes darted for a moment from one wall to another, unable to find the source of this tiny salutation. Had he imagined it, this voice of a child? For certain it was, he would never allow a child within these walls of pain. This place was X rated, for adults only. Things indescribable had happened within these premises.

But in a moment, unbelievably, he understood. It *was* the voice of a child, his beloved little Sabra. "Wha— what? Sabrina? . . . Is that you?"

"It *is* me, Daddy. Will you take my hand?"

"Take your— I can't take your hand! You mustn't be here, Sabra! You leave this instant! Your Daddy is busy right now!"

"No, Poppy, I'm not leaving. I'm just here, right outside your –your prison. But if you take my hand, I will lead you out. Give me permission to do that, please?" she begged.

"My— prison? But I'm not in prison. Your grandfather is though, and for good reason. You don't know, Sabrina, but he is an evil man; unpredictable as a wounded rhinoceros. I never told you this because it would have scared you. But I've trapped him now behind this wall, where he can't harm you or anyone else ever again. You must trust me on this. I know what I'm doing, Sabrina, my love."

"Father," she said with renewed emphasis, "Please do look at this fortress you have built. I'm asking you to look and see if it still serves you. I'm all grown-up now and don't need protecting. Look and see what you have made; how much effort it has taken to keep it in place. You have been standing guard at this gateless wall for too long, Daddy. Please, for your own sake, can you see this another way? You really can let it all go now. It's that easy. And something else, Poppy . . . Your father needs your forgiveness. He needs more love, not less, –and . . . and deserves it too, I think."

"Easy now, Sabrina-girl," The Teacher whispered in her ear. "Don't push too hard. *The giving up of judgment, . . . is usually a fairly slow process, not because it is difficult, but because it is apt to be perceived as personally insulting.*[69] One has to admit to being wrong about so many things. Remember, in his world judgment is the criterion for wisdom, maturity and strength. What we are asking him to see is the opposite. A 180 degree turn; that wisdom, in fact, is the relinquishment of judgment, and the necessary condition of his own sanity."

"Personally insulting, is it?" she whispered back. "Yes, I remember that feeling."

Then turning toward her father again, and touching her forehead against the fortress wall, her arms spreading out across the span of it, she said, "Okay. So, Daddy? Where is your father right now?"

"Why he's— He's here in this— this prison, like you said. I've got him walled up in here so he can't hurt you, my love. But you've got to listen to me and do exactly as I tell you."

Her Teacher nodded an affirmative consent. "Agree," he whispered.

Hesitantly, she did. "Alright, Daddy. Tell me what you want me to do."

"You must leave me here to handle this. Leave this place and don't look back. And another thing: you've got to return to your spiritual roots; to Mormonism. You'll be safe there. Will you do it, my darling? I must have you safe before I—"

"Before what?" she asked.

"Before I take care of this monster, once and for all," he cried. And he clutched at his heart, for it was burning with uncharacteristic venom.

"But Daddy, can't you see that I am already and always safe? Show me this monster."

"There! Look there! Do you see? He is vial; a demon with horns and a— a knife, a belt, and a vicious backhand!" A large shadow with claws and a dagger stretched across the imaginary wall; so large that it towered above them. "Don't go near him, Sabra! Get back! Go back to the safety of the life I gave you, the one I raised you in. The one I taught you to love!" His fear had projected onto the wall an image like the primitive drawings in cave dwellings, large and menacing to a small child's eyes.

"I do love that life, Daddy, I do! Nothing could have been sweeter or richer than the one you made for mother and me and our family. And I am here with you now, back in the warmth of that safety and love. Look here now, and turn away from that evil specter. It's not real, Daddy! I am real. The love that you gave me and our family is real. Your fear is not! Fear is not even possible without your consent. Remember, 'perfect love cast-eth out fear?' What do you think perfect love is, Daddy? It is the full appreciation of everything we thought to judge against, isn't it? Come to me now. Let Love hold you while we watch these shadows of fear fade into the light."

Sabrina reached for him, grabbed and held him like he was a little boy, a babe in the arms of the Mother. Now she was the parent, the adult, the protector. In that Eternal Present, *he* was now the child, rocked in the arms of a mother he had never known.

Sabrina found, odd as it was, that she knew this role of The Mother very well indeed, and knew it by heart. From some inner life it came forth; an instinct, clear and profoundly deep, as she cradled and shushed him in the full and generous lap of the feminine that was hers, as sure as it were Eve's, the Mother of All Living. Or Mary, the Mother of the Christ child. It issued forth from her as if she were the Archetypal Goddess herself, possessing the primal power to heal and comfort every wound of the human condition.

After a time, when the little boy's fears were somewhat put to rest, she pointed to the walls of the prison, the shadows that now flickered small and harmless in the dim light. "Watch now," she said. "Look at the story of that little boy who was once your father—a boy like yourself—and how he was made into that scary monster you have been so afraid of."

And they watched while silhouettes told the tale of a boy who— once innocent and curious—had had those qualities entrained out of him by hard and vicious blows, burns and beatings, much more harrowing than even his son had experienced. And how this boy learned to fight back and yet somehow grow into a different kind of man. A slightly better man. Except when he was crossed. Except when he drank to forget. Except when his wife ran away and left him with 4 little boys to raise.

Then came the miracle of the first of those boys, who somehow—though he could have passed into adulthood with the same propensities—had found another way. John Ryder Jr. broke the pattern, that awful chain of violence which had been passed down from generation to generation until then.

It had only required a whole village—perchance a Church—to make the shift. And such a Church it was, carrying the weight of certainty, the precision of loyalty, devotion, honor and duty. What else than such a Church could heal this generational misconduct, this Grand Illusion of Suffering? None else! It had to be a church that carried the banner of Family—the Perfect Family Life of God. And what Perfection it was; the evolution of the human experience into something so fine, so ideal, so good; a marvelous work and a wonder, indeed! A leap in consciousness for the collective, conditioned mind of this heretofore psychologically medieval earth. And who could blame them for wanting it to last forever? After years of trial and error, the human race had finally got this one thing right: this concept of the Ideal Family that the Mormons had brought to life; its own precious contribution to the evolution of human consciousness.

Sabrina and her father sat side by side and marveled at the way Love had grown itself in this corner of the world, this Mormon Aspect. And they watched the way it seemed to advance into more and more perfect versions of itself, until at last this perfection took on a slightly inflexible, caricature of itself. Indeed, it seemed that the vision of the Ideal Family was busting out of its skin; that a new, more malleable, workable model was wanted. Something that would include more, exclude less. Family yes, loving kindness yes, but extending outward to other, more varied models of relationship: diversity, not adversity.

"Father," she said, "It's beautiful isn't it? And don't you think that everyone deserves to experience our family, even those who don't fit nicely into it? What do you say we forgive him, this father of yours? Don't you think he deserves a break after all he's been through?

John Ryder looked into the eyes of his daughter/mother/wife and friend. They saw lifetimes together in each other's eyes: 'pre-existences' indeed. Sabrina was—in this illuminating moment— a representation of the magnificent Feminine Principle, asking him if he wanted to join her in this "seven times seventy" experiment; this crazy-ass request made by an amazing Teacher some 2000 years ago. And he saw that she was right. Forgiveness was the only way to make whole, to find peace, and—just incidentally—get himself out of this life sentence imprisonment. Spirit prison, the Mormons called it; the imprisonment of Wholeness/Spirit/God into a tiny body, a story ancient with pain, affliction and anguish. And all issuing forth from *a tiny mad idea,*"[70] when the son of God forgot to laugh.

And so he stepped out into the open, hyper-conscious, intelligent, rarified air of forgiveness, and took a deep breath. And as he exhaled, he gave this breath to God. To Wholeness. To Freedom.

It was the last breath in the sometime painful, stormy, erudite, but exquisite lifetime of Bishop John Ryder Jr.

36

Sleeping Beauty

It was the still of the midnight hour with monitors humming, tiny lights blinking on and off, the sound of a computer keyboard ticking off reports somewhere in the nurses' station, a clip board slipping into a file cabinet, and occasional hushed conversations down the hall; all the ordinary sights and sounds of a smooth running hospital slipping into its nighttime routine.

Sabrina was sleeping soundly—too soundly—after a week and a half in the ICU and still in a coma. Except for the one time with her father several days ago, she'd not said another word, moved a finger, a toe or even opened her eyes again for a single moment. It was all quiet on the third floor of the University Hospital. But just now, that wasn't especially a good thing.

George was on watch again and was trying to fall asleep in the large recliner chair next to her bed after reading the newspaper and eating a rubbery hamburger from the hospital cafeteria. It had been a long day with friends and family in and out, and once again he had volunteered to stay with Sabrina.

Lying there with her hair just washed (her mother and sister had done it with a bowl and pitcher that afternoon), Sabrina was a fairy tale version of herself. The whole room smelt of the fresh scent of shampoo, and Nathan had dubbed her the Sleeping Beauty when he'd come to visit that afternoon, which everyone would have found quite charming if not for the anxiety they were feeling.

It was starting to make them all nervous; this extended nap, this deep sleep. At first they understood it to be medically induced. But now, even after taking her off the high doses of morphine, she still remained silent and immobile. Was that moment when she had awakened with her father just a fluke, an anomaly? Should they have done something then to keep her awake longer? Could they have? The doctors were stumped and it was beginning to give everyone the jitters.

Her brother had already left for the "missionary training center," which George found out, involved quite a sacrifice of time and talent for a boy so young. It was wonderful on the one hand, to go visiting other countries while still so young, but quite a strict regimen: no dating allowed and a highly structured schedule too. George marveled at the devotion to duty, to belief. And he thought as how Sabrina had some strong programming to address if she were to integrate these newer ideas that he'd been reading about. Having read the Lazy Man's Guide in its entirety, George couldn't see how both thought systems could reside in one head; even a beautiful, comprehensive and intelligent one like Sabrina's. It would be difficult to reconcile one with the other. What use were doctrines and tenets after all, when one concept was equal to any other—maybe not in actual physical practice—but in terms of value to experience?

He looked at Sabrina lying there like a princess, and he thought he saw a faint smile on her face, like the one he had seen just after she'd been shot by that fool. Was he only imagining it? Sleeping Beauty indeed. He didn't know why he liked her so damn much. He didn't really even know her, did he? But it felt like it. Why? Anyway, her family had taken him in, and he had really wanted to be there when she woke up. But he would have to be going back to work soon and it was starting to feel like a hopeless teenage wish, this expectation of his. Why was he giving it so much meaning after all?

In the dark, barely lit room, he stood up with his hands in his pockets and bent over her, leaning in to smell the fresh chamomile and hibiscus in her hair. He looked at her plump red lips. Someone had applied some lip gloss. It was tempting to— Well, why not? Just try it. No one was around. If it was the one of the stupidest things he ever did, it was not the first stupidest thing. The first stupidest thing was kissing her in the first place. Stupid, stupid, stupid.

But how about it? Would another kiss turn everything around, bring everything full circle and back to normal? And what was normal anyway? He thought about something he'd read in The Lazy Man's Guide:

"The entire universe is made of beings just like ourselves. Every particle in every atom is a live being. Every molecule or cell is a tribe of beings. Energy is a large number of us vibrating together. Space is an infinite number of our brothers and sisters in perfect bliss."[71]

"Are we vibrating together, you and I, Sabrina Ryder?" he said softly. "If I kissed you, would the 'tribe of beings' that live and breathe as your beautiful, wounded body, wake up? Or would they stay in 'Space' in that perfect bliss? (And I wouldn't blame them if they did, by the way.)

"And why is it such a dreary world without you?" he murmured. "I feel bored, unmotivated, restless; wanting to catch up to you in some way. If I fell off a ladder for instance, and hit my head? If I was in a car accident? Would LSD do the trick? How can I reach you, you whimsical—"

And he touched her mouth with his, ever so lightly, blowing on it back and forth. "I don't know how I know this, but I think you are supposed to escort me through this life. Wake up, damn you, or I'll have to come get you."

Then suddenly—inhaling a sharp deep breath—Sabrina opened her eyes and spoke: "My father! Where'sh my— my father," she said, her voice squeaking past the tube hanging from the corner of her mouth.

George jumped back in surprise. "Sabrina! You're awake—"

"Where'sh . . . my . . . . fath-er?" she asked more insistently this time.

"Your father? Well, he's— Damn. He's not *here*. I am."

"Who—?" She starred at him a few seconds, as though she'd never seen him before. "Ish he alive, my father? Where ish he!?" She seemed to be more insistent than someone in her condition had the right to be.

"Alive? Of course, he's alive! Well, anyway, I think so," George said, rubbing the back of his neck anxiously. "He— he was alive last night," he stammered, a little flummoxed by the question. In fact he was really kind of irritated that she had returned to consciousness already making demands. Where was all the romance that was supposed to accompany a kiss like that anyway? And why was he so goaded by her response? He had a few questions of his own, as a matter of fact. Where the hell had she been all this time? And why was she so worried about her father? Christ. Was she completely unaware of her own condition? But she seemed clearly awake in every other respect.

He couldn't believe he was so aggravated at this girl for whom he had just felt some kind of starry-eyed devotion a few moments before. And he said with no small irritation, "Well, the assertiveness hasn't been taken out of you, Miss Ryder, wherever you've been!

"Where *have* you been, by the way? Do you know you were in a coma for ten days? And why are you so concerned about your father? He's in a world of hurt, it's true, but no more than the rest of us. You've pretty much spooked us all, I can tell you." He felt like releasing a tidal wave of emotion that he'd been holding down since—well since childhood probably, or maybe even from another lifetime. And she just happened to be on the receiving end of it all. He paced the floor to keep from focusing all his anger on Sabrina.

Then out of the blue, she asked, "Did you just kissh me?"

He stopped, and stared at the floor in embarrassment.

Is that really what woke her? The kiss? What are the chances? Were they in some kind of fucking fairy tale? Whatever. He definitely did not feel like the charming—you know—prince. And he started to pace again.

"I guess I did. Yeah," he said awkwardly.

"Who are you?" she whispered.

"Oh, God. I was hoping you'd remember. It's a long story, Sabrina, and I'm sure you aren't ready to hear it all just yet. I'd better go get the nurse anyway. Are you— are you okay? Do you need—I don't know—some Jello? Morphine? A drink of some kind?"

She tried to chuckle, but it appeared to hurt. "Ugh," she winced. "I'm . . . okay. Could you . . . shit? You're . . . . making me . . . . dizzshy."

At this, he laughed and all the tension seemed to be released. "Alright, I'll shit. But are you sure you don't want the nurse or something? I mean, you've been in a coma for—"

"I know. You shaid. Ten daysh." She spoke slowly and yet clearly. "It didn't sheem like it though. It was more . . . like . . . ten shcenturies where I waszh. . . . I've been . . . bus-shy."

"Busy? Busy? That's an odd thing to say. How could *you* have been busy?"

She clamped her teeth around the tubing in her mouth, swallowed hard, and pointed to a cup of water on the table. He put it gently to her lips. Those beautiful lips. His hand was shaky though, and she tried to steady it with her good one. Twisting a little to look at her left arm and shoulder, she asked, "What'sh thish?"

He couldn't decide where to start and she said, "Don't . . . tell me . . . it's a long . . . shtory. . . . Because it looksh like I'f got shome . . . time on my— my handsh," she said, indicating her left shoulder and arm. "And I know who you are. . ."

"Yeah?"

"You're . . . the Handshome . . . Princsh."

He smiled in spite of himself. "Alright. But I don't know where to begin. What's the last thing you remember?"

"The Kissh."

37

Awake

Was she playing him? That would mean she was feeling alright anyway, and he was glad about that. He pulled his chair around so she could see him while he talked. Leaning on his elbows, his arms across his knees, he began.

"Well, we were on a camping trip, a bunch of us. You were with Nathan. Nathan Bridger. You remember him at least? You and I had just met," he said before she could answer. "God, I hate to have to tell you this, Sabrina. Because this whole thing with your shoulder and the hospital? It's all my fault. So . . . let me introduce myself—"

Looking up at the ceiling, she interjected, "I'm sho . . . glad . . . you're alive. I wash afraid they . . . were going . . . to— Georgshe. . .You. . . are . . . Georgshe, right?"

And swear-to-God, he thought he saw one of her tears plunk right onto the pillowcase.

"You remember," he said.

"I ha- help."

"Help? Where do you think you've been, for God's sake?"

She moved her good right hand slowly and wrapped her little finger around the wrist of his left hand. Then she closed her eyes and smiled. Only this time it was a real smile, and she looked entirely satisfied with herself, like she was as happy as anyone had a right to be. "Let me tell you a secret, Georgche. You will . . . never experience . . . yourself . . . as dead. Just different." Then she closed her eyes and seemed once again to fall into slumber.

He stood up and whispered in her ear, "Sabrina?" No response. Only that smile. He would have tried to kiss her again if he'd thought it would work a second time, but it seemed too ridiculous to imagine. Anyway, she needed her sleep, and so did he.

Instead, he reported to the nurse that Sabrina had been awake for a moment there, which was very welcome news. They came in to check her vitals, and after getting her to respond faintly with a few words, they decided to let her sleep until morning. George only hoped he would have a chance to talk to her again, before her parents came back the next morning.

Around 6:00 in the morning, George was awakened by Sabrina, moaning. He dashed for the nurse and she showed them both how to manage the pain with the button on a little remote. The doctor came in at 7:30 and ordered the feeding tube taken out. After some prodding and probing, and asking lots of questions about what day it was, and who was the president of the United States (Martin Sheen, she said), a light breakfast was sent up. She couldn't eat just yet, but George was starving and she insisted he take her food, such as it was. Even at her most vulnerable, she was a force to be reckoned with.

He ate the thin oatmeal, anxious to see how much she remembered. That part didn't take long actually. But then there was this other thing. Could he establish—in the short time he had left?

For George, it seemed like a thousand years since he had buttonholed her up on that cliff. But the feeling of urgency was still there. Why did he feel so insistent? What could it matter anyway? He was probably just a lovesick idiot, but it didn't feel like that. First of all, he was thirty years old, and even in his youth he hadn't felt like this about any girl. In fact, he'd always been a bit aloof.

In his experience, girls had been pushy and sort of needy and angry when they couldn't get him to respond to their little melodramas. And he'd never been able to stay in a relationship too long before it had become suffocating. Why would this girl be any different? Yet there was a burning; an earnest, whole-hearted desire that had taken him beyond rational thought. What the hell? Now he was the one doing the pushing, being needy. What a fool. Still, he couldn't help trying to establish a case, a raison d'etre for this awkward discontent; something that would make sense of it.

The moment came when he knew he must speak openly and give it his best shot. He was certain her parents would show up any time now and he had to find out if she shared any of the feelings that had been incubating in him since he and Sabrina had first been introduced; every day, a little deeper and more persistent, a burring into his heart with — *"I don't know,"* he thought, *"but it's something I'd never have invited in consciously. In fact, it's so uncomfortable I wish I could excise it. I wish it could be operated on, like a ruptured appendix. If this is what love feels like, to hell with it. Who needs it?* "I'd rather have a heart attack," he had sometimes said to himself in the days he'd spent by her side.

So now was the moment.

"Sabrina, there's something I want to say. It might seem presumptuous or out of order, but I have to leave soon and—I wonder if . . . if . . you remember that we— If you'd consider thinking about . . ."

She made a snoring sound. "Are you going to kiss me again Mister? Because your conversation skills are seriously lacking. If you had on a necktie, like all good boys do on Sunday mornings, I'd use it to reel you in, and I'd ask you to do that thing you do with that amazing . . . mouth . . . of yours . . ."

"Sabrina. Listen to me, will you? I know this is outrageous, and I have no idea where it will take us, but will you join me in this—" he said, between exquisitely wet kisses—"will you do this—" more kisses this time, so tender he couldn't remember what the hell he was trying to say. "This—" And his mind wandered off to wherever minds go on that drug.

Disengaging a few minutes later for breath, "Yes, you sap. But why so dramatic and urgent?" she said, touching her forehead to his. "Honestly, I thought you were the strong, silent type," she laughed, and then gently pushing him away she said, "Do I know you?"

If she hadn't been swathed in bandages and so damned full of needles and tubes, he would have shown her a thing or two about being strong and silent. While contemplating his next words, Mrs. Ryder suddenly burst through the doorway. Then came her father and her sister, Sadie.

"Oh, hi," he stammered. "I was just asking Sabrina if—"

In point of fact, no one really cared what he was just about to ask Sabrina, because they had a few questions of their own, and he backed up as they pushed right past him, and fell on her like a bunch of groupies. Each one gave her a delicate half-hug, and Sabrina looked over their shoulders to see George standing there sheepishly, leaning against the doorway, hands in his pockets, smiling back at her.

God, he was glad no one had listened to him. What would he have said anyway? "I've asked your daughter to move to California with me as soon as she gets well?" And suddenly, he realized that he hadn't asked her this at all. He hadn't got to it yet. And all she'd said was "yes," to something, but what? Damn. This was not going the way he'd planned.

He turned and walked quietly down the hall toward the waiting room where he could make a call to his boss and report that Sabrina had turned a corner; that it looked like she was going to be okay, and that he'd be coming back to work on Wednesday.

38

Icons and Infidels

"So what is he on about, this 'George' character?" asked Abby, taking a bite of the Café Rio salad she'd brought to share with Sabrina. "I let you out of my sight for three days and he only brings back half of you, then. And you stayed out way past the curfew; ten days in coma! What were you thinkin' girl?! Not a good start, I can tell you that. Next time I won't give permission so heartily. And, by the way, what did the doctor say about goin' home? Will he discharge you anytime in the next year or so?" Abby had honed the skill of exaggeration, as though she had a copyright on it.

"I hope so. It's getting tired in here," Sabrina said. "Plus I've got to get back to work or they'll—I don't know—fire me or something, right?"

"They're not going to fire you," Abby said with a flip of her hand. "What do you think this George fellow wants anyway? Does he know you just bought a townhouse?"

"I told him yesterday. He's been calling every night; hasn't missed a day in a week. I always think we're going to have a hard time finding something to talk about, but it's not that way. There's something so deep and rich about him, Abby. Actually, I could sit for an hour without hearing him say a word and be satisfied. Silence with George is like a . . . an aphrodisiac."

Noah rounded the corner in a wheel chair, navigating it like a pro. "Let's go for a walk, shall we? They said we could borrow this." He screeched a wheelie in the space between her bed and the chair Abby was sitting in.

"Watch out, you idiot!" Abby yelled. And then to Sabrina, "How did you get to know him anyway? Didn't you say that he with some other skirt? And he's a friend of Nathan Bridger's, did you say? A friend of Nathan's is not necessarily a friend now, you know. Look at him, he's already taken you for the ride of the century! All this time, trying to get you to look his way and then—before you turn 'round—he's telling you he's gay! What took him so long to figure that one out, may I ask? By the way, 'herself' could have told him, it's that apparent! I saw him once by the water cooler with Jeffery Wilder. Hmm," she said, nodding her head as though she knew exactly what they'd been up to.

"Oh, Abby. You couldn't possibly have known any more than I did. The guy's got magnetism bleeding out all over the place, and you know it. Girls were always coming on to him and he seemed to love it and act on it too. Besides, we never know why things happen the way they do," she said, "I really love Nathan. But now I've met his friend, and I think I've got the better deal. Nathan finds his Gay Truth, and I find—I don't know—a shiny object named George, that absolutely fascinates me right down to my existential—sexistential—core!"

"Oh please, don't use puns to make your point! Now you're only embarrassin' yourself," Abby said. "When's he coming back then?"

"He said he'd try to come in three weeks. That was a week ago, and it'll give me time to get out of most of these bandages I hope. I'm not sure about the stitches though. They look so ugly. I'll never be the beauty I once was," she said with dull sarcasm.

"Oh, don't you even think about that, darlin'. They've got all kinds o' ways to fix *that* up. I imagine they'll start as soon as you are ready."

"That's just it. I don't want to spend one more hour in a hospital. How am I ever going to get to the place where I'll want cosmetic surgery? Ugh. And they say it'll take months of physical therapy too before I'm even fully able to use my arm again. It would be all so bleak if I weren't so absolutely happy. Why am I so happy?"

"That's not hard. You're in love," said Noah.

"But that can't be it. I've been in love before and this is different," she said. "Besides, it's not entirely about The Boy. It's much more about my own inner well-being. There's a sense of serendipity to everything. I'm telling you, it's way beyond the norm; as though Life is not random. Like everything is 'Kismet'; 'the Will of Allah'," she said with a dramatic flair. "And I think I'd still be happy even if I never saw George again. Of course, I'd ache inside something awful, but I'd still be happy beyond all description. It's that sort of happiness!"

"The will of Allah?" said Noah. "Why use that expression? Don't let anybody hear you say that. It's not funny, Sabrina."

"I didn't mean for it to be. It's an apt expression, that's all."

"No it's not! Not today. You have to take these things more seriously, girl."

"Why?"

"Why? Are you kidding? Because those guys do. They take it really seriously and they don't like it when you take the name of their god in vain."

"I wasn't—"

"It doesn't matter! As long as they think you are, you are."

"Whatever've you been readin' there lad?" said Abby. "You sound a bit daft. A little paranoid are you then?"

"As a matter of fact, I've been reading, Infidel, by Ayaan Hirsi Ali. She's really clear about some things. The old Law is weighing heavy on the world—and not just the Muslim one either. We're all feeling the side effects of the dark side of fundamentalism. You haven't forgotten about 9/11, have you?" he asked, seriously wondering if she'd lost track of the world as it is.

Just then, Nathan peeked around the door and walked in with his friend, Richard; Richard, whom Sabrina had heard about in long phone conversations.

"Did someone say, Hirsi Ali?" Nathan asked. "Infidel? Richard here was just saying he had read it and highly recommends it. The End of Faith, by Sam Harris, too. Yes, folks, 'Mikey likes it!'"

His friend, Richard looked askance at him and seemed a little uneasy. "I— I did," he said, as he arched his neck to look outside the room.

"What's the matter old boy? You gave me the Cliff notes only yesterday, remember? You said it was a very cogent—"

"It's just that I noticed a couple of Muslim women out there in the hall," he whispered, as he discretely closed the door behind him. "I don't think this conversation would amuse them. Can we use our indoor voices?"

"Really?" Nathan countered. "You're going to lower your voice on the subject? You weren't so soft spoken the other night!"

"I just don't want to offend. Excuse me, I'm Richard," he said, turning to Sabrina and the others with his hand out. "I think your next line is, 'Oh yes, we've heard so much about you, Richard— all good of course!'" Then looking directly at Nathan, "Why don't we do first things first, hmm? Then maybe we can launch into a full scale debate at the top of our lungs, (his voice went up two decibels here) on the most vulnerable topic of the century while the 'opposition' (back down to a whisper) listens in!"

"Well, I didn't know you were so sensitive on the subject, my friend." Nathan retorted, seemingly unaffected by Richard's outburst. An intimate tete`tete` you'd prefer?" he said, closing the door. "Then let's sit down, shall we?" They all took their seats and Nathan offered his friend the last chair in the room.

"So, <u>Infidel</u>, is it? Said Richard. "I mean, is that the subject of the day, because I do have some thoughts on the matter. 'Women should be available to men at any time,'" he quoted from the Quran. "'Even on the saddle of a camel. Except of course, during the days of the month when they are unclean.' Thank Allah for those days, I'm guessing," he said, rocking back on his chair, with his hands behind his head. "Of course that was good advice in the 13th century, no doubt," he said ironically. "Very sexy even.

"Ali's question is why is this book still such a page turner for so many today? The passages about killing the infidel are legion, but no one has a thought to cut them out because they're regarded as the last and direct words from the mouth of Allah Himself. And for some, they are the most revered passages because of the base chakra arousal factor. Those 70 dark-eyed virgins—casting their gaze away timidly, mind you—are images that catch in the throat and stick in the groin. I ask you, what can be done about a bunch of young bucks who go to bed masturbating to those fantasies? Anyone for a Coke?" he added dryly, as he dug into his pocket for some change.

Nathan spoke up. "It seems to me that, where infidels are concerned, the fundamentalist way is to use any means available for getting rid of them; that in fact, getting rid of them is the thing, which takes it out of the realm of religion, and into a political arena. Guns and war, bombs and strap-on dynamite. The end justifies the means; an ethic we *have* lived by since time immemorial, but has it ever worked? In fact, can't we see now that the end and the means are the same? That is, whatever system we use to eradicate a supposed evil automatically becomes our nemesis in the end? 'Live by the sword, die by it'"

Noah responded, "But if you've been taught that the book which contains the message, 'Kill the infidel' is a living thing; a cherished member of the family even, and that it is sacred above all lives—all Life – as a matter of fact. Better than living in this world at least, which I can see could be true for lot of them. They live in such a restricted mindset with a future Heaven that calls to them in their dreams. Not unlike the fundamentalist right-wing Christian who hopes for the 'end of days' because he/she will be taken up on the right hand of God to a Heaven that—well, let's just say it's way better than whatever's in second place. Life here on planet earth is second rate to that Heaven they've conjured up. Nothing Here compares to what they can make up about There. So instead of living in the present, they're focused on future rewards. And damn the current landscape, literally. The mind is a wonderful thing for time travel; and it's entirely possible to make Somewhere Else into such an Eden, that we forget to tend the garden we're in."

"Well put, brother," responded Richard.

Don't spiritual archetypes, like the 72 virgins just represent psychological dynamics?" Sabrina chimed in. "And they mature as we do. Maybe the best gift to any subculture then, is to let them truly live by their own devices; to test these adolescent theories. The end justifies the means? They can't be told otherwise if they believe it. A friend once told me that the seduction of evil is simply that it tries to enroll us in engaging with it. But what if we didn't?"

Yes, "said Abby. Haven't we finally come to a place where we can talk it out instead of duke it out?"

"No," said Richard, quite sure of his opinion, "because there's this crazy notion that if we have bombs and guns, why would we ever want to use less potent means of getting our way? We could hardly acquiesce to lesser forms of power; what would be the point? Good sportsmanship and forbearance? Come on. That's too subtle. No, we like the good fight! Besides, we want to use our expensive toys after all the trouble and expense we went to making them. 'Build it and they will come,' works here, as well as in saner projects."

"Never quite got over the living room scuffle with the plastic soldiers and tanks, did we?" interjected Nathan. "Plus now there's this new thing: a bizarre satisfaction in pushing a button that triggers a huge explosion somewhere distant from where one is actually standing. Remote revenge, I call it."

"Unless you're a Jihadist," retorted Noah, "and then you like being right at the heart of it, because the reward is so compelling. And there's nothing like the promise of great honor and money to give a kid the kind of courage it takes to stand with a device taped to his genitals, ready for a trip to another dimension. Plus great sex after."

Just then someone knocked on the door. Nathan opened it. And there stood a beautiful Muslim woman, dressed in a full-length skirt and head scarf. Everyone froze for a second, looking at each other with—what? Chagrin? Guilt? Fear?

"Oh, hello," she called in. "My father was just asking about Sabrina. He's the one in room 206? He wanted me to ask her if she is going for a walk soon so he could look for her in the gardens."

Not one of them in the room seemed to have anything to say. They stood gawking at this exotic beauty, as though they were holding one extended collective breath.

At length the woman said, "He is the one with no hair and lots of hook-ups? Cancer you know."

Still no response. Even Sabrina was befuddled. The Lortab had just kicked in, and it seemed to slow her response mechanism a bit. She opened her mouth to speak, but nothing came out. Instead, she waved weakly to have them come in.

Out in the hall, a small man sat curled up in a wheel chair, tubes running everywhere onto two different rolling stands. He smiled broadly and waved. Sabrina motioned again for them to come in, but they could not be entreated when they saw how full the room was already.

"Next time my friend," he said. "This is my daughter, Moshda. I wanted that you should meet. But I see Allah does not favor it today." And off they went, down the hall.

When Nathan had closed the door again, Sabrina finally found her voice.

"He's— he is a dear friend. We talk like children. He may be the kindest man I've ever met."

39

Paradox

All the opinions and ideas that they had bandied about the room so cavalierly a moment before, seemed now trite and insignificant in the light of actual experience. Concepts paled in the presence of reality. Sabrina saw an image in her mind of the Samaritan who had taken no interest in particulars. Yet there was still the dogma and the clash of cultures, and the need to reconcile them. But there was no ready answer and her friends left without resolving the dilemma, even in an academic armchair fashion.

Later that night, Sabrina talked to George on the phone about the strange coincidence of the conversation and the knock at the door.

After a moment's consideration he said, "I've always thought that no one point of view could commandeer the Truth; that paradox was, in fact, the hallmark of truth. I mean maybe Life knows what it's doing. Maybe there's a natural intelligence to the way these things happen. The synchronicity alone is stunning," he said. "All I know is that things only *seem* to conflict. Seen from a wider perspective, it might all fit together somehow."

"Well, okay, you may be right. But if we're speaking about serendipity," she said, "there's something even crazier I have to tell you. Before Nathan left, he asked Richard if we could have a moment alone. Of course, Richard obliged and went into the hall. He struck up a conversation with Noah and Abby, I think. I'd like to have been a fly on the wall for that one, incidentally." "Meanwhile, Nathan told me something very strange. He said that when he first got to know me, he thought maybe he wasn't gay after all, that maybe he could really be straight."

"I told you, didn't I Miss Popularity? Up on that cliff? When I—"

"Except," she interrupted, "that one night a few weeks after, he'd had this strange dream. It was about you –and me. This was before we ever met, mind you. He dreamt that we were a house; not that we lived in a house. —We *were* the house! And it was full of people all living together and they were artists or something. Like some of them were writers, some painters, some chefs, all kinds of creative types."

"Well, that's weird. How did we look as houses?"

"Not hous*es;* we were both of us one house. And the weirdest thing was, he said he couldn't actually see either of us in his dream. He just knew that together we were this beautiful, beautiful mansion that was full of life and creativity. Not children, mind you. It was full of adults he said, and the feeling he had about it was more than just expansive and loving, although it was that too. He said that it had the feeling of a kind of Knowing beyond the ordinary sense of things, a sort of mystical certainty that kept his mind reeling for days. He looked it up in all kinds of books on dream interpretation and couldn't find anything that really seemed like an apt explanation.

"Still he felt that it had huge significance, like maybe it had a symbolic meaning. And he kept feeling that he was supposed to introduce us and let the chips fall where they may. Apparently he struggled with the idea for days, but the impulse to find a way to get us together became stronger and stronger. The lowercase that he had for both of us together, he said, won out over the love he had for either one of us separately. That's when he suggested that you all come out to Utah for the camping trip, because he couldn't think of a way to get me to California."

Sabrina and George were both quiet for several seconds. This wasn't unusual for them; they often gave space for insight to reveal itself.

"I *thought* he was a little insistent about getting us out there," said George. "I remember I was up to my neck in a project and—well, he had to do some fast talking for a couple days to get me on board with the idea. I really wasn't keen on it. Then somehow Marty convinced me I should go with her; said I owed her for a favor she'd done me a long time ago. I couldn't even remember the incident, but I guess I felt guilty. Truth is, she told me once she thought we are a perfect match, but I've always been reticent. And it just seemed to make her miserable every time we got together. I think of her as a sister, quite frankly. So it's amazing that I even came along. 'Kismet', I guess.

Sabrina said nothing. Kismet indeed.

"But there's this other thing; something I haven't told you myself," George continued. "I told you about *my* dream that day standing in the Indian ruins. But I didn't tell you everything and I certainly didn't tell Nathan this; it would have been entirely inappropriate since you were his date on the trip. But I had seen you in a—well I don't know what to call it—a vision of sorts, I guess? It was a few weeks before Nathan even proposed the idea for us to come to Utah. Of course I didn't know it was you at the time, and I'd almost forgotten the incident until I met you that day in the diner.

I kept trying to remember where I'd seen you, and then suddenly it came to me, the vision.

"I have a habit of sitting at my desk at work, looking out the window. My office is on the fifth floor and I like to stare out onto the San Francisco cityscape. I can even see the ocean on a really clear day. Anyway, sometimes when I squint my eyes, I get this strange feeling; like I'm entering another dimension. Mr. Golas would know what I mean, I'm sure.

"Anyway, this day that I'm talking about, I was staring out the window, doing my squinting trick, just to see if I could achieve the effect I'm talking about. It had become a favorite pastime; to see if I could slip into this other world, the one where I become a Self that transcends the small one called George. And it often gave me access to a kind of creativity that wasn't typically available to me. That's the only way I can describe it really.

"Then suddenly, you were standing there on the other side of the window. You."

"Wait," she said, "You are on the fifth floor? Where was I then? Standing in the air?"

"Not exactly. You were standing in a . . . library? A bookstore, or something. Talking to someone. You seemed quite upset at this person. You and this man were talking quite rapidly. I couldn't see him very well; his back was to me. Anyway, it was only for a moment, and then it was gone. But I felt as though I had known you for—for—well—ever, I guess. But that you were just in another 'room' it seemed. Another parallel universe? In fact, it wasn't any distance at all. It was right there next to me, yet unavailable to my immediate senses except through the—shall I say—internal visionary ones? Anyway, I remembered all this when I met you the first time, in the diner. I tried to make sense of it, but couldn't. You must have sensed my agitation.

"I did sense something. . ." she said. "I thought you were intense, maybe that it was the way you were with everyone?"

"No! That's just it, Sabrina, I'm not. I like to think of myself as steady, logical and grounded. But suddenly I felt giddy and wary of some kind of trick being played on my mind.

"Tell me about it," she said. "I've been having those experiences for a couple of months now. In fact, I think I know what you saw. It was—"

But suddenly George asked if he could get the other line. He came back a moment later saying that his boss was calling about something important, and that he had to go. "I can call you back in a while, but honestly, Sabrina, I think this is a conversation we should have in person, don't you? We'll talk about it at length when I come in a couple of weeks. Very strange business, this," he said. "My darling girl, do I know you? Yes, I do! I know you from an alternate fucking universe! But now that we've met up in this one, I'm not going to let you to slip away from me! Can you promise you won't?"

But before she could answer, he said, "Try something for me, will you, Sabrina? Try setting the intention of dreaming about us tonight. I'll do the same. Nathan isn't the only one who has 'the gift of sight'. Are we a House? Is that a symbol for what we are? Dreams speak in symbols, don't they? Do this experiment with me, will you?" The phone kept beeping in between his words. "I'm sorry—I Gotta go, Babe!"

"Of . . . course," she said to herself, after he'd hung up. And she thought that in the next conversation they would have—whether on the phone or in person—she would tell him about her inter-dimensional travels with Mr. G. She'd been reticent to say anything up until now. It wasn't something one brought up in conversation with someone you were just getting to know. Crazy-making, that.

Preparing for sleep, just as an exercise she allowed her mind to abide peacefully in a place where two opposing ideas could live as equal possibilities without conflict: Love for a prophet and his teachings (Jesus, Mohammed, Joseph Smith) or love for the ordinary person standing directly in front of you? Or how about this: Standing for a cherished dream, or the transcendence of the cherished dream?

She noticed that from every point of view, a different set of opposites emerged until she finally chose peace and only peace. Sifting anxiously through all the opposing realities, she stood at last apart from them all. Could she simply observe the effects of choosing, and just let all things be as they are?

In fact only two weeks ago, hadn't she just been in a lively phone conversation about this very thing with her mother? They'd been talking about how hard it was to hold two different possibilities in mind; in this case: 'God's will vs 'My will'.

Blanche Ryder, in her wonderfully idiosyncratic way, had said, "Through this whole thing with your brush with death, I wasn't comforted when people told me to have faith. And I couldn't figure out why. Then one day after fasting and praying, I thought I'd try meditating a bit; you know, just sitting in silence, in honor of you sweetheart. Of course I don't know how to do it, and I didn't expect anything to happen. But I thought that you had told me once that it wasn't about getting answers really, but coming to some kind of peace? And by this time, that's all I wanted. The outcome was so uncertain and faith was getting me nowhere, because it was entirely focused on, 'The Thing I Wanted to Happen'. In this case, on you sweetheart, staying alive and getting well.

"So I was just sitting there, not knowing what to expect, when this idea floated to the surface of my mind: faith wants an object or an outcome to hope for, to believe in. In other words, we 'have faith' that things will turn out the way we want them to. And if they don't, we think we didn't have *enough* faith. Or that we were somehow unworthy.

But then from way down deep underneath all my fears, this beautiful wisdom—the one I always thought resided in a mind separate from my own?—said this: 'Isn't it much easier and simpler just to trust? Trust has no object. I could just trust in whatever happens, like something much bigger than my little life is going on here. And maybe I don't know what is the best outcome. I couldn't believe it, Sabrina," she said tearfully, "But I got this sudden and astonishing peaceful feeling after that; like it was the answer to . . . well, everything. To just trust things as they actually happen, instead of plying Heavenly Father with all my special requests. And the thought of Trust filled my mind with a kind of—I don't know—exquisite 'bliss'? And I didn't even know if that meant you were going to live or not! Oh, don't take this the wrong way, Sabrina, dear. It's not that I didn't care; it's just that I really, really knew for the first time that I could trust things as they actually happened. And that the only prayer I would ever have after that was to accept things as they are.

"Isn't that the craziest thing? But it gives me such peace. And I guess, after all, that's the only thing I want. Peace. I was practically ecstatic for three days, kind of like King Lamoni in the <u>Book of Mormon</u>. You remember the story, don't you sweetheart?"

"Of course I do, Mother. I love that story," she said. And she noticed in the following weeks and months that her mother seemed much stronger than even her father. In fact, from then on Mrs. Blanche Ryder fairly lit up the room whenever she walked into it. She was, Sabrina thought, in some essential way, changed; changed in her need to be certain about things. She seemed instead to be lighter and more curious about life, as though the Great Unknown was a delight instead of fearful. The old Blanche had died and had exploded into a brilliant radiance, annihilating every other altar (devotion) but this: *Trust would settle every problem now.*[72]

Her father, on the other hand, seemed ever so slightly more despondent and troubled, no matter how much Sabrina tried to cajole him out of it. It was a strange puzzlement indeed, like something had invaded their bodies and switched them out. What a wild ride Life could take you on! Change, the divine catalyst.

Who'd have guessed? Her mother enlightened, because she could no longer be certain about anything? And her father—in his sudden need for certainty—had become the grist of some unyielding set of beliefs that would no doubt grind him up and spit him out when it was time.

"Out beyond all right-doing and wrong-doing, there is a field. I will you meet you there. When the soul lies down in that grass, the world is too full to talk about . . . Why do you stay in prison when the door is so wide open? . . . Sell your cleverness and buy bewilderment!"[73] said Rumi, the poet.

Maybe 'bewilderment', Sabrina thought, is about being so confused by our own interpretations of life, we finally begin to see them as meaningless. So we just simply start trusting the world to be as it is. And in this strange bewilderment we learn to love life as it happens,

*instead of trying to control it or even figure it out. And maybe that . . .
is 'the peace that passeth all understanding?'*

In Biblical mythology, after all, it wasn't the fruit of the Tree of Good and Evil that God had forbidden in the Garden. It was the fruit of the <u>Knowledge</u> of Good and Evil; thinking we know what is good and what is not. And we begin to imagine a physical world with solid facts, solid truth; solid walls, immovable, immutable, imprisoned in our own concepts of right and wrong. Then comes the Exodus from the Garden, lies and the propagation of lies. Sacrifice. Lack. Who's God's favorite? The first kill. Scrabbling over land and borders. Wandering in the Desert. Fighting to the death over real estate and philosophical differences. And the carnage never seems to end.

But in the myth, hadn't God Himself pronounced it all Good in the beginning?

Love nurses a child or straps on a bomb. Either way, it is explosive in its brilliant radiance. Either way, the altar of our devotion is obliterated. Because the child will eventually grow old and die. And the bomb will take innocent hostages. And the only thing one can do is stare in wonder at this world that Adam made, all because he pretended to know.

And she began to talk to the wisdom inside herself.

"To Whom it may concern: How can we get back to the Garden where we see everything as Good? How can we integrate this strange world of opposites? Oh, and what is the meaning of George in my life? And could I have a dream about us please?"

And nodding off, she thought as how her questions had very little to do with each other. Yet somehow she knew that if one of them could be answered, so could they all.

40

It is Written

Two weeks later, Sabrina was preparing to leave the hospital, thanking all the nurses with flowers, candy, and little holiday gifts that her mother had purchased for her. Not a few tears were shed as she said her goodbyes to all the night nurses that would be gone in the morning when she would take her leave.

One to whom she did not have to bid adieu was the Muslim; the grandfather, kind and gentle, whose Paradise had called him home a few days before. Right on schedule, apparently. With eyes that sparkled, he gave Sabrina the honor of holding one of his frail hands, while he waited for Mohammed to come for him in his chariot.

Tomorrow she would walk out of the hospital for good, still needing some serious rehabilitation, of course, but mentally and physically ready for the challenge. The real healing was always internal, Sabrina knew, and that seemed to be unfolding every day in some new and incredible way. And George had become an essential part of this unfolding.

At bedtime, she read from The Lazy Man's Guide, as a prelude to meditation. She especially loved the last sentence in the book: "But if one of you whom I never hear about gets a little higher and happier, then I would write all this again a thousand times over. I hope you find the vibrations pleasant."[74] This was ever his kind intent she thought; that she feel "a little higher and happier". And she did. But there hadn't been a visit from him for a few weeks now and she was starting to wonder if he would ever show up again. And neither had she had a dream about George and herself. Were the sliding doors between dimensions beginning to close for good?

George was coming in the morning to ride home with her and to stay a long weekend with her family for Thanksgiving. Her mother had insisted that Sabrina stay at the family home for the holidays, and she had happily acquiesced.

Her father and George got along famously it turned out, even though there was a slight urgency in her father's repartee now, unlike the easy going attitude he used to have when he and Sabrina would "talk shop," as he called it. The Bishop had tried several times, in fact, to get George to come to church with them while Sabrina was in the hospital, hoping it would eventually transfer over to her when she felt up to it. But George had protested that he was only there for a few hours each time, and it would be imprudent to spend any of it anywhere but by Sabrina's side.

"Sir, I will take you up on that when Sabrina can come with me," George negotiated. And Bishop Ryder seemed mollified.

It was comforting for Sabrina to know that the problem of her father's melancholy and his relief were in the same place. A reconciliation—an 'at-one-ment'—had already been accomplished. The Jews had a saying: "It is written". And that's the way it felt to her, ever since she had awakened out of her coma. Still, it wasn't easy waiting, seeing how much despair could ride on the backs of beliefs that were supposed to give one comfort. Painful as it was, however, she was determined to give her father the same courtesy he had always given her; to allow him his own process.

"This is the hardest thing anyone ever does," she thought, "to give a loved one the space to work it out for themselves. And she was starting to appreciate all her father and mother had gone through on her behalf. "He even has Jesus on his side and still it seems hard." Of course, Sabrina knew that this psychological symbol, this beautiful 'cryptogram' called Jesus, was on everyone's side, but she couldn't say that to her father. For one thing, he needed to have this Savior Man as his very own right now. It might have been his only real consolation.

"Why don't we question our beliefs rather than suffer through them blindly?" she'd asked George one night on the phone. Sabrina loved listening to him talk to her father about philosophy and religion when they visited her together at the hospital. But whenever Bishop Ryder felt he'd lost the high ground—which frankly was seldom— it was different now. He didn't have the same gentle unassuming manner he used to have. Their conversations had become a serious endeavor, and sometimes he seemed exhausted by the effort it took to make his point. It was no longer the easy, enjoyable and entertaining pastime when she and her father had bantered ideas back and forth of a Sunday evening. And though she didn't like having to choose between these two brilliant men, still she often found herself taking George's part in her mind, agreeing silently with him. She thought as how her father was drawn to him as much as she, for to hear them talk together was to see and feel an unexplainable connection.

And how should she and George manage the 'special relationship' thing? In fact, neither of them could figure out what was driving their need to be with each other. They understood, at least intellectually, that it was almost impossible to know another person, especially in the short amount of time they had spent together. Yet they both could see that engaging in relationship—special or otherwise— was a wonderful way to know *oneself*. In any case, it would be a grand experiment, and one they agreed would be the prime focus of their time together, whether expansive or diminutive. That part was uncertain.

*'We have said that to limit love to **part** of the Sonship is to bring guilt into your relationships, and thus make them unreal. If you seek to separate out certain aspects of the totality and look to them to meet your imagined needs, you are attempting to use separation to save you. How, then, could guilt not enter?"* [75] *ACIM*

Yet their love felt so uncommon, so exceptional, they wondered how they could keep from projecting onto each other these 'imagined needs', suffering therefore the requisite guilt. In this new egalitarian view of love, moving parts (the constellation of friends and family), how could they navigate with ease? And how she could see every person in her life as equally lovely, when this 'George aspect' was still blinding her to any other?

As these thoughts turned round quietly in her head, she slipped into a lucid meditation, drifting away from the world of hospitals and nurses and relationships. It seemed that she stood in the center of a maelstrom of mental activity, waiting for the dust to settle. She watched her thoughts, trying hard not to attach to any of them; curious but not involved. Except possibly for that one called George. How would she ever disentangle herself from that one?

41

Lovers don't finally meet somewhere. They are in each other all along.[76] *-Rumi*

As Sabrina closed her eyes, a figure appeared on the horizon of her mind. He floated into her line of vision and stopped short just in front of her, although she suspected he could have gone right through her if he wanted. Well of course he could. This was her dream after all. Still, she couldn't shake the idea that he was the one running this show. It was designed that way, she supposed, to give him an aire of authority, because usually she wouldn't give *anyone* that kind of leverage over her, especially a man.

Yet here she was, face to face with one who always got the drop on her. What did he want now? Was he going to tell her that she had to give up the George Toy? Fat chance. Did he think he had *that* much influence?

"There you are. How's the shoulder?" he asked.

"I'm pretty sure you know the answer to that one. In fact I think you probably know the answer to everything."

'Is that so? Well, you might be interested to know that I've developed a particular skill set which makes it possible for me to almost always be surprised by Life; a most interesting way to live."

"Oh yeah? Well then, my shoulder is mending quite well, thank-you. Can't you make it so the scars go away without surgery, Golas? I'm asking for a miracle here. How-s-about it?"

"I don't deal in magic. But if you care to move on up to my dimension, you might see some pretty spectacular results where that is concerned."

"Oh no you don't. I have work to do here, with someone who really thinks I'm swell, mind you. *He* seems to want a relationship," she chided, "sex and everything. Duality—I know. Apparently, I'm not done with it. So I guess that's what you came here to talk to me about, right? Whadaya think? 'Will it change some vast eternal plan' if I stay awhile in the 3rd dimension?

"I think I want to see him become President of the United States, Golas. I want little clones of him running around my ankles. –Well maybe not. I don't know. Actually, I think I want to do something much more creative than having children. I want to walk with him into a new world; one where the child in everyone comes alive as the Essential Fact of existence. I want to pioneer this world, help establish it. I want to watch it open up before our very eyes, and then play with some notion of Utopia. Community, as good as it gets, you know? Like the city of Enoch rising up into the clouds? What would that be like!? Truth is, I *want* to play in other dimensions, but I don't want to skip over this part.

"I want to be here when man discovers that his thoughts can turn to form in a Holy Instant.

In fact, I want to *be* that Man. And I want Georgie-boy to be with me when we do it. Have sex after and smoke a cigarette."

"Tall order."

"It's a joke, Golas. You know about jokes, don't you?"

Taking her hand and turning it over in his own, he said, "Sabrina, you and he are going to be great friends, maybe even life partners, although I hate to predict anything about the future. Bad business, that.

"You can practice everything I've taught you, on him. You can practice loving him the way he is. You can practice not resisting him. You can practice loving yourself, even when you're hating him, which believe me, you will think you do sometimes. You can practice being *willing to see things differently*,[77] *letting all things be exactly as they are*,[78] *choosing peace instead of anything else*.[79] You can practice remembering that *your safety lies in your defenselessness*.[80]

"Then by all means, go forth and set things right in the world, doing whatever makes your heart sing. You can practice learning to love hell until it becomes Heaven. And you know what else? You can practice The Eternal Pause. You really couldn't ask for a better deal. And quite frankly, George is the best we could come up with; The Ultimate Illusion, you might say, present company excluded, of course.

"Sabrina, darling girl, look at me," he said as he tucked his hand under her chin and raised it.

Was she imagining it or was he shifting softly back and forth from Golas to George, right before her eyes?

"I'm going to count backwards from 10 and then you are going to wake up (in the dimension of your choice), holding my hand. Only it won't be my hand exactly. It will be his, this George of yours, who, as it happens, is my own extension of love in this world; a creation I'm rather proud of. He's got a good grasp of Universal Principle by now, I made sure of that. He thinks he wants to be an architect. But there are a lot of surprises in store for him, I think. For you both.

"Remember, there's nothing you need to do first to be enlightened; just to know that the experience is always within you right now, as is my voice which you will learn to think of as your own."

She squeezed his hand in appreciation without saying anything, remembering that to emphasize the pause would be her greatest gift to him. Then suddenly an inexplicable grief tore at her, as she understood what he was actually saying.

"Wait Golas!—you're not going to keep being my Guide? I really need you and I've finally gotten used to being jerked around all those tricky inter-dimensional rabbit holes. I won't complain anymore, I promise! Really I think I've got the hang of it now, so—"

"Sabrina, darling, I can't let you cling to me like this or there's a danger you'll get hung up on *our* relationship and value it more than the ones you'll actually be having in your own world. That's the dis-ease of your world, you know; always emphasizing some far-away god in lieu of the one standing right in front of you. So you're going to have to forget all this for now, I'm afraid. Forget me and our travels together. Oh, but not the lessons.

"Remember that Love doesn't care how you get to it; so when in doubt, just go—"

"Beyond logic to Love," she said, her voice choked with tears, repeating the lesson as she had learned it.

"And remember, you can't do this thing wrong, my love. Not ever."

And counting backwards, he began to fade from her sight . . .

10-9-8-7-6-5-4-3-2-

One.

She woke the next morning into a world of family, friends, and a certain young architect named George Wright, and all the feelings attendant to him. It was 8 o'clock AM and he was holding her hand and reading, as he often did while she lay sleeping. But here was the deal: Sabrina was glad she had a moment to relish him before he turned to notice her. She wanted to savor the image of him, preoccupied and unaware of anything but his book. She couldn't know that this was a portrait she would cherish many times in their lives together, giving her the sweetest pleasure and sometimes the greatest challenge. In this moment though, she thought that he—just as he was—might be the most beautiful man she had ever seen.

Presently, he felt her focused attention and turned from his book. "Darling, you're awake! The nurse let me slip in while you were sleeping. Your dad picked me up at the airport and drove me straight here. He's out getting us some breakfast. Are you ready for the big move home?"

"I am. I am. I most certainly am! George, are you sure you're real?" she asked. "Because sometimes I wonder if I just made you up, and you're going to vanish one night, like a dream, while I'm sleeping."

"I'm real enough, sweet girl. You needn't worry about me leaving anytime soon; we have work to do together, you and I, don't we? A world to save, to cherish, and re-create? And how will we accomplish this impossible task?" he exclaimed with comic passion as he stood and planted an imaginary flag on imaginary soil. "I don't know, but it's a hell of a mission we've envisioned for ourselves, isn't it? Sabrina, my love, in the words of Edward Rochester, (and here he turned to face her, leaning forward on the foot of her bed,) *Will you 'be my second self and best earthly companion?'*[81]"

With eyes aglow she laughed, "Indeed Sir, I will."

And this was marriage, as sacred and beautiful as any altar in any temple, she thought. And she said, "You know what? You're sort of a modern day musketeer, aren't you, George Wright? A kind of . . . Swashbuckler?!" she said, cocking her head to one side and looking at him with relish, although from where she had got *that image*, she did not know.

42

Land Mines

"Do you think that we'll ever be released from this crazy romantic overload?" he asked. "I hear it doesn't last. And why does that *scare* me, by the way?" he said as his voice buzzed through her head. He was spooning her, doing that thing where he ruffled his mouth in her hair when he talked. It was "Sunday in the Bed with George", and he was staying at the townhouse for another extended weekend.

In the habit of spending half the week with her, and the other half in San Francisco, he had set up a drafting table in her dining room so that he could work from Salt Lake, and give moral support to Sabrina during her year of cosmetic surgeries and shoulder rehabilitation. His firm had agreed to let him work from Salt Lake at least eight days of the month, plus he had the weekends, so that gave him about four days a week to be with Sabrina. With all the new technology, it was easy to send renderings back and forth and to communicate ideas. And when necessary, he could go to a prominent architectural firm downtown, where (in trade for a little consulting on the side) they were more than happy to let him use their space and printing equipment.

Sabrina turned over in order to face him. It was early, but they were accustomed to waking up with the sun, around 6:00 am.

"What an odd opening line, Mr. Wright. Where have you been spending your nights? What dream world?" And she searched his face for clues.

He let his question stand, gazing at her with a hint of mischief.

In her imagination, she saw an image of herself in a voting booth somewhere, punching out a straight ticket. All the little boxes on the ballot had only one name: George Wright. And with every poke of the stylus she marked her fierce, lunatic love for him.

She couldn't decide whether she liked him better clean shaven, or like this, with a scruffy morning shadow. Sometimes she begged him to let it go for the whole weekend. She liked begging him. Just now, for instance, he looked like he belonged on a TV detective series, and she wished he was handing her a warrant to search her for something; anything really, just so long as it was *thorough*.

Still she tried to make him squirm. "You're telling me that it's possible for *you* to be scared like a little girl?"

He pushed some strands of hair out of her eyes.

"Romance—so trying, isn't it?" she said sarcastically. "I wonder if it's just a necessary evil, something we have to go through before coming into a larger love, a broader understanding of it anyway. But it *is* a little bit like walking though a field of land mines isn't it?"

Yeah, he thought. *She understands.* "That's an interesting visual," he said. "Is that the way it feels to you sometimes?"

She contemplated the image in her mind. "Well, for instance, I see how *you*—in your innocent, gorgeous way—tend to attract woman. Of all ages, mind you. Men too, actually. I saw one of Nathan's buddies looking at you across the room the other night. I think if you'd turned around and smiled at him just in that moment, his knees would have buckled right there in the entrance hall.

"Sabrina, you are waxing satiric again. You don't really—"

"Let me finish darling. I know you don't see it. That's part of your charm. And the funny thing is, it might be what I love most about you: that you're attractive to lots of people, that you appear to command their attention and admiration with such ease. But I also watch my mind get all twisted up in jealousy sometimes. I hate to admit it, but it's as though you are this Field of Amazing Focused Attention, and I can hardly bare it when that attention is turned away from me and given to someone else. Oh my gosh, do I sound mad, selfish; unreasonable? Well. It's embarrassing, and not easy to admit."

He propped himself up on his elbow and laid his hand on her stomach beneath the sheet. Even after a year it still felt like the hand of God, and she sensed the warmth of it like it was nature's way of saying, "I've got you. You're safe with me."

He smiled at the prospect of pleasing her with just one touch.

She went on. "I think we humans have trained ourselves to believe that love comes from somewhere outside ourselves; from God or parents, lovers, or whatever. But I'm starting to see that this Loving Attention is something I've got to learn to give myself first— in spades probably; so that I can learn to feel it moving in and through and as me. What would *that* be like? So maybe the trials of romance are there to turn us back on ourselves, so we can really learn to love properly, from the inside out? Because, for you to expect love to always come from me—for instance—in just the way you like it, well that's insane, isn't it? And vice versa?"

He seemed amused, but said nothing.

"Are you horrified?"

His response surprised her. "I had no idea you felt jealous, you little minx. I feel like such an unconscious dolt. You've never said anything."

"Well, of course not," she said, teasing him with a smile, "I wouldn't want you to change for my sake, and anyway I love and hate it, all at the same time, like I said. It's bewildering, confusing. And why would I speak from that confusion? So while some woman is adoring you and you just happen—in your accidental charm—to be looking at her, adoring her in your own way—"

"But I don't—"

"You do, Georgie. You are so good to those you speak to, kind and considerate, they can't help loving you and then it sets up a cycle of respect and love that can't be denied or stopped, nor should it be. And honestly? If people—women in particular—weren't attracted to you in just that way, I probably wouldn't be either. Isn't that crazy?"

"I think I understand," he said. "It's almost exactly how I feel. I just hadn't thought of it that way. I see how other men are attracted to you and it makes me proud and a little afraid at the same time . . . But I guess I sooth myself by fancying that you 'sparkle' more when you're with me," he said with an uncomfortable chuckle. He was rarely uncomfortable about anything.

She tried to think what she did that made him believe she was sparkling. But he was right; that was *exactly* how she felt when she was near him. Sparkly.

"But what if one day you should stop?' he continued. "I do worry about that sometimes, when I wake up in the middle of the night and see you lying there so unaware of my desires. I realize that in some wildly odd compartment of my mind, I have it wired that you're supposed to always be attendant to them," and he laughed. "My desires, that is. It's like you were taken from my rib—I can see why the story is written like that now. It's the way it literally feels, like you still belong inside me, where no one can get at you. There. That's my embarrassment. And I don't even know if I want it to be different."

"I'm not sure we can do anything about it anyway," she said quietly, as she reconnoitered his body with her eyes. "Except to observe and be aware of it; to love ourselves when the other seems preoccupied? Which happens for me, as often as not, when you are reading a book, by the way. Go figure. Those books are lovers too and they take you so much further away from me than any woman ever could. But I use those times for . . . hmmm . . .mindful masturbation." And she laughed her own choice of words. "I'm talking about this as a mental process, of course. I know how to take care of myself, Mister. It's a great zen practice.

"I notice I'm there with myself," and she kissed him in between each 'notice'. "I notice I'm still alive. I notice I am breathing. And I notice I can feel Love anytime I want, maybe not *from* you, but certainly *for* you. And oddly then, I'm fulfilled, without a single prop from anywhere outside myself.

"And after watching how you are with women, I sometimes practice it myself (what I see you doing) with other men; being present with them and loving them fully, right where they are, without making it into a flirtation or a sexual thing. I've even tried it with women. *Especially* the ones who seem to groove on *you*," she said with a rueful sideways glance.

He laughed and she fell right into it with him like they were caught in a strong current swirling towards—who even cared—oblivion?

They spent some time there, lost in pleasure. And after a delightful ride in the rough country of the sexual wilds, Sabrina flopped breathlessly onto her back with her arms spread open and exhaled, *"It's alright to have a good time!"*[82] And they both went down the laugh tunnel again. What a way to spend the Sabbath; not exactly a day of rest, but hey—a day of play? Could have the same effect.

Kissing the scars on her shoulder as though they were the most beautiful thing about her, George said quietly, "So. Should I be worried?"

"Hmmm?" she said lazily, not catching his drift at first. Then walking her fingers up his chest, she said, "Well I think you better, Skippy. I might get the hang of this thing so well, that I won't need to be 'the beautiful reflection of my love's affection'. You know what? I think it will all work itself out if we just keep taking care of our own feelings, instead of taking our cues from each other."

"I'm with you on that. But it's a big assignment, isn't it?" And after a moment's silence, he said with a smile, "I like knowing you are jealous though . . ."

"I know, right? It's fun to feel this way as long as we don't get into trying to change each other or take it too seriously."

He waited and then dropped a little mortar shell into the quiet of the moment. "There *is* something I would like to change though, Sabrina."

She looked at him, pulling away just a little.

"I want you to consider coming to live with me in California. The days I spend there are dull and lifeless without you. You said once you that could find a publishing house in San Francisco that would give you more money and opportunity to move up than this little one here in Utah. Now that you are feeling stronger, wouldn't it be a good time to consider it? We could come back here as often as you like, I promise. But we'd be together and I have this weird feeling . . . like there isn't enough time—I don't know how to say it—but that I shouldn't waste a moment apart from you. Like 60 years won't be long enough somehow. It's probably just fear talking, unwarranted I know. But would you humor me, like the adolescent that I am?"

She was stunned, for reasons she had harbored in her heart from the first time they had met. "Really, George? Because I thought you liked it, this arrangement. I've always had the feeling that you liked your time alone there. And I'm really fine with it too, I am. Are you sure you won't feel . . . I don't know, trapped or held captive?"

"Whatever do you mean, silly girl? How could I feel trapped? Have I ever given you that impression even once in all our time together? Because if I have, I can't imagine how; I'm just about the most codependent, sorry son of a bitch I know. Just bringing this up makes me feel like I'm ten."

"But you said that you usually end up feeling pushed or manipulated by women. I heard you say that once and I've never forgotten it."

"Women! Yes! As a category. My mother—she— I was her only child, and she expected . . . so much. It's why I left home early. But you, Sabrina, *you* are not 'women'!"

"Oh. Well— I'm . . . I'm . . . Should I be flattered? Are you saying I'm more like a friend? A Man? Is it because I like to wear my father's old suits and ties?" she asked defensively.

"No! Sabrina, my love, no! You are the most feminine—oh how stupid I am for putting it the way I did. But you have taken me hostage alright. You're my muse, my friend, my lover, my perfect idea of A Woman. You are all that without having any of the negative qualities I've always attributed to the whole tribe!"

"Hold on there. I'm part of that tribe."

Well, of course. This is all coming out wrong. Forgive me, but there's something that women represent to me collectively that I've admittedly been suspicious of and I'm sorry about that, I truly am. But I suppose I needed to have one—just one—come to me the way you did. Whoever's in charge of these things—"

"Wait. You think someone is in charge; like there's a cosmic relationship bureau or something?" she asked with a hint of sarcasm.

"Sabrina. You know what I mean. It felt like serendipity meeting you, that's all. Anyway, 'the gods'—however you may interpret them—must have known I couldn't have fallen in love without the dreams, the uncanny kinds of things that happened to us along the way. And then you are so absolutely opposite from my idea of most women. You have a way of being aloof; objective, indifferent, quite as though you don't need me at all, yet you give the impression that you just sort of like having me around. That's comforting and very attractive to me somehow. You're an anomaly. You are a woman, but you are not 'women'."

"Hmmm," she acknowledged, and wanted to laugh, but thought better of it. Not just now. He seemed so serious, so earnest about it. And anyway she thought she understood what he was trying to say. She remembered her relationship with Ben, and that he had sometimes said he felt discounted by her. She even thought he had also used the word, "aloof". Back then, it often seemed like the only way to get through the trying times of their relationship without going mad or overreacting. And she thought that meant that there was something wrong with her.

Yet, she had encountered none of those ups and downs with George, and had attributed it all to his lovely steady nature. She never thought that she had been indifferent to him, certainly. But was it possible that she had been unconsciously watching out for the same dynamics she'd experienced with Ben, and had overplayed it a little? So now, it was a good thing? The world of duality was certainly unpredictable. What was 'bad' in one part of her life now seemed 'good' in another. Go figure.

Here she had been served up this passionate lover; one that actually thought there was something great about her 'indifference'. And she was content to see that when she had followed her heart, though it may have taken her far from the familiar and comfortable path she'd known, still it brought her here to this almost perfect man and his peculiar way of seeing things. Of seeing her. And she thanked the gods, the universe, and her own dear heart, for the journey.

She remembered her mother's epiphany, the one where Trust had suddenly burst in on her consciousness and changed her life forever.

"Trust will settle every problem now". That seemed like a promise Sabrina could hang her hat on.

43

Back to the Future

Her mother was weeping into the phone, "It's a heart attack, Sabrina! Please, can you come right away?"

Sabrina and George were just pulling out of a long winter's nap, after a Christmas Eve gathering with friends the night before. 4:00 AM said the digital clock on their bedside table. "Yes, Mom. You know we will. We'll book a flight and be there in a few hours, okay? What does the doctor say?" George forced himself awake as he watched her grab underwear and socks off the floor, staggering on one foot and then the other, listening to the particulars her mother rehearsed in amazingly clear detail without actually going to pieces.

Within 45 minutes, they were zipping along hwy 101, from Napa Valley to the Oakland Airport.

"It's not good," Sabrina told George, "He's in the ICU and they aren't expecting him to make it through the next couple of nights. No chance of a transplant for some reason. Neil will pick us up at the airport and take us right to the hospital. Sadie's coming down from Idaho this afternoon. Oh, George, I guess I knew this was coming one day, but 60! He's still so young. It's really unbelievable. Are you okay getting off work? I don't want to come back until— well, until everything is—" And she wailed like a child, giving herself fully to the Grief. It felt pure and cleansing.

Neil found them at passenger pick-up #7. Sabrina's eyes were puffy and red, and she hadn't eaten, even though George had made her toast and coffee before they left. He asked if Neil could stop to get her something on the way.

"No, please," she said, "Could we just go straight to the hospital? I can't waste a single minute. Is that okay?"

"Of course, honey, but it will just take—"

"I can *do* without food! I can't abide it if I don't have every last minute with him!"

George gave Neil the signal to get them to the hospital as fast as possible.

Individually, they were remembering the last time they'd all been together under similar circumstances, four years ago when Sabrina had been the target of a hoodlum's shotgun. After a couple of cosmetic surgeries, she still didn't look exactly 'as good as new', like the doctor had promised, but she was quite proud of the scars anyway. And George had been the kindest of caretakers in ways that no one ever would have imagined, least of all himself. Was it the guilt that had driven him to be so tender, so absolutely dashing, selfless, and attentive? Maybe. Certainly, he didn't know. But it had bonded them in a way—well, they just knew that they were in this time bound relationship for real, and for as long as Love held them there.

Sabrina's mother had gone home for a much needed nap just before they arrived. And when they got out of the car, Neil (a student at the U of U) explained that he had to leave for a few hours to take an important test.

Now, as Sabrina and George stepped out of the elevator and dashed toward the room where her father lay semi-conscious, she tried to calm herself, knowing that her anxiety would not be helpful on this holy ground. So she stopped and waited for a moment to compose herself, touching her forehead against the door.

That Eternal Pause

She had learned to do this with great elegance over the last few years. Though she couldn't exactly remember where she'd latched onto it, still it seemed to be the finest gift, a legacy from somewhere deep inside her heart. In the beginning it had been difficult, wrenching her untamed mind away from the 3D circus out there. But as she mastered this one little trick, it seemed to do more to change the quality of her life than almost any practice she had tried. It was a way of staying in constant meditation, while sometimes looking very busy in the world of doing.

"Help me, Father," she prayed, not knowing whether she was speaking to the Source of all Being or the earthly father she was about to encounter. Somehow, in this moment, it felt the same and she knew it didn't matter. The feeling was the thing. "Follow the feeling," her inner voice was saying. 'Father' was an altar of devotion so much bigger than most. As ideas went, it pervaded a significant part of her mind, and was certainly one that could take her into a world beyond words.

"George, can you give me some time alone with him? You won't take it personally if I ask you to wait a while before coming in?" she petitioned.

"Oh— no. Of course not. I'll go get something to eat. You take all the time you need. My place here is to get you through this in any way that suits.

"But you and Dad are so close. I don't want to keep *you* from saying *your* goodbyes. It's just that I have a distinct feeling that he and I need to—"

"Don't think of it, Sabra. Not now. Not in this moment," he whispered in her ear as he pulled her into an embrace. "I'll have my time with him, whether in the flesh or by some other means. Life is so remarkable these days I wouldn't be surprised if he visits both of us in separate dimensions at the same time. Why not? Anyhow, leave me to find my own way to him," and kissing her on the forehead he said, "This way is yours; through this door."

So in she went. And there he was, this cherished father, who had tried so hard in the last few years to get Sabrina to 'see reason', to come back to the life he had imagined for her. Long conversations, entreaties that went late into the night, until Sabrina could hardly bare to see him so distraught and strung out on beliefs that would not let him rest until he'd 'got her back into the church'.

Yet they had been closer than ever. And John Ryder had loved George like a son.

Finally, after two years, she had moved to San Francisco, partly because she and George simply couldn't live separate from each other even for a few days a week, and partly because it seemed prudent where her father was concerned. Perhaps he would find himself a bit more acclimated to her choices if he didn't see her so much. While living in Salt Lake, seeing him *less* had simply not been an option. He was such an integral part of her life.

And—wonder of wonders—her mother was so amazingly released from her old way of seeing things, that it was a delight to spend time with her also. Blanche Ryder could hardly have been more accepting of Sabrina's own way of thinking if she had left the Mormon faith altogether. Except that she hadn't. She loved the

Mormon culture. No, she would stay, often finding herself with tears flowing down her cheeks in the midst of a hymn or during the "sacrament" (the Mormon communion). Yet did she love Sabrina with all her heart, just as she was, without seeing a reason to change anything about her. Trust was a living thing in Mrs. Ryder's heart now. And together, she and Sabrina seemed to have their own version of church whenever they spoke in spiritual terms. It wasn't even necessary to choose their words carefully because Love was their first language.

Everyone noticed the change in Mrs. Ryder. Church members talked about it behind her back, in a good way. Although Neil, who had returned from his two year mission in Brazil, thought she seemed a little unpredictable. After all, hadn't she always taken the high ground in any conversation about right and wrong, good and evil? For all her nagging, she'd always been a rock of faith in his life. Now she seemed totally neutral about everything. Where was her moral compass anyway? He even missed the nagging a little. He might have said that she'd thrown the baby out with the bathwater, but she hadn't thrown out the bathwater. So what had happened? Sometimes he wondered if all women were just a little unstable.

Bishop Ryder, on the other hand, was grateful every day of his life for his wife's strange new way of seeing things. He couldn't have born this pain over Sabrina otherwise. Indeed, his wife seemed illumined, and completely disinterested in anything that emphasized their differences with Sabrina, or anyone else for that matter. It seemed she saw only love where ever she looked, like wearing rose-colored glasses, except that she never took them off. Even in bed she seemed lit up, almost as though there was some kind of ambient lighting in the room, shining from somewhere unseen. She held him at night with such tenderness, it helped him sleep. And she didn't even *try* to stop him from feeling this deep grief, knowing somehow that it was something he had to work out for himself, something

Patricia York

between him and his Heavenly Father. And John Ryder loved her for it; loved God for making her that way, however inexplicable the change.

Once a Bishop, always a Bishop. But he had recently been released from that position, because he had 'fulfilled his calling', as they said in church circles. Having a lay ministry meant that everyone did things in shifts. He'd been the 'father of the ward' (the parish) for seven years, a longer time than most. As a Bishop, he was first rate and the congregation loved him, but toward the end it seemed to everyone that it had taken its toll on him. Or maybe it was his heretic daughter who had brought him to such exhaustion? Everyone wondered.

But the Bishop didn't blame his daughter. It was all own his fault, he thought, and he was paying for it as well he should. "Pride goeth before the fall," the proverb said. The 'pride part'—his pride in Sabrina's intellect—had seemed right and strong and authentic, at the time—when he hadn't recognized it was pride. But later, after her near death, he was pulled up short, and realized that the 'fall' part was the more forceful dynamic in the equation. Now here he lay in this inter-dimensional purgatory, this life between lives, waiting for the worst. He was dimly aware that his wife had just left his bedside and so he had no touchstone, no voice to chant him home, and to remind him of the physical reality he was leaving for this other one, this uncertain one, the unknown path into oblivion.

The thing is, he hadn't really imagined it would be this serious in the end. He'd always thought things would go smoothly, that the journey would get brighter from here; more celebratory. Light beings and joyous— well, he didn't know. He'd never really thought about it that much. Well it wasn't supposed to be like this! Things he'd left undone haunted him; things left till the last minute, important things that should have been settled by now. How had he not accomplished them? It felt as though he were being pulled down into a pit of despair so deep that there seemed to be no way back to sanity, to the love he had known for most of the second half of his life.

Alone in this leaden misery, he was falling into something dark and dangerous with no one to hold his hand, to pull him back. And what was it that he could see down there anyway? A prison? A barricade of some sort? And a dark shadow crossed the landscape below. It was an old phantom he knew well. An avalanche of terror came thundering into his mind, paralyzing him with fear. For there it stood: this monster, the dragon who had reigned over his life with blood and horror for 17 years of his youth, and how many more in the lives of his three brothers? He descended slowly timidly into the depth of this terror with only one desire: to stop this ogre from hurting anyone else. If it took an eternity, he—John Ryder—would have to accomplish this one thing at least, to keep this fiend from hunting down more innocents; administrating more desolation, more agony and privation on helpless victims; like his precious heretic daughter, for instance.

Sabrina walked into the room and pulled down the railings of his hospital bed. Slipping off her shoes, she slid on top of the sheets, holding her father as close as she dared. He was white as the sheets on which he lay; his eyes roaming back and forth under the lids like little marbles. He seemed distressed beyond belief. Why would he be in so much anguish with the narratives of Mormonism so beautifully leading the way? She thought he must be suffering from the medications and she whispered into his ear.

"Father." She couldn't think of what else to say.

"Sabra? Wha— what? Sabrina? . . . Is that you?" he mumbled in a kind of hazy, uncharacteristic drawl.

"It *is* me, Daddy. Will you take my hand?" And she reached across his chest for his right hand, intertwining his fingers with her left.

"Take your— I can't take your hand!" he murmured wildly. "You mustn't be here, Sabrina! You leave this instant! Your Daddy is busy right now!"

"No, Poppy, I'm not leaving," she said with greater intensity. "I'm just here, right beside you and I'm not leaving." And she tucked her head beneath his chin, snuggling into the familiar Silence she had grown accustomed to, ever since he had challenged her to "meditate on it" those many years ago.

She wished he could realize how far into herself that one invitation had taken her. And she wished he could follow her there now.

44

Out Beyond Right and Wrong

The funeral was a typical deep-hearted Mormon one, with alternating elements of humor and touching sentiment. Stories of Bishop Ryder's life (strangely absent of any childhood tales) were full of good fun and the many kindnesses he had done over the years, in and out of his ecclesiastical term of office.

Generally, with very few exceptions, only Mormons were asked to speak for and about the departed, and since Sabrina was no longer an active church member, she was initially left off the roster of speakers. But Blanche Ryder wouldn't hear of it, and before it became a real problem that could cause hard feelings, as the current Bishop supposed, he gave in and didn't make an issue of it. How could he have known that Sister Ryder would never have let anything get in the way of her peace, her love for the ward and for Bishop Anderson himself? She was just simply very clear that Sabrina was to take part, and apparently her clarity carried the day.

The whole family gave short reminiscent talks and Sister Ryder even had the good Bishop Anderson—as a peace offering—read the eulogy. Of course he did the expected thing at the end—again, typical of most Mormon funerals—an earnest plea that each of them look deep into their heart and ask for a "testimony" of the truth.

Well, the Mormon truth, to be exact. And why not? It was their turf, wasn't it? In this building the truth was exactly as it was meant to be: an emblematic hall of mirrors reflecting infinite generations of family dynasties disappearing into the horizon, where Mormons sat and partook together the banquet of eternal life, notwithstanding the joke Sabrina had heard on occasion where St. Peter had said to an inquirer standing at the gates of heaven, "Shhhh. That's the Mormons. They think they're the only ones here."

Indeed, there was no end to this sweet domestic empire of love. Who sat at whose table? That part hadn't been worked out yet, Sabrina mused as she watched her own beloved family cry alternating tears of joy and sorrow.

She knew that her father would now chuckle at some of the literal interpretations of this picture of eternity that he loved so well. And he would have good-heartedly asked Bishop Anderson if he could work it out in his mind, the seating arrangements at the dining tables in those Celestial realms. Would the children who are grown and married have their own tables, or would they prefer to sit at the ancestral sideboard? And with each question so kindly put, so good-natured and humorous, his fellow priesthood holders would have had to laugh and agree that very little could be known about specific future seating arrangements from a factual, unvarnished viewpoint.

Which always brought one back to the truth of The Moment.

"My father was a marvel at finding beauty in each Holy Instant," Sabrina said in her short talk. "He was very much about experiencing the incredible feeling of being alive each minute of this amazing life he came to live. He rarely lived in the past or the future. In fact, I only learned about some of his extraordinary childhood hardships at the very end, watching at his bedside as he tangled with a few ghosts from his youth. My, how we never know the angels that walk beside us, that raise us to the light, so we can breathe the air infused with *their* hard-earned wisdom.

"I am the child of your wisdom, dear Father. I am that breath of your breath, and I would use it to bless the world, as you have taught me to do."

Sabrina had tried to find his brothers in southeast Missouri. The day before the funeral, she had finally got the youngest one on the phone. He was seemingly unmoved by his brother's death, having had no contact with him since he was very young. Apparently, all the brothers lived within hours of each other and had written their oldest brother off. And she found out a few things: her father had *tried* to communicate with them, but they judged him harshly for going to university and joining up with the Mormons. They were the product of an 'Ozarkian' backwoods upbringing, with pretty strong feelings about family loyalty and ideologies.

John Ryder Sr. had died several years ago and his oldest son had not attended the funeral. Sabrina thought she remembered her father worrying over that decision, whether or not to go. He had just made professor, but that didn't seem to be the problem. He was inordinately anxious, she recalled, which was not like him. He wouldn't talk about it to anyone, not even her mother. But now that she'd had this exquisite, tender experience with him on his deathbed, she understood it a little more. And it just seemed prudent to leave off trying to contact the rest of his brothers, knowing the way they felt.

Anyway, her experience with her father that day in the hospital bed certainly made sense now in the light of all this new information. That had been a week and a half ago, and Sabrina couldn't have let her father go so easily had she not given herself fully to that deathbed experience. As soon as she'd taken hold of him, he began to sob like a child. She was glad that no one else had been there, because it was such an intimate act. And when she had closed her eyes, she seemed to enter a sacred realm; sacred because she was privy to a sight she never thought to see: her father became a child again, and facing something so terrifying, he'd clung hard to her. At first, she thought his blood pressure would spike and that would be the end of it.

But that's not what happened. With her beside him, holding him, he was able to look directly at a thing he'd hidden for a lifetime. At first Sabrina didn't know what it was, but then she understood. It was his father; this beleaguered, lonely old man, who had waited all this time—in some kind of holding tank, it seemed—to see his son. Then she realized that the 'holding tank' was her father's own mind. And it really was a steel trap, the kind they always talk about when someone has held so much in for so long.

She encouraged her father to sit by and feel his feelings about this old curmudgeon, this dragon of a man. She kept hearing, *"The holiest of all the spots on earth is where an ancient hatred has become a present love.*[83]*"* And boy, did she have a front row seat to the Theater of Forgiveness. She'd never forget what it looked and felt like. And when all was said and done, she thought that she could forgive anyone anything. There seemed to be an angel there to help them through the process; someone she'd known from before? Or at least she thought she'd seen him somewhere in a dream or something, and he seemed essential to the process and very comforting.

When the task of dealing with his father was finished, John Ryder then turned to his daughter, and for several moments he was completely lucid. He appeared to have nothing left of the old anxieties or his need for her to come back into church activity.

He looked into her eyes and said, "'Out beyond all right-doing and wrong doing, there is a field. Will you meet me there,' Sabra?

I don't think Rumi was speaking in metaphor here." And then he seemed to drop into an illumined state, his eyes focused on some distant reality, like he was looking right through the ceiling.

"Love takes us beyond the walls we've built here on earth and lifts us up together as one," he said. Sabrina, my love, I'm so sorry I tried to get you to live your life differently for my sake. You are doing it just the way you should. How hard it must have been for you and George to hear me go on like I did, yet you were always so patient. . ."

"Shhhhh," she whispered.

Then he asked her if she would put his hand on her head so he could give her a father's blessing. And with a kind of wondrous strength in his voice, he blessed her with a continuation of the combination of genius and common sense that he'd always known her to have. He asked that she take good care of her mother, and he quoted Rumi once again, but this time it was from the poem, "Moses and the Sheppard".

"When you eventually see through the veils to how things really are, you will keep saying again and again, 'Ahhh, this is certainly not how I thought it was![84]*"*

Her father died in her arms that afternoon in such peace, and with such light-filled joy, that his countenance was lit up for hours after his passing, so that her mother, George, Neil and Sadie, could all see it for themselves, this miracle. There was no doubt he had been turning toward something in his final moments that fully engaged and delighted him in the most powerful way.

Nevertheless, Sabrina pondered the experience in her heart and kept her own council. She knew one day she'd share it. But not just yet.

45

The Gift

George flew back to California three days after the funeral. He'd been asked to speak at a small rally in California for Bernie Sanders, who was just gathering some political speed. Nathan and Sabrina were at once amazed, but not at all surprised, that George had agreed to do it since Sanders was a Democrat. George hadn't blinked, but accepted the invitation with wholehearted enthusiasm.

Because Sabrina needed to stay another couple of weeks to help her mother sort through her father's things and make some big decisions about what to do next, Nathan, who now lived in California also, accompanied George to the rally, and made a video of the event for Sabrina and her mother. They gathered with friends and family to watch it a few nights later.

"These are uncompromising principles we are speaking of here," George proclaimed with an orator's confidence. "Outrageous. I know that. But they are not new. The architect of these ideas was a real radical, a prophet on a hill. And two thousand years later, we're still talking about him. But to date, no one has seriously even tried living his revolutionary ideology." The crowd stirred, and he raised his voice so that he could be heard over the applause.

"This isn't about religion. It's hardly even about what we've called spirituality. It doesn't depend upon a personal God who champions our private points of view, rewards us for good deeds and punishes our enemies for bad. It comes down to simple, good environmental and psychological principles; living with each other in respect and trust and forbearance, for no other reason except that it feels good to do so!"

Here, the crowd went wild.

"Do you know what it is to feel entirely worthy of the air you breathe and the elixir of life that flows through your veins? The 'Kingdom of Heaven within' –is it just a metaphor? Or is it more factual than we dared hope; an invitation to an inner vitality, a synthesis of the romance of life and the peace of mind we all seek? Is it possible to achieve this in the external world through technology and a little good sense?

"And could we learn to welcome the Prodigal wherever he or she comes into view, whether in ourselves or out in the greater world? Isis, for instance; if we saw them simply as a collective Prodigal Consciousness, a misdirected devotion to a static ideal from the long ago past, could we somehow bring them home to sanity— just in our own hearts and minds? And would we kill the fatted calf? And how would this attitude change our world view?

"These attitudes I say have not yet been tried! And how can we seriously give up until—on this planet— we at least try them, once? And how might their application change our political and environmental landscape?"

Now people were standing up in front of the camera, so Sabrina could no longer see him, for all the frenzied multitude. She could barely hear the last few lines as he was completely drowned out by their cheers and shouts.

"And can we admit to the 'terrorist' in our own minds; the mentality that would rather launch little missiles of judgment onto the mental landscape, rather than extending a wholehearted desire to heal it?"

Sabrina saw in George Wright the beauty and strength of an authentic statesman, a leader of men. What would he do with this gift? Because even though he was pleased to help any campaign for equal rights, the environment, free public education and medical care, still he seemed less and less interested in politics. He'd even told her once that he, like H. D. Thoreau, felt called to a simpler life.

One night sitting together out underneath the stars, he said that he enjoyed his life with her too much to leave it for the greater dream he'd once envisioned for himself. And he was sure that the two of them could do the kind of good they were meant to do by simply living in congruity with life as it came to them.

Sabrina was embarrassed to admit that she could hardly wish for more than this herself. She loved their uncomplicated existence and yet she could see that he was meant for something more immense. There was this sense of him having been groomed by Life Itself for the healing of the planet. And sometimes she felt small and selfish when she thought of how little she wanted to give him up to this larger life.

However, that night, after watching the video, she opened her heart to the Universe, and put her devotion to this beautiful man—who'd been given to her for who knew how long?—on the altar of Love. It felt like an immeasurable sacrifice. And she knew there would be days and nights that she would wish that she hadn't been so magnanimous in this moment. It was entirely possible that this internal gesture would take him far away from the life they shared. Even still, she offered up The Gift, and the strangest feeling came surging back to her; that this was entirely appropriate, and that her acknowledgment and conscious good will was needed on some cosmic level.

She went to bed that night crying though she didn't know why. But a sudden grief bore down on her like the north wind blowing through her psyche. Yet her heart was strangely full of an abundant gratitude that felt like Generosity Personified; as though the Universe were rolling like a carpet at her feet.

46

. . .

Sadie was in her first year of college at BYU Idaho. And the night before she had to go back for end-of-term exams she and Sabrina sat together in the kitchen, talking and eating leftover homemade apple crisp that a friend had brought by. Perhaps because she was preoccupied with more important things, or maybe just because 19 year old girls are inherently self-absorbed, it had never occurred to Sadie that Sabrina's path was very much different from her own, even though she, herself, was still an active Mormon like her mother.

"Of course, each 'interior reality' is going to look a little different, don't you think?" she said to her sister as they chatted away while their mother wrote thank-you notes in another room.

"Careful, Sadie dear," Sabrina laughed. "You might be going down a slippery slope, allowing the Truth to be seen in different lights. It won't hold up in a church court," she said, referring humorously to that arcane ritual of excommunication still practiced by the Mormons.

"Why do you suppose they do that?" Sadie asked with a bit of bite to her words. "Just when someone needs our support, we ostracize them? Oh, not so you'd notice, by the way. They usually try to keep it secret. But it's pretty obvious if they aren't taking the sacrament or if they don't have a church job, so the guilt and shame must be terrible. I know it's meant to scare people into submission by losing something valuable—eternally valuable—but can fear and guilt really be the best motivators for good?"

"Why Sadie, you're a philosopher," said Sabrina. "And that's a good question. We know it's possible to be excommunicated from an institution, from a religion. But can one really be excommunicated from God? What say ye?"

"I'll tell you what, I've never thought about it before. But I'm going to. This is my church too, and I might have something to say about how it goes from here," Sadie affirmed.

Sabrina had never thought to stay and fight, or to think of the church as a society which belonged to its constituents. She'd always thought the constituents had belonged to *it*, and she supposed that was a big difference. She didn't care much for the idea of religion as a path for grownups, so she thought as how excommunication was as good an exit as any, though it surely seemed out of date and an old fashioned approach to modern problems.

The Church stood fairly well as a corporation, a village political posture, a charitable trust for third world countries and a support group for families. *And these are no small gifts,* Sabrina thought as she cleaned up the last of the dishes. But it wasn't a healthy psychological response to achieving adulthood; too much approval-seeking from authority (however deserving). "And there isn't a more emotionally co-dependent relationship than that between man and his Designated Experts," Sabrina whispered under her breath as she put away the cups and plates. Wisely, however, she had always kept these opinions to herself when Neil or Sadie happened to be in the room. This was a church about having no descent after all, and pretty good at presenting a united front in this. Keenly aware of discrepancies between old and new theological and political attitudes, Mormon scholars had picked their way carefully through historical documents, leaving the designated punctuation between words (. . .) when using direct quotes from the prophets of the earlier pioneering days.

In this way, Sabrina thought, the conditioned mind is able to hide inconsistencies, and it never has to look clearly at its own contradictions. "But there's nothing inherently wrong with contradictions, is there?" she asked out loud to Abby later that night, as they packed the last bit of her father's personal items into bins for storage.

And Abby had said, "I don't know, but it's how we evolve, isn't it? So why bother to cover them up? Why try to present a seamless face to the world as though it never had any problems growing into itself? My church has certainly learned that lesson, hasn't it now?"

"It looks like Sadie and her contemporaries might just be the ones to start changing social and political structures within the Mormon context." replied Sabrina. "And that would certainly be a new chapter in its history."

The next day, after seeing Sadie and Abby (who was now living in California also) off at the airport, Sabrina and her mother had some time to themselves. Neil was out with friends, and they decided to order Chinese and hang out in the quiet of the now empty house.

Blanche had been lit up with love through the whole funeral and for some days after, but tonight she needed to cry a bit. She wanted to begin releasing all those feelings that had taken a lifetime to accumulate, and she knew it would require some tears, maybe lots. Crying didn't scare her. She was acquainted with grief in her own way. Both of her parents had died in the last few years, and a sister as well. She was one who understood that love welcomes sadness as well as joy.

"Mother, why don't you come and stay with us in the wine country for a little while," Sabrina offered tentatively. "The Mormon community there is wonderful, I hear."

"Hmmm?" her mother muttered as though she were being called out from another world. "Oh, that sounds nice in a way, Dear. For a while anyway, while I do some personal grieving, I'd love to be near you and George. I could give myself a good cry in the day, and we could eat dinner together at night," she said, laughing through the tears. "But how would it look for me to live there? Don't you live with a bunch of other people? Do you have an extra bedroom or would I need to rent a place of my own somewhere in town?"

Excitedly, Sabrina said, "No, we have a bedroom/kitchen suite, a really nice one that no one has rented yet. There's nine of us altogether, some single, and three couples. And there's one couple—a man and his wife—who are just little younger than yourself. We met them working at a community garden center when we were buying some organic plants for our vegetable garden. They were interested in our idea of community and said they'd always wanted to live like that. We were immediately taken with them and so they joined us, and now we get all our plants for a discount. They also take charge of the vegetable garden while George and I fool around with the landscaping. You'd love it Mom! It's right on hwy 101 in the most beautiful part of the wine country.

"Oh, but you don't have to drink wine to appreciate it. Come to think of it, I think Susan—the wife in the couple I'm welling you about—said that she used to be a Mormon. She's very sweet; I think you'd like both of them. Oh we'd be so happy if you'd come! Should I call George? He could fly over to help us move your things.

47

The Expression Session

In the last year, Sabrina and George had made a momentous decision. One of the projects George's architectural firm had contracted to do, suddenly had the bottom drop out of it. A man who owned a small realty company had funded a high end bed and breakfast project with four houses on a three acre property in Napa Valley. When he had died, rather suddenly and unexpectedly, the whole endeavor had fallen apart. Apparently, everything hinged on this one investor's interest; the wife not so much. Faced with certain financial collapse and/or foreclosure, his wife had offered to sell it to the anyone in the firm for just a little over half of what they had put into it.

Since George had been doing most of the renderings for the undertaking, he was one of the first to hear about it. He had gone home to Sabrina that night and put the idea on the table; the little kitchen table that Sabrina had brought with her from Salt Lake; the one which had been the centerpiece for that lovely meditation years ago: "A table shares the purpose of the universe".

They were renting a small apartment in San Francisco, and Sabrina had secured a good job as an editor with Neil and Sons, a wonderful new publishing company based in San Francisco, that seemed hitched to a rising star.

So they both were making money and saving. In truth George had been saving for years; for what he hadn't known. Then one night, as they sat talking with friends at Harbin, a little hot springs healing resort near Calistoga Springs, he thought he suddenly understood the meaning of Nathan's dream: he and Sabrina were to be the innovators of a new way of living; for them at least. They would be 'parents' of a brainchild that had been floating around in his mind for years; an intentional living community based on mindfulness and creativity. Turned out Sabrina had been entertaining similar thoughts since her move to the west coast. And all the way home from Harbin they'd talked of nothing else. Talk about creation! Talk about an embryo seedling theory! Talk about your Immaculate Conception.

Sabrina told George about a pioneer community that had been conceived by her Mormon progenitors called, The United Order. "I know. It sounds a bit militaristic. And well, it didn't work out in the end because of some bad fashion design; they wanted everyone to wear overalls. Wouldn't you know it was the teenagers who dissented?" she laughed. "But I've always loved the idea and if we could have it be a less controlled environment, a more creative milieu, I don't see why it wouldn't flourish!"

As a matter of fact, couldn't they base it on nothing more than just being mindfully aware, and then supporting each other in whatever else they wanted to do individually? With an emphasis on creative energy, inspiration and deep insight? Perhaps sitting in meditation before making any big decisions? And the little ones—who cares, just go for it? A place of freedom from fear, from judgment, and from contracted, small ideas. It could become their statement to the world, their own social and political experiment for world peace.

George could feel hundreds of little synapses firing in his brain all the way home, thousands of crazy-ass conceptual sperm wiggling their tiny tadpole tails wildly upstream through some kind of Universal Vaginal Canal where they would pierce and impregnate some great big fat Soft Furry Ovum that would grow into—into what? Who knew? Networks of communities? Technologically based societies instead of money-driven? A whole new world! It was Disney-esque that was certain.

After meditating on the notion of buying the Napa property, they decided to place an offer which was accepted almost immediately. George had a good grasp of the problems involved for the remodel and he spent the month in escrow redesigning aspects of the project to suit their purposes. They added some kitchen appliances to the large bedroom suites, even though everyone would probably eat most of their meals together in the elegant dining room that was originally going to be a restaurant.

It was a big risk to jump in with both feet, but George and Sabrina decided to go with their gut and in a short time they had enough friends interested, that it would almost pay for itself. Nathan and Richard were up for it, and one of their other closest friends, Josh Levinson, and his girlfriend were also interested. Abby even said she might want to be included once they got it going. She'd always wanted to live in California anyway, she said, and was the first one to move in.

Josh and his girlfriend were pushing to use the restaurant for exactly that, say two to three nights a week. They'd always wanted to have a little bistro and there it was, right on the highway. Lots of Tuscany curb appeal too. Joshua thought that using it for public dining just three nights a week and one week-end night would give it a sort of specialized, "home grown" reputation. And they agreed to prepare food for the community on the other nights—the best organic foods—as a trade for the use of the restaurant until they could get it going. Sundays would be 'everyone for themselves'.

Sabrina sold the little townhouse in Salt Lake—which she'd been renting to Neil and some of his college buddies—and with the improvements she had done on the kitchen and the wonderful old closet—she made a tidy little profit to help with the down payment on the Sonoma property. Letting go old structures, psychological, spiritual and physical had become her delight. What could be better than what they had already? They were always just finding out, it seemed.

Meantime, these three acres on Hwy 101 in Napa Valley, with friends as 'family-in-residence', were just a little bit of Heaven.

And now Blanche Ryder was about to step into it with a gusto that would probably surprise even herself. As she and Sabrina packed her things the next few days—some small pieces of furniture, three suitcases of clothes—and found a young couple at church to house-sit for a year or so, she felt a sweet anticipation. As she lay in bed the night before they were to leave her beloved Utah home, her feelings were bitter-sweet, yet buoyant in a way that gave her solace. Who here would understand this crazy desire she had to step out into a new life and at her age too? Not entirely risky, since she could always come back, right?

Yes, she could always come back to this very, very ordinary life she had lived for sixty-some years; ordinary because—well—it had always been hers, just the way she'd wanted it. The ideal one. The Mormon one. The safe one. And it had never disappointed.

But now . . . now Life might serve her up some real adventure. And she wouldn't be entirely alone. She had her precious daughter beside her, whom she had learned to trust in a way that felt entirely appropriate. Everything was changing, and all she had to do now was to follow this Change into whatever uncertain future it was leading her. Yes, uncertainty was now her friend, her ally. It marked—not so much a path—as a way forward without promises and euphemistic sentiments. And all there was to guide her was her amazing, unpredictable Curiosity.

Grieving might take on an entirely new dimension in a community where all her conscious thoughts and feelings would be respected and encouraged into awareness; to be embraced by the collective heart of friends who would learn to know her from the inside out. In fact, she could feel herself sinking into the sumptuous sadness that would be her constant companion for the next few months; tears that would accompany her as she weeded the gardens, wrote in her journal, and took long walks. It was a picture she liked to imagine, although she didn't have the slightest proof that it would actually turn out that way. But for some reason, that was part of the joy of it, the exploit. She had no need for assurances and proofs anymore. It was enough to have the breath of life pulsing through her veins in this present moment.

They picked up George at the airport at 6:20 AM the next morning. Sabrina drove the first few hours, while George slept in the back seat.

"Now tell me about the community," Blanche said as she tried to put her makeup on in the car. "You said something about an 'expression session'. What is that exactly?"

"Well I guess you could call it ten minutes of uninterrupted public self examination," said Sabrina. "We can say whatever we want, but we're encouraged not to try to fix each other or comment on another's sharing unless it brings up something you want to look at in yourself. A community with a particular focus is called "intentional". The Mormon community is intentional. It focuses on the family as a path to God.

Our focus is on four main things: revealing thoughts we've hidden from ourselves and others; no 'people pleasing'; personal accountability; and supporting each other in our creative endeavors."

"What do you mean – 'no people pleasing'? That sounds rather mean spirited. Shouldn't we try to please others when we can?"

Sabrina smiled. "Well, I know we've believed that our best hope for a civilized society is that we try to get along by pleasing each other. However, that's based on the insane idea that if we revealed our true thoughts about anything, we'd never be pleasing to each other. So our values have been built on saying and doing what we *imagine* other people want. But how can we really know what that is without communicating clearly? So we're trying to take communication to a deeper level, you could say. Hopefully, we'll be able to please each other *and* be authentic as well; to tell our personal truth, while being completely accountable for the way we see things.

That's an important part of it. Turns out, you can live with almost anybody under those 'guidelines'. Remember 'guidelines' Mother?" she said with a little wink. And her mother laughed out loud.

"We often like to say: 'no private thoughts'. That is, no hidden agendas, not even from ourselves. The theory is that if each person is given 10 minutes to speak, to 'free-associate' in Freudian terms, our real feelings will bubble up to the surface and we can actually hear our own voices in a way that is very revealing. Personally, I think it's a key component to self-realization. I try not to have anything in mind when I start to speak for my ten minutes, unless I've had something floating around in there for a while; a persistent thought, call it 'good' or 'bad'. In that case, of course I want to get it up and out. The expression session is not for fixing problems though, nor working out problems. It's for pure expression. Sometimes I'm as surprised at the words that come out of my mouth, just as if they were someone else's."

"But then how *do* you work out problems?" asked Blanche. "Surely there must be a lot."

"Believe it or not, there are much fewer when we all show up for a short meditation and the 'expression session' *every morning*. So in our community, it's a kind of a deal breaker if you don't. But yes, when problems still persist, we use a forum similar to the expression session. We each start with ten minutes with the goal of getting out our feelings about the specific problem, after which those involved keep going around in 5 minute increments until every idea and feeling is heard.

"If the answer to the problem isn't obvious by the end of the session—say within an hour or so—we separate and take some 'tub time', a phrase coined by one of our friends who likes to sit in the bathtub to reflect on her feelings. Usually, after meditating/reflecting on it, clarity comes, and we reconvene later that day or the next. It's kind of like the Mexican Train Dominos game. We don't move on to the regular expression session until this one dynamic in the game is handled: the matching domino is found; that is, the problem solved. Usually, it doesn't take more than a day, although I've seen it take as many as three or four on occasion. But the results are spectacular and the love quotient is always bumped up several notches each time (maybe especially if it's been a difficult one to resolve), so that we're all so high we're floating on air.

Of course, then there's always this slight collective fear that the bubble will burst. So we just get very aware and try to move through it without resistance. It's pretty amazing. Since we've incorporated this process into our daily lives, we've become much clearer in our intentions, less reactive. We know better what we are looking for in the experience of living together, and what kind of commitment we'd be requesting when we look at any new applicants. We meet every morning in the main house at 7 or 8, depending on our personal schedules."

"That is amazing, honey. But what about people who have to work? Is everyone required to come every morning?" her mother asked.

"Believe it or not, with very few exceptions, it is a requirement to be there. People who live with us make the expression session, and our intention for a peaceful life, a priority. Most people would see the way we live as a huge luxury, and write it off as undoable. But that's the experiment — the whole reason we've created it, to see if it's possible to organize our lives around these principles. Even in the problem solving process, we don't focus so much on the problem as we do the quality of the actual experience. We've seen that problems generally take care of themselves when everyone has agreed to emphasize a peaceful outcome.

"Individual minds express from personal filters, and they aren't always easy to see through. But when we see conflict as meaningless, and peace as essential, problems are dispatched with a lot more ease and elegance. Everything else in the community flows from these three things: meditation, expression session and the problem solving forum. We often ask ourselves, "What is our purpose here?" And if the answer *isn't* to obtain a new level of peace and creativity, we know we're off somewhere. I don't mean peace at any cost, mind you. True peace doesn't cost anything," Sabrina emphasized, "and it can include a great many points of view. But the ego can get backed up sometimes, and what might start out feeling like a sacrifice to one or more of us in the beginning, usually turns out to be a gift after we've worked it through."

They stopped for lunch and afterward, George and Sabrina traded places. While Sabrina napped, Blanche and George continued the conversation. "We have a life that just about peaks at perfection," he said. "My idea of it at least. For instance, one of the bedroom suites we offer as an arm of service to the community. Usually it's reserved for women, just out of prison. We give them a place to 'reset', a chance to get a job and interface with life on the outside. We provide free rent and food up to a year, and they have to agree to come to expression session as well. After that, they'll find a place of their own. But they're always welcome to join us for the sessions and our many get-togethers. Or they might start their own communities.

"This beautiful woman who lives with us now—Sheila—is twenty-four, and she has two children."

"My – but what does she do with them while she works?"

"Oh, they go to school, but someone is always around to watch them when they get home if she is still at work. They even come to the meditations in the morning. It's a wonderful way to achieve a traditional family atmosphere, since no one in our group has any children and there are doubts that we ever will."

This was a subject which had raised Blanche's hackles in the past. "Why not?" she'd asked so many times, they were tired of finding answers. The truth is, they didn't know why not. They all pretty much loved children. Bob and Susan who were closer to Blanche's age, had children and grandchildren that came over once in a while, and they had even fostered children at one time and said that it was a great experience. So the idea of fostering children in the community was an on-going conversation in the community.

New ideas were always presenting themselves, and it was a delicate balance to give room to them while being available for everyone's input. Decisions were made together and they waited until everyone reached agreement, kind of like a jury deliberation. Unlike juries, however, they didn't always go by outward evidence, but often intuited answers from within, and waited for a consensus.

"This is an experiment that has sometimes led us deep into introspection," Sabrina explained to her mother later that day when they stopped for dinner. "It often produces the most astonishing personal insights. For instance, I realized at once that I had huge beliefs about the time it takes to come to common agreement on any subject with this method of deliberation—often longer than I thought necessary. But my attitude about it started changing as we practiced the art of going into Silence and retrieving the collective wisdom there. Now all of my beliefs about time and conflict have been laid on the 'Altar of the Conditioned Mind,' you could say, and *its* devotions are highly suspect. I put them aside until they are either discarded altogether, or given another chance to prove their efficacy.

"Nathan told me once that the idea of time is just a belief in past and future. It doesn't really exist when you think about it. If we stay present, enjoying the moment as it is, the time is always NOW. And that doesn't preclude us imagining or planning the future. It just keeps us from dragging all our baggage from the past into the future with us, and making decisions based on old limitations. Now when I have fears about getting things done in a certain time frame, I place them on this imaginary "table of contents" in my mind. I leave them there, sometimes taking a peek at them in moments of distress. Once in a while I feel tempted to pick them up again. But I'm determined that they stay there until 'the last judgment'; that's the day I judge all fears as unworthy of me and let them go entirely.

Her mother agreed that would be a fine letting go.

And as they turned into the driveway of their Italian Villa-like borough at the end of the long day's drive, the lush California vegetation fading into the now deepening sunset, Blanche Ryder found she was facing a new life. She would be living with her daughter—oh, and her boyfriend, who were still not married after four years—with no children to speak of—in the wine country—with ex-Mormons—who love to meditate, by the way—and would be unleashing her deepest sorrow; the loss of a cherished friend and husband into the Great Unknown.

Now what could be better than that?

Epilogue

Something wasn't right.

There was a strange smell coming from the engine and Sabrina pulled off the 101 to check it. Her little Mini-Cooper was starting to show its age and it was probably time to think about trading it in for something more environmentally friendly anyway.

She and George had been meaning to go looking on one of the weekends, but there was always something more interesting to do. Last week, for instance, there was a student film festival and the week before they'd all gone sailing with friends.

In the six months since her mother had moved into their little community, there wasn't a day gone by that didn't bring a sense of wonder and amusement. Lately, it had been chilly in the evenings and they usually had a fire going in the main house (where Sabrina, George, Nathan and Richard lived). Migrating over to the lodge in the evenings for conversation, popcorn and wine, everyone had grown into this community kinship, this 'family of man', as George liked to call it. Life was sweet, mainly because they were learning to take it on its own terms.

"Seems if you just let Life live *you* instead of the other way round, things have a way of turnin' out better than the way you thought you wanted it," Abby said one evening, as she put the dishes away after pot luck in the bistro.

Abby and Nathan had both landed jobs in the same publishing house in San Francisco. Sabrina worked at a different one, but they rode together with George into the city each morning and home again at night. If it were possible for them to be any closer, Sabrina didn't know how. Richard Hughes, Nathan's partner, was a computer programmer who worked from home. Robert and Susan Collins were retired and spent most of their time gardening and taking care of things around the place. Josh Levinson and his new wife, Jules, ran the Bistro four days a week.

Then of course there were the favorites: the young woman just out of the prison halfway house down the road; Sheila and her two children, Max and Millie. She'd been imprisoned for three years for making and selling meth with her boyfriend; getting off early for good behavior. The children had been taken from her and farmed out to foster homes, which wasn't much better than living in a drug house, but at least not worse. Now they could be together again, hopefully to regain some sense of family. And with the extended community all around them, psychological and financial healing seemed imminent.

After listening to Sheila's story, George and the other men had begun to talk about building another house on the property; to give a few impoverished souls a chance to change their lives before it came to the kind of circumstances in which Sheila had found herself.

Prevention. What would that look like?

George didn't know, but he was consumed by the desire to find out. His love for community living spilled out all over the place. It seemed he couldn't stop thinking about it, talking about it; how to make it better, how the world could benefit, and how it might be a solution for future social and political dilemmas. How to get these ideas into the hands of men and women in congress, in third world countries, and to people with influence and money? Even now he was writing a grant for some Bill Gates venture capital.

Sabrina had been spending her free time writing a book, a novel about community living. And in spite of the nasty little literary critic that lived inside her head, the editors at Neil and Sons were all over it. They were as encouraging as the inner critic was disparaging. Still she had slogged through the barrage of harsh, censorious condemnations every day that she wrote, stepping in fresh shit almost every paragraph of the way. Embarrassingly, she experienced the geography of her mind—not as the panoramic view her father would have wanted for her—but as a narrow, unfriendly environment, throwing up walls and barbed wire fences wherever she dared venture in her imagination. It was part of the rough terrain of writing that first novel, Sabrina supposed. Thank God she could find her way out at the end of every session, and leave it behind.

And today was a milestone. Today she had finished the first rough draft. It actually wasn't even that rough. Just because of the persistent nagging of that irritating inner critic, she'd done a deal of editing along the way and it was pretty much ready to hand over to a really fine production editor, to whom she was taking it this morning; someone she knew would be unbiased and scathingly honest.

Nathan had offered, but she felt too much in his good graces for him to give it a thorough distillation. The lines between them were blurred by love and high regard, and it was difficult to say whether that was a good or a bad thing where the book was concerned.

"Oh, come on Cheri," Nathan said in a fake French accent, "let me take a look at it at least!" And he whined as she had hurried out the door that morning. It was Saturday and they had just breakfasted together on the patio. He'd done everything possible to get a peek at it, but she wouldn't hear of it.

"You can see it if it ever gets published. In fact, you can have a signed first edition, but don't get in my way now, Buster. You're not qualified to do this one."

"Not qualified?!" he yelled after her, "Not qualified? What the hell do you think I do for a living and how much do you think I get paid there, Skippy?"

"This isn't about your aptitude, genius. It's about objectivity," she yelled back.

"Well, I never," he grumbled, and Richard gave a loud snort, knowing his partner's obvious infatuation for the woman and her work.

Blanche Ryder spent her days writing too, in her journal. She also did a lot of walking, and helping to take care of the two children. The evenings she usually spent with Sabrina and George, or else went into town with Susan and Bob Collins, with whom she was now fast friends.

Susan had indeed been a practicing Mormon only a few years ago, and she had nothing ill to say of the experience, and much good. So she and Blanche were often locked in conversations about spiritual topics of one kind or another. The three of them had even gone to church together on occasion. But that happened less and less now. An inner life had taken Blanche over it seemed, and "there is just no need to add anything to it," she often said to the others. Something spacious and rich was opening up within her. And in the moments she needed companionship, other than the community and her own dear Self, —well, there was a whole wide world out there. The Church of the Living God: Life Itself.

Patricia York

The four houses on their little estate now had all the renovations finished. Of course there were hitches and bumps here and there, but who was counting or taking issue with that? Things seemed to be humming along as though there was an orchestra playing in a pit somewhere, and everyone following the music with the exact skills of first chair musicians. No prima donnas though. It was Harmony as good as it gets.

What happens when everything is so good, that you think it can't get any better, Sabrina wondered to herself— as she stood looking under the hood of her car, for what she didn't know. *We always think there's going to be a downside, but what if that's not the way? What if we could see things differently? Is that how you transcend a world of opposites?*

She decided to call George and ask him if he thought she should drive her car to a station a couple of miles away or just call roadside service. Down the highway, a large truck came barreling into view. It looked for one moment like it was leaning to one side like in a cartoon. Crazy. But no, just an optical illusion.

"George? Listen, Houston, we have a problem. Something's wrong with my car. It might be overheating. I can't see it if it is, but it smells funny." And she turned her back to the road, plugging her other ear so she could hear his answer.

"What did you say? Oh never mind. You know what? I really just called to say that I love you and that this is the best day of my life—my whole entire life. What? Well, I know I've said it before, Mr. Correcto—so what? You know when they say that life is so good, it can't get any better? Do you think that's true, because I was just wondering,—like where do we go from here? Some people would say we're just waiting for the other shoe to drop.

"Maybe we should get divorced and start over or something," she said, and waited for his laugh, that beautiful laugh that always made her want to fuck him right where he was standing. "Yeah. I know. It's going to be hard, since we're not married. But it's the idea, don't you see?" She heard him say something, but couldn't tell what it was. She smiled, completely lost on her planet, the one circling that brilliant George sun. Oh, that man.

He had somehow turned his attention in the last few years toward a deep philosophic inquiry. Still working at the same firm, he was now one of their top architects. It satisfied his creative juices to do one project a year, but then he opted to use the rest of his time for his own purposes.

His father—a wealthy St. Louis industrialist, who had little interest in compliance with requisite environmental restrictions, had just been hauled into court for some major infractions, when he had suddenly died of a heart attack. His mother, a woman of the old school (stay-at-home and surf the shopping channels) was not interested in anything about the company except maintaining her annual stipend; one million plus benefits. George was the only child, and had inherited the whole bloody mess.

In this last few months, he'd hired a new CEO and CFO who were willing to figure out how to pay the massive fines his father had been dodging. If they could make it through these next few months, it just might be a source of income that would permit George to strike out on his own, do some of the things he'd dreamt about. It would be better than politics, better than philosophy, better than architecture, because it would be a synthesis of all of them. And better than— well, just about better than anything except his exquisite little life with Sabrina Ryder and Company.

They had decided not to marry because they wanted to make a statement: why should they live from a contract signed by a county courthouse clerk, whose supposed authority gave them the right to have an intimate relationship? Who could tell them more about their rights to live as partners than they themselves? Nathan and Richard felt the same. But it hadn't keep any of them from celebrating their respective relationships, admirably and often.

A colossal thundering crash shook the road where Sabrina stood and she turned around to look. The truck was sliding toward her, skidding on its side and pushing another car in front of it. What the—? There had been something weird about that truck. Maybe it—

You know when they say that life is so good it can't get any better? a voice whispered in her ear. She was so glad that she had figured out the time thing; how to stop it with her mind, so that a whole life could be lived in one Holy Instant. Because she thought of her mother now living without a safety net, probably resting out by the pool with Millie and Max; how happy she'd been these last few months, her beautiful clear eyes so often shining with tears of joy.

And she thought of Abby and Nathan who had been the dearest friends ever, each in their own relentless way. The Collins and Sheba and Richard, who were most likely laughing and gulping down some strange concoction that Jules had just made to heal the digestive tract.

The car was so close now she could see the license plate, except she knew that a vanity license plate could only have seven letters, but this one had nine— the sign of completion, she knew:

R U RDY 4 THS

And then there was that face of the astonished driver; a beautiful young man she was about to encounter with more intimacy than it looked like he was prepared to embrace. In less than a nanosecond they would become intimate friends, just to put a kind of welcoming spin on it. And why not? A soul relationship like that doesn't happen every day.

She saw George in his beautiful corner office, squinting his eyes, trying to peer into another dimension, the dimension she would occupy in a moment? All these thoughts ran through her head the instant before the crash, like a thousand words written on the head of a pin.

"Darling, can you see me? Are you watching?" she shouted mentally into the din. "I'll meet you in a moment, just outside your window, my love—because apparently I am expanding into something really, really amazing and I can't seem to stop it!"

But wait— Would someone get her book to the publishers? Was that guy that Abby liked going to ask her out again? Will her mother remember to water the hydrangeas? So many questions, so little time. And none of them were about God. They were all about the little things. Will Millie and Max get into that new school?

A highway sign appeared inside her head: 'Go right past Kolob and straight on to the North!' And then she began to laugh. Because laughing was always the way she liked to exit a room.

What happens when life is so good, it can't get any better? Well, here was the deal: Sabrina Ryder was just about to find out.

BEST DAY EVER!

"I am God's Son, complete and healed and whole, shining in the reflection of His Love. In me is His creation sanctified and guaranteed eternal life. In me is love perfected, fear impossible, and joy established without opposite. I am the holy home of God Himself. I am the Heaven where His Love resides."[85]

Endnotes

Chapter second:

1   T. Golas, <u>The Lazy Man's Guide to Enlightenment</u>, Gibbs Smith Publisher, 1995, p. 109

2   Ibid.

3   T. Golas, <u>The Lazy Man's Guide to Enlightenment,</u> Gibbs Smith Publisher, 1995, P. 110

4   Ibid.

5   Bible, King James Version, Matthew 5:45

6   T. Golas, <u>The Lazy Man's Guide to Enlightenment,</u> Gibbs Smith Publisher, 1995, P. 98

7   Ibid., p 99

Chapter Fifth

8   <u>https://www.mormon.org/beliefs/articles-of-faith</u>

Chapter Sixth

[9] https://www.lds.org/media-library/video/2011-03-044-peculiar-people?lang=eng Russell M. Nelson explains Exodus 19:3-8

[10] Bible, KJV, Romans 2:11

Chapter Seventh

[11] A Course in Miracles (ACIM), Foundation For Inner Peace Publisher, 1992, T-16.V.3

[12] Ibid., T-5.VI.12

[13] Ibid., T-26.IX.6

[14] Ibid., T-26.VIII.9

[15] Ibid., T-16.V.3

[16] Ibid., T-16.V.7

[17] Ibid., T-16.V.11

[18] Ibid., T-16.VI.2

[19] https://www.youtube.com/results?query=fran+lebowitz+on+gays+in+the+military

[20] ACIM, Foundation for Inner Peace Publisher, 1992, Workbook, Lesson 29.2.1-3

[21] Ibid., Workbook, Lesson 28.3.1-3

[22] Ibid., Workbook, Lesson 28.5.1-3

Chapter Eighth

23 Ibid., T-9.VII.3

Chapter Tenth

24 Ibid., Workbook, Lesson 42.2.3

25 Bible, 21st Century KJV, John 14: 15-17

Chapter Eleventh

26 Attributed to Byron Katie

27 <u>ACIM</u>, Foundation for Inner Peace Publisher, 1992, T-3.VI.5

28 T. Golas, <u>The Lazy Man's Guide to Enlightenment</u>, Gibbs Smith Publisher, 1995, p. 104

29 Ibid., p. 65

30 Ibid., p. 106

31 Ibid., p. 63

32 Ibid., p. 77

33 Ibid., p. 78

34 Ibid., p. 78

35 Ibid., p. 78

36 <u>ACIM</u>, Foundation for Inner Peace Publisher, 1992, Workbook, Lesson 325.1.1-3

[37] T. Golas, The Lazy Man's Guide to Enlightenment, Gibbs Smith Publisher, 1995, p. 78

[38] Ibid., P. 79

[39] Ibid., p.79

[40] Ibid., p. 79

[41] Ibid., p. 106

[42] Ibid. p. 106

[43] Ibid., p. 106

[44] Ibid., p. 107

Chapter Twelfth

[45] Bible, KJV, Proverbs 22:6

Chapter Sixteenth

[46] ACIM, Foundation for Inner Peace Publisher, 1992, T-8.VI.9

[47] W. Whitman, Leaves of Grass, Franklin Mint Corporation Publisher, 1979, based on the "Deathbed" edition of 1892, p. 88 (Children of Adam)

Chapter Twenty-first

[48] ACIM, Foundation for Inner Peace Publisher, 1992, T-14.III.I

⁴⁹ T. Golas, <u>The Lazy Man's Guide to Enlightenment</u>, Gibbs Smith Publisher,1995, Introduction, p. 9

⁵⁰ Ibid., Introduction, p. 10

⁵¹ Ibid., Introduction, p. 10-11

⁵² Ibid., Introduction, p. 13

⁵³ Ibid., Introduction, p. 30

⁵⁴ Ibid., Introduction, p. 16

⁵⁵ <u>ACIM</u>, Foundation for Inner Peace Publisher, 1992, Preface, viii

⁵⁶ http://www.scottwoodward.org/bookofmormon_witnesses_emma_smith.html paragraph 4

⁵⁷ https://krusty1960historysstory.wordpress.com/2015/04/14/april-13-handels-messiah-premieres/

Chapter Twenty-forth

⁵⁸ T. Golas, The Lazy Man's Guide to Enlightenment, Gibbs Smith Publisher, 1995, p. 54

⁵⁹ <u>ACIM</u>, The Foundation for Inner Peace Publisher, 1992, T-1.VII.1

⁶⁰ Ibid., T-10.II.1

⁶¹ Ibid., Workbook, Lesson 80, 4.1

Chapter Twenty-fifth

⁶² Ibid., Workbook, Lesson 268, p. 429

[63] T. Golas, The Lazy Mann's Guide to Enlightenment, Gibbs Smith Publisher, 1995, p. 110

Chapter Twenty-sixth

[64] ACIM, Foundation for Inner Peace, Publisher, T-22.I.I.7

[65] Ibid., T-31.I.3.1.1-4

[66] Ibid., T-31.I. 3.6

[67] Ibid., T-31.VIII.1.1-6

[68] Ibid., T-31.VIII.12.8

Chapter Thirty-fifth

[69] Ibid., M-9.2.4

[70] Ibid., T-27.VIII.6.2

Chapter Thirty-sixth

[71] T. Golas, The Lazy Man's Guide to Enlightenment, Gibbs and Smith Publisher, 1995, p. 57

Chapter Thirty-ninth

[72] ACIM, The Foundation for Inner Peace Publisher, 1992, T-26.VIII.2

[73] The Essential Rumi, translated by Coleman Barks, HarperCollins Publishers, 1995, p.36

Chapter Fortieth

[74] T. Golas, The Lazy Man's Guide to Enlightenment, Gibbs Smith Publisher, 1995, Forward, p. 53

[75] ACIM, The Foundation for Inner Peace Publisher, 1992, T-15.V.2

Chapter Forty-first

[76] The Essential Rumi, translated by Coleman Barks, HarperCollins Publishers, 1995, p. 106

[77] ACIM, The Foundation for Inner Peace Publisher, 1992, Workbook, Lesson 28, p.43

[78] Ibid., Workbook, Lesson 268, p.429

[79] Ibid., Workbook, Lesson 34, p. 51

[80] Ibid. Workbook, Lesson 153, p.284

[81] C. Brontë, Jane Eyre, Currer Bell, Original Publisher, 1848; Portland House Illustrated Classics, 1988, p. 152

Chapter Forty-second

[82] T. Golas, The Lazy Man's Guide to Enlightenment, Gibbs Smith Publisher, 1995, p. 68

Chapter Forty-forth

[83] ACIM, The Foundation for Inner Peace Publisher, 1992, T-26.IX.6.1

[84] The Essential Rumi, translated by Coleman Barks, HarperCollins Publisher, 1995, p. 165

Epilogue

[85] ACIM, The Foundation for Inner Peace Publisher, 1992, Workbook, *What Am I?*, p.479

CPSIA information can be obtained
at www.ICGtesting.com
Printed in the USA
BVHW031221281119
565085BV00005B/9/P